LETHAL BLOSSOM

a novel by

Stephanie Serrano

Lotus Pond Press
Hilo, Hawaii

Lethal Blossom
published by Lotus Pond Press, LLC
PO Box 4457, Hilo, Hawaii, 96720

ISBN: 9781931383134 (trade paperback edition)
ISBN 10: 1931383138

author photo by Shasta Rose
cover design byVenus de Hilo
tulip photo © BooHoo - fotolia.com
cat photo © Tinka - fotolia.com
heading graphic © Roxanne Black - fotolia.com

This is a work of fiction. That means I either made up the people, places, things, and events in this book or used them fictitiously. Any resemblance to actual persons (living or historical), events, organizations, or locales is entirely unintentional and coincidental.

Thank you for your support, and I hope you enjoy the story!

Stephanie Serrano
June 17, 2011

LETHAL
BLOSSOM

Rose eases into her gardening gloves, the canvas fingers wriggling with delight as she slips them on over swollen knuckles. What a treat it is to be outdoors again. The curved brim of her old straw hat smiles with her as she sets it into place over thinning hair.

Last winter, when Dr. Banana (oh, that's not right… *Burana*, that's it), when Dr. Burana's prognosis turned grim, Rose had been sure her gardening days were over. Then a friend suggested she try those herbal formulas from South America. Rose isn't one to jump at alternative remedies, but faced with terminal decrepitude she'd thought, why not?

Rose likes the herbs. Those nasty medications Dr. B. had her on made everything taste like rancid glue. Now that she's cut back on the pills she enjoys food again. And she has the energy to do a little gardening on a fine day like today. So here she is, back on her feet and back to her Monday afternoons at Riverview cemetery.

Rose putters around the family plot, trimming and pruning whatever she can reach without having to bend or stretch too far. So what if those last test results were dismal and people think she's getting spotty (no, *dotty*, that's the word) dotty in her old age. She's not in her grave yet. Thank goodness she can still drive. And she has that blasted cell phone her husband makes her carry, as if there'd be any kind of emergency in this peaceful place. She feels just fine, thank you, and just as well because look at that gum wrapper in the pachysandra.

Picking it up is not as easy as you'd think, and there's an iffy moment as she gets back to her feet. Once that's accomplished it seems a good idea to rest on this bench and peel the gloves off again and open her thermos of tea. Now, where's that lemon bar Hanna packed for her?

Rose made the lemon bars herself yesterday evening. They looked so delicious, cooling on a rack on her kitchen counter: meltingly crisp shortbread pulled from the oven just as it started to brown, lemon curd as smooth and yellow as a buttercup's wing, a snowdust of powdered sugar across the top.

Rose takes a bite, expecting to be delighted.

Oh dear. Clearly she made some horrible mistake.

It's the shortbread. She must have measured salt instead of sugar. That's a disappointment, and now she doesn't have a sweet to go with her tea. Rose looks in her handbag, hoping for a butterscotch, but finds only crumpled twists of cellophane.

She considers the lemon bar again. The lemon curd layer is every bit as delicious as it should be. Does she dare?

No one is around. Who would see her, anyway, in this private plot behind the overgrown podocarpus?

The breeze whispers, "Go on, then."

Rose has raised the lemon bar to her lips when a crunch of footsteps on the gravel path saves her from embarrassment. What on earth were you thinking, she chides herself as she slips the pastry back into its ziplock bag. That nice young woman from the Garden Club almost caught you licking that lemon bar like a (cough drop? no, *lollipop*, that's it), like a lollipop.

"Hello, dear," Rose says. "How nice to see you." Now what is this one's name? Not Rose, of course, but some other flower, she remembers that. "Come sit for a minute and keep an old lady company."

The young woman lets herself in through the gate that bridges the gap in the tall hedge. She'd been weeding the tulip bed over by the elms there, she says, saw Rose's car and thought she'd say hello.

Getting up can be a trial, so Rose pats the bench beside her and offers (Daisy?... no that isn't it) some tea before remembering she only has the one cup. Her visitor declines. She's brought a Snapple Green Tea with her.

Rose sampled a bottled tea once out of curiosity and thought it a remarkably horrid beverage. She tries not to let this affect her opinion of not-Daisy but it does. That opinion goes back up when (Iris, perhaps?) takes a white paper bakery bag from a spotless canvas gardening tote and asks if Rose would like to share a brownie.

Rose is very fond of brownies, so long as they don't have nuts in them. She once loved nuts, but developed a terrible allergy when she was five, and could never eat them after that. The allergy is so bad that Dr.

Bana— Burana insists she carry one of those Epi-pens with her, not that she's ever had to use it. Rose is careful about that.

She's about to explain the nut allergy when (Dahlia? … no, that doesn't seem right) smiles and says, "I hope you don't mind it doesn't have nuts. I don't like them in brownies."

"Without nuts is perfect," Rose agrees. "My, doesn't that look good."

"It's mocha espresso," not-Dahlia offers. "Do have some."

Rose wavers. Espresso in brownies is a fine idea, but she doesn't know (Pansy?) at all well, and feels she ought to refuse.

"There's plenty to share," not-Pansy says. "I really shouldn't eat it all myself."

"Oh, pshh," Rose replies, sounding exactly like an old lady. Well, she is an old lady. Not that sixty-eight is ancient, but a decade of poor health has left her creaky beyond her years. "You have a lovely figure, dear," she assures (Petunia? no, "p" is all wrong). "Surely you don't have to worry about what you eat."

"I have a lovely figure because I worry about what I eat," not-Petunia says with a wink. "But brownies are so hard to resist."

Rose is taken aback by the wink—surely that's not ladylike behavior, even these days—but she, too, finds brownies very hard to resist. Especially when frosted, as this one is.

Oh my. That is heavenly.

She takes a second bite and savors it, evaluating this time, prolonging the pleasure. Good dark chocolate flavor, dense and smooth as a brownie should be, and with that lovely espresso kiss. Is the icing a simple bittersweet ganache, as she suspects? Yes, and there's a hint of something else, something faintly familiar, something she hasn't tasted in a very long—

oh dear—

oh my—

oh this shouldn't be—

Rose tries to protest as she feels her throat begin to close and her face puff up. Her vision blurs as she scrabbles for her purse, for that (peppy? Epi, that's it, Epi-pen). Oh, where is it, she knows it's there, she'd felt it earlier when she looked for a butterscotch.

"Let me help you with that," (Aster, maybe?) says, as though the problem were no more urgent than a stubborn pickle jar lid.

Rose, struggling unsuccessfully to breathe, thinks it quick-witted of her companion to slide the purse from her weakening grasp and turn it bottom-side-up to dump the contents onto the grass at their feet.

There it is: the peppy-pen!

Rose reaches for it and, oh my goodness, topples right off the bench, her focus so firmly on the Epi-pen that she almost doesn't notice the nudge that sends her to the ground.

"This must be what you're looking for," not-Aster says.

Rose, vaguely aware that her slip is showing and that something distressing has happened to her hip, is relieved to see the young woman pick up the Epi-pen and—

"Oh, too bad," not-Aster says, tossing it under the bench. "It must have rolled out of reach when you dropped your purse."

Rose is astonished that the woman isn't helping her. She's picking up Rose's cell phone and placing it, too, out of reach. Rose manages one twitch of protest and then stops struggling to breathe, breathing is no longer necessary at all and—oh yes, of course, that's it. She sees the flower vividly now, the colors so glorious, the curves of its petals so precise, the delicate stamens frosted with pollen: flawless, a perfect beauty. The woman leans down, and Rose is shadowed by an exquisite blossom reaching for her with poisonous petals.

So distressed is Rose by this vision that some moments pass before she understands that she has died.

She doesn't feel dead. But surely that ungainly heap is her body.

It's a curious sensation. Freed from the familiar embrace of the meat suit (such a hideous phrase, and so perfectly apt) Rose is … not alive as she's understood it, but aware still, somehow, and something more: vibrant, in a way she can't put words to.

Rose has always thought that death would be an endless, dreamless sleep. She hadn't expected it to be so   floaty   and shimmery, and so very, almost, (it seems wrong to think this) delightful.

When Rose finally understands that she's been murdered she is at first astounded and then, briefly, furious. There were nuts in that brownie, and that woman knew it! And knew Rose was allergic, too. What on earth did she do that for? Of all the nerve!

But Rose has never been comfortable with strong emotions, and as her spirit grows lighter the anger falls away. Such a heavy sensation, anger, and so earthbound. Not like Rose, untethered now, inflating with a serenity that leaves no room for resentment.

My goodness, isn't this something, to be drifting upward as if there really is a Heaven beyond the sky.

There, where that light beckons.

Which is all very well, but Rose—despite having been a proper lady while alive—isn't about to just drift off to Heaven and let some wink woman get away with murdering her. She's dismayed to see that the wink woman, pressing a finger to the throat of Rose's discarded husk, is so far below now. Rose concentrates, and after a time is able to reverse her ascent.

Oh. That was a surprise, that pang of regret as whatever had lifted her beyond let go.

For a moment Rose doubts her decision, and then it is too late, and she is adrift between not-here and not-there.

I'm no expert on reincarnation, but this much I know for sure: karma you gotta watch out for. Anyone who hasn't figured out that bad behavior has a way of circling around to bite you in the ass—usually long before the question of another lifetime arises—is either a saint or not paying attention.

Picture me sitting at my kitchen table, wrestling with temptation. It's seven-thirty on a Friday morning in early June and sunlight is pushing its perky way through the leaves of the maple tree outside my window. Birds are probably chirping around out there, too. It's going to be a glorious day, but I'm not looking forward to it. I'm waiting for the coffee water to come to a boil while facing down a dozen hollow golf balls and the box containing my late husband's ashes.

The specific bad behavior I'm tempted by is of the sins of omission kind. What I'm wondering is, first, what I could possibly have done in a previous existence to have brought this particular hell upon myself, and, second, whether failing to comply with Brad's last wishes is the sort of bad behavior that will trigger a year of lousy parking luck (annoying but tolerable) or the kind that will bring me back next time around, if there is a next time, as a bat.

Greed, Envy, Sloth, Lust… is procrastination one of the seven deadlies? I've had six months to tackle this loathsome chore, and time is running out. Brad's birthday—the day he wanted us to play one last round of golf with him—is tomorrow. I wish I hadn't agreed we would do it, but the creepy moral authority of last wishes is difficult to defy.

"We" is supposed to be me and Brad's two kids from his first marriage. They were in college when Brad and I hooked up so I'm more dad's wife than step-mom to them, but we get along okay. Predictably, Amanda freaked out and refused to have anything to do with the golf ball lunacy, while William had shrugged and said, "You gotta admit, it's pretty funny." Too bad his job's taken him to Shanghai for the summer. To his credit, Will seemed genuinely sorry to be missing the fun. I told him I'd save a goofball for him, but that hardly makes up for being stuck doing the honors by myself. My own daughter, Olivia, would have stepped up, but she's headed for summer vacation in Italy with my parents.

Olivia is a treasure from my first marriage, and good company for a teen, but now that she's in high school she's turned into one of those over-scheduled over-achievers who's hardly ever home. I could have tagged along on the annual Italy trip, but the only thing worse than spending most of the summer alone would be spending eight weeks in a too-small villa with my parents. I love them, but Mom and I would get snippy with each other in about five minutes, so why spoil summer for the both of us?

A cloudburst of yapping from outside the patio door jolted me to attention just as the kettle shrieked its alarm. I turned off the flame and saw a pumpkin-colored flounce of fur bouncing around on the other side of the slider.

"Where did you come from?" I wondered aloud, stepping outside to confront the fuzzball. It was kind of cute, for a dog, but sheesh: that yip yip yip would drive a saint insane.

"I'm not feeding you, if that's what you're after," I told it.

It stopped yipping and gave me a look that I interpreted as stunned disbelief.

"Just so we're clear: I'm not much of a dog person." I admit I've been thinking of getting a pet, but had something of the feline variety in mind. A yippy little dog isn't high on my list.

The dog yipped at me again and started humping my leg.

"Hey! Get the hell off me!" I snapped, shaking it off and stepping back. Geeze. As if that would change my mind.

"Fiona, leave the lady alone."

A gangly kid with a mop of unruly hair the same color as the dog's leaned over the privacy fence between my yard and the neighb's, making come-hither gestures to the dog. He teetered and grabbed for balance. The kid was either standing on a plastic lawn chair or nine feet tall.

"Sorry about that." He grinned through a scrim of freckles. "It was a good one, though. Check it out."

He held out his camcorder so I walked over for a look. I noticed in the image that my red toenail polish was beyond chipped, and mentally scheduled a visit to the salon for that afternoon. I had big plans for the weekend, and the weather forecast predicted sandals for at least one event.

"Fiona?" I handed him back the camera. "I don't think that dog's a girl."

"Stupid pet story," he said with a shrug. "We tried renaming him, but it didn't take."

"How did he get in here?" I asked, with a wary eye on the mutt. It had given up yipping in favor of panting in a way that only a dog person would find charming. "Did I leave the gate open again?"

"I think he dug under back there, by those bushes."

Those bushes are floribunda roses that astonish me every year by blooming in spite of my gardening skills, which are a lethal combination of ineptitude and inattention. I hoped no damage had been done. Now that my neighbor, Rose, is gone I've lost my source of green-thumb advice.

"I'm Ansel, by the way," the kid said, proving he was better trained than his dog.

"Nice to meet you, Ansel. I'm Lena."

"Hi, Lena." He shook my hand with the solemnity of a child performing an adult duty. "It's very nice to meet you, too."

"Ansel's an interesting name. Don't hear that one very often."

He grimaced. "Stupid parent thing," he said. "I'd like to change it, but Mom won't let me."

I laughed in sympathy "My real name's Magdalena. That's privileged information, by the way. I go by Lena as much as I can."

"At least you get a nickname. Ansel totally blows."

"Suitable for a photographer," I suggested, with a nod toward his camcorder. "Though that may not qualify as art photography." Oops, shut my mouth. Adolescent egos can be fragile, and he seemed like a good kid.

"Oh, this is totally not art," he said, unperturbed. "It's for my website."

"Your website?" I tried to sense where that was going, and crashed into the caffeine jones that had dogged me ever since I'd stepped outside without stopping for coffee.

"Yeah! I have this site called—"

"Hold on, Ansel." I raised my hand like a traffic cop. "I can't survive another minute without caffeine. Come around to the gate. You can retrieve your dog and tell me about your website while I get some coffee in my system."

The kid disappeared behind the fence and reappeared at the gate and I let him in.

"Hey, you have a great pool," he said. "Ours is kind of dinky."

"You want a soda or something?" I asked as we stepped into my kitchen.

"Coffee's good," my guest said, feigning maturity. I looked him a question. "I'm old enough for coffee," he assured me. "I drink coffee all the time."

Yeah, I bet. "Do you drink coffee all the time at home?"

Big sigh. "No. Mom thinks I'm too young, or it will stunt my growth or something."

Didn't seem like that would be such a bad idea, but I wasn't his mother. "How old are you, anyway? And how tall are you?"

"Thirteen next month, and almost six feet." He sounded worried.

"Is that a bad thing?"

"Mostly it's good, 'cause I used to get picked on a lot. But Dad says most boys get their big growth spurt at fourteen or fifteen and I don't want to turn into a freak."

"Let's see what we can do about stunting your growth, then." I put two more scoops in the French press. "If your Mom asks, we'll say I gave you a soda."

He looked horrified. "Oh, no, don't tell her that! Mom's totally against soda. She'd rather I drank beer than a soda."

"It's a little early in the day for beer. Tell her I gave you bottled water then."

I checked that the dog was settled down outside and not humping the patio furniture or digging up any more shrubbery. The water boiled again and I filled the French press and set the timer for four minutes.

I leaned against the counter and gestured to his camera. "So, tell me about your website. Is it like a MySpace thing?"

"MySpace is lame," he said. "You gotta have your own domain to run a commercial site. I totally scored with MyHumpingDog.com. Here, check these out." He passed the camcorder to me. "Push that button."

Huh. "These are all of Fiona, ah, getting friendly," I said, squinting at the tiny screen.

"Yeah." He giggle-snorted. "I added a function to my site so anyone can upload a video clip. You know, like YouTube?"

I nodded my comprehension. Every now and then Olivia insists, "You gotta see this," about some especially fine example of YouTube idiocy.

"…and last month I had over two hundred uploads."

"I see," I said, although I didn't. How could video uploads of randy dogs be a commercial enterprise? Whatever. Sounded like a good project for a geeky, way-too-tall, almost-thirteen-year-old. I tried to think of a web-type question to ask.

"Um, do you get a lot of traffic?"

"Awesome numbers. I optimized the home page for dog training and obedience, and I've already made over five grand for my college fund in affiliate commissions." He looked thoughtful. "I think I can get that up that to 3K a month by the end of the year through social marketing, without increasing my pay-per-click investment. Hey, you wanna check it out? Where's your computer?"

I brought my laptop into the kitchen and we logged on. Most of what he'd said had gone over my head, but three grand a month? Maybe I should become a dog person.

The timer dinged so I poured elixir of the morning gods and handed him some.

"You want milk and sugar with that?"

"How do you take yours?" He peered cautiously into his mug.

"Light cream, no sugar." I prefer my sugar on the side, preferably in the form of cake. I try not to eat cake for breakfast more than once a week.

"I'll try it that way." He held out his mug and I poured in a dollop. If the dude didn't know how he liked his coffee, no way he drank it all the time. Probably he snuck energy drinks past his mom and figured caffeine is caffeine. Amateur.

He stirred it and took a wary sip. "That's pretty good."

It would be even better with a shot of brandy and some whipped cream, but I'd done enough corrupting of youth for one morning.

"This is organic, shade grown, dark roast Sumatra," I said. "Not as good as Blue Mountain or Kona, but a fine everyday brew."

"Wow. You're a real… what do you call someone who's into coffee?"
Caffeine addict, for sure. "'Bean head,' maybe?"

"You're a real bean head. My mom's like that about her tea."

"Tea drinker, huh." Wimp.

"Yeah. She likes green tea and herbal stuff."

Even wimpier. Sensing a golden opportunity, I opened a cabinet and pulled out a dozen unopened boxes and canisters of green tea in multiple flavors and varieties. I found a plastic grocery bag under the sink and put the tea in it.

"Here." I handed the kid the bag. "You can give these to your mom."

"But that's your stash."

"I hate green tea," I said. "My grandmother thinks I'll change my mind if she sends me enough of the stuff." Never gonna happen. "I'm thrilled to have someone to give it to. Where do you live, by the way? Do you need a ride home?"

"We just moved in next door," he said. "A couple days ago."

"Next door? On that side?" Duh. Alan and Rose—well, just Alan now—are on the other.

He nodded.

Geeze. A whole family moved in next door and I hadn't noticed. How out of it have I been? Maybe it was time to snap out of my widow-funk before too much more of life passed me by.

"That's great," I said. So much for swimming in the nude this summer. And that tea stash had become a house-warming gift which meant a reused Safeway bag wouldn't do. I found a wicker basket in the broom closet and transferred the tea to it.

"Is your mom going to be up for a visit from a neighbor at this hour?"

"Oh sure," he said. "We're early risers. She'll be done with her Pilates by now."

Early riser, Pilates, green tea: Mom sounded scarier by the minute. Although I'd bet a box of Krispy Kremes that Ansel would hit the sleep-'til-noon phase any second, no matter how many early riser genes swam in his pool.

"I'm going to freshen up," I said. "Let Fido in and take him out the front door, will you? And make sure he doesn't hump anything on the way. I'll meet you out front in three minutes."

I re-scrubbed my teeth and gave up on taming my unruly hair. Mom takes credit for passing on to me her "glorious auburn locks," though mine are darker than hers. I'd have settled for tresses I could get a brush through. I wondered, as I changed into cropped jeans and a fresh tee, what Ansel's folks had paid for their place. This neighborhood is holding its value pretty well in spite of the recession and, as Ansel pointed out, my pool is way better than theirs.

2

The day was almost over and I still hadn't mustered up the fortitude to cross goofball prep off my list. So I called my best friend, Suzette, to rope her into helping out and to tell her about Ansel and his freaky mom. In the ten minutes I was next door that morning I'd learned that Tulip is vegan, home schools her son, grows sprouts on her kitchen windowsill, and sews her own clothes from organic fabrics. I find all that earnest goodness a bit hard to take, plus it's a mystery how anyone can be so relentlessly cheerful yet show no trace of a sense of humor.

"I didn't know ... you had new neighbors." Suze was puffing in my ear like the little engine that could.

"Neither did I, until this morning. Where are you, anyway, and what are you doing?"

"I'm power walking—" puff "—uphill—" pant "—on my way—" gasp "—to your house."

"I admire your enthusiasm for exertion," I said. "But save your breath until you get here and I'll go take the quick shower I've been meaning to get to all day."

Twelve minutes later I was clean and changed into yoga pants and a fresh top, and Suzette was sprawled in a chair in my kitchen, catching her breath.

"Ahh, that's more like it." She drained her water bottle.

"You power walked a whole half-mile," I observed. "That's hardly a marathon."

She shook her head. "I went to the gym this afternoon. Burned a gazillion calories in kick-boxing class. All those skinny young bitches jumping around, I felt a hundred years old."

"Well you look good." I knew my lines. "I can tell you've been working out more." Not that she needs to. Suzette's half Chinese and annoyingly slim. I wouldn't mind if she were petite, but her lithe 5'10" tops me by three inches and makes my curves feel excessive. I try not to hold it against her.

Suze tilted her head at the supplies on my kitchen table. "Last I heard, you were going to do this on your own. Light a candle, say a last goodbye, all that good stuff."

"A grand plan, destined to fail. It's just too creepy. I need moral support."

"Immoral support's more like it." She surveyed the last wishes paraphernalia and pronounced swift and accurate judgment. "You're trying to do this sober? What's that about?"

I shrugged. "I was sticking with my plan not to drink so much."

Two months ago I'd decided that the short-term benefits of numbing sudden widowhood with a few cocktails every night did not outweigh the headaches, fatigue, and unwelcome spare tire that came along for the ride.

"I have a major sugar rush planned," I added in self defense. "Hanna brought over one of Rose's Cinnamon Caramel Bundt Cakes."

I tipped my head toward the cake carrier on the counter. Suzette oohed over and flipped the catches on the lid, and a wave of sweet, buttery, cinnamon aroma rushed me from across the room.

"It's for after," I said, as Suzette succumbed to the gravitational pull of sugar and butterfat. "If I have to earn it, you have to wait, too. You're right about the booze factor, though. We're deep in whatever-it-takes territory."

After a mieu of disappointment at delayed cake gratification, Suzette mixed up a batch of cosmopolitans while I fetched martini glasses from the pantry. Cocktails in hand we stood and looked at the two boxes (one of ashes and the other of "goofballs") and a teaspoon from my cheap picnic stash (no way was I using good flatware for this) on my kitchen table.

Suzette, always ready to appreciate the ridiculous in any situation, grimaced, snorted, glanced my way, and surrendered to a full-out guffaw.

"God, Brad was an idiot sometimes," she gasped. "Why didn't he arrange for the funeral home to do this part?"

Six years of marriage to Brad provided the answer. "Innovative thinker, sloppy follow through." Brad was a big-picture guy who could see a million different ways to solve a problem or close a deal but preferred to delegate the details. Fortunately, he'd had a great assistant. And he'd recently partnered with Alan on a big renovation project. Alan's a retired real estate lawyer and a whiz with minutae, so in that respect they were a good match. In his personal life Brad had wives like me to make sure there were clean shirts in the closet and beer in the fridge and the cable bill got paid on time.

"If he'd put Martin in charge of this," I mused, "it would be all ready to go." Martin, the astoundingly capable assistant, had headed for greener pastures a few weeks before Brad's death, lured away to be personal assistant to a B-List celebrity in Hollywood.

"Mahvelous Mahtin," Suzette drawled. "Too bad he took that job with what's-her-name. Wouldn't it be great to have someone to pick up the dry cleaning and go to the Post Office for us? If we'd split his salary between us maybe we could have shared him."

"Not at the salary the new boss offered. Not unless those golf balls are made of gold and filled with diamonds."

"That much, huh?"

"Close enough."

"Well, he's worth it."

We toasted Martin and pondered the task at hand.

"I think we're stalling," Suzette said.

I stalled further with another sip of my cosmo. "You got a better idea?"

"There's something to be said for getting it done." Suze gave me a sidelong look I'd seen a lot in recent months. The one that assessed what I needed on a coddle-or-tough-love scale.

"Baby steps," she said. "First, pull out a chair and sit down."

That I could handle.

Now what? I picked up one of the hollow golf balls and twisted it open, but the resolve I was looking for did not materialize. Instead, I felt a terrifying emptiness

"I can't do this," I said, choking up. "You know," I stuttered, unable to hold back the tears that had threatened all day, "Brad was an idiot sometimes, but he was my idiot and I loved him and I wanted to do this for him, and I just ... can't." I dropped the goofball and lay my head down on the table with my arms crossed over my head.

Some guardian angel took pity and delivered a telephonic distraction. Suze tipped her chair back to check the caller ID box.

"It's your mother," she said, as I raised my head and wiped my eyes with my sleeve. "Want me to pick up?"

I tore a corner off a paper towel to blow my nose and nodded yes. Not that I wanted to deal with Mom, but anything was better than the task at hand. Suzette waited one more ring for me to signal I was snot-free, then handed over the phone.

"Hi, Mom."

"Magdalena, are you crying again? I wish you would pull yourself together."

"We've had this conversation before, Mom," I replied, with an eyeroll for Suzette's benefit. "Do you think we could move on?"

Mom is a woman of intellect (her words) to whom tears signal an overwrought state from which one ought to retreat as quickly and decorously as possible. I think feeling weepy is a reasonable reaction to my late husband's first post-mortem birthday.

Suze lifted her empty glass at me and waggled her eyebrows in question. Big thumbs up for that idea. I took the cordless into the living room, not to keep secrets from Suzette but because it was a cremains-free zone.

"Everything okay with your trip?" I asked, hoping to direct the conversation away from me. Mom, Dad, and Olivia were headed for Europe in the morning.

"Well." Mom endowed the word with dramatic inflection, followed by an even more dramatic sigh that meant she was about to ask a favor I wouldn't want to do. "Actually dear, that's why I'm calling."

"Mom, it's late…"

"It's your grandmother, dear. She's had a fall."

"Granimi?" My heart lurched. "Is she okay?" Granny Mimi is Mom's mom. She became Granimi when I was three and hadn't yet mastered enunciation. She lives in San Francisco but travels a lot and had been at Mom and Dad's for a couple weeks. "What happened?"

"Your grandmother, who thinks yoga is an appropriate activity for an octogenarian, lost her balance doing some pose that only twenty-year-olds should attempt and thank God broke nothing more serious than her wrist."

"I'm glad it was just her wrist, Mom, but still."

"Exactly. The woman is 82 and should know better."

Sheesh, I'd meant the woman broke her wrist, how's she doing with that, but whatever.

"She was supposed to fly home tomorrow when we leave for Italy," Mom plowed ahead, "but she shouldn't be on her own so I've booked her a flight to Orchard City. She can stay with you while she recovers."

I muffled the phone in my shoulder while I groaned and rolled my eyes so hard they almost popped out my ears. My irritation was more at the way Mom had roped me in than at the prospect of a visit from Granimi, who is more fun and much easier to deal with than my mother. The shadow of a thought lurched across my mind that one day Mom might be 82 and brittle-boned and in need of extended home care, possibly with her only daughter. That prospect so horrified me I snapped back to the present dilemma.

"Of course she can stay with me," I said, eager to stockpile good karma by caring for the more immediate and amenable patient.

"If you ask me, you could use the company," Mom said. "Besides, your brother is off on some rafting trip with that new wife of his, so he won't be any help."

"That's fine, Mom." My brother is famous for his ability to be legitimately unavailable whenever family duty calls. It's uncanny, and I wish I knew how he did it, 'cause I'd sure like to try it for myself sometime. "Really."

"That's settled then," Mom said, as if it hadn't been a done deal before she'd picked up the phone. She relayed Granimi's flight info and, when asked, said my grandmother was resting comfortably and already asleep. "Olivia's still up, if you'd like to talk to her."

That sounded good. Sometimes it's easier to be a mom than to deal with one. "Sure, put her on."

I heard, "Olivia, dear, your mother's on the line," in the background and then my favorite voice in the universe came on.

"Hey, Mom, guess you heard the latest."

"I got the Adriana version," I said, feeling mushy. I missed my baby already and she hadn't even left the country yet. "Care to fill in the gaps?"

"Not much to fill in. Granimi and I were doing yoga and she lost her balance."

"You were doing yoga?" It didn't seem like Olivia's kind of thing.

"It wasn't my fault, Mom! Granimi was teaching me some poses for jet lag. Honestly, it was her idea."

"I'm not saying it was your fault, honey. God knows she's tried to get me into yoga enough times over the years." I've developed a fondness for yoga clothes as loungewear, but haven't done much yoga. "I didn't know she was still into it, though."

"Mom, where have you been? 'Yogini Granny' is all over YouTube. She's got her own blog and everything."

YouTube seemed to be the theme of the day. I wondered if a quick look at Yogini Granny would be worth the oh-my-god-that's-my-grandmother factor.

"Seriously," Olivia went on. "The woman is a pretzel. I'm surprised it wasn't me who fell over and broke something. I might not be able to walk tomorrow."

"I'm sure you'll live," I said, shaking off the YouTube revelation. "How's she doing anyway?"

"Word is she'll be okay. She may need physical therapy when the cast comes off."

"Did you get a chance to talk to her?" Any broken bone at 82 is bad news, no matter how good the prognosis.

"No. She was pretty doped up when they got home, and she's asleep now. She just…"

"She just what, honey?"

"Oh, Mom, she just looked really old."

Damn it. Olivia sounded as if she were about to cry and if she did it would get me started and I didn't need to add a mother-daughter sob fest to the evening.

Olivia took a breath and pulled herself together. "I mean, I know she's ancient, but she's got such a spark, you know?"

"Yeah. I know."

"It was just gone, Mom. It was like someone took Granimi away and left a shriveled old lady in her place."

"Oh, sweetie, I'm sure that was just the medication. I've been on that stuff and it would turn the Energizer Bunny into a zombie. She'll be as sparkly as ever by the time you get back." I hoped. I didn't want to see Granimi as a tired old husk, either.

"Okay, Mom. Thanks. Hey, Mom?"

"What, dear?"

"I'm sorry I won't be able to do the Brad thing with you tomorrow. I forgot to say that when we talked earlier. I'll be thinking of you."

Look at that. My teenage daughter actually realized her mom was facing a difficult day, and would have liked to help out. Then I really did get teared up. My baby was growing up, and tomorrow she would fly away to the ends of the earth.

"Tomorrow you should be thinking about what a great time you're going to have in Europe," I said.

"Okay, Mom, will do. I love you."

"I love you, too, pumpkin. But if you hitchhike anywhere I'm going to come over there myself and kill you."

"I know the rules, Mom! No hitchhiking and no solo overnights. Seriously, why would I wander around by myself when Tina and Rory are the next country over. I swear."

My mom thinks Olivia's staying with them all summer. I predict a dash out the door with a backpack within 72 hours. Fortunately, Olivia is capable of looking after herself, a trait I planned to remind myself of every five minutes for the next two months.

Olivia said goodbye and put me back on with Mom. I wished her a safe flight and an enjoyable stay at the villa they've rented every summer since I was in high school. What with cell phones and email it isn't as far away as it used to be but while there Mom relaxes enough to stay mostly incommunicado, which is a nice break for the rest of us.

I clicked off the phone and looked at the flight information I'd scribbled on the back of a magazine. Tomorrow was already over-scheduled, and now it included a house guest. Who needed to be met in Orchard City, which is the next town over from Laurelton, where I live. It's not much as cities go but is big enough for a regional airport and close enough to be only moderately inconvenient.

Suzette wandered out from the kitchen and handed me a refill. "Everything all right at home?"

"Granimi broke her wrist. She's coming to stay for a while."

"Oh, poor Granimi," Suzette said, with genuine affection. She's met my grandmother a bunch of times over the years. "When's she getting here?" she asked, noticing the flight scribbles I held in my hand.

"Midday tomorrow. We'll just have time to pick her up between Rose's funeral and Carlos's wedding."

Suzette looked at me. "As if there weren't enough going on tomorrow."

In the morning we would attend the memorial service for Alan's wife, Rose, who passed a few days ago "after a long illness," as they say. There's more to it than that, but I'll fill you in later. Then, in an abrupt change of mood, the afternoon would bring wedding festivities for Carlos and Rhianna, close friends whose nuptials I genuinely wished to celebrate. Followed by Brad's final golf game, which I wasn't looking forward to at all.

"On the bright side," I pointed out, "meeting Granimi at the airport means we can skip the interment."

"That's good news. Unless you want to pass on the whole thing," Suze offered one more time. "I'm sure Alan will understand if it would be too much for you."

I shook my head. "I'll be okay," I said, testing my bravado. I hadn't been that close to Rose, but the prospect of attending a funeral rattled my equilibrium on the Brad issue. "I'd feel I was letting Alan down if I didn't show. And Rose, too, of course."

I drained my cosmo and decided I'd better switch to water if I were going to get through anything without a headache in the morning. And it might be a good idea to eat something.

"I need food," I said, feeling tipsier than I'd wanted to be. "Let's go see what we can find in the fridge."

I threw an arm around Suzette's waist and we sashayed back to my kitchen, where I discovered what a wonderful friend she is.

"Taadaaaaah," Suzette announced with a flourish as I saw that the top was back on the box of cremains. The goofballs were back in their box, too, which was tied up with a purple ribbon I recognized as one I'd left on the counter.

"All stuffed and packed and ready to go," she announced. "Now all we gotta do is knock 'em around the golf course and you're done."

"You did this for me while I was on the phone?"

"You don't mind, right? It's not overstepping any bounds or anything?"

"God, no!" I wrapped my arms around her and planted a shmooshy kiss on her cheek. "It's the nicest thing anyone's ever done for me."

"Good," she said. "That means we've earned cake."

*   *   *

For an unknown time—a day, a century, one flutter of a hummingbird's wing— the consciousness formerly known as Rose had drifted from the place of her death toward this glimmering knot in the sea of vibration that the living identify as the world, a nexus once known as home and garden.

The essence that had once been Rose wanted … something. There had been a moment when it could have gone … beyond. But it had resisted slipping away. Resisted because …

Something wriggled on the far side of comprehension, a whisper of wrongdoing in want of correction. But there was so little now that resembled thought, and without thought how could there be memory?

As what was left of Rose hovered near the place that had been her home, its scattered attention coalesced enough to sense a potential source of assistance. A consciousness still enrobed in sufficient density and cohesion to possibly be able to do … something. Something about the wink flower.

Someone here, where a sparkle of sweetness and spice traced its way through the echo of the world and drew the shimmer of awareness that was all that remained of Rose toward a once-familiar aroma that it no longer perceived as cinnamon and brown sugar.

3

Midnight found us beached like walruses on the lounge chairs by my pool, washing down seconds of Cinnamon Caramel Bundt Cake with mugs of decaf. Zapping the cake in the microwave had been a brilliant idea: warm up all that brown sugar and cinnamon until the aroma wallops you in the face like a pillow. I expected lights to appear in windows on the next block as late night appetites awoke and wondered what that heavenly smell was.

Hanna, Rose's housekeeper, had brought the cake over, she said, because she needed space in Rose's fridge. As if CCBC wouldn't go over well at the post-interment reception tomorrow, or keep perfectly well on the counter. Didn't fool me. The cake was a reminder that Hanna was now available for a housekeeping gig at my place, should I decide to share the joy of cleaning up after myself. I figured one underemployed person in good health—current sugar overdose excepted—shouldn't need help tidying-up. Plus, there was the effect maid service would have on The Incredible Shrinking Budget, as I'd begin to think of my finances.

My house was less than immaculate, though, and I had a guest arriving. Oh well, Granimi is too polite to say anything about my feeble attempts at dust management. More important, she wouldn't rat me out to Mom, who would think a vigorous round of cleaning was just what I needed to get me out of my slump. I figured I'd crawl out of my slump when I was good and ready. Which I wasn't yet. Maybe tomorrow. Or the day after.

I plucked a stem from the arrangement of rosebuds I'd gathered that afternoon and twirled it between my fingers, thinking about global warming—these seem to bloom earlier every year—and that I should go indoors and clean up but was too sated with cake to move.

Now that was odd. I could have sworn that a half hour ago these had been tight buds, several days from opening. Yet this one had unfurled. Rosebuds don't open in the middle of the night, do they?

I turned my head to look at the arrangement, and practically jumped out of my skin when another bud eased its petals open as I watched. I shivered abruptly with that goose walking over your grave feeling. Like déjà vu, but freakier, and without the déjà part.

I tried to shake off the creeps. What do I know about roses, anyway? Rose had been the flower maven of the block. A rose is a rose is a … I shivered again, and something rustled at the far end of the yard, and a ripply feeling came over me that a crack had appeared in… what? Reality, perception, understanding?

It felt like something was about to happen, but the rustling stopped and the night went still again and the feeling was so nebulous that as soon as I tried to grasp it, it was gone. I stuck the rose back in the vase and told myself I was just feeling maudlin. Flowers open up all at once like that, if they're ready; just usually not when you're looking. Right?

"What a beautiful night to be out here," Suzette said. She gestured at the glimmer of underwater lights shimmering up through my pool. "The pool looks so nice all lit up."

If Suzette—who claims to be a wee bit psychic—hadn't picked up on the shivery vibe, surely it was all in my head. And the pool did look nice.

"That water's seriously cold," I said. "If you're thinking of going in." Technically it's heated, but as a result of Brad's demise I now live in fear of my electric bill. I'd turned the pool lights on tonight as a treat.

"So, Lena, any further thoughts about the house?"

I shrugged and shook my head to express my ambivalence. "If I'm going to sell it I should put it on the market soon. I'm just not ready to face that yet. And with Granimi showing up tomorrow…."

Widowhood hadn't exactly cast me into the poor house, but I wasn't close to as well off as I'd thought I'd be given Brad's confident assurances that if I stuck with him I would never have to worry about money. I knew he'd invested a lot in a big project—converting an old mill building Alan and Rose owned into condominiums—but I'd been floored when our accountant told me the project was "in debt up to its eyeballs" and in danger of losing its financing and that Brad had been "lucky to get out when he did." I'd thought Brad was still in the thick of it when he died, but apparently he'd seen the writing on the wall and had traded his part of the deal for some undeveloped land outside of town, staying on as project manager instead of a partner. Which was a drag because no one's buying undeveloped land around here these days and even if they were that parcel isn't worth much. Unlike my house. Yeah, the market sucks right now, but it's a nice place in a good neighborhood and the mortgage is almost paid off. I'd do okay on it, if I decided to sell.

I wondered if I should take Tulip up on her offer to introduce me to her "terrific" real estate agent. I'd risked offending my new neighbor by bluntly asking how much they'd paid for their place, but Tulip hadn't minded. These days we're all in the concerned-about-equity boat together. The number she quoted wasn't encouraging, but their place is smaller than mine and not as well maintained, if you overlook the dust bunnies under my couch.

Too bad the pampered wife years hadn't lasted longer. My plan was to wring every last drop of satisfaction out of what remained of them as I could, even if I did end up moving into a condo in a few months and going back to work. It's not like I've never had to earn a living. For most of my adult life I've struggled to make a living as an artist. Mostly that had meant I'd painted in what free time I had between raising Olivia and working as a waitress or sales clerk or, for a few miserable months I do not wish to repeat, a telemarketer. It was only since marrying Brad that I'd had the luxury of pretending to paint full time. A full time that started out as a few hours every day, slipped to a few hours a week, and eventually dwindled to not much of anything.

Lately I'd been trying to revive my career as a painter, but without much success, because somewhere along the way I'd stopped feeling inspired. At the time it hadn't bothered me because I'd been too busy enjoying life. I hadn't even minded when I overheard Amanda (before she got to know me better) refer to me as "Dad's trophy wife." I'm far enough from young, blonde, and a size 2 that I felt more flattered than offended by her words.

In spite of the financial crunch that accompanied my descent from trophy-ish wife to widow, I was so much better off than most of the world that stressing over money felt self-indulgent. That didn't mean, though, that I was eager to move out of my cushy house and get a job. Maybe a miracle would occur and I'd start making money from my paintings. If I could find whatever back corner of my being I'd stashed my inspiration-receptor in. So far I hadn't had much luck finding it.

4

"What the hell is he doing here?" Suzette asked.

"Huh?" I turned to see what was up. "Hey, there's Bob." I waved but he was looking the other way.

"Stop that!" Suzette hissed, giving me a scornful look. "'There's Bob.' There's Bob who couldn't be my date for the wedding this afternoon because he's working today."

"Well, maybe he is." It seemed unlikely, but what did I know about police work? Other than how it had felt to be suspected (briefly, thank God) of spousicide. Which was how Bob and Suzette met, but that's another story.

"Oh sure," Suzette said. "Like there's something hush-hush going on he can't tell me about. At Rose Braska's funeral? Come on."

"How the hell would I know? Why don't you ask him?"

"Because he's pretending he doesn't see us, dummy. What if he's avoiding me?"

"Then he'd be hiding behind one of those potted palms, Suze, instead of standing right there where you can see him." I fiddled with the strap to my sandal, which had twisted so the buckle dug into my foot. "This is a funeral, not a stake out. We've got a few minutes. Go say hello."

Suzette edged her way out of the row and I used the elbow room to get my sandal refastened correctly. I took my time with the task, glad for any reason to keep my head down for a few moments and pretend I was somewhere else.

"I used to wear pretty shoes like that."

I turned to see the elderly lady in the aisle seat next to me hold up a sneaker-shod foot for inspection.

"These may be pretty, but yours look more comfortable," I said.

"When you get to be my age, you appreciate Velcro," the old lady said.

I was glad to be young enough to be a slave to fashion, but envied my neighbor's privilege to opt for Velcro and cushioned soles regardless of occasion.

She nodded toward the front of the room. "They do a nice job with the flowers here, don't you think?"

"Um, yes, the flowers are lovely." There sure were a lot of them. No surprise there. Rose Braska had been known for two things: an astonishing talent for baked goods and her love of all things floral. The big surprise, now that I'd noticed, was the absence of the guest of honor herself.

"Where's the casket?" I'd been making such an effort to distract myself rather than look at the front of the room that I hadn't noticed there was no box up there.

"Oh, dearie, didn't you hear? The coroner hasn't released the body."

"Really?" That was strange. And if so, why had they scheduled the funeral already?

"The delay was unexpected," the old lady said, as if she'd read my mind. "But her children have jobs to get back to so they decided to go ahead with a memorial service today."

It sounded haphazard to me, but I wasn't the one planning things. I was more interested in what was up with the body. An administrative glitch, or something fishy going on? It hardly seemed credible that there'd be questions about Rose's death. She'd been ill a long time, and although she'd died of an allergic reaction you had to figure that just about anything might have done her in. Besides, if you lined up the entire population of this town and one by one picked out the person most likely to die under suspicious circumstances, Rose Braska would be among the last ones standing. Or so I'd thought.

As I pondered the unlikelihood of Rose's death raising any kind of question, Alan came into the room through a side door and stopped to clasp hands and accept condolence from someone in the front row.

"Oh, there's Alan," I said to myself. He was as neatly groomed as always, but appeared tired, a fatigue I too well remembered. He walked further into the room and turned to shake hands with a man I recognized as someone whose wife had been on the Friends of the Library board with me a few years ago.

"I wonder if I have time to say my regrets," I pondered aloud, without making a move to get up. I'd seen Alan in person a few days ago, and could catch him after the ceremony. Plus I couldn't remember the other guy's name or why his wife wasn't on the board any more. I decided that was enough reason to keep my seat.

"He killed his first wife, too, you know."

"Excuse me?" I turned to my neighbor in astonishment. Killed? First wife? Too? I could not have heard that right.

"It was quite the scandal," my neighbor said, eyes lighting up. She leaned in and gave me a close look at rose pink lipstick seeping into the deep lines around her mouth. She had eyes like a three-hundred-year-old tortoise. A tortoise with shiny eye shadow that matched the lilac turban covering up what looked, from the tendrils seeping out around the edges, like hair that hadn't been washed in a week.

"He got away with it," she said. "But everyone knew what really happened."

"Oh," I said, stunned into monosyllabic dismay. Had I missed out on some grisly back story, or was this old bat delusional? I wondered if she had confused Alan with some long-forgotten reprobate. Or maybe she was talking about the guy whose name I couldn't remember.

"Hello, Mrs. Lander." Suzette was back, leaning across me to greet the old bag. "How are you this morning?"

Mrs. Lander was just fine, thank you dearie. I gestured to Suzette to switch seats with me. I didn't believe Mrs. Lander for a minute, but the idea that there might be something off about Rose's death wigged me out.

"I'm afraid I don't remember your name, dear," I heard Mrs. Lander say as Suzette skooched past me and settled into the buffer seat. "You look familiar, so I'm sure we've met."

"Suzette Wong," Suze said. "We've crossed paths around town."

"I hope I'll do better with your name next time, dear," the biddy said. "My memory isn't good for much any more."

"I understand," Suzette said. I latched onto the bad memory comment as proof that Mrs. Lander had no idea what she was talking about.

"You're very exotic looking, you know," the old woman said. "Where are you from, dear, if you don't mind my asking?"

Suzette is from Albany, hardly an exotic locale, but when she whispered in Mrs. Lander's ear the old lady gasped and drew back. Then

Reverend Peabody took his place behind a podium at the front of the room and gestured to everyone to settle down and listen up.

"What on earth did you say to her?" I hissed.

"'Pluto.'" Suzette grinned at me. "She wanted exotic, so I felt I should do better than 'upstate New York.'"

I managed to muffle a snort, glad for the distraction. It wasn't until the minister had droned into his opening remarks that I remembered to wonder what Suzette might have learned from Bob that could put turtle-face's gossip into perspective.

5

Such an abundance of flowers! What need was there of Heaven in this wondrous place?

The spectral wisp of consciousness so delighted in burrowing among the blossoms that it forgot to hold to the faint memory of being human. Oh what a lovely place this was. How right it had been to follow awareness here.

Color, shape, and fragrance, while no longer distinct from one another, were so vibrant and intoxicating now. Look how it can wind itself around the blooms, becoming one with them. This one, and this one, and... not that one.

For a moment it felt trapped, anxious, uncertain, twined too tightly among the floral exuberance, and it almost remembered there'd been a reason for coming here... here, where there was rapture and joy among the petals... and where sorrow and loss lurked beyond the flowers' embrace, a cold and empty resonance close to which it did not care to linger.

* * *

After the service we hung around long enough to share condolences with Alan, who muttered Rose would be happy we'd come while looking too stunned to notice whose hand he was shaking. They say practice makes perfect but it was hard to believe his numb display was anything other than genuine.

Except wasn't it possible that guilt and remorse could be as numbing as grief? I couldn't quite convince myself that my doubts were based on impossibilities.

As I turned to go a long-stemmed lily in a large arrangement swayed and dipped its head toward me, a little bow that to a credulous soul might almost seem an affirmation that all was not well in Roseland and I was right to entertain questions. I told myself it was just a draft as members of the thinning crowd made their way out the door. The cloying fragrance of funeral flowers seemed to fill the spaces where mourners had been, and I felt a headache coming on.

I told Suzette I was going to dash to the loo (frequent bathroom trips being the downside of a vigorous morning caffeine habit) and would meet her at the car. As I reapplied lipstick I tried to recast Alan in my mind as a serial wife-killer. Pffft. It just didn't seem possible.

I dismissed the idea as nothing more than the effect of gossip on an overactive imagination, and was striding toward the exit to the parking lot when that pesky sandal buckle snagged on my trouser hem. I braced one hand against the wall and tried to disentangle the buckle without tearing a hole in my navy silk slacks. No hole, but a length of hem came undone. The sandals, pretty or not, were going into the Goodwill bag in my closet as soon as I got home. I'd paid enough to expect more from them, but maybe whoever snared them from a thrift store for five bucks wouldn't mind wrestling with a tricky buckle.

I remembered, from dealing with Brad's final arrangements, that the funeral home office was back here somewhere. Maybe they'd have a stapler or some scotch tape I could use for emergency wardrobe repairs. Probably there was a needle and some thread on the premises, too, but I didn't want to fix my trouser hem with the same tools that replaced buttons on a suit destined for the grave.

Around a corner I found what I thought was the office door, slightly ajar and labeled PRIVATE. A pale pink rose petal rested on the carpet by the door, probably fallen from one of the many arrangements that had been delivered to fill the front of the chapel. I'd raised my hand to knock when I heard someone on the other side of the door say, "We shouldn't be seen together here."

For a moment I thought the comment was addressed to me, but unless the speaker had X-ray vision that wasn't possible. The odd thing was, it sounded like Alan. Sort of: a generic well-spoken-older-guy voice. I couldn't be sure. And it wasn't any of my business.

By the time I'd told myself that, I'd taken a step to the side and aimed my ear toward the gap on the hinge-side of the door. So prepared was I to believe that I'd misheard the comment—that the next would be something like, "That one's done, who've we got for this afternoon?"— that I was surprised to hear the murmur of a woman's voice, and then the man again: "I really can't have this conversation right now."

She must have turned toward me, because her voice became clearer. "I know this is a difficult time for you, darling,"—darling?—"but we need to talk about it soon." I imagined her moving closer, her face turned up to his with a beseeching look. Which just proves I've been watching way too much daytime TV lately.

"Alright, if we must," might-be-Alan said. "I'll see if I can come by your place later."

"Don't see if," the woman pleaded. "Just come. You know I'll make you feel better."

This was getting soapier by the second. Do real people say things like that?

"I've got a house full of family," he said. "It's not like when…," his voice faded.

When it was just you and Rose? I wondered.

"That's the perfect excuse," the woman said. "Tell them you need some air, that you're going for a drive. No one will question that."

"Alright," maybe-Alan said. "I'll be over sometime after eight."

"Alan, are you back here?"

I moved quickly toward the exit as a stout woman in an unflattering gray suit rounded the corner from the lobby.

"Oh hello there," she called out.

I turned back as if I'd just noticed her.

"I'm looking for Alan, have you seen him? I thought he was back here."

I shook my head no. "I was just on my way out," I said, and hurried out the back door, bumping into Suzette, who was on her way in to see what was holding me up.

"You'll never guess what I just heard!" I blurted, embarrassed by my shameless eavesdropping and eager to spill the beans. "Come on, I'll tell you in the car."

The parking lot had emptied out to just a handful of cars. I was tempted to stick around to see what stragglers emerged and whether any had bimbo-in-the-back-room potential, but we were running late to pick up Granimi. I settled for taking a picture of each car with my phone as we walked through the parking lot. I'm not much of a phone person, and hadn't used that function before, but pushing the button with the camera icon on it seemed to do the trick.

* * *

"Alan a wife-killer? Stodgy old Alan? And a mistress? I don't believe it."

"Suzette! Eyes on the road, please!" I begged, as we swerved across the yellow line. Thank God traffic was light. "And no, I don't believe Alan killed anybody. That's just wild rumors. It's gotta be. I mean, consider the source."

Suzette shrugged. "Mrs. Lander may be a few stems shy of a bouquet but that doesn't mean she made it up."

"No," I pointed out. "But come on, she half-believed you're from Pluto!"

Suzette snorted. "I feel kind of bad about that," she confessed.

"You're a terrible person, we're agreed. I'm just not 100% sure it was Alan in the office back there." I pondered whether or not that was a bad thing, and came to no conclusion. "By the way, what did Bob have to say about why he was at the service."

"Told me to mind my own business," Suze admitted. Fat chance that would happen. "Then he tried to distract me with a make-out session in the viewing room across the hall."

"You didn't! Eeuw."

"There was nobody in there," she said, then giggled. "No body, get it?"

I rolled my eyes. "Seriously, a funeral parlor?"

"It was just a quick kiss," she said. "Get your mind out of the gutter. Besides, I could tell I only had half his attention. Usually he's a way better kisser than that."

"At least you know he really was on the job. And now we know something's going on."

"Something's hinky, that's for sure."

"But, as you pointed out," I said, "this is Rose Braska we're talking about. Made the world's best cookies, wouldn't harm a fly, last person on earth to be involved in anything 'hinky.' I bet it's a funeral home scam or something."

I didn't really believe that. I thought about how my guest room window overlooks Alan's driveway. It would be interesting to see if his car pulled out around eight o'clock that evening.

"You're forgetting that dear old Rose had beaucoup dear old bucks," Suzette said.

"It was Rose's money?" I knew the Braskas were well off. Rose was a major cheddar on the local charity scene, and that doesn't happen unless you have dollars to donate. But I'd never given any thought to who or where that money came from.

"Alan brought something to the table," Suzette said, flicking her blinker to make the turn to the airport, "but the big money was Rose's. I heard she was a toothpaste heiress. Or mouthwash, maybe. Dental floss? I forget. Some kind of oral hygiene product."

Toothpaste heiress? The things you find out about your neighbors.

Suzette dropped me off and went to look for a spot in the short-term lot. I hustled over to arrivals, scanning the area for an elderly invalid in a wheelchair. I should have known better. If Granimi hadn't waved hello I would have walked right past her.

6

Granimi had chopped off her hair since I'd last seen her, and has been shedding her conventional wardrobe over the years since Grandpop passed. Still, it was a big step from the Chanel suits she still wore in my mind to mold-green cropped cargo pants topped with a particularly unattractive hoodie that appeared to be made from shredded garbage bags. The half-cast on her left forearm was hot pink. Buttercup-yellow platform flip-flops matched the Hello Kitty tee peeking out from under the hoodie.

"Granimi!" I gave her a gentle hug and a kiss on the cheek. I suppressed a shudder as the jacket rustled under my touch like a nest of cockroaches. Eesh, what was she thinking?

"You're looking, uh, cheerier than I expected," I said. She did look well, considering Olivia's comments the night before. "How are you feeling?"

"Oh I'm fine, dear," she said. "Feeling my age a bit more than usual, that's all."

"It takes a lot to slow you down, G.," I said. "How's the wrist? Mom says you broke it?"

She waggled the pink cast at me. "Cracked a bone. It's a little sore, but not enough for all the fuss everyone's making."

I picked up her carryon and noticed something stuffed in the outside pocket. "Any chance you're supposed to be wearing this?" I pulled out a blue nylon sling.

"Oh, that's such a nuisance," she said, waving it away. "I took it off when I got on the plane," meaning the minute she was out of my mother's sight, probably. "I must have forgotten to put it back on."

Forgot, my foot. G. is as old as the hills, but still sharp as a tack. "Mm-hmm. Why don't you wear it while we're moving around."

"It's just so ugly," she said as I helped her into the sling, the plastic bits of her hoodie whispering like windblown refuse.

This from a woman who'd shucked a fifty-year accumulation of couture for a Hello Kitty tee and something that could win Worst of Show at a trash-to-fashion challenge. I hope at her age I have half her energy and at least four times her fashion sense.

Suzette met up with us at the baggage carousel, where it eventually became apparent that Granimi's bags had taken a side trip to destination unknown. By the time we'd filed a lost bag claim it was close to wedding ceremony time. I'd planned to take Granimi home but there wasn't going to be time for that unless we skipped the vows and went straight to the reception. Good thing we'd planned for a time crunch and had our wedding attire with us. Suzette had RSVP-ed "and guest" in case Bob could make it, which he wouldn't, and Granimi said weddings are fun and she was up for anything. Which was more than I could say for myself. By the time Suze and I had changed into our party garb in the airport bathroom, I was ready for a nap.

"Whose wedding is this again, dear?" Granimi asked as we approached the chapel.

"Carlos owns The Pear Street Gallery, where I show my work," I explained. Used to show, that is. Claims of ongoing representation might stretch the truth just a bit.

"And Rhianna," Suzette added, "is a textile artist. They've been together for decades. No one knows why they're finally getting married, she swears she's not pregnant, but we're happy for them. It should be a fun wedding."

"It's a shame the airline lost my bags," Granimi said. "I would have liked to dress up."

"I'm sure you'll fit right in." I wondered what her idea of dressing up was these days. "It's an artsy crowd. Suzette and I will probably be the most boring people there."

"Speak for yourself!" Suzette shimmied her silver lamé hips. "I plan to prove that a woman pushing forty can boogie with the best of them."

* * *

I'd been looking forward to the reception for weeks but by the time we were tossing birdseed at the bride and groom, tired and cranky had moved in. "I am so not in the mood for this," I muttered as we arrived at The Pear Street Gallery, where the reception was being held. Thank god the ceremony had been short. I needed a nap, and to scrub the idea of Alan as wife killer out of my cranium. I wished I could reach in there with a toilet brush and get rid of all the doubts and unpleasant innuendos grunging up the inside of my skull.

Suze handed me a glass of champagne and reminded me that if I stuck it out there would be cake. "I know it's a rough day for you, but this is supposed to be the fun part, remember?"

"You're right," I admitted. "I'm just so freaking tired. I was up half the night worrying about Granimi"—needlessly, as it turned out—"and thinking about Brad. He loved a good party. I wish he were here." My mood slump was partly due to the unavoidable fact that when this reception was over Brad's final golf game was next up on the agenda.

I looked around. Getting the receiving line started would take an hour. I'd give a million dollars to anyone who could corral a roomful of artists into order any faster than that, especially when half of them hadn't arrived yet.

"I'm going to steal a cat nap on that couch Carlos keeps in the storage room upstairs," I said. "If I disappear for half an hour, can you keep an eye on Granimi?"

"Sure, honey," Suzette said, "although I don't think Mimi needs to be chaperoned." She gestured to the far side of the room where Granimi was showing off her hoodie to the bride.

Rhianna, dressed in a pink lace micro-mini and tent-sized veil, fingered the hoodie admiringly and made a comment to several 20-somethings who appeared to be wearing fancy underwear in lieu of clothes. It occurred to me that G.'s jacket might be the latest thing from some hotshot Tokyo designer, in which case it probably cost ten times as much as my last electric bill.

"If I were you," Suzette advised, reminding me of my nap plans, "I'd keep that scarf between my head and any part of that couch. It's seen a lot of recreational activity, if you know what I mean."

"Eeuw," I said, recalling a few choice rumors and a certain evening reception a few years back when Brad and I had gotten carried away. "I'm not sure I wanted to be reminded of that." Wasn't gonna keep me from my power nap, though. I'd curl up on the floor if I had to.

* * *

Twenty minutes later I stretched and rubbed the nap wrinkles out of my face and got up off the infamously comfortable couch in the gallery's storage loft. I could hear a swell of good cheer from downstairs, but felt no immediate urge to join the fun. Instead, I found myself looking through the paintings stashed in racks along the back wall. I recognized some as the work of painters I knew or admired, and was surprised to find one of my older paintings there. I propped it up on a display easel and contemplated the evidence of my past talent. I'd forgotten how close I'd come to being really good.

Why and how had I lost my focus?

I'd been distracted by being happy for once, maybe that was it. Had I paid for that happiness with my talent? Is it true that an artist has to suffer to be any good?

If that's the deal I should have churned out half a dozen masterpieces these past six months. So much for that theory.

I put the painting back where I'd found it and headed down to the party before I could get any more depressed.

7

I found Granimi discussing *anime* with a fiercely pierced and tattooed young man and his equally embellished girlfriend. G. looked a little tired around the edges but assured me she was having a wonderful time.

"My goodness, dear, there are so many interesting people here," she said. "I didn't realize you had such a fun *milieu*."

Lately my milieu, if you want to call it that, has consisted of Ben and Jerry and the TV remote, but it was nice someone thought I led an exciting life.

We made it through the receiving line in something less than an eternity, and then it was time for more champagne and lots of finger food. The room was full of friends, many of who I'd not seen in a while, and at some point the band picked up steam and dancing took over the main room. Waiters stopped circulating; a buffet, for those who required continual sustenance, was laid out on a table in one of the back rooms. I needed a break from conversation and went to see if any more of a particularly delicious phyllo concoction had materialized.

On my way to the nosh room I remembered that Carlos had mentioned turning what had been a small storeroom on this floor into another exhibit space. I was curious to see what he'd done with it.

A man I'd noticed Granimi chatting with earlier was in the new gallery. Older than me, early fifties maybe. The kind of lean that ages well. His long dark hair, pulled back in a pony tail with a strip of caramel suede, sported just enough streaks of gray to avoid looking like an attempt to be young and hip. He wore an embroidered vest of plum velvet and a silver-and-turquoise squash-blossom necklace (both of which I instantly coveted) that only a guy with Native American genes could pull off. I'd interrupted his study of a painting while a slim young blonde talked about the iconography of patriarchal-political aggression in her art. Pretentious twit. I started to back out of the room, remembering why, in spite of my fondness for Carlos and Rhianna, I don't hang out much with other artists.

"Hey there," the man said, noticing me and offering a friendly smile.

I returned a polite mouth-twitch back, on the verge of slipping away. I'd check out this room another time.

"We've almost met," he said, taking a step forward, which earned me an annoyed glance from his companion. As if I had any intention of stepping on her toes.

"You're Mimi's granddaughter, correct?"

"Yes," I admitted. Instant best friends with everyone, that's Granimi for you. She was probably on a first-name basis with half the guests by now. Being sociable with people I already knew was proving enough of a strain for me, and I did not feel like making small talk with strangers. I reluctantly shook the hand he offered and introduced myself. "Lena Wells."

"And you're a painter?"

I suppressed a grimace. Granimi has an irritating habit of playing matchmaker when I'm between marriages, and I suspected she was at it again.

"Yes," I said, to answer his question. "Or I was, at any rate." These days I mostly just felt like a widow, which was neither as interesting nor as fun as being an artist.

"You've given it up?" he asked, with a raised eyebrow. He was still holding onto my hand. Ordinarily I find that beyond annoying, but something about this man's touch had a soothing effect on my prickly psyche.

I shrugged. "It's been a difficult year for me," I heard myself say. What was I doing? The whole point of checking out this room had been to avoid other people for five minutes. I did not want to get sucked into conversation.

"Of course," he said, now clasping both my hands with both of his. Normally an even more annoying gesture that was making me feel confused and almost happy. I gently extracted myself from it.

The blonde, recognizing that she'd lost his attention, stalked out of the room, pausing to say, "I'll catch you later, Raven," in suggestive tones.

You've got to be kidding me. I mean, he had the look for it, sure, but Raven? That was a bit much, no matter how well he pulled off the pony-tail-and-vest thing.

Raven didn't look at blondie as she left, so I guess no competition there, not that I cared.

"Your grandmother told me you've lost your husband," he said.

Of course she did. Probably she also implied that her idea of a requisite date-free mourning period had expired.

"I didn't misplace him," I said. "He died."

It came out more sharply than I'd intended. The guy seemed nice, actually, and his sympathy appeared genuine. "Sorry. I didn't mean to snap at you. I've been feeling sorry for myself today, and it's made me short-tempered."

"No need to apologize," he said. "I'm Raven Santiago, by the way. Now," he touched my elbow and guided me further into the room, "tell me what you think of this painting."

He positioned me in front of the same work the blonde had been spouting off about. A dreary mess, if you asked me. Which he'd just done.

"No sense of composition," I said. "And the colors are muddy." I saw from the wall label that it was titled War Crimes #3, so I guess those murky blobs were meant to be corpses, or prisoners, or maybe just turds of some kind.

"Pompous and dreary," I summed up, stepping back and turning to my companion to gauge his reaction. "I'm not a big fan of bleak abstraction."

"No reason you should be," he said with equanimity and a hint of a smile.

According to the label, the creator of the dismal canvas was a Cybil Andersen, probably the departed bimbette. Raven won back the points he'd lost with his silly name by proving he'd seen past the long blonde hair and thong-flaunting. Although they could be why he'd chatted with her in the first place. You can't blame men for noticing.

"Are any of your paintings on display here?" he asked.

"I don't think so."

"Because you haven't been painting much lately."

"Because what I've painted lately is gloomy and depressing and imitative, and the world doesn't need any more of that crap."

"I prefer cheerful paintings myself," he said. "Something with a little color to it."

I'd been wondering why Carlos had displayed Cybil's work; usually he shows an unerring eye in what he selects for the gallery. The other pieces in the room weren't much better. Then I remembered something Carlos had said a while back about what he'd do if he ever had a few extra square feet to put to use. I looked around the tiny room and a laugh slipped out.

"I realize I don't know much about art," Raven said, "but is a fondness for color really laughable?"

"Oh, no, no. I'm sorry," I apologized. "I wasn't laughing at you. I like bright colors, too." I held out the skirt of my boho-chic dress to display its rampage of oversized florals.

"Then what did I say that's so funny?"

"It's not what you said," I explained. "It's what this room is."

"And that would be…"

"The Loser's Gallery." I put my hand over my mouth, remembering, too late, that Carlos had sworn me to secrecy.

"Loser's Gallery?" Raven looked around began to smile as he got the joke.

I drew my fingers across my lips in the universal keep-it-zipped signal. "It's supposed to be a secret."

He winked at me. "Gotcha." Something outside the door caught his attention. "Stay right there," he said, and ducked out, returning a moment later with two flutes of champagne.

"Okay." He handed me a glass, "I know it's supposed to be a secret but, since you've already let the cat out of the bag, explain to me what this Loser's Room is about."

I hadn't quite had enough to drink to blame it on the champagne, but what the hell. "Carlos is a softie. He hates saying no to anyone. So his idea was to create a space where artists who aren't likely to make it could have a piece on a gallery wall and feel good about themselves for a while." I gestured at the dozen or so small paintings in the tiny space. "Until recently this was a closet. And none of these are close to Carlos's usual standard, so I think he's turned that rather peculiar dream into a reality."

I gave a silent prayer of thanks none of my stuff was in there. I'd slit my wrists if that ever happened.

Raven looked around with an expression of suppressed mirth, and when he caught my eye we both let out a chortle.

"Seriously, though," I begged him. "Carlos swore me to secrecy. If word gets out, the whole point of this place will be lost."

"I imagine someone will figure it out eventually," he said. "But I'll keep your secret."

"Thanks," I said. "I'm probably only one of many who are in on the joke, but I'd rather not be the one who gave it away."

A drumroll followed by applause and whistling from the front room interrupted our pact. "Sounds like we're missing something," Raven said, taking my elbow again and ushering me from the room. "Let's go see if they're serving cake."

A man who likes cake. I was almost tempted to be interested. Not that I'd do anything about it if I were. Being interested could lead to flirting, which might lead to dating, which would require making an effort, and I couldn't imagine dredging up the energy for any of that kind of behavior.

As we edged back into the crowd someone stopped Raven to say hello and I eased away to hook up with Suzette, whom I could see accepting a plate of cake from a guy in snakeskin patterned jeans and a leather vest. Nice look with the shaved head and tribal tattoos.

"Hey, it's Lena!" Suzette hailed me with a tipsy enthusiasm that implied she'd forgotten she was our designated driver. "Lena, this is Spike," she said, talking around a mouthful of cake and gesturing at snakepants with her spork. "Spike's a musician," she added, as if that explained why she was flirting with him, which maybe it did.

"I'm sure he is," I said. Husband number two had cured me of the musician thing. Brad had been hubbie three, if you're wondering. I agree that's a lot for someone still a couple years shy of forty but it's not like I'd planned it that way. Shit happens.

"Where's the line for cake?" I followed another wave of the forkette and edged my way toward the good stuff. It wouldn't be a proper wedding until I'd eaten two pieces of cake. At my wedding to Brad, I'm pretty sure I'd had three. God forbid I find another husband, or I'll be up to four.

I can eat a lot of cake, but even for me four would be a lot.

8

I edged out to the periphery of the crowd with my second slice (almond pound cake with white chocolate mousse and raspberries: yum) and scouted around for Granimi. Her stamina for social interaction is much greater than mine, but I did wonder if maybe she'd had enough partying on top of a morning of air travel.

"I'm fine, dear," she said, when I caught up with her. "I took a short nap in Suzette's car a while ago. At my age the batteries need to be recharged more frequently."

"I'm a big fan of naps myself." I looked at my watch and calculated travel time. "If your recharged batteries can keep you going for another fifteen minutes, Suzette and I will be ready to go."

I hadn't told G. about the scheduled goofball fun, and planned to settle her in at my place before Suzette and I snuck off to smack Brad around the golf course. Or we could take her with us, if she was up for it. Might put ideas in her head, though, for when her own day came. Who knows what the Granimi version of goofballs might be.

"That sounds just fine, dear. Oh excuse me," she said, moving away, "there's Christy again." She waved at a redhead wafting past in a billow of gauze and glitter. "I told her we would schedule some Pilates sessions while I'm here."

We? At least the "get more exercise" part of my long-postponed self-improvement program would be taken care of.

"I see you found cake."

Raven had come up behind me.

"I know you haven't been painting lately," he said, "but I would be interested in seeing your work sometime."

Yikes. I didn't want to show my recent work to anyone. I was on the verge of concocting an excuse when I realized I didn't want to just brush him off, either. Was I interested in this man? I didn't think so. I was a long way from being over the widow thing. And while he was pleasant enough, and seemed genuine, he wasn't anyone's idea of gorgeous: tall and straight, yes, but a little farther into the middle years than I felt like venturing, and with looks that were interesting at best, rather than handsome. Plus the whole 'Raven' thing was ridiculous.

I had to admit, though, that the man had charisma. And he'd passed up a buxom young blonde with a navel ring to chat with a 37-year-old who ate too much cake and wouldn't wear a thong if it came with a million bucks pinned to it.

Well, maybe for a million.

Somehow, while I was calculating my thong price, the words, "There's a painting of mine in the upstairs storeroom, if you'd like to see that one," slipped out of my mouth.

"Let's start there," Raven said.

I found his presumption that viewing one painting would lead to more irritating, and recognized what I was doing: looking for flaws because I didn't want to admit I might be just a teeny bit more intrigued than I wanted to be. So cut it out, I told myself. Show him the painting and then you can get back to being bitter and lonely.

God. What had happened to getting on with life? If not now, when?

Raven waited.

"Come on then." I flashed what I hoped was a confident smile, but my smile muscles were rusty and I wasn't sure they pulled it off.

I realized, as we headed up the stairs, that I'd left my scarf on the couch up there. That scarf had been a gift from Brad, and was a favorite: a wisp of orange silk with a subtle ikat pattern in yellow, the ends embroidered with gold thread. I'd hate to lose it, and by the time we got to the top of the stairs I was thinking more about finding the scarf than about showing Raven my painting.

"It's not here," I groused, lifting the sofa cushions and looking around the floor.

"You left your painting in the couch?"

"The painting's back there," I said, waving a hand toward the rear wall. "I left a scarf up here earlier. An orange one. I'd like to have it back."

Raven raised an eyebrow.

"What?"

"Uh, nothing," he lied.

"Ohhhh," I said as the penny dropped. "You've heard about The Couch."

He gave me a considering look. "You don't strike me as that kind of a person."

It's possible I'd impressed him as being too snippy and caustic to get laid, but I chose to believe he meant I was intelligent and pretty and clearly above such skanky behavior.

"I'm not the Couch type," I assured him. Other than that one time with Brad, but we'd been married so probably it didn't count. "I had about an hour and half of sleep last night," I explained, wrenching my brain away from the past, "and snuck up here for a quick nap before the festivities began. Alone, although that's not any business of yours."

My ornery mood wasn't helped by the realization that if the couch had been put to its customary use at any time after my nap, one of the many other women at this event could be going home with my scarf.

"You're right," Raven said. "Not any of my business at all. So," he turned to look around. "Which one of these is yours?"

I gave up on the scarf and led him to my painting. "This one's from four or five years ago." I tried to remember exactly when I'd painted it, but it was like trying to remember life before you were born.

"I like it," Raven said. "There's something about the light, how you've painted the sky, that's very... " He gave up. "I don't know how to talk about art."

"But you know what you like?" I prompted.

"Yes," he said. "I know what I like. And this is nice."

From someone fluent in art-speak I would have bristled at "nice" as high praise, but his sincerity was apparent. Nice was fine. "What would you have said if you didn't like it?"

He grinned. "Oh, something like, 'it looks very accomplished, but is not a style I relate to.'"

"Fair enough."

"And you say your recent work has been 'gloomy and depressing.' That's because of your husband's death?"

"Thank you for using the D word," I said, avoiding the question. "I know people mean well when they say 'lost your husband,' but it's not like he'll turn up in the back of a closet. I don't know why people can't just say 'died.' That's what happened: he died. Tiptoeing around it doesn't make me feel any better. Much as it sucks, though, it's been six months, and I'm starting to believe that some day I'm going to get past it." Maybe not over it, but past it. Probably.

"So it's something else that's keeping you from painting."

Ouch. The man is insightful.

I take a deep breath and nod that he's right. "What I've lost," I hear myself say, wondering why I'm spilling to a stranger, "is the part of my soul that knew how to paint." I've never put that into words before. It feels good to have confessed it. "Well, not how to paint, exactly. That's technique; I still have that. It's the vision thing that's gone. I used to look at the world and see a million things I wanted to interpret on canvas. Now all I see is the same old place everyone else is living in."

Saying it makes me feel jittery and off balance inside. "There's this—," I flail a hand in a random gesture. I don't know what to call it. "A feeling that I get. Like I'm plugged into something as big as the universe. Like it's not me painting, I'm just the hand that moves the brush."

I teeter on the edge of an abyss, remembering. How long has it been since I've felt that connection?

"It's like breathing," I whisper, as if I could coax it back. "Or sleep. Or the taste of an orange. It's life. And I've lost it, and I don't know how to get it back."

I choke up and I don't know whether I'm crying for Brad or for the painter I used to be, or for the lost child from my past who's been on my mind so much lately. A tear makes a dash for freedom down my cheek.

"You know," Raven said, "I might be able to help you with that."

9

Are you kidding me? I bare my soul to you, I tell you things I've never said to anyone, not even to myself, and you come back with the come-on I've been half expecting since we met?

I guess I overreacted, because the next thing Raven said was, "I'm leading a journey seminar next weekend. I think you might find it interesting, and possibly even a little bit healing."

"What's a journey seminar?" I asked, sniffling, wishing I'd stuffed some tissues into my cute little purse.

"I teach shamanic journey work," he said, pausing to see if I had a clue what he was talking about.

And there it was: the woowoo factor. The one that goes with the whole I'm a Native American in touch with my soul—and yours, too, vibe.

"It sounds very New Agey, I know," he said when I didn't reply. "But the techniques are accessible, and the process can yield remarkable insights."

I didn't respond. I felt wrung out and idiotic and I wanted to go home but I couldn't because I had to go knock fake golf balls containing my husband's cremains around a golf course before I could crawl into bed in a dark room and pull the covers over my head. I don't even play golf. I've never even liked golf.

"It seems to me," Raven said, gesturing to my painting, "that being a good artist requires more than technique. It takes soul. And getting in touch with your soul is what journey work is about."

It sounded good put that way, but a lump of fear or grief or regret or too much wedding cake welled up in my throat and I yearned so much for the wholeness his words promised that I forgot how to breathe.

"I don't have a seminar brochure with me," he said, fishing a finger around in a vest pocket. "But here's my card. There's a seminar description on my web site."

I took the card, and muttered something about looking it up, feeling a familiar cloud of overwhelm coalesce around me. I'd had enough of being with other people, and couldn't imagine voluntarily attending a group activity like a seminar. Crawling into a cave for about a thousand years was looking good.

"Yoo-hoo, Lena? Are you up here?"

I recognized Suzette's voice before her face appeared at the top of the stairs.

"Over here," I called.

"Come on," she said, climbing up the last few steps. "It's time to go. Oh. I didn't know you were with someone."

"This is Raven," I said. "He talked me into showing him one of my paintings."

She teetered over to have a look for herself. "Oh, I remember this one." She peered at it. "Gosh the light's terrible back here."

She was right; the loft is a huge space, spanning the entire length of the building, and we were in the darkest part of it, toward the back.

Suzette picked up the painting and turned to the front of the room. "Let's look at it in the light."

She led the way to where several large windows pierced the street wall. I trailed behind trying to parse what Raven's hand was doing on my back when Suzette let out a yelp and clutched the canvas to her chest.

"Oh my god."

I couldn't see what had alarmed her, because it was behind a Japanese screen partitioning the corner of the room. A few more steps and I let out a gasp myself.

Of all the necks I thought my scarf might be draped around, this was not one I'd imagined. For a long moment the three of us gaped at what had recently been a skinny, greasy-looking man in a cheap blue suit. My lovely orange scarf was wound tightly around his neck, the bold color contrasting obscenely with the deep rose hue of his face and the swollen purple tongue protruding from his mouth.

"Oh my god," Suzette and I squeaked in unison. Raven, the only one of us capable of motion, knelt beside the body, checking for a pulse although the man was clearly dead. Those wide open eyes hadn't blinked once in the hours we'd been standing there unable to look away.

Downstairs the music stopped, as if our discovery had halted the festivities, and we heard a distant call for single ladies to congregate for the tossing of the bouquet.

"What do we do?" Suzette asked.

For one surreal moment I thought she was asking if we should go jostle for good bouquet-catching positions.

"Call Bob," I said, so she did.

*   *   *

"I know you get a kick out of seeing me do my job," Bob said to Suzette when he arrived with a couple of other officers. "But finding a body is going a bit far, even for you. That's more down Lena's alley."

I glared at Bob. I hadn't exactly found Brad's body. Brad had fallen into the river from the River Bend Terrace mill-to-condos project. I'd found the spot where he'd been standing. Brad had washed up on some rocks about a mile downstream. I didn't like the reminder that some had wondered at the time whether I'd helped Brad over the edge.

"Any idea who this is?" Bob inquired. We all shook our heads no.

"What's that around his neck?" a uniform asked.

"Uh, that's my scarf," I volunteered. No point dodging the question.

"And you are?"

"Lena Wells. I was up here a couple of hours ago and dropped my scarf. We'd come back up to look for it when we found him." Not the entire story, but enough of it for now.

Bob noticed the squeamish expressions on Suzette's and my faces as we tried not to look at the body. "Is there some place you could stay put until someone's ready to speak with you?" he asked, so we and Raven relocated downstairs to Carlos's office.

Bob came down with us to negotiate the early release of the bride and groom from the wedding hostages, so they could catch their flight to Puerto Vallarta. The three of us were left to cool our heels until someone was ready to ask more detailed questions. With some negotiating and pleas for mercy, I arranged for Granimi to join us so she wouldn't get lost in the shuffle of guests waiting to be interviewed before they could go home. After a half-hour that felt like a month, a glance at the clock told me that we weren't going to get to Brad's last golf game anytime soon.

Eventually we got a chance to tell our tales. Separately, and several times over. Raven disappeared at some point, then Suzette and G. were done and graciously said they'd wait for me to get the okay to go home as well.

"Sorry we kept you so long," Bob said at last, almost managing to sound sincere. "The scarf thing raised a few eyebrows, but you're cleared to go."

I knew from prior experience that "cleared to go" did not mean "cleared of all suspicion." All those canapés and second helpings of wedding cake felt like cobblestones in my stomach.

10

Suzette pulled up in front of my house and I gently woke Granimi. One upside of our delayed departure from the reception was that Suzette had sobered up enough to drive us home. The other was that stumbling on a corpse was a great excuse for postponing Brad's final golf game. I got the goofballs out of the back, and G. and I waved our thanks to Suzette and dragged our sorry asses up my front walk.

A folded sheet of white paper was taped to my door. What now, I thought, assuming yet another scolding notice from the Homeowner's Association: my lawn is an eighth of an inch overgrown? I ushered Granimi inside and ripped the paper off the door, planning to throw it out unread. Until I saw the message hand-written in purple ink:

> *Your niece is at our house.*
> *Tulip van A.*

My what? Where?

It took a moment for my tired brain to dredge up the relevant facts that I do have a niece—Valerie, my brother's kid—and that Tulip van Alstyne is my new neighbor.

What was Val doing next door? I hadn't seen her since Thanksgiving, which we'd made the mistake of spending at my brother's house. Alcohol, impending divorce, and an overcooked turkey had been a miserable combination. As best I could recall I'd given Val a hug before Brad and I fled the premises, telling her that if things got really bad at home she should call me. Since last November the divorce had been finalized, Pete had moved out and remarried at the speed of light (confirming our suspicions he'd had someone on the side), and Val, living with her mom, hadn't called. I'd sent her an Old Navy gift card for her twelfth birthday in February, for which I'd received back a one-line thank you email.

I remembered I'd turned my cell phone off during Rose's memorial service and hadn't looked at it since then. Yikes: twenty-three voicemails. Probably all from or about Val. I figured I could ignore them until I'd talked to her.

"Hey, G.," I said, "I've got a surprise for you."

"What's that, dear?"

"Come next door with me and find out."

Tulip must have been keeping an eye out, because her front door opened before we'd even stepped across the yard. Valerie peeked out from behind her, looking chastened and unsure of her welcome. Until she saw Granimi, and then she came bounding down the path to greet us.

Granimi, who's had prior experience with teenaged runaways, slipped right into her role of unconditional love. "Why Valerie, I didn't know you were going to be here! What a delightful surprise."

Tulip smiled at us. "This dear child was sitting on your front step for over an hour!"

Then you should have invited her in sooner, I thought.

"Thanks for looking after her until we got home," I said. I had to fake the friendly bit. Something about the woman made my inner bitch itch. Probably it's that glow she's got from being so healthy and happy.

Val released her hold on Granimi and I set aside my mixed feelings towards my irritatingly nice neighbor and gave the kid a hug of my own.

"I wish you'd told me you were coming, sweetie!" I said. "I'm so sorry I wasn't here to greet you."

Val had sprouted into the gawky stage since I'd last seen her. Brown hair that I remembered as long and glossy was now chin-length, tangled, and in need of shampoo.

"It's too bad you haven't had your cell phone on," Tulip pointed out.

"Tulip," I struggled not to snap at her, "it's been an extremely long day, and we're here now, so could we just get on with getting Val home to my house?"

"Sure," she said. "Come on in, her bag's inside."

Tulip stepped inside and I turned to Val. "I'm happy to see you, kid," I whispered. "But what are you doing here?"

Valerie gave me a pleading look I remembered using at that age, the one that means I know I screwed up and I already feel bad about it so please don't come down on me too hard.

"I ran away from camp," Val said.

Ran away from camp? I didn't know whether to be alarmed or impressed. Whatever camp she'd been at couldn't be nearby or I would have been pressed into weekend visit duty.

When I didn't explode at the news, Val went on in a rush, "I just had to get out of there and I didn't know where else to go and can I stay with you for a while, please? Pleasepleasepleaseplease?"

"You came to the right place," I said, maybe fibbing just a little. "My house is way better than camp."

We stepped into Tulip's front hall, and were greeted with enthusiasm by the horrid little dog, who halted a scant yard away and looked from me to Granimi as though deciding which of us to assault first.

"Don't even think about it," I growled. Fiona slunk back half a foot.

I kept a close eye on the dog while confirming with Tulip that Valerie's parents had been called with the news that their daughter had turned up unharmed, and then we said thanks again and goodnight and retreated to my house.

"Who's hungry?" I asked, ushering Val and Granimi into the kitchen. I felt we all needed to decompress, and food's always good for that.

Granimi said she'd had plenty to eat at the wedding, thank you, but Val perked up at the mention of food.

"Mrs. Van Alstyne made me a sandwich," she said, "but it had sprouts in it."

"And you don't eat sprouts?"

"They're like little green hairs!"

"Uh, yeah. I guess they are." I rather like sprouts in a sandwich, hair-like or not, but I'm not twelve.

"Can we have pizza?" Val pleaded. "The pizza at camp was horrible."

Pizza. Funny how your feelings about a food can change overnight. I hadn't eaten pizza since the night Brad died. Which was no reason to deprive Val. I handed over some cash and told Granimi and Val to order in from Celeste's—takeout menu in that drawer there, salad fixings in the fridge—and retreated to the living room with the phone.

I called my brother first, to let him know I'd surfaced, that Val was settling in at my house, and that it probably would be best for everyone to have a quiet night and for details of revisions to Val's summer plans to be put on hold until morning. Peter, always happy to let someone else handle the tricky stuff, agreed. He did step up and offer to call his ex-wife for me, but I gritted my teeth and told him it would be better if Patty heard from me directly.

Val, when I checked back in at the kitchen, was telling Granimi about some interesting character she'd met on the road from camp to my house.

"I just spoke to your Dad," I told her, "and I'm about to call your Mom."

"Is he mad at me?" she asked. "He said he isn't, but I think maybe he is."

"He was worried about you, honey." I sat down in the chair next to hers. More likely he was worried he'd have to cut his rafting trip short. Pete's a decent dad, and he loves his kid, but he has an unshakable things-will-be-fine attitude that can look a lot like irresponsibility.

"I don't think he's mad," I told Val, "but your folks were scared when they didn't know where you were or what had happened to you."

"I'm sorry," she said in a small voice. "I didn't mean to scare anybody."

"I know you didn't," I said. Twelve-year-olds aren't known for their sharp appraisal of future consequences.

I got up to make the next call.

"Are you calling my Mom?" Val asked.

"I think she'll feel better if she hears from me that you're at my house now and everything's okay," I said.

"Oh." Val said. "Am I going to be punished?"

"Not tonight," I assured her, "and not by me." I wished I could tell her that she'd wake up in the morning and discover this had all blown over. "Why don't I have a chat with your mom, and we'll take it from there."

"Okay," she agreed. "Do I have to talk to her again?"

And here we are, I thought, caught between a moody twelve-year-old and her equally difficult mother. What a lovely place to be.

"If you want I can tell her you've gone to bed," I suggested. "I know it's really early, but I can say you're tired from all the excitement." I sure felt worn out. I looked at my watch: 6:47 seemed like a fine bedtime to me.

I'd expected drama from Val's mom, but Patricia sounded as tired as I felt. In spite of excessive concern with the fact that I hadn't immediately made plans, the moment it became clear that Val would be my guest at least overnight, to attend an "appropriate" church service in the morning—whatever that meant—Patty agreed that next steps for Val would be better dealt with in the morning. Thank God for that.

I occupied myself until the pizza had arrived and been consumed by moving my things back into the master bedroom. I'd been sleeping in the guest room since my own bed had suddenly become too empty. Granimi had seen through my offer to stay put and said six months of dodging my own mattress was long enough. So I stripped and made up beds—Val would stay in Olivia's room—and put fresh towels in the bathrooms and puttered around until pizza hour was over.

We all hit the sack early. I gave Val and Granimi a brief tour of the cereal shelf and told them if they woke up before I did to get their own breakfast. I considered a nice soak in my Jacuzzi tub but was too tired to get wet, so I settled for brushing my teeth and splashing some water on my face. I'd wake up with mascara smudge on face and pillow, big deal. I pulled on a favorite sleep tee and slumped on the side of my bed to make sure the alarm was off. The clock said it was only 8:14, which couldn't possibly be right. In my personal universe it was at least 2 AM.

Something bothered me about the clock, and I stared at it, watching it blink to 8:15 before I remembered my plan to keep an eye on Alan's driveway to see if he went for an evening drive. But Granimi was in the guest room now and I was on the other side of the house and eight o'clock had come and gone. Compared to the horrible experience of encountering a real dead body that afternoon the nasty rumors about my perfectly nice neighbor seemed ridiculous.

11

I'd expected my first night back in the master bedroom to feel sad and strange and lonely, but after a long day in the company of too many others it was a joy to have the room—any room—to myself. I crawled under the covers and melted into the pillow, thinking that a comfortable mattress is one of life's greatest pleasures.

Not that a comfy bed does a whole lot of good when your brain is gnawing away at the issues of the day, which include nasty innuendos about your neighbor, on top of which there's the image of a certain gruesome dead person you can't manage to shut out of your head. I tossed and turned for what felt like forever, haunted by thoughts of death in all its permutations, and eventually I must have slept because I woke at something after two in need of a pee.

I was drooped, semi-conscious, on the throne, when my inner voice spoke up. This has happened a handful of times, usually when I've been under stress and am half-asleep. It's as though someone has spoken, but I only hear the words in my mind. I guess it's my intuition bypassing an overloaded waking brain to make sure I get the message. Which is usually short and to the point.

This time the Voice said, MAKE IT RIGHT.

"Make what right?" I grumbled, feeling unfairly put upon at being bossed around by whatever part of my psyche had chosen that glorious moment to speak up. Any number of things could use some adjustment, it seemed to me: Val's flight from whatever was so unendurable, which probably wasn't just camp; my Incredible Shrinking Budget and all the worries that went along with that; Brad's goof ball idiocy, which I'd made a good-faith effort to follow through on (wasn't my fault some guy had turned up dead with my favorite scarf around his neck, add that grisly scenario to the list) but which still lurked in the to do column; my inability to paint worth a damn any more; and oh, let's see, why don't we throw in the possibility that my neighbor may have killed at least one wife.

Make It Right, I heard again, or thought I heard, fainter this time.

"Up yours," I muttered, ignoring the fact that the Voice is, I assume, in some way me. "Why don't you fix it, whatever it is?" I flushed and heading back to bed. "And leave me alone." I added. "I don't want to hear any more about it."

*   *   *

At 3:08 AM I conceded defeat, slid my feet into slippers, and padded out to the garage to look at my recent paintings. My conversation with Raven had reinforced my worst fears: I wanted to believe that inspiration would come back and was desperately afraid it wouldn't. But maybe the paintings weren't as bad as I'd thought, now that I'd had a look at what Carlos had chosen for the Hall of Shame.

When the belt-tightening began I'd sold Brad's BMW and traded in my Lexus for a used Honda CR-V. If I park in the driveway, that frees up the garage to be my painting studio. The Homeowners Association frowns on cars left in the driveway overnight, their point being that's what the garage is for, but until they take me to court over it I don't care.

I pulled out the canvases I'd finished, abandoned, or was theoretically still working on and lined them up around what free space remained in the center of the garage, which was looking more like a storeroom than a studio these days. There were quite a few canvases, because I kept starting a new one in hopes it would turn out better than the last. The crappy lighting didn't help. If I was serious about resurrecting a painting career I'd either have to find a decent studio space or install better lighting in the garage, either of which would make my budget squeak.

I paced the garage. The paintings weren't awful, or even all that bad. Well composed, decently executed, competent though not outstanding. Seen all together, though, the problem was clear: I'd been painting my grief, even when I hadn't intended to do so.

The only people who would buy these, I thought, were ones who were already depressed. "Yes," they'd think, looking at my pain, "this one speaks to me."

A wave of nausea swept through me at the thought that my work might poison someone else's experience. Bad enough that my favorite scarf had just been used to kill; I wouldn't let my paintings inflict damage, too. I stalked into the kitchen—hoping focused activity might push the horrid vision of that strangled stranger from my mind—pulled my largest knife from the block, and returned to the garage. I grabbed the first canvas I came to and slashed it from the frame, balling the canvas up and tossing it to the oil-stained cement floor behind me. I would not paint unhappiness any more.

I moved on to the next painting, and then the next, tears starting to flow as I shredded the evidence of my failure. I only slowed down when I stumbled and decided that falling on my 8" chef's knife was not part of the plan. I wiped my eyes and pushed my hair from my face and opened the bay door to let some air in before continuing at a saner pace. When all the paintings had been destroyed I picked up a frame in each hand and tossed them into a pile beside the open garage door, going back for more and then gathering up all the crumpled canvases until I had a knee-high heap ready for disposal.

At which point I ran out of gas and sat cross-legged on the cold cement floor. The grand gesture had felt great, until reality set in. I remembered I should be thinking like someone on a budget, which meant not throwing away a couple hundred dollars worth of frames that could be reused if I got the remaining shreds of canvas off.

Come to think of it, if I'd had any sense I could have just scraped the paintings down and painted over them. For a moment I stressed over the cost of replacing all that canvas, too.

Nope, destroying them was the right thing to do.

I thought about burning the tattered canvas remains but at some point during my catharsis a light rain had begun to fall. Probably a bonfire in the back yard, even in the rain, wasn't a good idea. The humbug association would love that.

I wanted to go back to bed, but also wanted to finish what I'd started. I got a screwdriver from the utility shelves and pried staples from the back of a frame, pulling the remaining shreds of canvas off and setting the frame aside. The aroma of damp earth revived me as the drizzle continued, piercing the night with the fecund smell of hope and possibility.

I settled into a groove, prying and pulling as my butt went numb and my fingers cramped. I had just finished up the final frame when a mangy looking gray cat I'd seen skulking around earlier in the week slunk in through the open garage door and settled on its haunches just this side of the damp, a curve of wet tail wrapped over its front paws.

"These were all crap," I explained, in case the cat wondered what I was up to. "So I trashed them."

We regarded each other for a silent while. In recent lonely moments I'd considered getting a cat again, now that Brad's allergies were no longer an issue. But I'd had in mind something with a higher adorability factor, like, say, your basic kitten. The feline that had crept into my garage was long past any cute phase and looked more likely to hiss at me than purr.

The kind of mood I'd been in lately, that made us a good match.

The cat licked rain from its tail, then crept up to the far side of the pile of canvas shreds and sniffed at them and turned to look at me. One eye was swollen shut, something icky oozing from the corner. The missing half of one ear appeared to be an old injury. Nettles nested in thick tangles in shaggy fur. Being a cat, it maintained an air of dignity in spite of advanced scruffiness. It sniffed at the corner of a painting again, then turned to look at me and gave a toss of its head before slinking out the door and around the side of the house.

That was weird: I got the distinct impression the cat had been telling me "good job" on destroying my work. Okay then. I had the feline stamp of approval and the pile of shredded canvasses could go in the trash.

I opened the bin to dump it all in, and came face-to-face with the take out box from Celeste's Pizzeria. Brad's—and once my—local favorite. The receipt was still taped to the top of the box: peppers and olives, a fine combination. Judging by the weight of the box it still held a few slices. I'd told Granimi to put any leftovers in the trash, and felt a wince of shame at my wasteful request. Maybe it was time I got over the pizza thing.

I opened the box and considered the withered slices remaining. Congealed and disgusting, not a good barometer of how ready I was to face pizza again.

The night my life veered off the good times highway, Brad had called to say he was leaving the jobsite in ten and what did I want on my pizza? He'd pick up from Celeste's on his way home. Pepperoni and olives was my first choice, but I never got to eat it. It had been snowing, weather and road conditions deteriorating. So when I called Brad back a few minutes later to say I'd decided on spinach and mushrooms instead, and he didn't answer, I figured he was hustling home. And then that the roads must be slow, and his cell battery dead, and every other reasonable excuse I could think of, and eventually that something must have happened because he wasn't home yet and he hadn't called and he wasn't answering his cell.

I'd called Celeste's and they said he hadn't picked up our pie yet, they'd reheat it for me. The police said there'd been a couple of fender benders, nothing involving a BMW. I'd felt foolish and frantic. In the big picture, he wasn't all that late. But it felt wrong. I was almost relieved when Suzette called to say she'd just driven past the mill. Brad's car was in the lot so he must be working late, did I want to meet up for dinner? I'd said we had plans for pizza and Netflix at home and called Brad again, still no answer.

Usually he stayed after the crew left to hit a few golf balls into the river, his way of winding down at the end of the day. But if he was still there, why wasn't he picking up? I grabbed my keys and headed over there, telling myself I was being an idiot, that Brad was on his way home by now and would tease me for years about that night I had a meltdown 'cause he was late showing up with my pizza.

I swung by Celeste's to see if he'd maybe picked up our pie. They handed it over and I drove the rest of the way to the jobsite with the smell of pizza making me sick because my stomach was in a knot. The snow had let up but the roads were slick and nasty. I almost sideswiped a dumpster when I slid into the River Bend Terrace lot, the gate in the security fence wide open, Brad's car parked by the office trailer with an inch of wet snow on it.

The lights were on in the stairwells and at the top floor of the old six-story structure, where a golf club lay on the unfinished floor at the open river side of the building, near a white plastic bucket and a half-dozen golf balls. Orange security netting was pulled aside where Brad had practiced his swing and listened for the satisfying plop of a ball hitting the water. I'd called out for him and walked down to the L at the far end of the building, thinking maybe he was down there, around the corner. From there I had a clear view downriver to where the strobe of emergency lights danced on the water, a mile downstream where the river curved around a bend and I couldn't see the shore.

"Should I have saved that for you, dear?" Granimi asked. I jerked back to the present, and turned to see her standing in the kitchen door. "I thought you'd wanted me to throw it out."

"I did," I said, wondering what she was doing up at this hour and if my burst of destructive activity had woken her. "I didn't want it in the house."

"You used to love pizza, dear," she reminded me. "I was surprised you wouldn't have any tonight. Are you on a diet?"

"No, G.," I said, before realizing the diet excuse would have been a good one. Although then I'd have to watch what I ate for a week. I closed the pizza box and put in back in the bin.

"What are you doing up?" I asked. "It's the middle of the night."

She gave me a look. "It's after 5:30, dear."

I noticed then that the sky beyond the open garage doors was no longer black, and that the rain had stopped and early risers in the trees were celebrating a new day.

12

I put water on for coffee. Granimi opted for green tea. Good thing she'd brought some with her, as my tea shelf was bare. We talked about Val for a few minutes, both of us wondering what had happened at camp to make her run away. I'd hoped she might have opened up to Granimi over pizza the night before, but no such luck. After a bit Granimi took her tea out to the pool deck to do some stretches, while I enjoyed a refill of coffee in the kitchen. I remembered that I'd left the goof balls—brought in from Suzette's car the night before—on the hall table. Retrieving the wooden box, I padded into Brad's office and placed it back on the shelf where it had waited out the past months.

"Sorry, honey," I said, giving the box a pat. "We'll get that last game in some day."

I could have used his help with the multiple remotes, but I managed to get his TV turned on and tuned to the Golf Channel with the sound down low—a gesture of my intention to make Brad's last wishes right, even if righting everything else on the "needs attention" list seemed likely to prove beyond my powers.

Val showed up a little after eight as I was topping off my caffeine reservoir and browsing through the Sunday paper for details on the dead guy at the wedding. All I'd learned was he'd been identified as a local building inspector who'd gone to high school with Carlos. It seemed unlikely I would be a person of interest, but if so the cops weren't saying. Curious as I was for details, I was glad to set the paper aside and say good morning to Val. She was still in her PJs, looking half asleep and less like the almost-teen who'd shown up yesterday and more like the little kid I remembered her as. Probably the old teddy bear of Olivia's she was clutching had something to do with that.

"Are we going to church today?" she asked.

Church? I only ever go to church for weddings and funerals and the occasional christening, and I'd managed to fit two of those three into yesterday.

"Uh, we, uh, could go, if you'd like," I stuttered.

She shrugged and fiddled with the bear's ears.

"Tell you what, think about it while you have breakfast," I suggested. The cereal selection was grim: stale All Bran, which Granimi had been content with, or instant oatmeal. I'm not much of a breakfast person, unless you count cake. I'd had leftover CCBC for breakfast.

"Toast is fine," Val said, sliding into a chair. "Do you have peanut butter?"

Everyone has peanut butter. I asked Val what church she attended at home, and she answered with such a lack of enthusiasm that I was able to coax her into admitting she didn't especially want to go to church but was afraid Mom would be mad if she didn't. Patricia's rebirth as a bible thumper had been a contributing factor to my brother's divorce, so I wasn't in any rush to put church at the top of the agenda.

Val was halfway through her toast when she looked around the kitchen and asked, "Where's your cat?"

"I don't have a cat, honey." Well, there was that stray who'd skulked off into the night before I could do something stupid like try to pick the nettles out of his fur, but he didn't count.

"Are you sure?" Val looked perplexed.

I laughed at her odd comment. "Yes, Val, I think I would know if I had a cat."

"Oh." She finished her toast in silence, then hopped down from her chair. "Can I go outside?" She pointed out the slider to the back yard.

"In your PJs?" Why not. "Sure," I said, opening the door for her. "Stay where I can see you and don't go near the pool." Dear god, I hoped she could swim. I don't have a safety fence.

"Okay." Val was already out the door. I watched her run to the back corner of the yard and was wondering what on earth when she crouched down and picked something up. She trotted back toward me carrying the mangy stray in her arms. Its bad eye looked better but it still wasn't anything you'd let your kid get close to.

"Here he is!" she said with a triumphant grin.

"Val, that cat's a stray!" Visions of her little forearms marred by infected scratches ran through my mind. "Put it down, now, before it bites you."

"But he likes me," she said. "He won't bite."

The cat did appear docile, but I wasn't convinced it was friendly.

"Can we keep him? Please?" The cat wriggled and she put it down. It rubbed its head against her ankle and she giggled and leaned over to pet it.

"Val." I felt like a meanie, but seriously. "We are not keeping that cat." I barely felt capable of caring for myself, much less Val and Granimi, and she wanted to add a cat to the list?

"I'm going to name him Shadow," she said, ignoring me, crouching down to stroke its back.

Clearly "no" wasn't going to work, so I sighed and tried a different tactic. "Do you think Shadow might be hungry?"

Shadow meowed that some tuna would be good, and Val jumped up to usher the creature into my house.

"Uh uh, the cat does not come in the house. You may take some food and water out to him, but Shadow stays outside." At least until he got a clean bill of health from a vet. Assuming he stuck around for a while and we could convince him to go for a ride in the car.

"But—"

"No. House rules," I summoned up my stern mommy voice. "Shadow stays outside." For now. We'd see how long that lasted.

Val scowled but didn't put up a fight, and I rummaged for a plate and something that could be used as a water dish. Shadow waited outside the kitchen door, occupied with self-grooming but stopping every few moments to check on the progress of his breakfast.

The phone calls began while Val was outside watching Shadow eat a can of albacore tuna. Val crept back in and hovered by the door when she realized my lengthy chat was with her mother.

Patty went on and on about how much trouble Val had been lately, "making up stories" and "telling lies to her own mother." It was an odd strategy because it seemed to me that what Patty really wanted was for Val to stay out of her hair—if not at Bible camp, then with me—so she could go on a cruise with her new boyfriend. You'd think she'd have the sense to highlight or manufacture a list of angelic qualities instead.

I thought it unlikely that Val was as untruthful and misbehaved as Patty implied, but was aware the girl had been on her best behavior since arriving on my doorstep. When Patty started on her third repetition of how thoughtless and selfish and disrespectful Val's behavior was—the kid was twelve, what did she expect?—I passed Val the cordless phone and told her to talk to her mom in the living room while I did the breakfast dishes and tidied up the kitchen.

Val returned some minutes later and handed me the phone. "Mom wants to know if you really mean it about me staying with you for a while."

I assured Patty—again—that Val could stay as long as she wanted. Meaning within reason and don't expect me to keep her all summer when you've told me you'll be back from your cruise by the middle of July. All that remained to be resolved was how I would ensure that Valerie didn't spend her entire stay slouched on my couch with the TV remote. I'd figured out that "appropriate" was Patricia's favorite word, so I started throwing it into the mix as often as possible.

"I'll start looking for appropriate summer programs right away," I assured her.

Granimi who'd been listening in while reading the Sunday paper, waggled the arts section at me and pointed to something on the page.

"In fact," I squinted at the paper, "there's an article in the paper today about a kids' art program Val might like." I raised my eyebrows at Val, who shrugged indifference. Then she caught on and her face lit up as she pantomimed swimming. "And she's already asked about swimming lessons." I watched Val switch to air guitar. "And we're going to look into guitar lessons, too."

Val smiled and gave me the thumbs up. Which was all very well, so long as I wasn't expected to foot the bill for all that.

I half listened to Patty say roughly the same thing. What we needed was a fairy godmother. I sent a pleading look at Granimi and rubbed my fingertips together in the universal moolah gesture. Luckily for us, moolah is something Granimi has plenty of, and she's happy to spend it on family. She nodded and mimed making out a check. Val laughed, so Granimi tore the first phantom check out of the book and tossed it in the air and rapidly wrote another and another. Val bounced around pretending to catch them until we were all laughing.

"I'd like to know what's so funny about losing an entire summer's worth of camp tuition," Patty said.

I said we'd been laughing about something else, and passed on the good word that Granimi would underwrite Vals' summer activities. After only another twenty minutes of reviewing already settled details I was able to get off the phone. Granimi, I discovered, arming myself with a fresh mug of coffee, had earned her angel wings by talking to my mom so I wouldn't have to endure another rendition of recent developments.

"Bless you, I said, kissing her on the top of her spiky head. "You are unquestionably the world's greatest grandmother."

"Well, that's my only job these days, dear," she said.

"Except for being the world's greatest great-grandmother," Val pointed out, which earned her a pinched cheek.

"Yes," I said. "Thanks to the generosity of the world's greatest great-grandmother, you, Valerie, are hereby declared an honored guest of this household."

Val clapped and said goodie and bounced in her seat.

"There are certain terms and conditions upon which this arrangement is contingent," I warned, looking at my list of Patty's demands. "To whit—"

"That means 'listen up'," Granimi translated.

"No more than one hour of TV a day."

Val looked concerned about that until Granimi and I guffawed.

"TV within reason," I amended. I figured that meant no 2 AM creature features and fending off soap opera addiction. "What else... okay, bedtime is 8:00 PM—"

Val rolled her eyes.

"—or later." Val could figure out for herself when she was tired. "Supervised internet use only." I looked at Val. "We'll figure something out that doesn't require me to look over your shoulder every minute you're online."

She nodded okay to that.

"Only non-fat dairy products," I read from my notes. "No red meat. Only organic poultry and vegetables." What was she trying to do, double my food bill? "No white flour or refined sugar." What kind of a life is that? "Tell you what," I tossed the pad on the table. "You can eat what we eat if you want to, or something else if you'd rather, so long as you consume at least one fruit and two vegetables a day. How does that sound?"

Val jumped up and hugged me and said it sounded great, and I said it was time we all changed out of our PJs and did some grocery shopping.

13

When we returned from essential errands Granimi disappeared for a nap and Val and I decided our exercise for the day would be a swim in my pool. After completing a few half-hearted laps we clung to the edge and swished our feet in the water. Val was just being a kid; I was thinking that even small movements might burn off a few cake calories.

"I get that Bible camp's not for everyone," I said, shuddering internally at the idea, "but what was so bad about it that you had to run away?" I expected some reluctance to open up, but the scared look she gave me was a surprise.

"Honey, I'm on your side. No matter what. I want you to know that."

"The other kids hated me," she whispered. "They called me names."

"That's not very nice." I decided to hone my detecting skills by practicing the "stay quiet and the suspect will talk" technique I'd learned from TV. Either I wasn't patient enough or it doesn't work as well in real life.

"I went to camp when I was your age," I said to break the silence. Jeeze, about a million years ago. I cast my mind back to the summer I'd discovered that my clothes were all wrong, my favorite music was lame, and I watched dorky TV shows.

"Did you like it?"

"I didn't at first." Going to camp for the first time had been like teleporting to another planet. "All the stuff that had been cool at my school wasn't cool at all at camp, so I felt awkward and self-conscious."

"Were the other kids mean to you?"

"I got teased a bit," I admitted. An unpleasant nickname had been involved, and no, I'm not telling. But it hadn't been all bad. "After a few days I made some friends and then I had a good time."

Val kicked at the water for a while. "I don't have any friends." She sounded so lonely and sad I didn't know whether to hug her or run out and buy her a BFF.

"That's tough." What had happened to the cheerful, outgoing kid I remembered? Last year Patricia complained that Val was always on the phone or texting or wanting someone to drive her and her friends to the mall.

Val blinked back tears, and it struck me as odd that I hadn't yet seen her pull out her cell phone to call or text anyone.

"When I was your age," I confided, "I used to worry about being popular." One of the great perks of growing up is outpacing that anxiety.

"The popular kids at camp are the meanest," Val said. "Why is that?"

"That, my dear, is one of life's great mysteries." We splashed our feet some more. "Who was the most popular kid at camp?" I asked.

Val thought about that. "Shannon Wilson."

"Was Shannon one of the girls who was mean to you?"

She nodded.

Watch out, Shannon, I thought. Karma can get to you, any time, any place. "What was the meanest thing she did?" I asked casually, not making the question specifically about Val.

Val thought about that one, too. "She put a spider in Alice Keeney's bathing suit."

"Eeuw!" I shuddered. I don't like spiders one bit. "That's nasty."

Val nodded.

"If she keeps being mean, she won't stay popular forever," I said. Only through high school, college maybe. Which at Val's age was as good as forever.

Val swished her feet and giggled.

"What?" A giggle was a start.

"Shannon broke her leg," Val said. "She fell off the rope swing." She ducked under the water so I wouldn't see her smile. I might have felt Val was just a bit too pleased, but clearly Shannon had it coming.

Or did she? Sure, Val is family, and I wanted to believe she's a good kid, but the truth is I hardly knew her. And her own mother had basically called her a lying, scheming bitch.

When Val came up for air I had a stern look waiting. "Tell me you didn't have anything to do with that," I said.

Val looked so genuinely horrified that I felt like a heel for giving Patricia's comments a milligram of weight.

"It wasn't my fault!" Val said, on the verge of tears.

Something had touched a nerve. "I believe you, sweetie," I said. Maybe. "But did Shannon breaking her leg have anything to do with why you left camp?"

After a long pause, she nodded. "We had to prepare skits," she said, "from Bible stories. I was in Shannon's group."

"Let me guess: Shannon got the best part?"

Val nodded. "But the skits are for next weekend, and I knew she wouldn't be there, and I when I said that they all laughed."

I didn't get it. And then I did.

"You mean you knew something was going to happen to her? Before it happened?"

Val nodded. She wouldn't look at me.

"But you didn't make it happen."

She shook her head no.

"I don't understand." Not entirely true. I thought I understood, but was having some trouble believing it. "How did you know she would break her leg?"

"I didn't," Val said in a small voice. "I just knew she wouldn't be in the skit, because she wouldn't be at camp any more by then."

"How did you know that?"

Val shrugged. "Sometimes I know things."

Yeesh. That's a freaky talent. Potentially useful, but freaky. Were we really having this conversation? My brain tried to dissociate by pointing out that I was cold and turning into a prune and this would be a good time to get out of the pool and make lunch.

But sometimes you do know.

I'd known when Brad didn't come home that night that something bad had happened. And we've all heard stories about the person who has a gut feeling not to get on the plane that crashes, that sort of thing. Was Val's story any different? Maybe it happens a lot, and we all never talk about it because we don't want to be laughed at.

"Mostly you keep it to yourself, huh?"

Val nodded. "It gets me in trouble if I say anything."

"So, what happened when Shannon broke her leg?"

Val looked into the water and swished her feet. "They said it was my fault."

"Oh, sweetie! How could it have been your fault?"

Val began to leak tears, so I pulled her into a hug and maneuvered us over to the steps and out of the pool. I wrapped her in a towel and sat down with her on one of the lounge chairs in the sun.

"Is that why you ran away?" I asked, just to be sure there wasn't more.

Val nodded. If we didn't wrap this up soon her head was going to fall off from all the nodding. "They called me a witch," she said. "They said they were going to brand me."

"What!" I slapped a hand over my mouth to keep the swear words from getting out, and stomped around in a circle for a while. If karma didn't get the lot of them, I'd go after those kids myself.

Okay, calm down, deep breaths, stop scaring the girl.

I sat down next to Val again and took her hands in mine and looked her in the eye. "You did the right thing to get away from there," I told her. Okay, so she could have involved a responsible adult earlier in the adventure, but she'd arrived at my house safely and that's what mattered. "And I'm glad you came here."

I let go of her hands and pulled the towel closer around her neck. "You and me and Granimi will have our own summer camp here, no mean kids allowed. Okay?"

*   *   *

Forty minutes later Val and I were showered and changed and sitting at the patio table in the shade of a sun umbrella, enjoying a semi-healthy lunch of turkey sandwiches on whole grain bread with a side of Terra Chips, a compromise between the pleasure of potato chips and the less appealing goal of eating more vegetables. Tomorrow we'd substitute carrot sticks for the chips and ease up on the desserts, but first we had to finish off Rose's bundt cake.

"Who's that lady?"

I looked up. "What lady, honey?"

"The old lady in the flowered hat," Val said. "She wants to talk to you."

"Who does?" Granimi was inside catching up with friends, which I presumed meant phoning or tweeting or writing a blog post or possibly even letters, if anyone did that any more. I didn't see her, though, and a flowered hat didn't sound like the kind of thing that would be featured in her current wardrobe. Besides, Val wouldn't ask who Granimi was.

"Val, I'm sorry but I don't know what you're talking about."

"Oh." She pretended to be fascinated by the sandwich crusts on her plate. "Never mind."

"Val." I pulled the arm of her chair to turn her towards me, feeling creeped out. I remembered Val's certainty that I had a cat and the sometimes-you-know reason she'd run away from camp, which were putting Patty's comments about her problem behavior in perspective. "Honey, do you see someone in the house?"

"Not in the house," Val said. "She's over by that tree."

"Your eyesight must be better than mine." I looked at the sun dappled grass under the maple tree, trying to keep my tone as light and sunny as the perfect June afternoon, but my arms were covered in goosebumps. Was that a shimmer in the air over there?

In spite of midnight messages from my inner voice and the occasional sometimes-you-know episode of my own, I don't believe in ghosts or UFOs or any of that. Not that I'm a die-hard skeptic, it just all seems unreal to me. In theory I'm open to the idea that something bizarre might be going on, possibly, but only to other people and only somewhere far removed from my own experience. But an invisible (to me) lady by my maple tree?

I put my hand on Val's to reassure her that I didn't think she was crazy or lying or just being bad. "Honey, do you sometimes see things that other people don't?" I asked.

She nodded.

I didn't want to think that my niece might be a budding medium, but it was preferable to the only alternative I could rustle up, which was schizophrenia. An equally freaky topic which I know even less about, except for a vague idea that it usually surfaces in adolescence. Most important was to make Val feel safe. Focusing on an insecure twelve-year old in need of love and acceptance made it easier to ignore how freaked out I was feeling.

"I bet a lot of people don't understand it when that happens," I said.

She nodded again.

"Okay then. Is the lady in the flowered hat still there?"

Val nodded.

"Does she have a name?"

Val was silent for a moment. "She's pointing to one of the flowers on her hat."

I thought then of Rose Braska as I'd often seen her, kneeling in her yard by the garden beds, hands busy with the many flowers she grew, wearing a battered old straw hat to keep the sun from her face, turning to wave hello as I drove or walked by. I could almost see the soil griming the palms of her yellow canvas gardening gloves.

"Do you know what kind of flower it is?" I asked, queasy with dread. Rose had been fond of hats. I'd seen her several times on dressier occasions, I was sure of it, in a pink straw hat with a garland of roses around the crown.

"It's pink," Val said. "Rose pink, that's it. She's pointing to a rose."

My heart raced. How could Val be so calm?

"She's your neighbor." Val turned to me, and this time she looked concerned. "I didn't know your neighbor died."

But that time I was trying very hard not to freak out. I took a deep breath and looked over to the tree under which Rose's specter was reported to be lingering, and didn't see a thing out of the ordinary, other than that hint of a shimmer that I'd hoped was a cloud of gnats. Then I saw the cat, who'd been lurking under the table hoping for edible fallout, slink across the grass toward the tree, belly low, tail twitching.

I leaned closer to Val and put my hand over hers. "Rose Braska died last week, honey," I said. "She'd been ill for a long time so we all knew she might not be with us much longer. It certainly doesn't have anything to do with you being here. I'm very sure of that."

"Why do I see her, and you don't?"

"I don't know, honey." I gave her shoulders a squeeze. I could have done without the freaky stuff, but I was feeling increasingly protective toward Val. If freaky came with the territory I'd just have to lace up my freak-proof boots and wade in.

"It's good you can see Rose," I said, "because I'm curious," if curious means feeling like throwing up, "why she's here." Rose and I had had the kind of polite neighborly friendship that doesn't invite intimacy. I wouldn't have expected to be the person Rose would make an appearance to.

"I think she wants to tell you something," Val said.

I waited for more but there wasn't any. "I think she'll have to tell you," I said to Val, "so you can tell me." Please God Rose wouldn't start talking to me directly. I didn't think I could handle that.

Val frowned. "I don't really hear things with my ears," she said. "Just kind of in my head. So I don't know if she can talk to me."

"Maybe you can just understand what she wants me to know," I suggested, trying to keep uneasiness out of my voice.

Val was still for a long moment. "She says it wasn't what everyone thinks," she said at last, "about how she died."

Val gasped then, and turned to me, her eyes full of alarm.

"It wasn't an accident," she said. "Someone killed her."

"There you two are." Granimi stepped outside and crossed the patio. "My goodness," she said, coming closer. "Whatever's the matter, Lena? You look like you just saw a ghost."

14

Dead silence reigned as Granimi looked at our shocked faces and then Val and I burst out into a splutter of only slightly hysterical laughter.

"No," I gasped, when I felt capable of speech. "I didn't see anything." I made the mistake of looking at Val, which brought on another round of hilarity.

Granimi smiled at us, waiting to be let in on the joke. "You two are certainly enjoying yourselves," she said as we struggled to stifle our giggles. I knew that was as close as she would come to letting us know that our exclusive laughter was just a bit impolite.

I felt deliciously limp and almost dizzy after the laughter catharsis. "Sorry, G., we didn't mean to be rude, but you couldn't have said it better if someone had scripted that for you."

"What on earth is so funny?" She took a seat at the table and skooched her chair a bit to get out of the sun.

I was fine with telling Granimi everything, but felt it was Val's secret to share, so I gestured it was up to her.

Perhaps sharing her ability with someone who'd managed not to be judgmental had been a good experience, because Val sat up straight and told Granimi, "I saw the ghost." She looked over at the tree. "It's gone now. Aunt Lena couldn't see her. That's why it was so funny."

Granimi, understandably, didn't have a response other than to look from Val to me to see why we were pulling her leg.

I nodded. "It's true. Val saw a woman in a pink flowered hat standing under that maple tree. I couldn't see her, but I think the cat did." The cat was now under the tree, sniffing at the grass.

"That's right where she was standing!" Val jumped up to go ask Shadow if he'd seen Rose, too.

Granimi took the opportunity to ask what was really going on.

"I wish I knew," I admitted, and told her what had happened.

"Your neighbor, Rose?" she said, when I mentioned the name, as if still only half-believing she'd heard correctly. "It makes sense—," not the word I'd have chosen, "—that her spirit would linger if she died suddenly."

"It's too weird for me," I said. "When I think about it I'm totally freaked out." I was more concerned about Val's mental health, which was just as scary a topic as ghosts. I shivered and rubbed at the goose bumps on my arms.

"Chicken skin," Granimi said, touching my arm.

"Chicken skin?"

"That's what they called it when I was a kid, in Hawaii. I haven't thought of that expression in years."

Granimi so rarely spoke of her childhood that I sometimes forget she hasn't always lived in California. She seemed lost in reverie for a moment.

"My father used to tell me stories," she said, turning to watch Valerie play with the cat as if nothing had happened, "about my Granny Sullivan. She had a gift for knowing things. She'd say, 'Bring the laundry in, it's going to rain,' on the most beautiful day. Sure enough, in a little bit there'd be a sudden shower. Daddy told me she saw ghosts sometimes. To her they'd look as real as you or me. She didn't always know they weren't living people unless someone else was there who couldn't see them."

"Granimi, that's creepy!" Although it was, perhaps, slightly reassuring to think that what Val was experiencing could be a psychic ability that runs in the family. So long as that didn't mean I'd wake up some day and start seeing ghosts myself. For a nanosecond the idea that if I could see ghosts perhaps I could see Brad again flashed across my mind, but I shuddered it off.

Granimi smiled and patted my arm. "Dead people are much less likely to harm you than living ones," she said. "I never really knew Granny Sullivan—she passed when I was about five years old—but Daddy said she was never frightened by the ghosts she saw. She'd say mostly they wanted their loved ones not to be so sad that they were gone. Although one time…"

"One time what?" I prodded, eager to hear the story and not sure I wanted to.

"One time she saw someone who'd been murdered," Granimi said. "Everyone thought it had been an accident. I don't remember the details. It involved one of the plantation workers, not anyone we knew."

"Did they catch him?"

"Catch who, dear?"

"The murderer."

"Oh, yes," Granimi said. "They did. Someone convinced the authorities that it might not have been an accident, and when they investigated the killer confessed. It wasn't a him, though, dear. It was a woman who'd done it. A crime of passion, I suppose." She shrugged it off. "I didn't mean to bring up something so morbid."

"Morbid or not, I'm starting to think maybe Val really did see Rose," I said.

"Did you think she made it up?" Granimi asked, as if it hadn't occurred to her to doubt that a ghost had shown up in my yard in the middle of the afternoon while she'd been inside lacing up her orange high-tops.

"Yes, I thought she might have made it up," I said. "It could all be a bid for attention. Or a cry for help."

"I don't think she's in any danger, dear," Granimi said. "And she looks perfectly happy right now."

"Happy?" I turned to G. in disbelief. "Granimi, her parents recently divorced, her mom's so determined to force Jesus down her throat that she won't let Val see her old friends, the kids at camp made her so miserable she ran away, and god only knows what else is going on. I don't think it's accurate to say that kid is 'happy.'"

"I didn't say she doesn't have problems. But look at her right now and tell me that child is unhappy."

I looked and saw Val lying on her back in the grass under the maple tree, laughing while the cat licked her face. She did, indeed, look happy. I'd been so sure that she was a kid in trouble that I hadn't even noticed her laughter.

"Okay, you win that one," I said. "But what if…"

"What if what, dear?

"What if it's not some odd inherited ability? What if it's something else, like schizophrenia? Don't you think we should take her to a doctor?"

"And tell the doctor what, that she sees ghosts? How is being deemed crazy by a physician going to help her?"

"But what if she's sick, Granimi?"

"If she's sick, we'll make sure she gets the help she needs," Granimi said. "Valerie has been in your care for less than a day. Let's not rush to slap a label on her that might be hard to peel off. What she most needs is to be allowed to be a normal kid for a while. If something is really wrong and she needs professional care, I'm sure we'll be able to figure that out."

"Granimi," I said, feeling uncertain how best to fulfill my responsibility to my brother's child, "normal children don't see ghosts."

"Maybe they do," she said. "Maybe they're the normal ones, and it's the rest of us who are missing out."

"That's a lovely thought." Then I remembered my inner voice, the one that pestered me in the middle of the night, and how it felt so clearly a part of myself, something mostly unknown and unacknowledged that I knew I should listen to. "'Make it right,'" I whispered.

"What was that? Don't mumble, dear."

"Have you ever heard a voice in your head, like there's someone else in the room, when no one's there, but you hear words anyway?"

Granimi started to shake her head, no, and then I saw a spark of recognition in her eyes. "You know, I did once. A long time ago. Oh, my goodness me. I haven't thought of it in so many years."

"Thought of what, Granimi," I prodded. Setting Val's issues aside, I was eager to not be the only person hearing voices.

"Oh, this was way back before the beginning of time," she said, with a glint of humor. "When I lived in Hawaii. I was still a girl, about the age you were when you came to live with me in San Francisco that year."

I nodded for her to go on.

"Oh, I was a handful back in the day," she said with a wistful smile. "You should have seen me, so pampered and willful and full of fun."

I smiled. It was still a good description of her.

"No one could tell me what to do," she said. "I was in love with a Local boy, and if I say he was inappropriate that wouldn't begin to describe it. Which is why we kept it a secret."

"Granimi! You had a secret forbidden love?" I was thrilled to be hearing bits of her history. Granimi has always been full of stories, but they're about people she knows or someone she's met or read about, almost never from her own past.

She laughed. "I wasn't so swept away, even then, that I didn't realize that half of what I saw in the boy was how horrified my parents would be if they knew I was spending time with him. It didn't hurt that he was beautiful, skin like honey and thick wavy hair and dark eyes that were like diving into the sea at night. We could have brought him to California with us and dropped him down in the middle of Hollywood and he'd have been a screen idol overnight.

"Anyway, my parents may have suspected something was going on, or maybe they just sensed I might get into trouble if they didn't get me settled early. So when your Grandpop showed up and took a fancy to me, they decided it would be a good idea for me to marry him."

"But you were so young." I'd known Grandpop was older, but not that Granimi had been a child bride.

"I had just turned seventeen, dear, which was considered plenty old enough to get married in those days. Your grandfather wanted a younger bride. He'd already been married, you see. His first wife had died without bearing him any children, and he was eager to start a family."

I was stunned by this revised vision of my grandparents' marriage. Grandpop had doted on Granimi, and she'd appeared to adore him equally.

"You and Grandpop had an arranged marriage?" I could hardly believe it.

Granimi nodded. "I'm sure I could have gotten out of it if I'd wanted to," she said. "Daddy could be strict but he was also a pushover where I was concerned. Oh my, were they prepared for a fight!"

"So what happened?"

"Well, I knew my father had been spending time with a businessman from California," she said. "The night he came to dinner, which the housemaid told me had been arranged so he could meet me, I waited in the upstairs hall to get a look at him when he arrived. I was prepared to hate him on sight, you see. I was determined to be modern and independent then. In spite of my infatuation with the boy, what I really wanted was to go to college on the mainland and have a career and travel the world. So the idea of my parents picking out a husband for me was preposterous, especially when I found out the man they'd chosen was closer to my father's age than to my own. All the same, I was very curious, as you can imagine."

I nodded, eager for her to go on.

"That's when I heard the voice," she said. "I was peering through the banister when your grandpop came in the door. At first all I saw was his dark hat and fine suit. Men still wore hats in those days, and dressed well for dinner. Then he took his hat off and handed it to the maid. He wasn't as old as I'd thought, and appeared quite handsome and sophisticated to a young girl from Hawaii. I'd expected to dislike him, and instead a voice in my head very clearly said, 'Marry him.' And I knew that I would."

"And that's how you and Grandpop got married?"

Granimi laughed. "Oh, the look on my parents' faces when they sat me down to share the plan with me and I just nodded and said 'okay.' I don't think they'd ever been so astounded in their lives. It wasn't what I'd been planning to do, I can tell you that. But when I heard that voice, I knew it was how things were supposed to go. I knew that if I ignored it my whole life wouldn't turn out as well."

She paused then, and I let her reminisce in silence until she was ready to continue.

"So" she said at last, "I married your Grandpop and when the war ended he took me back to California with him. And I came to love him because he was a good man and worth loving. We were very happy together."

I almost expected her to say "The End," as though she'd told me a fairy tale. I couldn't shake the feeling that during that last pause she'd been thinking of some aspect of the tale that she'd decided to leave out. That was alright. She'd shared far more of her history than I'd heard before and I was entranced.

"I've gone my whole life without hearing that voice again," Granimi said. "Lord knows there've been times I would have loved an authority like that to tell me what to do. But I only heard it the once, so I guess that was the time that mattered for me."

"Aunt Lena, can I use the computer?" Val asked. I'd been so engrossed in Granimi's tale I hadn't noticed her come up to us. She was carrying the cat in her arms. It looked very pleased with itself.

"Sure honey," I said. I remembered I hadn't adjusted parental controls on the computer, and decided to trust Val for the time being. "But the cat stays outside."

She pouted but didn't put up a fight. "You have to stay here," she said to the cat, which jumped out of her arms as soon as she began to set it down. I watched Val go into the house. She seemed so young. I could hardly remember what it was like to be twelve, and couldn't imagine what it was like to see a ghost, but she appeared unaffected by the experience.

"Thank you for telling me your story," I said to Granimi. "I'm glad you listened to that voice." If she hadn't, I wouldn't be around to be hearing voices of my own. "I've heard a voice like that, too," I confessed, and told her my recent experience.

"So maybe that's what the voice was telling me," I concluded. "That Rose's—," the word felt wrong in my mouth, awkward and scary and hard to get out, "—murder, if that's what it turns out to be, is what I'm supposed to make right."

"That could be, dear." Granimi didn't sound convinced.

"I guess I'm not sure," I admitted. "Maybe I'm just reaching for something to fit."

"You'll know when you know," G. said with equanimity.

"You don't think it's important for me to figure out?"

She shrugged. "You'll know when you know," she said again. "If you think you should be figuring it out, you don't know yet. Maybe you're right that it's about Rose. Or maybe it's about something else."

I felt confused. Much as the whole Rose's ghost thing wigged me out, I'd liked feeling I knew what the voice had been talking about. Granimi had undermined my confidence.

"Lena, dear," G. said, "it's wonderful that you've had these messages from your inner guide, or whatever you want to call it. So many people are closed to their soul wisdom, and that's no way to live. But sometimes the making sense of it happens later. Source is talking to all of us, all the time, and sometimes we understand it better than others. You think I'm here," she went on, "because I broke my wrist. Your mother thinks I'm an old fool. And you're both right, in your way. But I think I broke my wrist when I did because I'm supposed to be here with you and Val. If I'd been meant to go home to San Francisco, that's where I'd be now."

"'Everything happens for a reason,'" I quoted.

"It sure does," she said with a conviction I wished I shared.

"So what's your reason for being here?"

"I'll know when I know." She reached over to pat my hand.

"It all feels very mysterious to me." I felt nostalgic for my days of lying on the couch, channel-surfing with the shades drawn.

"You say that like it's a bad thing," Granimi pointed out. "Why not relax and enjoy it?"

Shadow sat up from where he'd been sprawled on the sun-warmed flagstones and began grooming. Our lunch plates were still on the table, a yellowjacket nosing around the remains of Val's sandwich, and a few houses over I could hear the noise of a lawnmower. The patio umbrella luffed in a passing breath of breeze. If you'd asked me at that moment what I believed, I would have been unable to answer. It was the most ordinary of summer Sunday afternoons, the kind of day you can't help but relax and enjoy, but it all seemed brittle and unreal. I felt that if I reached out and poked at the air with a fingernail I might rip a hole right through to some other reality.

I pondered Granimi's question. Why not relax and enjoy it? Was there any good reason to feel frightened and at risk?

Well, how about the idea that maybe Rose Braska had been murdered. That wasn't a comforting thought. Not to mention the way we got that information.

"Seriously, Granimi, Val says she saw my neighbor's ghost and it gave her a message. That doesn't strike you as a bit weird?"

"This kind of thing takes some getting used to, I suppose," G. said. She adjusted the brim of her hat and I turned the umbrella to give her more shade. "But it's just as odd to believe that what we call normal is all there is."

Maybe Granimi wasn't the best person to go to for a reality check.

"According to quantum physics," she said, "our conventional concept of reality is way off. In fact, everything we experience is various wavelengths of vibration, and our senses are vibration receptors. But those receptors are limited in what they can interpret for us. Take infrared light, for example, or those dog whistles that humans can't hear. It's ridiculous, really, to think that what we perceive with our physical senses is anywhere close to all there is." She raised her eyebrows at me and ate a Taro Chip from Val's plate. "I saw some very strange things when I was in India a few years ago," she said. "Your hair would stand right up on end if I told you."

I laughed, not taking her seriously. I knew she'd traveled in India with a companion my mother had disapproved of, but he'd stayed over there and was no longer in the picture. "Is that what inspired your new haircut?" I asked.

She took her hat off to fluff her hair and strike a pose for me.

I heard the familiar squeak of the backyard gate.

"Hey gals, I heard you laughing back here," Suzette said, letting herself in from the driveway. "What a gorgeous day, huh?"

We waved hello, and Suze came over and air-kissed Granimi hello and plopped down in a chair. "So, what's up with the two of you today?" she asked, her eyes sparkling with unshared gossip.

15

"No way! That is awesome," Suzette said when I shared news of Val's arrival and what my niece had seen in the shadow of the maple tree and how I'd recognized her description of Rose's hat. "I can't believe I missed it! I'm so jealous."

"I missed it, too," I said. "And I was sitting right here."

"You know what I mean. I would have liked to have been here, even if I didn't see any more than you did."

I hadn't yet mentioned Rose's message, and Suze had a theory of her own. "I bet she showed up because they released her body, and she's about to be buried."

"They did? She is?"

Suze grinned at me. "Bob and I made up," she said with a happy smirk, "if you know what I mean. He wouldn't tell me squat about the guy at the wedding—"

Oh yeah, that guy. I'd managed to almost forget about him, and was sorry to be reminded. Boy, I sure hoped no one else would turn up dead for a few days at least. Not anywhere near me.

"—the righteous prick, but he did get beeped this morning and he told me the coroner had released Rose's body. And guess what?" She paused to savor our impatient looks and get-on-with-it gestures.

"That allergic reaction she died from was triggered by the nuts in a brownie. They think she ate it on purpose! Apparently she was much sicker than anyone—well, anyone but her doctor—knew. She'd relapsed, and the prognosis was bad. She hadn't even told Alan about it."

"Poor Alan," I said, forgetting for a moment that maybe he should be under suspicion. It seemed selfish of Rose to have denied him the chance to say goodbye. That wasn't like her. Which inclined me to believe that maybe dying hadn't been Rose's choice, no matter how it looked to the professionals.

"Anyway," Suzette went on, "she didn't leave a note, so there's no way to know for sure. She could have eaten the brownie by accident, so it's being called an 'unattended death.'"

Granimi and I exchanged a glance.

"Gee," I said to Suzette. "That's not what Rose said."

Suzette's astonished yelp was everything I'd hoped it would be. "She said something! Oh my god, tell me everything. What did she say?"

"She didn't speak, exactly. And I didn't even see her, so it wasn't like we had a conversation. Val said Rose wanted to tell me something, and she picked it up telepathically, or however it works."

"So what did Rose say telepathically?"

"She said it wasn't an accident," I told her, my smile fading. "Suzette, Val said Rose was trying to tell us that someone killed her."

"Oh my God!" Suzette leaned back in her chair with a hand over her mouth, looking from me to Granimi. "She really said that?"

"Suze, I just told you, she didn't say anything. That was the message Val got."

"Well—," Suzette waggled her fingers for more.

"Well, what?"

"'Well, what'?" Suzette sat up very straight and glared at me. "Who did it, that's what! What else did you find out? Come on, spill!"

Holy crap. I'd been so freaked out by the idea of messages from the dead that I'd completely missed the obvious. My heart raced as I finally comprehended it: if Rose had been murdered, that meant someone had killed her. Duh.

"There isn't anything else." Geeze, had we missed an opportunity there or what?

"She didn't tell you?" Suzette could not believe it.

I shook my head no. "Um, I think that's when Granimi showed up. She took one look at us and asked if we'd seen a ghost—"

Suzette let out a bark of laughter.

"—and that kind of set us off and then Val said Rose was gone."

"We've got to talk to Val. Where is she? Do you think she could contact Rose again? Maybe we could—"

"Suze!" I held a hand up for her to stop. "Chill for a minute, okay. Maybe Val can help and maybe she can't. But she's had a rough time about stuff like this from her mom and other kids, and she needs to set the pace."

"Of course. You're right," Suzette said. "Still, Lena! If Rose was murdered…. We have to do something."

The ghost story version of events still struck me as supremely iffy. Mostly because I didn't want to believe it. I wanted the entire incident not to have happened.

"You're the one sleeping with a cop," I pointed out. "Isn't this Officer Bob territory?"

"That's Detective Bob," she reminded me with a glare.

I know that. Maybe I still harbor just a teensy bit of resentment for the way he'd looked at me when he'd thought I might have given Brad a push.

"Besides," Suzette said, "what do you suggest I do, call him up and say 'Rose's ghost told Lena's niece she was murdered'? He'd laugh so hard he'd cough up a lung."

She had a point there. Officer Bob, being the kind of manly man that Suzette gets hot for, gave us enough grief for not having real jobs and for doing girly stuff like shopping and lunching and getting our nails done. If we mentioned ghosts to him we'd never hear the end of it.

"You're right." As much as I enjoy reading a good mystery, dealing with one in real life wasn't nearly so inviting. "No one will believe us unless we dig up some kind of credible evidence. Or some clues, or … something." I had no idea what.

"We could start by thinking about who might want her dead," Suzette suggested.

"And why they were in a hurry," Granimi pointed out. "Rose looked half in the grave when I was last here. Why not just wait a little longer and let nature take its course?"

"That's a bit ghoulish, Granimi, don't you think? Besides, she might have hung on for years, for all we know. I know she was taking some herbal remedies from South America. Apparently they actually did some good."

"Why do you sound surprised?" Granimi asked. "Herbal medicine can work wonders. And without all those nasty side effects. I've been taking rainforest supplements for years. Where do you think my youthful vitality comes from?"

I'd thought it came from genetic luck and naturally high spirits, but whatever. "Anyway," I went on before I lost my train of thought, "We don't know that she was killed. I mean, what did someone do, force-feed her a lethal brownie? Doesn't that strike you as just a bit ridiculous?"

Granimi and Suzette gave sheepish shrugs.

"I think we ought to look into it," Granimi said. "After all, Val did see something. Do you really want to ignore that?"

It was my turn to feel sheepish. "You're right. I'll sleep better if we poke around a bit." Even if we ended up just making fools of ourselves, which seemed likely.

"We could find out more about her health issues," Suzette suggested. "I bet we can learn a ton on the Internet."

"Do we even know what was wrong with her?" I asked. "I mean, I'm pretty sure it wasn't cancer, because I think I'd have known if she was doing chemo or radiation. All I know is that she was sick for a long time."

Granimi waved her hand dismissively. "Not a priority," she said. "We should focus on the husband. Statistically he's the most likely suspect."

"Alan!" Suzette slapped my arm. "Remember what Mrs. Lander said, about his first wife? I bet that's it! And don't forget the mistress."

"What mistress?" Granimi wanted to know.

"I overheard a conversation at the funeral home," I explained. "And it sounded like it might have been Alan. It's not at all definite, though, because I didn't see who was speaking. It could have been someone else."

Suzette glared at me as though I were dragging my heels on the way to a sample sale. "Don't you want to investigate this?"

"Frankly? No. I wish this whole thing wasn't happening. I wish Val were making it all up and that we didn't have to deal with any of it."

Suzette and Granimi were looking at something behind me.

"I didn't make it up!" Val said, and I turned to discover that she'd heard my comments. "Why doesn't anybody believe me?" She burst into tears and ran into the house.

Add high-strung twelve-year-olds to the list of things I didn't want to deal with. Two days ago I'd been living a wretched, boring, quiet life and I wanted it back.

16

"Val, honey, I did not say you were making things up." I perched on the side of the bed in Olivia's room. Val was curled up, face to the wall, pretending I wasn't there. "I said I wished you were making it up, because it's scary to think that Rose might have been murdered."

Silence.

"Granimi and Suzette believe you, too."

"I'm sorry I saw her," Val muttered.

"Well I'm glad you did," I assured her, although it was an outright lie. "Without you I wouldn't have known that Rose needs our help."

"I thought I was supposed to make it up to you," Val said in a very small voice.

"Make what up to me?"

She was silent for a long moment. "About Uncle Brad."

"What about him?" Did she know something about Brad, too? Suddenly the room got very small.

Val rolled over and sat up so she was leaning against the wall. She wouldn't look me in the eye. "That he was going to be dead," she said in a small voice.

"Wha—?," all that came out was a squeak. She'd known Brad was going to die? I felt like running out the door except I was dizzy and could barely breathe and my arms and legs didn't belong to me any more. I took slow, deep breaths and tried again.

"Val, honey, your Uncle Brad died because he was careless and stupid." I sent a mental apology upstairs, but that's the truth. "He was hitting golf balls from one of his construction sites. He'd moved the safety netting aside, and it was snowing, and he slipped and fell out of the building and into the river. It was a stupid, stupid accident and absolutely not in any way your fault. It wasn't anyone's fault but his."

I'd been angry at Brad before, for abandoning me by dying and for being so stupid and careless, and now I realized how truly, royally, righteously, pissed off I was that he'd been such an idiot. I was breathing so hard I was practically spitting, and probably scaring Val again. I took more slow, deep, breaths and willed my heart to slow down.

Val looked more unconvinced than alarmed. "I should have said something."

She looked so miserable my heart melted. Plus, now that the shock was wearing off enough for my brain to function, I was curious.

"What exactly did you know?" I asked. "And when did this happen?"

At Thanksgiving, it turned out. When Brad had ruffled her hair on his way in to dinner. But all she'd sensed was that he would die soon, and that it wasn't a health thing. No details, or any kind of insight that might have been useful.

"Oh, Val, I'm so sorry you've been feeling badly about this." I gave her a hug. "But you know what? If you'd said anything, Uncle Brad wouldn't have believed you." Uncle Brad would have teased me for the remaining weeks of his life about my crazy niece. If Val had been wrong, and he hadn't died, he would have teased me for decades.

"You know what I think?"

Val shook her head no.

"I think knowing something isn't always the same as being able to make a difference."

"Then why do I know things? And how do I know if I should say something?"

"I think maybe you that answer is in here," I suggested, tapping her chest. "Sometimes, like today, it will feel right to speak up. Other times it will feel right to keep quiet."

She nodded, but appeared skeptical, and then her phone chirped for attention and Val looked at it as if it might bite her.

That was downright creepy. No twelve-year-old girl should be afraid of her phone.

"What if it's my Mom? What should I tell her?"

"Let's see." I mentally reviewed our day. "Tell her we bought lots of healthy stuff at Whole Foods, and Granimi got you some clothes at Target, and that she bought some things too but her lost luggage was here by the time we got home anyway, and that we swam in my pool and … how does she feel about cats?"

Val shrugged again. She'd develop shoulders like a linebacker if she wasn't careful.

"Tell her I'm letting you feed the cat who lives in my back yard," I suggested. "And be sure to say we're taking him to the vet tomorrow to make sure he's healthy before I let you play with him. She'll probably be happy if you complain that I won't let you bring him in the house."

"What about seeing Rose?" she asked. Her phone had stopped ringing.

"I think that sort of thing falls into the 'need to know' category," I said.

"What does that mean?" she asked.

"That means," I explained, headed straight to hell, "that if your Mom asks if you saw a ghost, you say yes and tell her about it. If she doesn't ask, and you don't think there's any other reason she needs to know, you don't have to tell her. Yet."

"She wouldn't believe me anyway."

"I'm not saying you should lie to her," I pointed out, flames licking at my toes.

"I know," she said. "Sometimes Mom's happier if she doesn't know everything."

I remembered then that Olivia was in Europe with questionable supervision, and wondered what kind of funky mom karma I might have called down upon myself.

"Val, if there's ever anything you need to talk about, and you don't want to tell your Mom, promise you'll tell me or Granimi?"

She nodded.

"Promise?" I wanted to be on record as having gained verbal agreement. Inwardly I prayed that Olivia had someone responsible to talk to about whatever she might be keeping from her mother.

"I promise," Val said.

"Good. Check your voicemail, and if that was your mom give her a call back so she doesn't wonder where you are."

I headed downstairs to do the lunch dishes and give Olivia a call and heard Val laugh and say something in a cheery tone. That was progress.

Val stuck her head over the banister and called down to me, "Can I go to Ansel's house? He's got a Wii system!"

"Sure, honey," I said. "Take your phone. If Granimi and I go out again we'll call you, okay?"

"Okay!" she was already skipping back to her room to grab her things.

This was an excellent development. The kid needed a friend her age, and Ansel seemed like a good choice. Maybe he didn't have many friends, either. I thought he was cool, but I'm old enough to appreciate geeky. And I couldn't imagine Tulip allowing inappropriate activities or video games of any kind. Which was the only downside of this budding friendship; it would inevitably mean more encounters with The Cheerful Vegan.

Suzette and Granimi had moved into the kitchen, where they'd found a pad of paper and were plotting detectively activities. They were disappointed that Val had turned back into a normal kid in search of Wii tennis.

"We need her to contact Rose again," Suzette said. "And ask who killed her."

"First of all, I don't think Val's very in control of her talent," I said. "So I wouldn't expect much from her." Although some additional inside information would be helpful, I had to admit. "Secondly, let's keep in mind she's a twelve-year-old kid, not our personal Ouija board."

"That's a great idea!" Granimi said. "We could use a Ouija board. Do you have one?"

Are you kidding me? Those things give me the creeps. "No," I said. "And I don't want one, either." Me and my big mouth.

"You are such a wimp," Suzette said. "I bet we can get one at that game shop downtown." She checked her watch. "If they're open on Sundays I might be able to pick one up this afternoon." She played with her phone for a minute, then held it to her ear and waited, eventually shaking her head. "Answering machine," she said. "Closed Sunday and Monday. I wonder if Wal-Mart carries them."

"Wal-Mart carries everything," I said. Although possibly not Ouija boards. I imagined a network of woowoo-phobic moms threatening a nationwide boycott if Ouija boards weren't pulled from the shelves. "We'll probably need some things from there tomorrow. I'll check it out." Reluctantly, but I might as well. Suzette and Granimi's enthusiasm made a Ouija session a sure thing now that the idea had come up.

"Tomorrow we should visit the scene of the crime," Suzette said.

"Which would be where?" I'd assumed Rose had died at home, or at a restaurant, or some other place where people eat.

"I don't know," Suzette said. "But since I'm sleeping with a detective, I can find out."

"Okay," I said, "but I'm taking Val to the Aquatic Center in the morning to register for swimming lessons, and we have to take a cat to the vet, and we've got to arrange some of the rest of these activities on her list."

"I'm giving a feng shui talk to the Women's Club lunch tomorrow," Suzette said, "so I won't be able to meet up until afternoon anyway."

"I thought you'd sworn off giving free lectures." I'd heard plenty about how eager those audiences are for free information and how reluctant to pay for a consultation.

"Business has been slow," she admitted. "I'm feeling desperate. Plus, they're printing one of my articles in their newsletter, which will help expand my market. This town just isn't the hotbed of feng shui interest it used to be. I need a new audience."

We brainstormed ideas for how Suzette could expand her business until she reminded us we'd strayed off topic. "We need the inside scoop on Rose and Alan's marriage," she said. "And I know just the person," giving me a meaningful look.

"Why are you looking at me?"

"Because you and Rose share a cleaning lady. Duh."

"Oh, right. Hanna." Hanna had cleaned for me in the past, although not recently. Hence the bundt cake reminder. "I had to give her up," I said, "for budgetary reasons."

"Housekeepers know everything," Granimi said. "Suzette's right. You should get her to come clean this week. I'll pay, if that's an issue."

"Deal," I agreed. Free maid service, courtesy of Granimi. Can't argue with that. I had to return the cake plate anyway. I'd take that over in the morning and have a chat with Hanna.

17

Monday morning Granimi and I hit the phones and in a mere two hours had swim camp, guitar lessons, and something called Nature Group for Val all lined up. Good thing G. has deep pockets. Too bad I didn't plan to let her get behind the wheel, as I'd be spending most of the summer in my car. I decided to look at driving Val around as a way to say I'd gotten out of the house without having to engage in any activities myself.

The bundt cake had been reduced to one last misshapen wedge, which I put out of its misery while indulging in a third mug of coffee. I gave the carrier tray a rinse and wipe rather than follow my usual strategy, which would be to leave it on the counter and look at it for a week while thinking I ought to return that one of these days. My normal impulse to procrastination had been shouldered aside by a mandate to pry into the personal lives of others. Plus I was eager to arrange for Hanna to come over and clean.

The prospect that someone else would scrub the mildew out of the shower put some bounce in my step as I headed next door, ducking down the driveway to peek in the kitchen window and see if Hanna was around.

"Hey, Hanna," I said when she opened the slider screen and gestured me in. "How's everybody holding up over here?"

"Is a sad house, for sure," she said, stepping back to the sink. Hanna's a squeak of a thing, a scrawny 5'3", and a cleaning dynamo. She never rushes about but if you keep an eye on her you'll notice she's always in motion, tidying or polishing or dusting something.

"You want to speak with Mr. Alan? He not home this time." Hanna sighed, wiped her hands on the dishtowel tucked into the top of her apron, and turned to put some serving utensils in a drawer.

Hanna says she grew up near Bakersfield but there's more than a trace of some kind of accent I can't identify in her speech and she wears her yellow hair in twin braids that would only be considered American on someone like Raven. I've never seen her dressed in anything other than cornflower blue poly-blend pants and a simple calico blouse with an apron over the lot. Her look is so timelessly fashion-free I can't figure out if she's a worn 40 or a youthful 60. You can picture her in high school, looking exactly as she does now—except younger, of course, and without the apron—the kind of person who's so self-contained it wouldn't occur to her to follow a trend or dress to fit in.

Probably why I like her. Although that self-containment makes any impulse to get to know her seem like a gross overstepping of bounds. I'd no more ask Hanna a personal question than I'd ask my mom when she last had an orgasm.

"That's alright, Hanna, I came to see you. Oh, and to return this." I handed her the cake carrier. "The cake was delicious. We really enjoyed it."

"You eat this whole thing already?" Hanna took the empty tray and cover from me and hefted them as if amazed by their weightlessness. "You gonna get fat for sure, missy, you not careful."

"I had help!" I said. True, I'd eaten too much of it myself, but still. "My grandmother and niece are both staying with me. And my friend Suzette's been over a couple of times."

"Mmm hmm, sure," she said, putting the carrier on the counter and lifting off the lid to give it a good scrub. "Old lady, one little girl, and that skinny Asian chic," she pretended to mutter, knowing I could hear her. "How much cake they gonna eat?"

I've been indulging in cake every chance I get my entire life, and don't plan to stop anytime soon, so I didn't see what age had to do with it. And how is it my fault I'm not a skinny Asian chic? "Yes, I ate a lot of it," I admitted. "I like cake. Do I have to tell you that?"

Hanna gave me a big smile. "What kind of crazy person don't like cake?" she said. "Is good you don't want to be so skinny you can't eat cake. What kind of life that?"

I smiled back. I sometimes think Hanna fakes the accent to amuse herself. Most of the time she doesn't sound much like the vaguely Eastern European heritage she claims. Whatever. As quirks go it seems harmless.

"We all liked the cake," I said. I had a sad thought. "I guess that's the last time I'll enjoy one of Rose's cakes."

Hanna made a *pfff* sound and gave a dismissive flap of her dishtowel. "I make that," she said. "Make one other for you any time you wanna fat out."

"You baked it?" I gave her a suspicious look. "If I remember correctly," I pointed out, "you said 'I bring you Mrs. Rose's Cinnamon Caramel Bundt Cake' when you brought it over."

Hanna looked at me as if I had the brain of a three-year-old. "That's what a recipe for, missy, so all peoples can make that same thing."

I know that. I also know, from turning out a few duds myself, that there's more to being a world-class baker than just following a recipe.

"Mrs. Rose didn't bake much no more," Hanna explained, talking over her shoulder as she washed the cake carrier. "The arthritis too bad most days, so mostly I do it for her."

"You did the baking?" I'd had no idea.

"That's right. Most all the cooking. For some years now. Mrs. Rose, she sit right there at that table with her tea and that big recipe book she got and tell me what to do. She say 'now stir it around so it thicken,' and ask 'how it look now?' and sometimes say bring her the pan so she can take a look. I get pretty good. Nobody know the difference."

"In that case, I hope you'll bring over another cake when you come clean for me this week?" I made it a question and waited for her response.

"Oh, I love to come work for you some days," she said, perking up. "Wednesdays I can come. Three o'clock, for a couple of hours. More some other days if you want."

Hanna, as I've hinted before, is a bit of an operator. It didn't surprise me that she turned my offer of an afternoon's work into a regular gig. So long as Granimi was paying I was happy to go along with it.

"Wednesdays sound good," I said. I watched her dry off the cake caddy and put it away in a cabinet. "The house is quiet. Have the family gone home?"

"They all at the cemetery. Mrs. Rose going in the ground this morning."

"Oh." I was surprised she wasn't attending the interment. She'd worked for Rose for many years. Hanna pretended to straighten something in the cabinet, and I saw her blink away a tear. "Hanna, I'm so sorry about Rose," I said. "I know she was more than a boss to you."

I'd meant to be kind, but Hanna began to cry, so I went over to her and put an arm around her shoulders and guided her to a chair.

"They don't let me go with them," she said, pulling a tissue from her apron pocket. "That Anna daughter, she say I have so much to do, so many peoples in the house, better to stay and clean up. As if I don't want to say goodbye to Mrs. Rose, too."

"That Anna's a bitch, then," I said. Yeah, I know, some people handle stress better than others, and maybe this Anna daughter wasn't one of them, but the sight of Hanna in tears didn't inspire me to cut her any slack.

"And she take Mrs. Rose's recipe book!" Hanna said. "Mrs. Rose always tell me that book gonna be mine when she gone. Now that daughter taking it home with her."

Hanna was more angry than sad now, and I didn't blame her. I knew the book, an ancient black vinyl binder with peeling corners, stuffed with stained and yellowing pages. I'd given Rose a new binder one year, with a floral cover in yellow and blue that went with her kitchen, but she hadn't seemed to realize I meant her to use it, and the black behemoth remained in action.

"Did you talk to Alan? Maybe Rose mentioned that she wanted you to have it."

"Pfff. Mr. Alan not gonna rock that boat," she said. "Anna already got the book in her suitcase." Hanna got to her feet, grabbed a sponge from the sink, and went at an invisible spot on the table. "She don't even cook for real, just heat up in the microwave. But she ask where her Momma's recipe book at, she want to keep it. She never going to use that. I tell her Mrs. Rose say it going to me, and she just give me this look like what kind of worm think she deserve something of Rose to keep, and she take it up to her room."

Hanna didn't seem the type not to put up a fight if she wanted something, so maybe she didn't want to rock any boats either.

I looked at my watch: 11:37. "What time do you expect them back?"

Hanna shrugged. "Mr. Alan taking them all to lunch someplace nice. So maybe one-thirty, two o'clock. Depends how much drinking going on. That son Stewart drowning his sorrow pretty good. A van coming at two-thirty, take them all to the airport. So they be back before then, pick up their stuff." She gestured toward the front of the house. I peeked into the hall and saw luggage piled by the door.

"We need that recipe book while they're still out," I said to Hanna. "Does Alan have a photocopier in his study?"

She nodded and then smiled, understanding where I was going.

"Grab the book and meet me in there," I said, and headed for Alan's home office to turn on the copy machine.

I looked around while I waited for Hanna to return with the recipe binder. I'd been in the Braska's home many times, but never in Alan's private lair. I recognized a few things from his old law office, including a nice color photo of the four of us—Alan and Rose, Brad and me—in a silver frame. The photo had been taken at… I didn't recall. Some awards function, or a charity dinner. We'd gone to a bunch of those together over the years.

It was a nice picture. Brad looked handsome, and I was wearing my favorite good dress. The green one that sets off the auburn tones in my hair. I'd done a fine job with hair and makeup that night, one of my better attempts at elegance. Helped that I looked so happy. I hadn't seen that kind of smile in the mirror in a long time. I wondered when I'd have an opportunity to get dolled up like that again. Not that I'd miss those dinners. If they were here in Laurelton it was either the Country Club or the Water Street Inn. Neither is known for the originality of its cuisine.

Where was Hanna? Perhaps Anna was a distrustful type who had locked her suitcase. I pictured Hanna jimmying a miniature padlock with a bobby pin. Seemed like the kind of thing she might be good at, but she didn't say when she appeared a few minutes later, binder in hand.

We worked silently for a while, Hanna handing me pages from the binder and putting the copies I ran off into a manila folder. I wondered how much Hanna knew about how Rose had died, and whether there was some kind of inventory of what baked goods were stashed in that freezer in her pantry.

"Hey, Hanna," I asked, "when was the last time Rose made brownies?"

She caught my drift, and didn't like it. "I no do that!" she bristled, shaking a finger at me, her voice shrill. "Don't you say I put those nuts in there that kill her! I love that woman like she my own mother. I never do that!"

"Hanna!" I said, making a placating gesture. "No, I didn't mean that at all." Yikes. Talk about foot in mouth disease. "I was wondering if Rose had done any baking on her own recently, maybe when you weren't here."

She looked only slightly mollified. "If she clean up good, maybe I wouldn't know," she admitted. "She make some lemon bars that Sunday, I know that." She shook her head sadly. "Mess up that shortbread something bad, too. Had to toss them all out. Not like Mrs. Rose to do like that. Probably why she ate that brownie. Take one bite of that lemon bar, look for something better to eat for sure."

"It's just that, Suzette and I wondered if maybe Rose had made the brownies herself, and put the nuts in on purpose."

Hanna was already vigorously shaking her head. "No. Not Mrs. Rose. She never do that."

"Are you sure? Because if her health had worsened maybe she couldn't face being so sick again."

"She never do that to herself. Nuh uh," Hanna muttered. She used the corner of her apron to dab at her eyes.

"Yeah, that's what I think, too," I said. Now that the foul play theory was in my head I didn't seem able to get away from it.

"All those people," Hanna said, gesturing toward the rest of the house, "they say 'Poor Rose, she not want to be sick no more.' But Mrs. Rose, she too much of a lady to go like that. Lying on the ground with her slip showing and leafs in her hair. She the kind that want to be in her bed, hair all brushed nice and her best nightie on, with Mr. Alan there to hold her hand. She not the kind to fall down on the ground and lay there til someone find her like that."

Sounded like Rose had died outdoors somewhere. I teared up a little, too, imagining her, always so dignified in life, ending as a heap on the ground, old lady undergarments bared to the world. And I noticed that Hanna cast Alan as the devoted husband right up to the end. Unless she'd meant how Rose would have liked to go, not how Alan might feel inspired to behave. I was pondering how to broach that tricky subject when Hanna suddenly perked up.

"Can't be Mrs. Rose made that brownie herself," she said. "We run out of baking chocolate Friday, use the last of it in those cupcakes she make for the church. Butter and eggs low, too. Those both on that list she give me to go to the store Monday before I come in. She want to make some crumb cakes for that Garden Club meeting."

"Unless she went to the store herself," I pointed out. I'd waved to Rose in the Safeway parking lot not so long ago. The way she drove it was a miracle no one had put her license through a shredder. I couldn't help thinking that the residents of Laurelton were all a little safer now that Rose was off the streets for good.

Hanna looked skeptical. "Maybe that happen," she admitted. "But where all that stuff she bought? Be some extra chocolate on the shelf, fresh eggs in the fridge. I don't see that when I come in Monday, put the groceries away."

Hmmm. Not exactly hard evidence, but suggestive. "So she didn't bake them." I checked the time again and wondered who'd made the brownie, but the clock was ticking on the binder project. "We need to get a move on Hanna," I said. "Let's get this binder finished while we have the chance."

* * *

After we finished photocopying the binder contents, Hanna and I sat for a few minutes in Rose's kitchen with cups of tea and a plate of ginger cookies. A breeze swept over the garden and in through the open slider, filling the room with the scent of warm grass and roses. The breeze caught the edge of the pantry door and slammed it open against the counter, a flutter of pink fabric falling from the back of the door to the floor. I recognized it as Rose's apron, an old-fashioned garment of faded red gingham and white eyelet trim. Rose was gone, and would never wear that apron again, and something was not right about that.

"Hanna," I said, picking the apron up to hang it back on its hook. "I think someone tricked Rose into eating that brownie, knowing it would kill her and that everyone would think it was an accident."

Hanna surprised me by smiling and grabbing my hand as she looked into my eyes. "You think so, too?" she said. "You don't believe this just some accident, she eat that by mistake?"

I hadn't intended to share the freaky bits, but something prompted me to spill. "My niece thinks she saw Rose yesterday, in my yard."

Hanna's eyes opened very wide, and she pressed her hands to her face. "You see her spirit? It come to you? For true?"

I shook my head. "I didn't see her," I confessed. "But Val described Rose's hat very clearly. The pink one, with roses around the brim."

Hanna looked, if possible, even more astonished, and then she snapped her fingers and jumped up from her chair and rushed from the room. I heard her footsteps padding up the stairs and a door opening. A minute later she returned and set a round hatbox on the table. Hanna lifted the lid to reveal Rose's pink flowered hat.

"This hat?" She lifted it out of the box, and I nodded agreement.

Hanna turned the hat in her hands and we shared a quiet moment. Then she put it back in the hatbox and disappeared with it into the pantry.

"I put that up on one high shelf," she said when she emerged a moment later. "That Anna daughter ask for it, I gonna say Mrs. Rose give it to a church lady, don't remember which one."

She took her seat again and looked at me. "I never believe Mrs. Rose die from some accident," she said. "She so very careful, always look out for are there nuts in it. And she not die on purpose, nuh uh. Never happen that way. Never."

"Val thinks Rose was telling us that someone had killed her," I said.

Hanna gasped again. "Rose say this?"

I shook my head. "Not in words," I explained. "More like thought beams or something. That's what got us thinking she was killed in the first place." I shrugged an apology. "I'd accepted the accident story like everyone else. But this ghost thing made me wonder. That's really why I came over, to talk to you and see what you think."

"I think same as you," she said. "I don't believe in no accident, and for sure she don't eat that brownie on purpose."

"Hanna, we need to figure out what happened," I said. "Or at least come up with a really good theory. If we can find a suspect, or a motive, something that could be backed up with evidence, then maybe we can get the police to look into it."

"Of course I help with this," she said. "Who you think do this thing? What kind of person be so nasty to Mrs. Rose?"

Drat. I'd been hoping she'd have some idea. I still wanted to get Hanna's reaction to Alan as a possible suspect, and was struggling with how to raise that topic gracefully—it didn't seem a neighborly thing to do while sitting in the man's kitchen—when we heard a car in the driveway.

"The family back," Hanna said, "I gotta go smile nice, help with that luggage."

I was curious about this Anna daughter and her drowning-his-sorrows brother, so instead of sneaking out the back door I hung around, pretending it would be polite to say hello to Alan, see how he was doing.

"Hello, Lena." Alan greeted me in the front hall as a herd of Rose-relatives lumbered up and down the stairs corralling luggage. He gave me a limp hand-clasp and introduced me to his stepdaughter Anna and her husband Mel, and her brother Stewart (flush-faced and visibly tipsy) and his wife Sarah (tense and snippy to Stew) and Anna's kids Jason and Emily (college-aged, neatly groomed and adequately polite, but visibly bored beyond reason and eager to get free of parents and drunken uncles).

Anna turned out to be the large woman I'd fled from in the back hall of the funeral home on Saturday. I wondered what, if anything, she'd seen or heard of the chippie in the office. Not the sort of thing you can ask a stranger over a handshake in a hall full of relatives. And how the hell I was going to ask Hanna if she thought Alan was having an affair or, worse, if he might possibly have killed his wife? Or wives. Still hadn't looked into that creepy rumor.

Anna gave me a damp handshake. "I don't remember meeting you at the reception Saturday," she said with a fake smile.

"I'm so sorry I wasn't able to come by the house after the service," I replied sweetly. "I had to pick up my grandmother at the airport." Grandmother trumps neighbor any day, hah.

"If you'll excuse us," Anna said, settling for polite dismissal, "we have planes to catch."

"Of course." I was surprised that any child of Rose's would be such an outright bitch, but it happens. "I'll see you Wednesday, Hanna," I said, turning my back on Anna and giving Hanna a kiss on the cheek. "We'll have a strategy session then," I whispered to her.

I said goodbye to Alan, scrutinizing his face for clues. He looked so genuinely sad and tired and lost that I felt terrible for even thinking of suspecting him. Didn't stop me from wondering, though.

*   *   *

"We'll see you this weekend, then," Granimi said into the hall phone as I came in my front door.

"Who was that?" I asked when she'd hung up, wondering if we included me, and what I might be doing that weekend."

"That was your friend Raven, dear," she said. "He invited us to a talk on Friday night, before the workshop he's giving Saturday. I told him we'd be there."

"*My* friend Raven?" I asked. "I only just met him. It's not like he's a buddy or anything."

"Maybe all you have to do is give him a chance," she suggested with a smile.

"First of all," I complained, "I don't want to be set up with anyone, thank you very much. Secondly, I refuse to date any guy who goes around calling himself 'Raven,' even if that is his real name. And thirdly, I am quite sure I didn't give him this number, so how do you explain that?"

I was curious about the workshop, though. It sounded interesting. And, while I'd never admit it to Granimi, there was something about that man. I'd meant to check out his website but hadn't yet done so and wasn't sure what I'd done with his card.

Granimi admitted, without a trace of shame, that Raven might possibly have gotten my number from her. "I do think the seminar will be interesting," she said. "Raven Santiago is a big name in the field, you know. I was so pleased to meet him at that party. I'm sure his session will be fascinating. I'll go ask Val if she'd like to come, too," she said more to herself than to me, and wandered off to further her plans for our time. And we wonder where Mom gets it from.

Whatever. I had other things on my mind. "Tell Val to come down for lunch," I called up the stairs after Granimi. We needed to leave for her guitar lesson in an hour. And take the cat to the vet, but come to think of it I didn't own a pet carrier, so the vet would have to wait until I'd made a stop at Hairballs-R-Us.

I paused, waiting for sounds that would indicate Val was on her way down, and noticed that the door to Brad's office was closed. I usually leave it open. Had I closed it last night? I couldn't remember. Then I heard a mutter of voices. My heart beat faster as I crept close and leaned an ear against the door.

The voices were coming from wherever the digital cable signal originates, and I remembered I'd left the TV on. Even goof balls don't need to watch that much Golf Channel. I reached for the door handle, and when I touched it got what felt like a tiny electrical shock. I snatched my hand back and looked at the door, suddenly a little freaked and no longer convinced the room was empty.

I'd thought my side yard under the maple tree was empty, and Val had seen Rose there.

I backed two steps away. Was Brad's ghost in there, sprawled in his leather club chair, feet up on the matching ottoman, a phantom glass of single malt in his hand while he watched Tiger devour the competition?

Val chose that moment to hop down the stairs.

"Hey Val, come here a sec."

"What's up?"

"You know how you saw Rose in the yard yesterday?"

She nodded.

"And you see other, uh, things sometimes, too. Right?"

Val looked at me then at the study door. "Uncle Brad's not here," she said. "Can we have lunch now?

"Sure, honey," I said. Queen of the Idiots, that's me.

Val skipped off to the kitchen in search of a sprout-free sandwich. I took a deep breath, opened the door to Brad's study, marched in like I owned the place, and reached for the clicker to turn the TV off. Enough of the Golf Channel already. We had a guitar lesson to get to and a killer to catch.

18

Suzette showed up as we were about to head out to Val's guitar lesson. She'd found out from Bob that Rose died at her family's plot at Riverview Cemetery. Rose was part of the beautification committee or whatever they call it, stopping by every week to remove dead flowers from vases and tend to the plantings around the family mausoleum.

"Seriously, Lena," Suzette said as I drove us out to take a look around the cemetery after dropping Val off at her lesson. "You'd think the location alone would trigger a flood of gossip, but I hadn't heard anything. Are people not talking to me anymore?"

That was possible. Gossip keeps Suzette's world turning 'round. Her fellow townsfolk may have learned to keep their mouths shut in self-defense.

Suzette was examining her cuticles, "I definitely need a manicure," she said. "I think I'll have time tomorrow morning, if Dolores can squeeze me in. Those girls hear everything."

"I thought you liked Heavenly Nails better," I said, just to be difficult. And what was this about 'if I have time'? Suzette works almost as hard as I do, which is to say hardly at all, thanks to the wonders of alimony.

"Heavenly Nails is better," she agreed, "but the manicurists are all from Laos or someplace like that. They talk non-stop but I can't understand a word of it. If I go to Dolores I might actually learn something. Turn here." She pointed to the open gates of the cemetery.

I was not happy about poking around a cemetery, even on a sunlit afternoon. We'd stopped by Wal-Mart for a pet carrier and essential cat supplies, and Suzette had snagged a Ouija board from the toy aisle. The presence of it in the back of my car was giving me the heebie-jeebies. Even as a kid I'd never fully embraced the spirit of Halloween, although I was a big fan of the candy part. I'd always dressed up as something girly like a princess or ballerina. Suzette, on the other hand, told me she'd loved her witch's costume so much she'd tried to wear it to school for a week.

I knew Rose's family had been prominent in the area for generations, and just how prominent became clear when we parked and strolled over to the mausoleum. We'd dressed nice for our excursion, in order to look like we belonged at a recent gravesite just in case someone was around, but the place was deserted. The plot occupied prime real estate on a rise at the back of the cemetery. The imposing crypt I could see lurking behind a tall hedge looked larger than my first house, and reeked of old money. Which was as good a motive for murder as any. I shivered and shook off a wave of the creeps.

I heard a distant voice call out, "fore!" and realized that if I never got Brad's last golf game in perhaps I could stash his ashes up here; apparently this part of the cemetery bordered one of the local golf courses. I strolled over to the far side of the plot and peered beyond it. Through the gaps between trees in the wooded stretch that separated the living from the dead I caught a glimpse of two pastel-clad gentlemen buzzing by in a golf cart.

"Is that the Laurelton Country Club on the other side of those trees?" I asked Suzette, as I made my way back to the front of the plot, where a wrought iron gate afforded access through the hedge.

"Must be," she said, after a moment's thought. "Huh. I didn't know the two places were back-to-back like that." She turned away from the trees to admire the view. "It's so pretty and peaceful here," she said. "No wonder people like to picnic in graveyards."

Pretty and peaceful, sure. But picnic here? No way.

The iron gate, while imposing, did not bear a lock, so we let ourselves in.

"That's where they found her," Suzette whispered. "Beside that bench."

"Why are we whispering?" I whispered back.

"Because it's creepy," she admitted, still in quiet tones. "Knowing that she died right here."

We shared a moment of silent appreciation for the macabre circumstance of our visit.

"Alan came to look for her," Suzette said, "when she wasn't home yet and hadn't answered his calls to her cell."

I felt a clench in my chest. That's what happened to me the night Brad didn't come home. Poor Alan. I wouldn't wish that on anyone.

Suzette had turned away and didn't notice my discomfiture. "He found her lying on the ground by that bench," she said. "Her purse was on its side with everything spilled out onto the ground. They think she was trying to get to her epi-pen, which had fallen under the bench, out of her reach."

"Oh God, that's so sad," I said, picturing the scene in my mind.

"What's really sad," Suzette said, "is that you or I would have easily been able to reach it in time, but Rose...,"

"The arthritis," I finished the thought. "She had flare-ups. She told me once it was like someone glued her joints together with broken glass."

Suzette nodded. "But if it was that bad—"

"—what was she doing here that day?"

"Exactly."

"Maybe it wasn't so bad she'd stay home," I suggested. "Just bad enough so she couldn't kneel down and reach under the bench like you or I could."

"That could be. I'm going to look up arthritis online when I get home. I bet Hanna can tell us what kind of symptoms Rose might have had. Let's remember to ask her that."

Something was niggling at my mind. "I don't get it," I said. "If they knew she'd died from an allergic reaction, what were they holding the body for?"

Suzette perked up at being the source of inside information. "Bob says they did some toxicology stuff, to make sure it really was an allergy thing."

"Would they normally do that?" If an elderly woman in poor health came into my morgue dead of a known allergic reaction, I don't know that I'd poke around much further. Then again, there are about a thousand good reasons why I don't work in a morgue.

Suzette grinned at me over her shoulder as she wandered to the other side of the tiny manicured yard fronting the mausoleum. "Apparently they were being extra cautious because the death was unattended. Plus, Bob says they asked the medical examiner to stall for a few days while they checked out Alan's alibi. That's why Bob was loitering at the funeral, keep an eye on him and watch his behavior."

"They really suspected Alan?" I looked around for some kind of obvious clue, seeing only grass, gravel and a leafy groundcover of some kind. I wondered if Bob or any of his cohorts had seen Alan sneak into the back office with a bimbo. Maybe Suze could find out.

"I think it was more a question of crossing t's and dotting i's," she said. "'Cause Alan was the one who found her, although she'd been dead for a few hours by then and he was with people before that. Although—," she drew out the word for dramatic emphasis, leaning over to look behind an azalea, "—I did some poking around online last night, and Mrs. Lander was right. His first wife died—," she straightened up and made air quotes "—'accidentally,' too."

"No way!"

"Way. A riding accident, in New Mexico. Snake spooks her horse, she gets thrown, head hits rock, end of story. And, guess what?"

"What?"

"She was loaded, too. He got most of it. Plenty of questions, but no witnesses. Family didn't like him, so it turned into a big to-do, lawsuits, the whole deal. When the dust settled Alan rode out of town two-and-a-half million richer."

"Holy cow. How come we'd never heard about it?"

She shrugged. "It was twenty-five years ago, in another state. Probably not something many people around here know about."

"Still, sheesh."

"Yeah."

"That's a pretty lousy track record." How many guys lose two wives to freak accidents? Even decades apart. Come to think of it, though, I'd already racked up one accidentally deceased husband, and I was still young, sort of. It could happen again.

"So either he's gotten away with arranging an accident twice—," Suze said.

"—or he's incredibly unlucky." Huh. Even if it was just bad luck it made me feel differently about Alan. Like maybe his icky karma would rub off on me if I stood to close. I'd feel bad about that, except for the lingering possibility it had been his doing. "Did you mention any of this to Bob?"

"He said stranger things have happened and not to get ideas in my head."

"I think it's suspicious," I said, before I remembered how sad and forlorn Alan looked. "Still, the man appears to be genuinely grieving. I'm not saying that means Rose's death was an accident, just that if it wasn't

I'm not convinced he had anything to do with it."

"Maybe he's a good actor."

"Maybe someone else did it."

"That could be, too."

"You know," I said, looking around, "it's really quiet and private here." I peeked out the iron gate. My car was pulled to the curb about twenty feet away. A couple power-walked in the middle distance, far enough away that even if I'd waved and called out they most likely would not have noticed me. "Seriously. If you parked somewhere else, no one would know you were here once you're on this side of the hedge. It's a really good place to kill someone."

"Especially if you make it look like natural causes," Suzette added.

"And you wouldn't have to get rid of the body. Just leave it lying here."

"Okay, now I'm really creeped out."

There was a matching bench to the one Rose had been found beside on the other side of the enclosure, in a nice patch of sun. I sat down and pondered the location.

"So, the theory is," I summarized aloud, wanting to be sure I had it right in my mind, "that Rose came out here and either accidentally or deliberately ate a brownie with nuts in it. Then, when the allergic reaction kicked in, she panicked and knocked her purse over and couldn't reach the Epi-pen in time."

It made sense that way. I could almost see it. I almost believed it, too. Then I remembered the look in Val's eyes as she'd turned to me and said, "Someone killed her."

"This whole thing is just incredibly sad." I felt a wave of regret that Rose was gone, and that I'd accepted her at face value for years: a sweet neighbor lady who loved to bake and was kind to everyone in a polite, upper crust kind of way. It's not like we'd ever have been best buds or anything, had I made the effort to know her better, but now that I no longer had that opportunity I felt bad that I'd missed it.

Suzette, who'd wandered off behind the mausoleum, reappeared, looking about as cheery as I felt.

"Are we done here?" I asked, getting to my feet.

"Yeah, I'm done," Suzette said. "Is it just me, or are you starting to feel really down?"

"I'm beyond 'starting to.'" I held the gate open for her and shut it behind us. The bench where Rose had died was now in deep shade. I wondered if anyone would sit there and think of Rose. It was a nice spot, in its way, though not somewhere I'd want to hang out. I thought for a moment that I smelled roses, and shivered. Time to get out of there.

"This was much more fun when I was pretending it was just an interesting theory," Suzette said. "Now it feels real."

"We could totally be barking up the wrong tree, you know," I reminded her. "So far we've got nothing but wild speculation and a twelve-year-old who says she saw a ghost."

"And our own intuition," she reminded me.

Suzette's a lot bigger on intuition than I am, but after my conversation with Granimi maybe I'd start paying more attention to it. It still seemed there was a good chance the only thing we would accomplish by exploring Rose's death would be to make colossal fools of ourselves, but I felt unable to let it go.

Outside the overgrown hedge I took a moment to look around. Another brisk walker powered past, and I nodded hello. The fitness fans were incongruous. I could appreciate the lack of traffic, though, and the park-like setting. If you don't mind dead people everywhere.

I counted a grand total of one other pedestrian and two cars within view, and one of those was my CR-V. "You could get away with anything here," I said. I looked around at all the grave markers and vases and bouquets of real and artificial flowers. "Seriously, why aren't we surrounded by drug deals and spies making dead drops?"

"Spies?" Suzette laughed. "In Laurel County? What kind of hotbed of intrigue do you think you're living in?"

"I bet there's fierce interest in prize-winning apple pie recipes, stuff like that." I turned away from the unused potential of the acres of quiet seclusion and headed for the wooded strip of land between the cemetery and the golf course, thinking about pie. I may be a cake junkie, but there's room for pie in my dessert pantheon.

"What are you looking for back here?" Suzette asked, swatting away a bug and keeping her Jimmy Choo knockoffs firmly planted on the manicured lawn rather than risk the unknown footing of the underbrush.

"I'll know when I see it," I replied, with more confidence than I felt. More likely I'd step on it or walk right past it.

And then I did notice something. A gap wide enough for a golf cart-sized vehicle to have come along and crushed the shrubbery. I fingered a broken branch and had no idea whether it had broken last week or a year ago. I wondered if Raven would be able to tell. He wouldn't be living up to that ridiculous name if he couldn't track a golf cart through a couple yards of underbrush.

Curious, I broke a twig off a branch beside the one I'd been looking at. Huh, it did look different. Which only told me that the first branch hadn't been broken off within the last five minutes, which I could have told you anyway.

"Hey, Suzette," I called out. "I think someone drove a golf cart in here and parked in these bushes."

"And?"

"And… I have no idea. But if you didn't want to leave a car on the drive there," I gestured to where my car was parked, "you could come through this way."

"Lena, you're showing promise as a detective," Suzette said. "Maybe you should ask Bob for a job."

I snorted. Maybe when pigs fly. Rose might want to appear to someone more competent than the two of us if she expected to see justice before her bones turned to dust.

I swatted at the shrubbery for another minute or two, hoping to find something exciting, like a tire track. It all just looked like woodsy stuff.

"Next time, remind me to wear slacks." I tried to pick twiggy fragments out of my pantyhose without starting any runs. Oops, too late. This pair was tight in the waist anyway. I looked around, saw the place was still deserted, and reached up under my skirt to pull them off.

"I'm done with funeral attire," I said, wadding up the nylon and stuffing it in my purse. "Let's go home and change into something comfy."

"I need a drink," Suzette said. "How 'bout we go to Oscar's for peach daquiris."

I looked at my watch with regret. A peach daquiri and some bar snacks would be perfect.

"I appear to have adopted a kid for the summer," I reminded Suzette, "and her guitar lesson is over in eleven minutes."

*   *   *

On our way home I tuned out as Val chatted about her lesson and went on about the loaner guitar she cradled in her lap, and how Gary, the guitar dude, said they could work on songwriting if she wanted, which she did. I'd hoped the Ouija board would have slipped everyone's mind, but as I started to pull away after dropping Suzette off I saw her in the rearview running after us and waving for attention.

"We forgot to plan our Ouija session," she said when I hit the brakes and buzzed down my window. "Wanna do it tonight?"

Not especially, no.

"Oh, cool!" Val said. "The Ouija board. Hey, is this it?" She wriggled around to lean into the cargo area and nab the Wal-Mart bag. "Awesome. Mom would freak if she knew about this."

What the hell, it wasn't like I had a chance of getting out of it. "Come over later," I told Suzette. "Or join us for dinner if you want."

"Yeah, come have dinner with us," Val pleaded. She was developing a girl crush on Suze, which was fine with me. There are worse role models. Better ones, too, probably, but none that hang out with me on a regular basis.

Suzette agreed to the dinner idea, and she and Val made wooooo sounds at each other at the prospect of a séance while I rolled my eyes and wished the whole thing were over already.

Ansel was in his front yard when we pulled into our driveway, tossing a ball for the yip-machine. Val jumped from the car and went over to say hello. I wasn't sure if she was interested in Ansel (another crush brewing?) or in playing with the dog. I lugged Val's guitar and the Ouija board and the cat carrier into the house, weighing the merits of cooking up some of the pricey organic groceries we'd purchased yesterday against the ease of ordering in. If we ordered in I could take a bath before dinner, which that an easy decision.

"Ansel's coming over after supper," Val said, skipping into the house and letting the front door slam behind her. "He thinks the Ouija board sounds really cool."

I retreated to my tub with a cold glass of pinot grigio, wondering how his mom felt about it. I figured if Ansel wasn't smart enough to just say he'd been invited over to play a board game and leave it at that, that was his problem.

19

"The main thing is not to invite the spirits in by asking them to prove they're here." Ansel had downloaded a bunch of Ouija tips in preparation for our session.

"I thought inviting spirits in was the whole point," I said. "Aren't they supposed to move that pointer thingie?"

"That's the planchette," Ansel said. "That doesn't count as asking for a demonstration. It's like, you don't want to ask them to rock the table, or flicker the lights or something like that. That's giving them permission to come into your home. Just ask questions that can be answered on the board."

I didn't get the distinction; if spirits are hovering around guiding the planchette, how is that different from them being in my home? If I'd had any sense I would have suggested we do this at Suzette's.

"There are some freaky Ouija stories online," Ansel said, "but they aren't very credible. I think they're just made up to be scary."

I think he meant to make me feel better—it was obvious I was nervous—but it wasn't working.

"We want to contact Aunt Lena's neighbor, the old lady who died recently," Val said to Ansel. "I don't think she's likely to cause any trouble."

"Did you ever meet Rose?" I asked Ansel. "Mrs. Braska? She lived next door on that side," I tilted my head in the Braska direction. "Her husband Alan is a retired lawyer?" Ansel looked blank, and I realized he'd probably moved to the neighborhood a few days after Rose had died.

Suzette managed to finish lighting all the votive candles she'd set around the room without igniting the sleeves of her caftan, and Granimi turned off the lights.

"Do we all do this together, or what?" Val asked, nudging the planchette with a finger. We were set up in my living room, with the Ouija board on the coffee table and the séance participants, both reluctant and eager, gathered around on cushions on the floor.

"One person should be the stenographer," Ansel said, flipping through his papers.

"I'll do that," I volunteered. If I were busy taking notes I couldn't be called on to wield the planchette. Perfect.

"The letters can come up really fast, so it's hard to keep track unless someone writes it down," Ansel said. "And you have to write down the questions we ask, too, or the answers might not make sense later."

"I'm on it," I assured him, getting up from my cushion to look for my notepad and pen in the kitchen. I poured myself another glass of wine while I was in there.

"This says you shouldn't drink alcohol before using the Ouija board," Ansel said, pointing at his papers when I returned to my seat with my full glass and topped off Suzette's from the bottle I'd carried in with me.

Suzette and I both burst out laughing. "Yeah right," she said, waving off his advice. "Too late for that."

"Any more for you, Granimi?" I asked.

She shook her head no. "I think I prefer a clear head tonight, dear."

Party pooper.

"And I think it would be a good idea to begin with a prayer," she suggested. "Let's all join hands. You, too, Lena." She bowed her head.

"Merciful spirits, guardian angels, Divine Source, we ask that you be present with us and guide our session so that only good comes from it. Bless this house, and all of the people—and any other entities—in it, and help us to be of service tonight in whatever capacity we can. Amen."

We all amen-ed after her, and then we got started. Consensus was that more than two people at a time was unwieldy, so Suzette and Granimi took the first shift.

Talk about anticlimactic. They sat for what seemed a very long time, hands on the planchette, nothing happening. Suzette asked several times if anyone was there, and Granimi asked for Rose to come join us if she were able. More nothing. I was stifling a yawn when the planchette suddenly jerked and stuttered.

"Is that Rose?" Suzette asked, sounding remarkably calm while my heart lurched into double-time. "If that's Rose, please announce yourself through the board."

The planchette wiggled some more, but didn't move.

"I think that's me," Granimi confessed. She lifted her fingers from the planchette and leaned back against the armchair behind her, resting her pink cast in her lap. "I'm sorry, dear. I don't think I have the stamina for this. Let's give someone else a turn."

Suzette looked at me to see if I'd changed my mind about more active participation, but I shook my head no way, so Val and Ansel took over.

"Rose, if you are with us, speak to us through the board," Suzette said.

A draft moved through the room then and I heard a door slam shut upstairs. My heart thundered around in my chest like a panicked rabbit as the candle flames flickered and danced. No one else seemed in the least bit alarmed. I felt like an idiot. What was I so afraid of?

Suzette whispered to Val that maybe she should try asking.

"Rose, if you are with us, speak to us through the board," Val repeated. And just like that the planchette started moving. I was so unprepared for results that I had to scrabble for the pen, which I'd dropped under the coffee table. Ansel reproved me with a sidelong glance as Val read off the letters indicated by the planchette.

S—W—E—E—T—S—W—E—E

I wrote it down on my pad, glad to have something to do.

"Sweetswee," I read back, when the planchette stopped. "Or 'sweet sweet,' maybe." Had the planchette stopped close enough to the T for it to count again? "Rose had a world class sweet tooth. For what that's worth," I suggested. One of the few people I've met who was in my league.

I was shushed and then we all waited some more, and the scared little bunny inside me calmed down a little. During a long pause while nothing else happened, I looked at the words again. Two sweets, maybe. Could they refer to the brownie? I was about to whisper this possibility when Val spoke up.

"Rose, is that you?" she asked.

After a long moment, the planchette slid over to the "yes" spot.

There was an intake of breath around the table, and wide-eyed glances were exchanged. Suzette and Granimi squirmed and nudged each other with their elbows.

"Who are you?" Val tried. "Tell us your name."

Another long pause, and then:

R—O
Long pause:
Z
Then some more dithering and a dash to:
S

Again the planchette seemed to lose focus. It headed toward the E but didn't quite make it. The letters were close enough to ROSE to elicit smiles all around. It wasn't clear to me that this proved anything, since we'd spoken the name several times. I was still telling myself this was just subconscious manipulation of the planchette, not some kind of entity pushing it around through our fingers.

"Val, do you see her?" I whispered.

She shook her head no.

Suzette shushed again, then asked, "Rose, were you murdered?"

Ansel's head popped up and he looked from Suzette to me. I guess we'd forgotten to clue him in to why we wanted to contact my dead neighbor.

Suzette's question didn't get a response, so she nudged Val to do the asking again.

"Rose, did someone kill you?" Val asked.

The planchette began to move again, more quickly this time.

W—I—N—K—W—O—M

I wrote it down, but it didn't make sense.

"Was that a yes?" Granimi asked.

I shrugged. "That was a 'winkwom.'"

"Wigwam?"

I shook my head no, before we got shushed again.

"Rose, tell us who killed you," Val instructed.

The votive candles flickered more wildly for a moment, although I didn't feel any draft in the room, and the planchette began to move again.

A—L—S—T—R—O—M

W—I—N

(K?)

"This doesn't spell anything," I whispered, earning another shush.

"Spirits forget how to use language," Granimi whispered. "We need to be patient."

I noticed no one shushed her. I tried not to feel put out by that.

The planchette began to move again.

O—T—H—R—F—L—O—W—E—(R?)

"Did that spell something?" Ansel asked.

"It looks like 'other flower,' if an E is missing. And I'm not sure about the second R." Given the spelling accuracy so far, it might just as easily mean "overflow." I scribbled that possibility on my pad, too.

"What does that mean?" Val whispered to us.

Several shrugs around the table. "Why don't you ask her?" I suggested, with a nod at the board.

"Why don't you ask her," Suzette said back at me with a wink and a smile. "Wink!" I said, looking at my notes.

"What?" All eyes turned to me.

"W, I, N, K: wink.' Those letters have come up twice. Maybe Rose is telling us she was killed by someone with an eye twitch."

"An eye twitch?" Suzette complained. "That can't be right."

"You just winked at me," I pointed out. "So maybe she means you."

"I winked after she spelled it. How does that make sense."

"Ladies." Granimi intervened. "Keep it mellow. Let's focus on the board, and hope Rose is still around."

A long moment of silence.

"I forgot what I was going to ask her," Val said.

"Ask if she's still here," Granimi suggested.

"Rose, are you still with us?"

The answer came right away:

H—E—R—E—N—O—T—H—E—R—(E?)

The planchette stopped again at an indeterminate spot, and eyes turned toward me.

"I'm not sure," I said. "It could be 'here, not her,' or 'here, not here,' or 'here, no, there,' or maybe 'her, another,' if it's misspelled."

"I read that misspellings are common," Ansel said. "So we should take that into account."

That sounded like license to make messages mean whatever you wanted, but I was willing to go with it.

"What's the last thing she said before that?" Granimi peered at my notes. Good luck. With the overheads out and the votive flames dancing and flickering I could barely read them myself.

"It looks like 'other flower.'"

"Maybe that means a name," Granimi suggested. "Like Rose, but a different flower."

"Oooh, good thinking, G. How many people have flower names?"

"My mom does," Ansel pointed out. He looked concerned, and I felt a thrill of possibility run through me.

"I don't think it means your mother," I assured him. Could it? "I'm sure there are lots of women with flower… hey! If it's a flower name, it's a girl, right?

"Yes!" Suzette agreed. "Nice call. So the killer's a woman. Excellent."

Yeah, narrows the suspect pool to only half the population.

"Val, ask who 'other flower' is." I suggested.

Val asked, and the planchette responded:

A—S—T—R—O

M—E—R—I—A

"'Astro' and 'meria'" I read back.

"Astro is star," Ansel said.

"And maybe meria is supposed to be Maria," Suzette suggested.

"Maria Star?" Granimi and I both wondered aloud.

Could it be that easy?

"Now we're getting somewhere." Suzette said. "Val, ask where we can find this Maria Star. Or Star Meria. Oh, wait. Lena, isn't there a Star of the Sea chapel out near Holtsville somewhere?"

"Mer is French for sea," Granimi said.

"So where is this getting us?" Val asked.

My sentiments exactly. "I think we need to keep going," I said. I imagined a spectral Rose hovering above my coffee table, rolling her eyes in frustration at our inability to decipher her clues. Fat help she was being. Why couldn't she just spit out a name, like a normal person?

"How are you kids doing," Granimi asked Val and Ansel. "Do you want someone else to take a turn?"

"I'm good," Ansel said, and looked at Val. She nodded okay.

"Val's getting a good response," I pointed out. "She should keep going."

"What should I ask her?"

"Ask again who killed her," I suggested. "That's what we want to know, and we still don't have a clear answer on that."

Asked and answered:

B—A—D—B—L—O—S—O

M

F—L—O—W—E—R

W—N—K

"There's 'wink' again," Suzette whispered.

"And probably that was 'bad blossom' before 'flower,'" I said. "We still don't know what that means."

"Rose," I asked, starting the question before I realized I intended to participate directly, "keep telling us who killed you."

B—L—O—N

D—I—E

"'Blon' isn't a word," Ansel said.

The "die" part we all got, and I felt a chill run through me that had nothing to do with the temperature in the room.

"It could be one word," I realized. "Those pauses don't seem to be reliable as word breaks. Which makes it 'blondie'."

"A blonde!" Suzette exclaimed.

That ruled out the women in this room. Unless you counted Granimi's hair as blonde.

Ansel looked fidgety, and I remembered that his mother was not only named after a flower, but also strawberry blonde. This time the thrill that ran through me was more of a sinking feeling. Did dark secrets lurk beneath Tulip's sweet exterior. Oh my god: "Sweet." No. Couldn't be.

Plus, it didn't seem right to put Ansel's mom on our suspect list when he was sitting right there. "Maybe it's blondie as in blonde brownie," I suggested, turning my thoughts toward fattening treats in hopes of putting both myself and Ansel at ease.

The planchette thought that was a question, and raced to spell out:

B—R—O—W—N—I—E

Blondie, brownie. A blonde killer with a brownie, or just an unquiet soul obsessed with baked goods?

"Rose, forgive us for being so dense," I said. "Could you try one more time to tell us who killed you?"

It seemed at first that my question wouldn't get a response, then the planchette answered.

A—S—T—R—O—M—E—I—A

"What did that spell?" Granimi asked.

"'Astro' again, with MEIA, all run together."

"Astromeia?" Ansel said. "That sounds like a constellation."

"Or one of the more obscure Roman goddesses," Granimi suggested.

"We can Google it later," I pointed out, as the planchette began moving again, on its own this time, without waiting for a question.

P—R—U

"Pru? That's a nickname for Prudence," Granimi said.

"No one's named Prudence any more," I said. "Not even in your generation, G."

"Well then, if we are looking for a Prudence she'll be easy to find."

"Rose, do you mean 'Prudence'?" Val asked, going to the source.

The planchette wavered, then spelled out:

P—E—R—U

"Peru!" We all got a little excited.

L—I

"This is like a bad cell phone connection," Suzette complained. "It would be nice to get a few more complete words."

"Lima? That's in Peru, isn't it?" I asked. Geography class was a very distant memory. Did that mean Rose was killed by some blonde flower woman from Peru? "Do we know anyone from Peru? Or anyone who's been to Peru?"

Ansel sat up very straight and looked even paler than usual.

"Is something wrong, Ansel?" I asked.

He shook his head, but his squeaky "no" was unconvincing.

"Do you want to stop? Someone could take your place if you like."

He hesitated for a moment, then took his hands off the planchette and got to his feet without making eye contact. "I have to go," he muttered.

I followed him to the door, said goodnight, and watched him run across the yard to his house. Something was wrong there. Did he think the clues pointed to his mom? Could Tulip really be the 'other flower'? And what did Peru have to do with it?

I rejoined the girls and surprised myself by sitting down in Ansel's place, resting my fingertips on the planchette as if I'd been born to it.

"What was that about?" Suzette asked.

I shook my head. "Not a clue," I said. I'd run the Tulip possibilities by her later. It didn't seem right to voice any more about it with Val in the room. If Ansel stayed friendly with her she'd probably be spending time at his house, and I didn't want to plant ideas in her head.

"Let's see if we can get something more useful here," I said. I'd stopped feeling scared sometime around the Star of the Sea theory. "Suzette, can you take the notes while I try this?

"Maybe we're asking the wrong thing," Suzette said. "Let's see if we can find out why Rose was killed. That would be useful to know, too."

"Rose, if you are still here, tell us why you were killed," Val commanded.

N—O, came the reply. I held my breath as the planchette moved across the board. I was so totally not pushing it! I looked at Val and she met my gaze with a shy grin and a nod. She wasn't pushing it, either. Holy shit!

"'No'?" Suzette exclaimed. "Why did she say 'no'?"

The planchette vibrated for a second, then moved again.

D—O—N—N—O

"Donno?" Suzette said. "Is that a nickname for Donald?"

"I think she means 'don't know,'" I said. I didn't know, either, how I knew that.

The planchette jerked and landed on the yes spot.

"She doesn't know why she was killed," Granimi said.

W—H—Y

"Oh God," I said. This was just too sad. "She wants us to find out why."

"It would help if she'd tell us who," Suze pointed out. "We're having trouble with that."

"Maybe she doesn't know that either," I said.

"Someone gave her that brownie."

I felt the planchette take off again:

W—I—N—K—W—O—M—A—N

W—H—Y

"I don't know why, Rose," I heard myself say in a soft voice. "But we're going to find out." And we'd find out who this Wink Woman was, too.

Further questioning was fruitless, and we soon gave up. By the time we'd put the board away and turned the lights back on Granimi was half asleep and Val was yawning mightily. We sent them off to bed and retreated to the kitchen where I made a pot of decaf and Suzette and I reviewed our scribbled notes.

"Wink woman seems to be the main clue," I said.

"And that astro thing was repeated twice."

"Here it is: ASTRO plus MERIA, which we thought might mean Star of the Sea, or possibly Maria Star. Then it comes up again as one word, without the second R."

We Googled all of them, without anything that looked like a relevant response.

"What about this," Suzette pointed to the top of the screen. "'Do you mean *alstroemeria*?'"

I looked at the strange word. "I don't know. Do we?" I clicked on it, and the search results that popped up were headed by a selection of thumbnail images.

"On my god, it's a flower!"

I clicked again. Alstroemeria: Peruvian Lily. "No wonder she couldn't spell it. I can't even say it."

"Whatever, it's Peruvian," said Suzette.

My thoughts exactly. "L—I came up on the board right after Peru. I bet it was for lily, not Lima. It's pretty. I've seen them in those mixed bouquets you get in the grocery store. I wonder if Rose ever grew any in her garden."

"Are we supposed to take it that literally?" Suzette asked. "How does that help us?"

"I have no idea. Maybe we should call some local florists, ask if they have any."

"And that will tell us what?"

"We won't know 'til we ask," I pointed out.

"I guess it's better than nothing."

"And we need to check out Tulie, too," I said.

"What's tooley two?"

"TULIP, van Alstyne, my new neighbor," I reminded her. "The happy vegan? Named for a flower? Blonde? Oh my God, I just remembered: I saw her at the memorial service. She does know Rose."

"Or Alan."

"Either way."

"And that's why Ansel freaked out," she nodded, catching up. "He thought these clues could mean his mother."

I nodded. Poor kid. "I hope they don't, for his sake."

"But still."

"Worth looking into."

We pondered that.

"And we do that how?" Suzette asked.

Excellent question.

I googled Tulip van Alstyne but forgot to put the quote marks around it, so we got pages for the Tulip Moving Van Company and the usual gazillion other useless and only vaguely similar results. A try with the quote thingies was a dud, too.

I clicked over to whitepages.com and searched for a van Alstyne in our zip code. Laurelton's on the small side, so there's only the one zip for everybody.

"Michael van Alstyne: 871 Mountain Laurel Crescent," Suzette read off the screen. "Only van Alstyne in town, apparently. Do we know that's the correct spelling?"

"Uh huh. Michael must be the husband. And that must be their old address. We could check it out. They didn't move next door until after Rose died."

"Again, that will tell us what?"

"I have no idea." I wasn't sure we'd learned anything useful from poking around at the cemetery this afternoon, but I was glad we'd done it. I felt we'd accomplished something, even if that was just crossing a task off our list.

"Where's Mountain Laurel Crescent?"

MapQuest knew. "Other side of town, out by the old quarry."

"Near the cemetery?"

I zoomed out a couple of clicks for a better view. "Kind of."

We looked at each other.

"I don't want it to be Tulip," I said. "I find her a bit much, but Val likes her, and Ansel's a good kid."

"Then instead of checking her out as a suspect, we can tell ourselves we're eliminating her from our possibles list," Suzette said.

"Our possibles list? So far she's the only one on it."

"What about Alan?"

"He's not a good fit for the blonde flower name," I pointed out. "Plus he has an alibi, remember?"

"I'm thinking about his mistress."

"If he really has one." Better her than my neighbor. Or maybe she was my neighbor, unlikely as that seemed.

"The mistress might be a blonde flower," Suze said.

"And maybe she doesn't have an alibi for that afternoon."

"We gotta find out who she is."

"Let's start with if she is, but yeah. And we should find out where Tulip was that afternoon, too."

"Any ideas how we do that?"

"Let's start with the mistress," I suggested. "Hanna's coming over Wednesday. I bet she'll know if Alan's been fooling around, although I don't know how I'm going to ask her that. Maybe Val can find out more about Tulip while she hangs out with Ansel. We don't even know if Tulip works. If she has a job, that probably rules her out of an afternoon trip to the cemetery."

"Depends on the job," Suzette said. "She could be a sales rep or a case worker of some kind, where she's out driving around in her car most of the day."

"Okay, we'll put Val on that," I said. "She can ask Ansel what his mom does or where she works. I'll talk to Hanna about Alan. You see what else you can get from Bob. Maybe there's something in the file that would help."

20

Suzette called Tuesday morning while Granimi and I were engrossed in the newspaper. "You've been cleared!" she announced, but I already knew that from reading the Orchard City Courier.

What with all the drama around Val showing up, followed by ghostly revelations and ensuing speculation, the dead guy at the wedding had been pushed from the forefront of our curiosity, although we'd avidly followed the story in the local papers. On Sunday we'd learned that the corpse in question was that of one Eugene LeJeune, a local building inspector. Eugene had attended Orchard City High with the owner of The Pear Street Gallery, my pal Carlos. Carlos had hired Eugene to make sure the 160-year old structure would support the combined weight of several hundred wedding guests.

Nice of Carlos to think of that before the dancing started.

Carlos reportedly acknowledged the high school connection by inviting Eugene and his girlfriend, one Deborah Constantine, to the reception. They'd attended, and at some point during the festivities Eugene had been strangled with a scarf belonging to "a local artist attending the festivities."

Nice of them to refer to me as an artist.

Details were juicier on Monday, when the Courier had informed us that Eugene was under investigation for using his position to—as best I could figure out from all the carefully worded allegedlies—arm-twist local contractors and property owners into footing the bill for his gambling debts. Rumored kickbacks, extortion, and bribery were expected to implicate at least one Laurel County Planning Committee member. Eugene's scheme of choice was to either detect or invent a (costly to correct) mold or asbestos problem, then arrange to overlook it for a (less costly) cash consideration. It was hard to believe he'd thought he could get away with it for long, but allegedly the guy had been shaking folks down for years. This led to some theorizing that one of Eugene's victims had wised up and struck back, but specific clues and likely suspects were scarce.

Probably because the girlfriend did it. As reported in the Tuesday edition Granimi and I were reading when Suzette called, Eugene had overindulged and become flirtatious with someone else, or maybe several someone elses. That part was unclear. It was clear that Deb had stormed out, met up with a girlfriend to continue drinking at a dive a few blocks away and, when all notions of sense and propriety had been thoroughly drowned, returned to the party to confront Eugene about his current and past indiscretions. The paper didn't say, but I could guess what Eugene might have been doing when Deb tracked him down in Couch territory. Deb admitted making a forceful argument to Eugene that she didn't like his behavior and no longer needed him around. That she'd used my scarf to do so was just bad luck. (I made a vow to be more careful about leaving my personal property lying around where anyone could use it).

The truth would have come to light sooner, but Deb, sleeping off a world class hangover in her new boyfriend's basement apartment, had been difficult to find. Reading between the lines, you could sense some disappointment on the part of the press that the crime had not been perpetrated by a town selectman. Probably that's why so much was made of Deb's employment history as a professional mud wrestler.

I consider myself open-minded, but I was glad to read that both Eugene and Deb were residents of Orchard City. Laurelton likes to think it's above such things as mud-wrestling.

Suzette congratulated me on being cleared of all suspicion, and invited me to join her and Bob for lunch. Granimi'd already asked if I wanted to tag along to her 12:30 Pilates session, so I was happy to accept Suzette's offer. We arranged to meet at Café Dijon after I'd dropped Granimi off at wherever her Pilates thing was happening.

"She certainly has nice muscle definition," Granimi said, examining a photo from Deb's championship season a few years back. She sure had a lot of muscles for a girl. "I wonder what her workout routine is."

"Thinking about a career in mud-wrestling, G.?" That would pack the house.

"I'm a little old for that, dear. Do you suppose they use a special kind of mud?"

I had to laugh. "Honestly, Granimi, is that the kind of thing you think I know?"

"I'm just wondering," she said.

Whatever. I was still in mourning for my favorite scarf and couldn't muster up interest in the finer points of mud varietals.

*   *   *

"Are you two nuts? Rose died of anaphylactic shock because she ate something she was allergic to," Bob said. "I'd say the case is closed, but there is no case. There never was a case." He chugged his iced tea, looked at the empty glass as though it should be full of beer, and signaled the waitress for a refill.

I was grateful that Suzette had omitted ghost stories and the Ouija session from what she'd shared with Bob, but without it we had squat. We had that Rose was wealthy and that her housekeeper didn't believe the suicide theory, and that someone at some time might have parked a golf cart behind that big-ass mausoleum.

"Yes, Rose had money," Bob said. "And yes, it's odd that she would eat anything with nuts in it, given her allergy. So either she didn't know she was eating nuts, or she ate them on purpose. Either one of those two scenarios makes perfect sense to me, and I don't see any reason—and let me remind you I am speaking as a police officer here—I don't see any reason to think there might be others."

He paused to start in on his iced tea refill and demolish half of his turkey wrap. Suzette and I were having soup of the day and sharing a large Mediterranean salad. I hoped it was a light enough meal to allow for dessert later.

"I have to agree with you though," Bob said when his mouth was clear, "about the potential of that location. There are worse places in this town to do a drug deal." He seemed lost in thought for a moment.

"Bottom line, though," he said, wiping his mouth, "is you have a deceased who's been officially declared not a homicide, no suspect, no substantial motive, and nothing that even qualifies as circumstantial evidence."

Suzette seemed undeterred by Bob's lack of enthusiasm for our suppositions. "That's why it would be helpful if you could get us a copy of any notes the police department might have about Rose's death," she said to him with a smile.

"Now you've completely lost it," he said. "There is no way, NO FUCKING WAY, that I am giving an official police file to unauthorized civilians!"

"Sir," the waitress leaned in. "Sorry to intrude, but please keep your voice down."

Suzette placed a placating hand on Bob's arm. "I didn't mean to upset you, sweetie," she said. "It's just that you said there wasn't a case. I thought that meant it wouldn't be a problem."

"'Wouldn't be a problem'? What are you trying to do, get me fired?"

I was sorry I was stuck in the window seat. If this turned into a full-blown spat I'd have to climb over one or the other of them to get away.

"I'm not asking for the file, if there is a file," Suzette said calmly. "Just a copy of anything you think would put our minds at rest, so we can leave you alone and let you solve any real murders that come up."

Bob grimaced at her.

"I'll make it worth your while," she said in a sing-song voice, pushing her chest out and waggling her tits at him. "I've got a new Victoria's Secret bra and panty set," she teased, "and I know you want to see it."

This time Bob actually growled at her, but it was a friendlier grrr, and his eyes were glued to her chest. "Bra and panties, you say."

Suzette nodded. "Pink satin," she said. "With black lace. And when I say 'panties,' that's kind of a stretch because there really isn't much to—"

"Okaaayyy, we get the picture," I said. "Bob: yes or no on the info? Suzette, if you arch your back any more it's going to take a year of chiropractic to get your spine back on straight."

Bob re-entered the earth's atmosphere from the fantasy land he'd been visiting, and sat back in his chair. "I give in," he said to Suze. "I'm your helpless love slave."

Suzette leaned over and gave him a kiss.

"What I'll do," Bob offered, "is take another look through the file and see if anything catches my eye that might convince the two of you there's nothing about Rose Braska's death to get excited about."

Suzette clapped her hands, while I settled for a smile and conventional expressions of thanks.

"I gotta get back to work." Bob lumbered to his feet. "Next time you want to buy me lunch, pick someplace that serves guy food. Enough of this quiche and tabbouleh crap."

"You think he'll give us anything worth looking at?" I asked, as the café door shut behind him.

Suzette waved and blew Bob a kiss through the window. "We'll get the whole file," she said confidently. "Or most of it." She waggled her chest at me and smiled.

"What have you really got on under there? Curious minds want to know."

"White cotton panties and an old beige nylon bra," she admitted. "I've got the satin and lace stuff at home, though. Bob's a pushover for the stuff, so I like to be prepared."

* * *

Suzette was right about Bob's susceptibility to fine lingerie. She called me after dinner to say he'd shown up with a pile of photocopies, and invited me to come have a look at the papers.

"Let's go back to the allergic reaction," I suggested as we started the review. "Any chance it could have been triggered by something besides the brownie? Or that something else mimicked the effects of an allergy?"

"It was the brownie," Bob said. "Believe it or not our coroner is known to be reasonably competent. Plus, we found a white bakery bag and a piece of uneaten brownie on the ground beside the body. As much as you might suspect I don't know how to do my job, that seems conclusive to me."

Suzette hastened to assure him that we had nothing but the greatest admiration for his professional skill, instincts, and acumen. I thought she was laying it on with a trowel, and Bob seemed amused by her excessive praise. It was odd to see this big, gruff potato of a man melt when he was the center of Suzette's attention. I recognized the special dynamic of an unlikely couple who suit each other perfectly. Brad and I had had that magic, and I felt the familiar clenching in my chest as I watched them tease each other with words and smiles.

"What happened to the half-eaten brownie?" I asked to distract myself from bittersweet memories.

If we got a look at that piece of brownie, maybe we could find where someone (if we were right, and it had been offered to Rose with malice aforethought) had purchased it. Unless it was homemade, in which case we were shit out of luck.

"The brownie was sent to the lab," Bob said. "So they could check it for toxins. There's a lab report in here." He tapped the folder on Suzette's coffee table.

"Who needs toxins when you've got a severe allergy," Suzette pointed out.

"I'm more interested in what it looked like," I said. "Any chance there's still a piece of it floating around somewhere?"

Bob gave me a look that questioned my question. "It looked like a brownie, Lena. You know: dense, brown, chocolaty? Damn, now I want one. Hey Suze," he called to the kitchen where she'd gone to refill our wine glasses and fetch him another beer, "you got any chocolate in the house?"

Suze stuck her head into the room. "You want supermarket chocolate or the good stuff from my private stash?"

"The good stuff!" Bob and I replied in unison.

She brought out our drinks then disappeared back into the kitchen, returning with a box of Valrhona dark chocolate squares. "86% cacao content," she said. "For adult palates only. If you prefer milk chocolate," she said to Bob, clearly suspecting him of plebian tastes, "I've got some M&Ms you can have."

"I can get those anywhere," he said, reaching for a square of midnight nectar. "M&Ms are as common as donuts. 86% cacao content will be a new experience for me."

We all swooned as the dark indulgence melted on our tongues.

"Wow. That's intense," Bob said. "Are you sure this is legal?" He reached for the box. "I think I need to take these in to the lab for analysis."

"You do that and we're through," Suzette threatened. "No more private lingerie shows for you."

Bob groaned and put the box back on the coffee table. "You've ruined me, woman!" he complained. "How can I go back to M&Ms after this?"

"You can't," she said mournfully. "At least, not right away."

"The good news," I chimed in to reassure him, "is that in a couple of hours, if you still want M&Ms, you'll find they aren't half bad."

"There's always a place for M&Ms," Suzette agreed. "But sometimes you need the good stuff."

We were silent for a while, savoring our treat. Suzette, in a grand gesture of generosity, offered us all another piece. We mmmmed some more, and basked in chocoholic contentment.

"So, Bob," I reminded him as I floated on a chocolate high, "about that brownie?"

"Highly unlikely, but I'll ask around. Once it tested clean, it probably got tossed. Or possibly eaten. What's your interest, anyway? A brownie's a brownie, right?"

Suzette and I gaped at him. There are brownies, and then there are brownies. How could he not know that?

"Um, some are better than others," I said diplomatically. "I'm curious about whether it was obviously a nut brownie, with chunks of walnuts or whatever clearly visible, or if it looked like a plain brownie."

"So someone with allergies would be more likely to eat it," Suzette said, catching on. "Lena, that's a good question."

We looked at Bob. He had personally been in the presence of the brownie.

He shrugged. "It looked like a half-eaten brownie."

So much for expert opinion.

"I'm troubled by the white bakery bag," I said. "I don't see Rose purchasing a brownie. If she wanted to bring a snack with her, she's got a full-size freezer in her pantry with a bakery's worth of choices in it."

"Maybe she also had a stash of white bakery bags around" Bob said.

"Maybe. Whenever I was over there I was focused on the baked goods, not the accessories." I worked on conjuring up a mental picture of the typical treat-from-Rose experience. "You know, when she gave me something to take home, she always put it in a ziplock baggie."

"That's what I would use," Suzette said, "if I were going to stick a brownie or some cookies in my purse."

Bob didn't see the reasoning behind that.

"Grease spots," I explained. "Baked goods are yummy because they're full of butter. That's why bakers wrap their goodies in waxed paper, or use waxed paper bags."

"Even in waxed paper, I wouldn't put it in my purse," Suzette said. "Unless it were in a plastic baggie, too."

"And if I had ziplock baggies in my kitchen," I carried the argument to the next logical step, "why would I use a paper bag?"

We both looked at Bob.

"I'm not a purse kind of a guy," he said. "What do I know?" Then his eyebrows went up. "Wait a minute, though, there's something in here...." He flipped through the photocopies and pulled out a sheet. "Here we go.

There was a lemon bar in her canvas tote bag. It had one small bite out of it and it was in a Ziploc bag."

Suzette and I looked at each other. "Rose didn't bring the brownie," I said. "I talked to Hanna yesterday, and she said Rose made a dud batch of lemon bars the night before she died. Hanna had to throw them out. So if Rose had one with her—"

"—she hadn't tried them yet, and didn't know they were funky," Suzette said, pursuing my logic.

"Which means she wouldn't have had a brownie with her," I concluded. "Because she had a lemon bar."

What a team. We high-fived our deduction.

Of course, Rose might have brought multiple treats. But then they'd have both been in plastic bags. My head spun. How do real detectives keep track of the details?

Bob shook his head. "I follow your reasoning," he said. "And it's somewhat persuasive, but a long way from conclusive. Way too easy to explain it another way. Maybe she ran out of ziplock bags. Maybe the brownie was in with the lemon bar, whatever."

Suzette and I shook our heads, no way.

"What?"

"You don't put a brownie in with a lemon bar," I said. "They'd get all smushed together."

Bob looked unconvinced. "Look into it further if you want," he said, "but there's no case here. I'm not gonna be able to help you with it."

"That's okay, honey," Suzette said. "You've given us lots to think about."

"There is one thing you could do," I suggested to Bob. "Just ask around about the brownie. See if anyone else who handled it—maybe the lab techs—can remember whether it had visible nuts in it or not."

"And that makes a difference why?"

"Because the lab report confirmed that the brownie had nuts in it, right? Let's say you're baking a batch of brownies," I explained. "And you decide they'd be better with nuts. You mix up the batter as usual, and at the end add some chopped nuts. When the brownies are done, and you slice them up, the chunks of nuts are visible. Kind of like chocolate chips in a toll house cookie, only in reverse."

"And most bakers," Suzette added, "sprinkle some chopped nuts on top, too."

"If the brownie your lab tested contained nuts," I went on, "but there were no visible nuts in it—"

"That means someone ground the nuts up really, really fine, so they wouldn't show," Suzette suggested.

"Or maybe they used a nut oil, like a walnut or hazelnut oil, instead of butter," I theorized, "so the brownie wouldn't look like it had nuts in it."

"And a person with a nut allergy would think it was safe to eat," Suzette concluded.

"Wouldn't it smell like nuts, though?" I asked.

"That's a good point," Suzette agreed. "Someone like Rose would be especially vigilant."

"I think we need to look into that, too," I said, adding 'smell?' to the list on my yellow pad, under the 'brownie' heading. "Maybe there's a nut oil that would trigger Rose's allergic reaction, that doesn't have much of an aroma. Walnuts are distinctive, she might have noticed those, but macadamias, for example, don't have a strong flavor."

"You two are starting to scare me," Bob said, looking at us with something that might have been respect. "Okay, I'll ask around, see if anyone remembers the brownie."

We brainstormed possible other avenues of exploration for a few minutes, and then it was time for me to get home. Suzette agreed to stop by in the morning, before I took Val to her swim class, to divvy up investigative tasks.

21

"We have regular, white-chocolate chip, or walnut," the counter guy at SweetiePies pointed out when I asked him what kind of brownies they sold.

"I'll take a walnut."

He used a piece of waxed paper to pluck a walnut brownie from the display case, and placed it in a plain white paper bag. The fat chunks of walnut nestled in chocolate deliciousness would be visible at a dozen paces. I made a mental note to inquire whether any waxed paper had been found at the scene.

"That'll be $4.26, with tax," he said.

That seemed steep for a brownie, but I paid up, dropping the change from my five in the tip jar, which made it an even more over-priced treat.

"Do you always put chopped nuts on top of the walnut ones?" I asked as he handed the bag over.

"Don't know why we wouldn't."

"What other flavors do you make?" I asked, to keep the brownie conversation going.

"We usually have marbled cheesecake on the weekends. Those go pretty fast. The white-chocolate chip are new. We're trying those out. Plain and walnut we always have."

I reached into the bag and broke off a small piece of brownie to sample. Not bad, although a bit on the dry side for the price. "This is delicious," I said around the morsel. "I bet you sell a lot of these."

"Chocolate chip oatmeal cookies and apple pie are our best sellers," he said. "We're famous for our pies."

He sensed me succumbing to temptation as I followed him to the pie part of the display. I hadn't had apple pie in a long time.

"Those do look good," I said, walnut brownies momentarily forgotten. This assignment was going to be trouble. What had happened to my vow to adopt healthier eating habits?

"We use all organic ingredients," he said, sensing a potential pie sale on the hook, "and locally grown apples."

That sounded healthy to me. For a pie.

"I'll take one," I said. "It doesn't need to be refrigerated, does it? It will be in my car for a while before I get home."

"Don't put it in the fridge," he cautioned, taking a pie from the case and setting up a box for it, "unless you're going to keep it for a few days. The flavor is best at room temperature. Or you can reheat it: fifteen minutes at 350 will warm it up nicely."

I took the opportunity to sample more of my brownie, as an excuse to change the subject back from pies.

"You know," I said casually, "a friend of mine brought me a brownie last week that was really good." I let my eyes wander up toward the ceiling in what I hoped was a reflective way. "I wonder if she got it here; it had nice big chunks of walnuts, like this one."

"We are of the big chunks are better school when it comes to nuts," he confirmed, whipping a yard or so of red string around the pie box.

"I wonder if you might remember her." Shit, it would help if we'd found out what Rose had been wearing that day. Or if I'd had the sense to bring a picture of her to show around. "Older lady, about five-six, solid build, grandma-ish? She would have been in around three o'clock."

He shrugged and shook his head no, knotting the thread and breaking it off.

Had it been cool last Monday, or sunny and warm? I hadn't done my homework. "Maybe wearing a beige linen barn coat," I guessed, "with big patch pockets?"

He shook his head again. "We get a lot of customers after lunch," he said. "Everyone wants a sugar fix in the afternoon, or they're picking up something to take home for dinner. Why don't you ask her?"

"I'll do that next time I see her," I said, accepting the pastry box he passed across the counter. "Thanks for your help. The pie looks delicious."

"Come back next month," he said. "We'll have fresh peach and sour cherry."

I'd taken steps toward the door, but turned back. "Real sour cherry, from scratch?"

"The real thing," he promised with a smile. He passed me a business card. "Give us a call early July, and we'll let you know when we'll have 'em.'"

"I'll do that," I said, and carried my apple pie to the car. I looked at my list of local bakeries and planned the next stop. Good thing I'd never started on that diet, because I would be in serious caloric trouble by the end of the morning.

SweetiePies' walnut brownie paled in comparison to City Bakery's. Their secret, the counter girl confided, was extra butter and half brown sugar rather than all white.

Ninety minutes later I'd hit two more bakeries, three delis, two of the three Starbucks in town, and had purchased two bunches of alstroemeria from local florists. (No, the flower isn't rare. Yes, they are often used in arrangements. No, they couldn't recall a special request for them; I was the only person who'd ever asked about them.) The florist angle was looking to be a waste of time, so I decided to leave the rest for a later date when we were out of ideas for what to do next.

The brownies were probably a waste of time, too, but at least they were edible. I'd taken a nibble from a number of purchases—as necessary to further conversations with counter staff—and had written on the outside of each bag where the goods had come from. The laundry basket I keep in the cargo area of my CR-V to corral small purchases was filling up with bakery bags and I was starting to worry that all the fillings would drop right out of my teeth. When I got home I'd have to brush and floss like a demon. I wasn't stepping on the scale for a few days, either, that's for sure.

Three of the bakeries I'd visited used plain white unwaxed bakery bags like the one found beside Rose. No one, at any of those places, remembered any older lady from last Monday. Much of the counter help had been in their early twenties at best. Rose, being of invisible-to-the-young age, could probably have stopped in every day and not been noticed.

I'd had no idea a town Laurelton's size could support the production—and presumably the consumption—of so many fattening baked goods. The upside of the day's adventure was that I was so thoroughly sick of brownies I doubted I'd ever eat another one. But I had one more stop to make before picking Val up from swim camp: the Starbucks in the bookstore at the Riverside Mall. It seemed an unlikely place to count on finding a brownie when you needed one, but Suzette had pointed out it wasn't far from the cemetery if Rose had had reason to be on that side of the river.

I ordered a decaf Americano and looked over the small display case of baked goods. A few cookies and pastries, a handful of salads and baguette sandwiches, no brownies.

"Do you have any brownies?" I asked the counter person, whose spiky bangs were so long it seemed getting them caught in that nose ring would be a problem.

"Just what's in the case," he said. Or maybe it was a she. Young and scrawny and dressed in the kind of cords and tee that make at-a-glance gender identification difficult. The affectless monotone didn't help.

"Do you ever have them?" I asked.

"I don't eat refined sugar," the cashier said. "I wouldn't know."

"Your customers eat refined sugar, so maybe you should know," I muttered.

In reply, I got a shrug and thirty-seven cents in change and a "pick up is down there."

I accepted the change and dropped the coins in my purse. No tip for you, pal, I groused to myself. I sidled down to the pick-up end of the counter feeling like a pathetic excuse for an investigator. I couldn't even pry the possible past or potential future existence of a brownie out of a Starbuck's cashier. Spencer would have gotten an answer. If he couldn't wear the little shit down with witty repartee he'd grab it by the nose ring and force a response.

Then I had an idea. "Hey, hold my coffee here for a couple of minutes will you?" I said to the (clearly female) barista manning the espresso machine, and sauntered off toward the information desk.

22

"Can you look in your computer for me," I asked the info clerk (clearly male, well groomed, no visible piercings) "whether you carry *Investigating for Idiots* or something along that line?"

"Checking up on someone?"

Only if I could figure out how. And who. "It's for my nephew," I said. "He thinks he wants to be a P.I. because it looks like fun on TV. He might benefit from a more realistic view of how he could be spending the next thirty years."

"Don't be a killjoy," the clerk said, clicking something on his keyboard. "Let the kid have his dream."

"Hey, don't blame me," I said. "His dad put me up to it."

On the other hand, it was possible I had a heretofore undiscovered talent for lying on the spot. That might come in handy. I resolved to practice on unsuspecting sales clerks and wait staff, so I'd be prepared if I needed to tell a whopper some day.

"Here you go," the clerk said. "We should have a copy of Detecting for Morons on the shelf. It'll be under Careers on the back wall over there, beyond Sports and Fitness."

"Excellent," I said, with a glance at my watch. "That sounds perfect. Thanks for your help."

I found and paid for the book, collected my decaf, and drove off to the Aquatic Center to collect Val. She wasn't waiting out front, so I parked and wandered toward the pool entrance, where I found her chatting with two other damp-haired tweens.

"How was your first day of swim camp?" I asked as we walked to the car.

"Good," Val said, sounding as enthusiastic as I'd hoped. "The coaches are really tough, but in a good way. Our relay coach made us swim really hard. Did you know she was an alternate for the Olympic team?"

"No," I said. "But she must be a pretty good swimmer."

I clicked the car doors unlocked and opened the driver's side and was assaulted by the aroma of baked chocolate.

"Oh my god, you bought brownies!" Val exclaimed as she climbed in. "Can I have one? I'm really hungry." She turned around in her seat to see where the tantalizing smell was coming from.

Once again I had screwed up the thinking things through part. For the bulk of the morning I'd carefully nibbled the corners off brownies (thinking that if I melted with rapture in front of the counter help they'd be more likely to chat with me) while preserving the length and width dimensions of each chocolaty square. Just in case something turned up from the lab that we could compare to. Not that I expected a match.

"Are they in the back?" Val asked, unclipping her seatbelt and reaching for her door handle. "I'll get out and get them," she said, one foot already on the ground.

"Val, wait up." I caught up with her at the back of the SUV and put a hand on the cargo door to keep her from opening it.

"Pleeeeease?" Val slumped against the back of the car. "I'm sooooo hungry! I'll eat something healthy when we get home, I swear."

"How 'bout some cherry streudel," I suggested, wondering if the plastic sporks I'd stashed in the CD compartment some time ago were still there. "Or maybe apple pie?" Those at least had fruit in them.

"I really want a brownie," she moaned. "Please? They smell so good!"

"Okay," I gave in and opened the cargo door. "Plain or walnut?"

"Walnut, definitely," she said, perking up. "Oh my god," she said, seeing the heap of bakery bags in the cargo basket and the white pastry boxes beside them. And the bouquets of wilting Peruvian lilies. "Are you having a party?"

"No." I reached for a handful of pastry bags. "Here's the thing, though. You can only have half a brownie from each bag." Val gave me a questioning look. "I'll explain in a minute. And you have to let me do something first."

Val hopped up and down with impatience, "Well, hurry uuuuuup! I'm huuuuuungry."

Personally, I never wanted to eat again, but I'd been there. I shut the cargo door and climbed back into the driver's seat, reaching into my purse for the blue Sharpie I'd wielded all morning. I took a brownie out of the first bag (Sunshine Bakery, 12th and Elm, not one of the best; I suspect vegetable oil instead of butter) flattened the bag on my knee and traced the outline of the brownie before breaking off half and handing it to Val.

"Why are you doing that?" she asked, stuffing the entire half in her mouth and wolfing it down.

"Suzette and I are playing detective," I said, starting on a brownie from the second bag. Clearly Val was going to need more than one. "We're trying to rule out that the brownie Rose ate came from a local bakery. There's a chance we can get a sample of the one that killed her from the evidence lab, to compare with these. So I need to keep part of each brownie, and the dimensions, for comparison. That's why I'm tracing the outline on the bag and only giving you half. Here's another one."

Val actually took a bite of that one (Deli Express, Baxter Street, between 8th and Division, I'd stopped sampling by that point). "Yumm, this one's nice and gooey."

I hoped that didn't mean it was undercooked. Visions of salmonella poisoning flashed across my brain. "Need another?"

"No, I'm good. Can I have a sandwich when we get to your house? And some milk?"

When we got home, Val downed half a chicken salad sandwich and a glass of low-fat milk and headed upstairs. I put the wilting alstroemeria in a vase and sat at the kitchen table to summarize the morning's findings. I opened a new Excel spreadsheet and set up columns to capture which bakeries sold what types of brownies, along with approx. size of same, description (nut chunks: large, small, abundance of, etc.), and the type of bag used.

Suzette showed up while I was in the midst of data-wrangling, with an armful of bakery bags of her own. She burst out laughing when she saw the state of my kitchen.

"Oh my god. Your haul is worse than mine!"

"I can't believe it only took a couple of hours to destroy my passion for brownies," I said.

"Me too," she agreed. "I'm never eating another one."

"So how'd you do?"

"There are way too many mediocre brownies being sold in this town," she said. "I hope Rose died from eating a really good one. Which place on your list was the best?"

I groaned. "I don't even want to think about it. Besides, we really didn't set out to do a taste test. I've been inputting my notes, so if the lab comes up with a sample we'll have something to compare against." I picked up my ruler and measured another brownie before putting it back in its bag.

"Here's my list." Suzette handed me a sheet of paper. "What are we going to do with all these?" she asked, waving a hand at the collection of pastry bags.

I hadn't considered storage issues. We only needed to keep a small piece of each one, I decided. I got up and removed the apple pie from its box. That would be a good size to keep samples in.

"You bought a *pie*, too?"

"It seemed like a good idea at the time." What had I been thinking?

"And what's in here?" Suzette pried the top off the other box.

"Cherry streudel," I admitted. I blame the nice man at SweetiePies for planting the cherry idea. I'd succumbed to temptation a couple of stops later.

"This looks good," Suzette said. She poked a fingernail at a window of exposed cherry filling. "Oh, look at that, I got my fingers in it. I guess I'll have to cut that bit off."

"Help yourself," I said. "You know where the forks and plates are around here." I finished typing in the last of my notes as she sat down at the table with a slice of flaky-gooey crimson goodness and a glass of milk. "That does look good," I said, wondering if it was worth just a taste, then deciding that I ought to eat something that wasn't mostly butterfat, white flour, and refined sugar. I retrieved the other half of Val's sandwich from the fridge. It was full of mayo, but I figured the protein in the chicken would offset some of the sugar carbs I'd consumed that day.

"How many grams of fat and sugar do you think we've eaten this morning?" Suzette wondered. "Oh, you should try this. It's really good." She pushed her plate toward me.

"Way more than we should," I said, waving the plate off. I wasn't going to eat pastry again for a month. Or at least several hours.

"I can't believe I ate that," Suze said a minute later, looking at her empty plate. "Is this what they call aversion therapy?"

"You mean where you make yourself sick on something, so you'll never touch it again?"

She nodded. "Remind me of this moment if I ever say I'm hungry."

"How much of a brownie sample should we save?" I decided on a square inch of each. I got a roll of plastic wrap from the cabinet and began cutting off a piece of each brownie and wrapping it in plastic. To each sample I taped a piece of paper on which I'd written the place of origin. The excess brownie portions got tossed into a Santa cookie tin left over from a past Christmas. I was all for throwing them out, but that wouldn't be fair to Val and Granimi, who deserved their shot at wretched excess.

I fit the last square into the apple pie box and taped it closed. I wrote "TOXIC: Do <u>NOT</u> eat!!!" in Sharpie on the top of the box and put it in the freezer.

"Let's just keep the plain white ones," I suggested as Suzette helped me collect all the empty bakery bags. We tossed the others in the recycle bin and I folded up the plain white bags and looked around for something to keep them in.

"Do you think this is going to do any good?" Suzette asked. "The problem with brownies is anyone with a box of Duncan Hines can make them at home." She lay her head down on my kitchen table. "Oh my god, I am having such a sugar crash."

I was feeling more than a little nappish myself, and was glad I'd eaten some chicken sandwich, even if it added to feeling overfull. I pondered Suze's question. The brownie adventure had seemed very clever when we'd come up with the plan. I now wondered if the effort, and calories, had been worth it.

"I'll be amazed if it leads us to a killer," I said. "But we have to convince Bob and his colleagues that Rose's death wasn't an accident. It would be good to know for sure that the brownie Rose ate didn't come from a local bakery, because I think that's what someone wants us to believe happened. That's why the bag was there."

"If the bag didn't blow in on the breeze from somewhere else on some other day," she said.

"I don't think it did. Maybe I'm crazy to trust my intuition on this one, but I think it was left there intentionally. Besides, it would have to be really windy for anything bigger than a gum wrapper to blow over that hedge. I don't remember any gale force winds this past week."

"I see your point," she said. "Hey, next time we go sleuthing, we should take a camera. I can't believe we didn't think of that."

I fished my cell phone from my purse. "We could use our phones. I finally figured out how to take pictures with mine."

I remembered that my photos of cars from the funeral home parking lot were still in whatever a cell phone uses for memory. What kind of lame-o detective forgets about the clues she's collected?

23

If we could identify the owners of the cars that had lingered in the funeral home parking lot when Suzette and I left, maybe we could find out who that voice in the office belonged to. Maybe Suzette could waggle her tits at Bob again and get his help with that.

First, I had to solve a technical problem.

"I don't know how to look at the shots I took," I said. "Or how to get them into my computer."

"Beats me," Suzette said. "I've never taken a photo with my phone that was worth keeping."

She pulled her phone out and snapped a shot of me, looked at the result, and burst out laughing. "Oh my god, I really don't think we want to keep that one. You look like that snake-head lady, Medusela, or whatever her name is. What's the secret to taking a decent photo with this thing?"

"Don't ask me," I said. "I'm just a middle-aged technophobe."

"Thirty-seven is not middle-aged," she reminded me. "Haven't you heard? Forty is the new twenty. We've got plenty of time to catch up on technology before we're over the hill."

We heard the front door open, and a "yoo hoo" that sounded like Granimi. A few moments later she joined us in the kitchen.

"I thought you were taking a nap," I said.

"I went out for a walk, and stopped for a chat with your neighbor, Tulip. Such a nice lady, we have a lot in common."

I couldn't imagine what. Oh, right: green tea. And Pilates. All that healthy stuff G. was so good about not pushing on me.

"Tulip takes the same rainforest herbal supplements I do," Granimi said. "She's built quite a nice business for herself with them. She even won a trip to Peru, to visit the villages where the herbs are harvested. She said it was incredible, really inspiring."

Suzette and I exchanged glances. Tulip had been to Peru? I remembered that Ansel had fled our séance just after the Peru clue came up. Granimi appeared oblivious to the import of her information, but she'd been half asleep by that point in the evening.

"How did the brownie expedition go?" Granimi asked. The kitchen looked suspiciously free of brownies, although the table was covered with dark brown crumbs.

"If you're looking for leftovers, they're in that tin," I said, pointing at the counter.

"Lena stashed a box of labeled samples in the freezer," Suzette said. "Those are the extra bits that are okay to eat."

"Somewhere in this house," I said, remembering I was trying to retrieve photos from my phone, "is the user guide for this. I wonder what I did with it?"

"Is your phone not working, dear?" Granimi asked. "Here, use mine." She reached into her track suit pocket and pulled out a slim rectangle that I recognized as the latest iPhone. Turned off it merely looked sleek and intimidating. Turned on, I suspected it could launch a space shuttle.

"My phone works fine," I assured her. "I just don't know how to get photos from the phone onto my computer." Surely that was possible.

"Just email them to yourself, dear," Granimi said. "That's what I do."

This was getting embarrassing. "I don't know how to send an email from my phone," I admitted. Email has its upsides—a message from Olivia with a link to travel snaps in her flickr album had brightened up my morning—but I've never felt the need to send or receive messages from my phone. That's what the computer is for.

"Let me put my other glasses on," Granimi said.

The doorbell rang. I left my phone in Granimi's capable hands and went to answer it.

"Is Val home?" Ansel asked.

I was glad to see him after his nervous flight from the house Monday night. "Val!" I yelled up the stairs, "Ansel's here."

"We could use some help eating brownies," I told Ansel. "Come on in the kitchen."

"What's your email address, dear," Granimi asked when I returned, Ansel in tow. I spelled it out for her. "Oh dear, it says 'unauthorized service request.'"

Not a surprise; I'd signed up for the bare minimum service plan. I regard my cell phone as an evil necessity and use it as little as possible. Why everyone's obsessed with being accessible twenty-four hours a day is a mystery to me. I prefer to be incommunicado as much as possible.

"What are you trying to do?" Ansel asked.

"Lena wants to get some photos from her phone onto her computer," Granimi said. "I was going to send them to her email, but she hasn't signed up for it."

"Can I see the phone?" he asked. Granimi handed it over.

Ansel confidently punched a few buttons and appeared to browse through a menu of some kind. "I can download these for you. Where's your computer?"

I pointed him to my notebook, open on the kitchen table. Ansel sat down and fiddled with the phone then shifted his attention to the computer.

"Can I close these programs? I have to install a utility and reboot."

"Sure, whatever," I said. Handy to have a computer geek next door.

We grownups left Val and Ansel in the kitchen with my cell phone, my computer, the tin of brownies, a quart of milk, and instructions not to make themselves sick, and retreated to the living room with a bottle of chardonnay and our notepad of flimsy detecting ideas.

"Am I the only one who thinks we don't have a clue what we're doing?" Suzette asked.

"No." I sank into the couch. Driving around eating brownies all morning had been exhausting. Oh! I'd left it in the car. "I got us some help," I said, getting back to my feet and grabbing my car keys from the key bowl on the hall table on my way out the front door. I trotted back into the living room a minute later.

"Tadaa," I held up Detecting for Morons for inspection.

"You didn't! Oh my god, hand it over, girl." Suzette leapt up and grabbed it from me. "Detecting for Morons!" she exclaimed, holding it so Granimi could see. "Exactly what we need. Lena, you are brilliant."

I noticed Ansel had come into the room.

"Um, I downloaded those pictures from your phone," he said.

"That's great, Ansel. Are they in the My Pictures folder?"

"Yeah, I made a subfolder called 'phone pics' for you."

"Okay. That's helpful, too. Thanks."

He lingered.

"Do you need something else?" I asked. "Do I owe you money for that thing you were going to download?"

He shook his head no, hesitated some more, and finally got the question out: "Why did you take a picture of my Mom's car?"

I left Suzette and Granimi to study detecting tips and followed Ansel to the kitchen, explaining that I'd been trying out the picture function on my phone.

"Which one is hers?"

Ansel peered at the tiny preview images and pointed at one, which I clicked open. A white Prius. What else would a planet-tending, granola-munching, grow-your-own-sprouts-on-the-windowsill tree-hugger drive? I wished I could remember if the voice in the office had sounded like Tulip, but that was four days ago and I'd been distracted by the ridiculous dialogue. I'd have to hear Tulip being intimate and seductive to be sure. So far, I'd just heard her being cheery.

24

I waited until Ansel and Val went upstairs to use Olivia's computer, then browsed through the rest of the photos and made a list of as much as I could see of makes, models, and license plate numbers. I passed the list to Suzette, who was confident she could get Bob to look them up for her. I wasn't sure what we'd do with the details when we got them, but it seemed like the kind of step a real detective would take.

Suzette and I divvied up the online research we had planned, she went off to her place, and I poked my head into Olivia's room to see what the kids were up to. Ansel sat sideways at Olivia's desk, her notebook computer balanced on his knees, focused on the screen. Val lay on Olivia's bed, on her back with her arms by her side and her eyes closed. What were they doing, playing therapist? Whatever I'd interrupted, it didn't seem frisky, so after a "Can't you see we're busy?" from Val, I left them to it until it was time to take the cat to the vet.

At 2:15 Val ventured into the yard, scooped Shadow up from where he'd been lounging under a peony bush and carried him to the house. I'd expected the cat to have nothing to do with getting in the box, but after an initial balk and an "are you kidding me?" look at Val, who murmured assurances, he allowed himself to be caged. I reminded Granimi that Hanna was coming over at three o'clock and that she knew where my cleaning supplies are and didn't need supervision.

At the vet's office, I filled out paperwork and handed over a credit card while Val talked to Shadow through the grille on the front of his box.

"You are being remarkably well-behaved," I told the cat as I took a seat beside them. Shadow gave me a satisfied look that seemed to imply awareness on his part that this visit to the vet was a clear step toward adoption. I wasn't entirely on board with that, but it appeared that any opportunity I might have had to protest was long past.

I left Val in charge and stepped outside to check in with Suzette on my cell, and got the good news that she had a name and contact number for the lab tech who had handled the fatal brownie. Bad news: he refused to talk to Suze on the phone, even if she was a friend of Bob's.

"He sounded young and nerdy," she said confidently, "so I'm going to confront him in person wearing something short and tight."

That could work, if he weren't so intimidated he lost the ability to speak. "Call me at home later," I said. "I want to hear how that goes."

Shadow eventually made his way back to an examining room, where he was given a clean-enough bill of health and couple of shots, which he endured with little more than a tail twitch. I found myself stroking his fur as I helped hold him still, and almost didn't mind paying the bill when we were done.

While we'd waited I enlisted Val to find out what she could, next time she was at Ansel's house, about what Tulip did for a living and on what kind of schedule. "Just pretend you think she's cool, and want to know more about her," I suggested. I felt slimy, involving a kid in this, but she was the one who'd seen the ghost, which put her in the middle of things. Right?

"Why do you want to know about her job?" Val asked.

"Process of elimination," I said. "Rose died on a Monday afternoon during working hours, so if Tulip has a regular job that means she couldn't have done it."

Val didn't like the implications. "Do you think she might have?"

"Of course not, honey," I said, wondering how far Val's talents might run in a mind-reading direction. "But I don't want to offend her or Ansel by coming right out and asking if she has an alibi; this is a more polite way to go about it."

"What if she doesn't have a job, or doesn't work on Mondays?" Val asked.

"No biggie." I played it cool with a casual flip of the page in the magazine I was perusing. "We'll worry about that later, if we have to."

*　*　*

By the time we got home Hanna's car was in the driveway, and as we let Shadow loose in the yard I could hear the hum of the vacuum cleaner running upstairs. I went up to let Hanna know I was home and ready to chat whenever she wanted a break from cleaning. She joined me downstairs a few minutes later, and I coerced her into sitting down while I poured us some coffee and fetched the Santa tin from the counter. Val and Ansel had made quite a dent in the contents, but there were still lots of brownie fragments left.

"Here." I placed the open tin on the table and passed Hanna a plate. "Sample these and tell me what Rose would have thought of them."

Hanna broke off a couple of pieces and ate them thoughtfully. "That first one pretty good," she said. "But the flavor a little flat. A touch more salt and you taste the chocolate more. Second one, not good. Too dry. Overcooked, and they use cheap ingredients. Maybe that flour a little stale." She picked up a third sample and took a bite. "This one got the nuts in it, so Mrs. Rose, she don't like that. I think it pretty good, though." She smiled at me. "You gonna become a baker too?"

"Not likely," I said. My talent with baked goods leans more toward consumption than production. I explained that we were trying to prove— to whatever extent possible—that the brownie Rose ate had not come from a local bakery, and that the white bag left at the scene was a decoy.

"So far, all the bakeries confirm that their nut brownies have nuts on top, as you would expect, so the counter help and customers can tell which are which."

I mentioned Suzette's plan to chat up the lab tech who had handled the brownie. "What bothers me is that Rose wouldn't have eaten a brownie with visible nuts in it. But if you used ground nuts, wouldn't that change the texture and flavor? I'd expect she would have noticed that in time to—," I tried to imagine Rose spitting anything out, ever, even if her life depended on it.

"Grind up the nuts would help some," Hanna said. "Still it would be speckled I think, and change the texture. Maybe use nut butter, or nut oil instead."

"Even with a nut oil, though, wouldn't she taste it?" I asked.

Hanna thought about that. "Peanuts or walnuts, for sure would taste different," she said. "Other ones, I don't know. Macadamias, the flavor not so strong. Especially if they're not roasted."

"Does that make a difference?" I thought nuts were nuts: you know, those cellophane packets at the grocery store, in the baking aisle next to the chocolate chips.

"Roasting brings out the flavor," she said. "Raw nuts are okay, but they taste better roasted." She shrugged, "Also, Mrs. Rose, she say to me some times how the medicine make it so she can't taste good no more. That made her sad, that the most delicious food all taste bland. Like gray color, she tell me. No joy in it."

We pondered the horror. I wondered what medications Rose had been on, and if I would ever be condemned to them when I got older. I really should take better care of myself, cut down on sweets, do some Pilates.

"So texture could be the most important factor," I said, returning to the matter at hand. "Hanna, could you make a brownie that has nuts in it, but looks and tastes like it doesn't?"

Hanna gave it some thought. Then she tapped the table with a finger and nodded. "Coffee," she said.

Always a good idea. "I'll make a fresh pot." I started to get up.

"Not to drink, I mean coffee is good to add to your brownies, very nice flavor."

Ah, yes. Hard to go wrong with any combination of coffee and chocolate. "And it would help mask the nuts?"

She shrugged. "I think maybe. We try it out, make some up and taste them. That way we know."

"That's exactly what I was thinking," I said. "If you're available for a few hours sometime in the next few days, let's bake some brownies with different kinds of nuts and nut oils, and do a taste test. I'd do it myself, but I'm not a great baker. I'd really like it if you could help."

Hanna nodded she was in. "I can come Sunday, after church," she said. "And you don't pay me. This I want to do for Mrs. Rose."

"I'll do the shopping," I offered. "Can you get me a list of ingredients to buy?"

Hanna nodded, and pulled a piece of paper from her apron pocket.

"Oh, wait a minute. Duh." I shook my head at my own stupidity. "We're forgetting that Rose didn't make that brownie."

"Why that matter?" she asked.

"I don't want to imply anything less than the highest admiration for Rose's skill in the kitchen," I said, sensing I treaded on hallowed ground. "But I think one reason she had such a reputation as a baker is because she made things from scratch. Not many people do that anymore. So anyone who does is considered a 'good baker.'"

Hanna nodded grudging accord. "How that matter to the shopping list?"

"Let's just get boxes of brownie mix," I said. "It'll be faster and easier, and that's probably what the, uh, killer did."

Hanna agreed. "Probably what I'd do," she said, crossing several items off her list. "Duncan Hines got one with the chocolate squeeze packet that pretty good. I make that before lots of times."

I'd turned out a pretty good pan of brownies from that box myself on more than one occasion. Damn, you'd think I'd still be sick of these, I thought, reaching for the tin.

"How many brownies we going to make?" Hanna asked.

"Let's see, first we'll need a batch of plain ones for comparison. Let's make a list of what kind of nuts we should test."

We decided on walnuts (common) and macadamias (subtler), ground and oil, with and without espresso. If we didn't have any luck with those, we could branch out to pecans, almonds, and brazils.

Dear God, and I was already drowning in brownies. I'd have to come up with someplace to donate what we baked. Or maybe hold my own bake sale. No way could I survive that many brownies in the house.

25

Suzette came by before dinner for another pow-wow, and I filled her in on plans for phase two of brownie overload.

"We should assemble a focus group," she said, "of people who don't know what we're up to."

"That includes us," said Granimi. "I'm not convinced we have much grasp of this detection business."

"Show some faith, Mimi," Suze said.

"A focus group's a great idea," I said. Then I had an even better one. "We should get some people Rose's age who are on similar medications, and do the taste test with them." I looked at Granimi. "How are your tastebuds, G.? Still working okay?"

"I can't say any part of me is working like it used to," she said, "but I can still tell the difference between mayonnaise and library paste, if that's what you mean."

"A nursing home!" Suzette said. "We'll go to a nursing home and ask for volunteers."

Granimi snorted. "Those folks are too decrepit. And they're all on special diets. You want one of those fancy retirement villages. Get yourself a bunch of bored retirees who are old enough to maybe not taste as well as they used to, but their brains aren't yet dripping out their ears."

"Geeze, Granimi!" What an image, ick. "Where's your sympathy for the aged."

"We mock what we fear," she said. "I may be zippy for my age, but I know what's coming."

We batted the taste test idea around some more, and in spite of our unseemly enthusiasm for elder-abuse-by-chocolate it did seem a good way to test our theory.

"How are we going to get in the door at one of those places without any medical or food-service credentials," I wondered aloud. "We might run into liability issues."

"What, some geezer gets a toothache and sues us?" asked Suzette.

"No, I mean some Associate Director of Corporate Butt-Protection doesn't let us in the door with food that wasn't baked in a properly licensed and inspected commercial kitchen."

"Lena's right," Granimi said. "It would be good to have an in."

We were interrupted by Val, who wanted to know when dinner would be.

I hadn't given a thought to dinner yet. "Probably not for a while," I said. And it was anyone's guess what we'd eat, but there were plenty of groceries in the house. I'd come up with something. "There are some brownies left," I suggested. "Why don't you have those and some milk, and I'll get started on dinner in a little bit."

Val sighed and stomped off to the kitchen in a way that made me think I should pay more attention to providing her with regular, nutritious meals. It's a sad day when even the adolescent in the house has had enough of brownies.

But I had an idea for the taste test. "What if we got Ansel and Val to say they're doing a summer science project on the effects of aging on taste? With parental supervision, of course."

"Play on people's reluctance to say 'no' to kids," Suzette nodded her approval.

"And, at the same time, to not take them seriously," I added.

We spent a fun few minutes brainstorming increasingly ridiculous ideas for brownie focus groups before I had a horrible thought.

"I think we may have overlooked something really obvious."

"What's that?"

"We've assumed that the nuts in the brownie had to be disguised so Rose would eat it. But what if I just held a gun to your head and said 'eat or I shoot.'"

Suzette groaned and put her head in her hands. "I can't believe we didn't think of that."

"I'd call your bluff," Granimi said. "I'd rather be shot than die from anaphylactic shock." She shuddered. "Besides, you'd have to have a gun. And be willing to use it."

Or at least wave it around with confidence. On TV it looks like everyone in America carries a gun, but I don't. As for terroristic threatening, I couldn't see any of us pulling it off. Suzette, maybe, if she didn't burst out laughing.

Granimi had a point about calling the bluff. Rose had a steely side. I could picture her sitting on that bench like the Queen Mum, legs decorously crossed at the ankle, saying, "Go ahead and shoot me then, if you really want to get rid of me."

"Okay," I said. "Maybe that's not as sure a thing as I thought. I'm still bothered, though, by all the time we've spent on whether or not it's possible to disguise nuts in a brownie. We haven't made much headway on why someone would kill Rose, other than maybe her money. At some point we should think about motive."

Suzette slumped in her chair. "But we're having so much fun with the brownie angle."

"Keep in mind we aren't doing this purely for entertainment and chocolate value, considerable as those may be."

"Money, sex, and power," Granimi said. "Those are the big ones."

"That's a start." I grabbed my trusty yellow notepad and wrote MONEY SEX POWER across the top of a fresh page and drew vertical lines to make three columns.

"Power seems unlikely." I tried to imagine Rose as a home-grown Imelda Marcos.

"She was queen of the Garden Club for years," Suzette said. "Maybe someone else wanted to be top dahlia for a change."

"Yeah, but who would kill for that?"

Suzette waved off my objection. "Some of those ladies could run a major corporation and have energy left to take over a third world country on the weekend. I hear the politicking that goes on at those meetings is brutal."

"That may be," I acknowledged. "But murder? Seriously?"

"Power struggles, sure," she said. "Murder, maybe not so much."

"I don't think that angle's likely, but if we run out of other ideas we can take a look." I wrote 'Garden Club?' in the Power column on my pad. "What else have we got?"

"Money is power," Granimi said. "Maybe someone wanted hers."

"Do we know for sure she had money?" I asked. "We know she came from a prominent family, but having the name doesn't mean she had the bank account."

"We should assume she did," Suzette suggested, "until we learn otherwise."

"Do we assume that a money motive points to Alan?"

"Only if he's the one who inherits," Granimi pointed out, yawning.

"And if he was in a hurry," I said. "G., you raised that point the other day: even if she hadn't told him about her turn for the worse, why not just wait it out?"

"Maybe he thought she was going to change her will," Suze said.

"Or he needed the money in a hurry," I added.

"How are we going to find that kind of stuff out?" Suze asked.

"Maybe that Detecting for Morons book will help." I didn't have a better idea, other than breaking into my neighbor's house and rummaging through his papers. I let myself wonder, for a moment, what might be in those file drawers I'd seen in Alan's home office while photocopying Rose's recipe book. "And we should take a closer look at those papers Bob brought over, find out what the cops did or didn't look into or follow up on, and take it from there." I added 'Bob/papers' to my pad under the Money column. It didn't feel much like progress.

"Okay, door number three: Sex." I lowered my voice to a whisper and tilted my head to Granimi, who was almost asleep. "Let's continue this in the kitchen."

"I can't believe Rose ever had sex," Suzette said as we retreated.

"She had a couple of kids with her first husband, so she must have boinked a few times. Maybe she was a hottie in her day."

"That day was a while ago. We need to consider this Alan and mistress angle. In fact, why did we just spend so long talking about other stuff? How sure are you that the person you overheard at the funeral home was Alan?"

"Significantly, but not entirely," I said. "The problem is that Alan didn't sound like himself that day. The fact that he's so down speaks against his wanting to get rid of Rose. He looks devastated."

"A mistress doesn't mean he didn't love Rose, or want to get his hands on her money."

"I can't see him coming up with the brownie scheme, though," I said. "Rose would have noticed him messing around in her kitchen."

"I barely know the man, but he strikes me as the kind of guy who doesn't know how to boil water."

I agreed. "Even starting with a box of Duncan Hines, I don't see it. He's smart enough, but he'd have figured out something clever that was within his sphere of competence, which the kitchen definitely is not."

"He probably wouldn't do it himself, anyway. He'd delegate."

"You mean hire someone?"

"It's been done, I know that much." Suzette sat back and sipped her wine. "I'm having a hard time," she said, "imagining who in this town you would go to for that."

"Maybe not in our version of this town," I said. "But there's an underbelly to everywhere. Even here. We just, you know, don't have a clue where it is."

"Being chicks with money, you mean."

I was thinking more of being terminally suburban, but I guess that's the same thing. We pondered our uncool quotient.

"Not that we're not hip, in our own way," I said.

"Oh, totally. You're an artist, after all. How cool is that?"

"And feng shui is still in. Besides, you've got that sexy Eurasian thing going on. Hard to argue with that."

"Totally."

"Killer-wise, though," I said, "I think outside help would be the way to go."

"Bring in someone from Portland, maybe, or Spokane."

"Gotta be a hitman somewhere in Spokane." I hardly even know where Spokane is, much less whether it's a hotbed of hitmen. I put my glass down. "I think maybe I've had enough wine."

"We do seem to open a bottle every time we sit down to talk," Suze said.

As had become usual, today's was almost empty.

"We're doing a lot more talking and drinking than detecting," I pointed out.

"The wine does encourage creative thinking, though. We need to have flexible minds if we're going to solve this thing."

"Yes, and one of these days we ought to get off our butts and go follow someone around and ask questions." I poured us both some spring water, then rinsed out the wine bottle and put it in the recycle bin. "Besides, if we ever have to chase someone, it will help if we haven't gotten too fat."

Suze contemplated her tummy, then looked away. "Let's not go there."

Happy to oblige. "So, where were we, anyway? We're supposed to be eliminating unlikely possibilities here."

We tossed ideas around some more and concluded that Alan most likely was not the killer (it helped that Bob had already ruled him out), although he might have hired one. All based on the assumption that Rose had not committed suicide by brownie.

"Sticking with the Sex theme, that brings us to jealousy," Suzette said. "Let's assume that Alan has been having an affair."

"Maybe his mistress wanted Rose out of the way."

"Because Alan wouldn't leave her."

"I believe he genuinely loved Rose," I said. "But I can also see him having an affair on the side with someone younger and friskier."

"Yeah. Maybe once Rose's health declined, there wasn't much going on in the bedroom area."

"Rose was older than Alan," I said. "A good ten years or more, I think. If he's still in his fifties and she was pushing seventy and not well…"

"Not enough Viagra in the world to cure that problem."

"So it makes sense that he'd be looking around."

"In which case there will be gossip."

"You're the gossip queen," I said. "Poke around. I'm going to chat up Alan's old secretary. She might know if he had something going on while she was working for him." I thought of the possible Tulip angle, also, and reviewed it with Suze.

"Those Ouija clues seem to point to her," I said. "And we know she was at the funeral home when we left, but I just don't see her hooking up with Alan. Although I gather her husband is away a lot."

"I wonder if that's why they moved to this neighborhood," Suzette said. "Maybe she was angling to be closer to Alan."

"Seriously," I said, shaking my head. "I know opposites attract, but Alan and Tulip? It's so unlikely!"

"So, maybe it's someone else."

"We might have her license plate number. So get on Bob about that," I reminded her. "If Alan's been seeing someone," I thought aloud, "it hasn't been at his house."

"Which means her place or a hotel."

"Hotels have lobbies, and lots of staff. Motels are better for illicit sex. I don't see Alan as the sleazy motel type."

"He might get a kick out of it."

I shook my head. "He's well known for being fastidious," I said. "Five minutes just standing, fully clothed, in a sleazy motel room and he'd burn his clothes and scrub himself down with bleach. I bet he goes to her place."

"And with Rose's family hanging around, he hasn't seen her for a while."

"So she's probably bugging him to get together."

We pondered the possibilities again.

"We need to follow him," I said. "See where he goes."

26

A full-on stakeout would have been impossible, given my chauffeuring schedule, so it's a good thing we got lucky. Early Thursday afternoon, as Granimi and I headed home from doing errands downtown, I saw Alan and a nicely dressed blonde come out of a restaurant on Beale Street.

"Watch out!" Granimi warned. I slammed the brakes and managed to avoid rear-ending the minivan in front of me, which had stopped at a red light.

"Sorry about that, G.," I said as we rocked to a halt. "Look out your side window. A man in a blue sport coat and a blonde woman in taupe slacks and a white blouse should be coming up the block."

"Are they friends of yours, dear?" Granimi started to buzz her window down. "I'll wave them down for you."

"No." I stabbed at the master window controls. "I want to see where they go, but I don't want them to see us."

"Oh," Granimi said. "This is exciting! Who are they, dear, and why are we watching them?"

"The man is Alan Braska, Rose's husband," I explained. "I don't know who the woman is, but if Alan's having an affair it would be convenient if she's his mistress."

"Convenient how, dear?"

"Convenient because they're right there, walking down the street where we can follow them." How was that not obvious?

Except that now they had turned the corner and I was stuck in the center lane. Shit. The light changed and I zipped ahead and pulled over to the curb, cutting off a guy in a black Saab who had some choice thoughts to share about my driving.

I reached over and popped Granimi's seat belt release. "Hop out and follow them while I drive around the block."

Granimi opened her door and climbed out of the car at a pace that was sprightly for an octogenarian, but somewhat short of swift. Safely at curb level at last, she turned to wave goodbye. I gestured furiously toward the side street. Go follow them! The fact that G. is spry for her age doesn't make her speedy. And she didn't seem as sharp on the uptake as usual. Which was worrisome, but one of the many things I wasn't going to think about just then.

The next street was, of course, one way the wrong way. Eventually I eased up to the corner on the far end of the block that Alan and his female companion had turned down. I crept across the intersection, trying not to veer out of my lane as I looked around. Parking was a bitch around here, no open spot for blocks, so if they were still on foot I'd have to creep along behind them, traffic piling up behind me, annoyed drivers leaning on their horns like this guy.

I pulled over as far as I could and waved the blue Acura past, peering around for any sign of Granimi and our targets. Where the hell had they disappeared to?

A flash of white in the rear view mirror caught my attention and I looked back over my shoulder to see a head of spiky white hair poking out the door of a commercial building on the block behind me. My cell rang.

"Where are you?" Granimi asked. "I followed them into an office building, and I'm here in the lobby."

"I'm up the street on your right." I flashed the blinkers so she'd see me.

"Oh, there you are dear." She stuck a hand out and waved. "What do you want me to do now?"

"Stay where you are and keep an eye out. Try to be inconspicuous," like not waving at me, sheesh. "If I can't find a parking spot, I'll come around the block again and pull up in front of where you are. Give me a few minutes."

"Roger that. Mimi out." The spiky white head popped out of sight.

Loony, but the edge wasn't completely gone.

The parking gods provided a space two blocks down and one over, as good as could be expected in this part of town. I hussled back to Worth Street. Granimi waited in the empty lobby of number 421, under a "no loitering/no menus" sign, trying to be innocuous. She looked like a five-year-old allowed to pick out her own outfit: orange plaid leggings, ruffled blue mini-skirt, and a droopy olive long-sleeved tee. She hummed to herself, affecting what I could only suppose was intended to be an air of nonchalance. Good thing this wasn't one of those big office buildings real cities have, with a manned security desk in the lobby. They'd take one look at her and call Social Services.

"Hello, Lena dear," she said, as though she hadn't seen me all morning.

"Yeah, hi G." I guided her across the street and under the awning of a housewares store halfway down the block.

"Oh, look at that nice tureen," she said. "Do you think your mother would like that?"

The tureen was shaped like a duck with orange and purple plumage. "Only if it comes with a personality transplant." I turned her away from the display. "We're not window shopping, G. Unless they walk out of that building while we're standing here, in which case we'll pretend to, okay?"

Granimi nodded. "That sounds like a good plan, dear. That way they won't know we're watching them."

"That's the idea. So what happened after I dropped you off? How did they act?"

"I didn't witness any PDAs," she said. "But something's going on there."

"Why do you say that?"

"Well, my eyesight isn't what it used to be, dear, but it seems to me that if they were just acquaintances or business associates she wouldn't have walked quite so close to him. And before they went into the building she touched his arm, like this."

Granimi lay her fingertips on my forearm, and tilted her head to look up at me. It was a simple gesture, and surprisingly intimate. If I were a guy and within several decades of her age, I might have thought she hoped I would kiss her.

It wasn't much, but it felt like something.

"What did he do?" I asked.

"Nothing."

"Nothing?"

"Nothing." Granimi nodded at me as if that meant something more than nothing.

"And what, oh great master, do you make of that?"

"I think," she said, "that they have a relationship. And she's used to having his attention when they're together. But he's grieving, and not thinking about her."

I'd been there, panting for attention from someone who had acted like he wanted me but who had disappeared, perhaps with someone else, into the sanctuary of his mind. I don't mean Brad, by the way. He'd been delightfully present and accessible, for a guy. Marital mistake #2 was another story. I was annoyed I even remembered he existed.

"So, in your professional opinion, you think she could be the mistress?"

Granimi nodded vigorously. "I'd bet my hat on it, if I were wearing a hat."

I restrained myself from ruffling her hair. "You're a pip, Granimi. Have I told you yet how much I like that haircut? It suits you."

"It is fun." She turned to check her reflection in the store window, fluffing the spikes back up with her fingers to make sure she looked as much as possible like a hurricane survivor. "While I was waiting for you I looked at the directory in the lobby. There are twelve businesses in that building: small places like CPAs and a graphic design firm, and a Realtor's office."

"So either she works in one of those offices," I said. "Or they have an appointment with someone. I don't suppose you got there in time to do something clever like watch the elevator indicator, or anything like that?"

"It's only a two-story building, dear. I do think they went upstairs, though, because when I came in the lobby was empty and I heard footsteps on the second floor, then a door closing."

"That narrows it down."

"I wrote down the names of the businesses." She handed me a folded takeout menu with what looked like spider tracks in the margin. "Suites 101–501 are on the first floor, so these must be upstairs."

"Great." Too bad her handwriting is so atrocious. I passed the menu back to her. "Granimi, can you read this?"

She peered at it. "Not without my reading glasses, dear."

Don't think the problem is entirely with your eyesight, G. I found a pen in my purse and wrote the building address on an empty bit of margin. Surely there were other ways to get a list of tenants.

"Oh, there he is!" Granimi grabbed my arm and spun around to look in the store window.

"Be casual," I reminded her. "No sudden movements." I pretended to point at the window display while trying to get a reflected view of the other side of the street. It looks easy in the movies. I gave up and risked a casual quarter turn and a peek over my shoulder. Alan, alone this time, walked away from us.

"Come on," I said. "Let's follow him again."

27

We stayed on the far side of the street until Alan had turned the corner, then tailed him another two blocks until he paused to take a remote out of his pocket and chirp his car unlocked.

"So what do you think?" I asked Granimi as we watched him drive away.

"I think they met for lunch and he walked her back to her office and stayed for a few minutes, and now he's driving away."

"I think you're right." My car was blocks away in the other direction, so following him wasn't an option. "I'm parked about a quarter mile from here," I said. "Are you good to walk that far, or do you want to wait here and I'll come pick you up."

"I will walk, thank you," Granimi said. "I may be old, but I'm no more than halfway to decrepit."

Granimi and I retraced our steps, and I tried to remember which side street I'd parked on. G. said something I didn't quite catch and when I half-turned, the better to hear her, I saw a tall man dressed in faded jeans and a chambray shirt leave the building we'd been watching. I didn't get a good look, but as he turned away from us and walked the other way the long hair confirmed it.

"Hey, Granimi, is that Raven over there?"

"Over where, dear?"

"Walking away from us, over there. Carrying a brown satchel."

We exchanged glances. Clue or coincidence?

"Let's see where he goes," I said. He had a head start, and his long legs set a brisk pace. We put a good hustle on and did our best to keep up.

"Is this an open tail, dear?" Granimi asked, puffing slightly. She was flippetting along in a fast half-shuffle in her yellow flip-flops.

"An open what?"

"'Open tail,' dear. That's when you don't mind if the subject knows you're following them. I read it in that book you got."

"I suppose so." I was glad Detecting for Morons was helping one of us. I hadn't done more than glance at the Table of Contents. I thought that if we could catch up enough to have a chance encounter with Raven—without being too noticeably out of breath, which might clue him in that we'd run after him—that might not be a bad thing.

Raven had waited for a break in traffic so he could cross the street, which gave us a chance to close the gap.

Granimi waved and yoo-hooed and he saw us and smiled back with a wave of his own.

"Hello Raven, dear," Granimi said. "What a nice surprise."

"Delightful indeed." He bowed over her hand while sending a wink my way.

I smiled a hello back that wasn't quite as coolly composed as I'd intended. That wink had flirtatious intentions, and I rather liked being on the receiving end of it.

"What brings you ladies into town today?"

"Just doing some errands," I said. "How 'bout you?"

"A business appointment, which is now done, and I need to pick up a birthday gift for my daughter."

"Oh that's nice," Granimi said. "How old is she?"

"She'll be 31."

Yikes, not a whole lot younger than me. I sort of, almost, wished I were older.

"What are you going to get her?" Granimi asked.

"She likes kitchen things," he said, "so my plan was to look in here." He tilted his head at the housewares store we'd loitered in front of earlier. "Perhaps you could help me pick something out?"

"It would be our pleasure," Granimi said, so he held the door for us and we went in.

The place almost made me want to become a chef, it was so full of clever gadgets and shiny stainless steel this and that and a rainbow of aprons and cloths of various kinds.

"Do not, under any circumstances, encourage my Grandmother to buy that duck tureen," I said to Raven as we browsed the interior side of the window display.

"You have something against ducks?" He lifted lid to look inside.

"What exactly is a tureen?"

"It's for serving soup."

"Really. And all these years I've ladled it straight from the pot into my bowl."

"We all do that," I said. If we use a pot. Mostly I just zap a bowl in the microwave. "I have no idea who would use a tureen these days, other than Martha Stewart."

I explained that Granimi is famous for giving lovely, expensive, and utterly the wrong gifts for all occasions. "That tureen, for example. She saw it in the window, uh, the other day, and thought of getting it for my mother. Who will hate it, and never use it."

"I see." He put the duck's top half back on. "And will your grandmother enjoy giving it to her?" He raised an eyebrow at me.

I hadn't thought of it that way. "Yes, I suppose she will."

"Then let her give it. And your mom can either use it or pass it on to someone who will like it. What's the harm in that?"

"None, I guess." I don't have a problem with regifting, if it's done thoughtfully. The downside was the good chance that, if Granimi gave the tureen to my mom, the person it would be regifted to is me. "How does your daughter feel about ducks? What's her name, by the way?"

"Dorothy, and she likes cows."

"I bet they have cow-themed stuff here. Don't get her a cow creamer, though. If she's known for the cow thing, she'll already have one."

"What's a creamer?"

I scanned the nearest aisle and gestured him to follow me. "It's a cow," I held the ceramic figure up by the looped tail, "for pouring cream." I demonstrated by tipping it nose-down.

"You're right. I've seen one of these at Dot's place."

Dot? What a horrible nickname. I'm not fond of Magdalena, but at least Lena is an improvement on the original.

Raven looked at his watch.

"Are you in a hurry?" I asked. "We haven't been much help with your shopping."

"I've still got a few minutes," he said. "I do need to get to another appointment, though. You and your grandmother are coming to my talk tomorrow night, I hope."

"Oh, right. I meant to visit your website but things got kind of crazy at home."

"If you come to my talk, you'll learn everything that's on the website and more."

"We'll be there," I assured him.

"Are you talking about Raven's workshop?" Granimi sidled up, holding an egg platter.

"Yes, I've just said we'll come to his talk tomorrow night." I hoped she didn't have me in mind for the platter. Deviled eggs are tasty, but I don't need a special plate for them.

"I'm sure your talk will be very interesting," Granimi told Raven. "I met a fascinating man in Prague a few years ago, who'd been researching shamanic rituals in, I think it was Siberia. He told the most interesting story, something about a reindeer. Or was it a bear...?"

"When and where is this talk taking place," I asked Raven.

He opened his ancient leather satchel and pulled out a flyer. "Orchard City Community College, seven o'clock. You know where that is?"

I nodded yes, wondering if Val would like to come. "My twelve-year-old niece is visiting," I said. "Is this something I could bring her to?"

"Absolutely, if she's interested."

"Do you think Val would be interested?" I turned to ask Granimi, but something at the end of the aisle had caught her attention and she'd wandered off. If not, I'd have to think about finding a sitter. I thought Val was old enough to be left on her own for a couple hours, but her mom probably disagreed.

Granimi waved me over, and Raven headed for the next aisle to continue his search for a cow-themed whatever.

"Do you think Raven would like this?" G. stretched for a large hand-painted ceramic plate on a high shelf. Probably placed up there to keep it out of reach.

I intervened before she could knock something over with that pink cast. "No heavy lifting, G.," I reminded her. "It's very nice, but that's probably meant to be a crow." Plus, Raven didn't strike me as a platter kind of guy.

"Oh," she said, disappointed. I almost felt bad for spoiling her fun.

"I could use some new dish towels. Let's go pick some out." I knew she'd insist on paying for them, which would maybe turn off the gift-buying impulse for the rest of the day.

We flipped through the display of dish towels, settled on a set of six that would go with my kitchen, and met up with Raven at the cashier.

"What did you find?" I asked.

He held up a handful of kitchen tools with a grin. "No cows," he said. "But I think she'll like these, whatever they are."

I laughed at the set of whisks with squid-shaped bodies, tentacles made of curled wire. "Those are so clever!" I immediately wanted one, but couldn't remember the last time I'd used a whisk. Maybe I should cook more.

Granimi of course wanted to know what I was laughing about, then had to find the whisk bin, too, although I'm quite sure she has even less use for a whisk than I do. I told the cashier to hold off on ringing us up, and waved Raven to go ahead.

"I'd better restrain her before she buys the whole store," I said. "We'll see you tomorrow tonight."

I caught up with Granimi at the front of the store, waving to Raven through the window as he walked out with his purchases. We watched him unlock the door of a sky blue Mercedes that predated keyless entry systems by at least a decade. The sedan was more battered rust-heap than cool ride, but Raven made it look good.

"I told you he likes you," Granimi said, jabbing me in the ribs.

"Ow, watch who you stab with those talons, G.," I said. "Maybe he's just drumming up business for his workshop."

"I expect he has no trouble finding people to attend his workshops, dear. You might find some competition there."

"I told you, I'm not interested in dating anyone yet, and especially not someone named 'Raven.'" And when did I agree to attend the Saturday workshop, too?

"It's a good name for him, if you ask me."

I didn't entirely disagree. "I'd feel like a cliché," I said. "Ms. Whitebread Suburbia enthralled by the exotic Native American. Please. I'd die of embarrassment."

"Don't knock exotic," she said, waving off concern for my dignity, and I remembered her story of forbidden love, or lust, or whatever it had been.

"It's not too soon for you to start dating again," she went on, "You're far too young and attractive to go through the rest of your life alone."

"I think some alone time might be good for me," I said, not realizing until the words were out of my mouth that they were true.

"You've been alone for half a year, dear."

"Yes, and I've spent that time crying and feeling sorry for myself. I'd like to find out if I can be alone for a while and enjoy it. Then maybe we'll see if I'd like to date anyone."

"Don't wait too long," she said. "I bet there are plenty of women who wouldn't mind playing Jane to his Tarzan."

"You're assuming Raven's single. For all we know he's married, or living with someone. We know he has a daughter." I had noticed he didn't wear a wedding ring, but that didn't mean he was available.

"If he were married," Granimi pointed out, "his wife would do the gift shopping. If there's a girlfriend, he'd have brought her along. And if he's got kids, he's probably not gay."

I hadn't thought of that. I couldn't fault her logic.

"He's something of a hottie," Granimi added, jabbing at my ribs again.

"Maybe," I admitted. "Or could be you're just falling for the hair. Are we done shopping here?"

The drawback of lurking by the window display to watch Raven drive off was that Granimi got another chance to decide the duck tureen was just what my mother needed. I thought about talking her out of it, but Granimi had a gifting reputation to uphold. While G. got out her plastic at the sales counter, I wondered how much to read into my conversation with Raven. I realized I wanted to attend Raven's Saturday workshop as well as the Friday lecture. The ridiculous name would take some getting used to, but was that reason enough to give up further exploration of the maybe-hot thing the man had going on?

28

All of our running around town had fatigued Granimi, so I took her home for a nap. I'd expected Val, who'd arranged for a ride home from a fellow swim camper, to be home but she'd left a note on the kitchen table that she was "hanging with Ansel." Hanging where, and doing what, she had not specified. I was suspicious of the note. It seemed to imply that she hadn't wanted to call me on my cell to apprise me of their plans, which in turn implied that she thought I might not like whatever they were up to.

"Any idea what's going on over there?" I asked Shadow, who kept a close eye on all kitchen activity—even when no can opener was involved—but he wasn't telling.

I called Val's cell, and she picked up. "I'm at Ansel's," she said. "We're doing some research online."

"What kind of research?"

She didn't answer right away. In the pause I heard the faint and distinctive sound of a computer keypad in use. "Ansel's typing up some notes, I'll tell you later."

Okay. A slightly sneaky response, but nothing to get concerned about. Yet. "Is Tulip around?" I asked, partly because I was curious about a work schedule, if she had one, and partly because my role as surrogate mom prompted concern about at what point the kids were spending too much unsupervised time together.

"She's at work."

Aha. "Doing what, do you know?"

"I'll tell you later."

"Fine."

While Granimi napped, I got online and did some research of my own. The list of business names G. had scribbled down was too far from legible to be of use. Between a Google address search and our town website I came up with a list of businesses with a 421 Worth Street address. I was about to start clicking links when Suzette called to see if I wanted to talk to the lab tech with her. He'd agreed to meet for a drink at a bar in Orchard City after work, but he'd sounded creepier this time and she was reluctant to meet him alone.

"Sure," I said. Drinks with a creepy geek in a sleazy bar, sounds like fun.

Granimi was up from her nap, so I okayed with her and then called Val again to say I was going out for a few hours and Granimi was in charge of dinner if I wasn't back by the time they wanted to eat.

*   *   *

The sleazy bar turned out to be more upscale than I'd expected and Corbin, the guy from the lab, was as young as expected, but only slightly geeky. He did look surprised to see two of us, which inclined me to believe that he'd done some Googling himself and that the photo of Suzette on her feng shui webpage had influenced his decision to meet in person. Not that it mattered, so long as he talked. We introduced ourselves and moved the party to as quiet a table as we could find and ordered drinks.

"Why are you so interested in this brownie?" Corbin wanted to know. "It checked out okay. No toxins or anything like that. I took a look at the results again this afternoon, and there's nothing off about it. It was just a brownie."

"A brownie that killed a friend of ours," I said.

Suzette glared at me to be nice. "We're not questioning the lab results," she said sweetly. "We just want to know what it looked like."

He gave us the same look we'd received from Bob. "It looked like a brownie, I guess." He started to wipe condensation from his beer bottle with a cocktail napkin, then stopped as though realizing it didn't help him look cool.

"We know there were nuts in it," I explained. "We're curious about what kind, and whether they were visible. There was no photograph of the brownie in the police report. Since you ran the tests on it, we thought you might be able to describe it to us."

Again, the baffled look.

"Uh, dark brown, about an inch thick, kind of cake-like?"

Are all guys this clueless about brownies? Good thing I'd brought show and tell. There'd been nothing left in the Santa tin but crumbs, so I'd grabbed a couple of samples from the freezer stash and stuck them in my purse. In a ziplock bag, of course.

"Exhibit A." I moved an umbrella-drinks menu aside and placed a plain brownie sample in the middle of the table.

"Exhibit B." A nut brownie, with chunks of walnuts clearly visible in the side, and a scattering of more finely chopped nuts on top.

"Which one did the brownie you tested look like?" I asked.

"Gee, I didn't really pay that much attention." He thought about it. "I don't remember anything on the top like that." He picked up Exhibit B, but appeared unsure.

"Hey Corb, what a day, huh?" The question came from a young woman about his age. She had a nice voice and a pleasant, almost-pretty face that could have used some makeup. Her mousy brown hair looked like she cut it herself but she had lovely hazel eyes. The girl needed a makeover, but perhaps she was a geek, too, and immune to such things.

"Oh, hi Michelle. Yeah, it's been crazy."

Was it my imagination or was he happy to be seen by her in the company of two hot older chicks?

"Another brownie case?" she asked, noticing Exhibits A and B.

"Same one," he said. "Not that it's a case anymore."

"Ms. Johnston was pissed someone ate that one we tested," she said. "If that was you, you'd better hope she doesn't find out."

"Probably Craig the Keg." he said.

"Yeah, most likely."

Maybe we should ask Craig the Keg about the brownie. Although if he'd eaten the evidence probably he wouldn't admit it. In the meantime, this chick was definitely trying to flirt. And Corbie was definitely digging it. We should help him out, right?

Suzette was on it. "Corbin's been great, helping us make sense of all this brownie stuff," she said. "Hey, why don't you join us?"

I grabbed an extra chair from the next table over and swung it around to put her next to Corbin. "Drinks are on us," I said. "I'm Lena, that's Suzette."

She hesitated, glancing over to the bar. The girlfriend she'd been hanging with signaled she was cool with it.

"I'm Michelle," she said, taking the seat. "I work in the lab, too. You probably figured that out."

"Hi, Michelle." We all ordered more drinks and a basket of chips. Corbin stuck to beer while the ladies got festive with frozen margaritas. Suzette and I asked CSI-groupie questions about working in a lab until the drinks arrived and had been sipped at.

"So Michelle," I asked when we were all relaxed and friendly. "Were you involved in testing that brownie, too?"

"Nah, I was working on other stuff," she said. "It wasn't a big deal thing."

"We're curious about appearance," Suzette explained. "Do you remember what it looked like?"

"Jeeze, it looked like a brownie," she said. "I remember when it came in, there were some jokes about why don't we just divvy it up and see if it makes anyone sick, that kind of thing."

"Which of these two did it look like?" I pointed to our specimens. "Visible nuts, or plain chocolate?"

"Oh, right. That one." She pointed to Exhibit A, the plain one, with no hesitation. "I remember that. I mean, I didn't pay much attention, 'cause it wasn't jobbed to me, but I did hear that it was the nuts that had killed someone who was allergic. Which was odd, because nut brownies look like that other one, you know?" This time she pointed to the walnut version, proving it's definitely a gender thing. If you've got brownie questions, go to a girl for answers.

Suzette and I smiled at each other and did a low-five under the table.

"Michelle, that's what we suspected," Suzette said. "Thank you for confirming that."

"Sure," she said. "Glad to help, I guess."

"Did you mention to anyone," I asked, "that it seemed odd to you, that what looked like a plain brownie turned out to have nuts in it?"

She shrugged. "I just kind of noticed and moved on. I'd forgotten about it until now. Why? Is it important?"

"It could be," Suzette said. "We don't know yet."

We played it cool while the drinks lasted, then thanked Corbie and Michelle for their time and saved our whoops of triumph for the parking lot.

"Yes!" Suzette and I hooted and pumped our fists in the air and did a happy dance, which caused a couple of guys on their way in to inquire whether we were sure we wanted to leave when joining them for another round was such an appealing option. We waved them on, declined their counter-offer to tag along to wherever we were headed next, and skipped to Suzette's car feeling ridiculously pleased with ourselves.

"This is huge." Suzette started up the engine and pointed us toward home.

"We have successfully proven that brownie subterfuge was a factor," I confirmed. "We are awesome."

"We deserve another drink."

"We do. And something better than stale chips for dinner."

"Luigi's?" Suzette suggested, naming one of our favorite local eateries.

"Perfect." I called home and learned that Granimi was teaching Val how to sauté a chicken breast and make a salad. I told them I was eating out and would be home later. After just five days of family duty it felt good to be on the loose with my gal pal.

*   *   *

"You ladies are in a good mood tonight," Devon said as he showed us to a table.

"Lena and I have been exceedingly clever today, Devon," Suzette said, "and have earned a nice dinner."

Devon wished us an enjoyable meal and sent over complimentary cocktails, having learned from experience that our good moods usually lead to a self-indulgent dinner tab and generous tip.

The giddy afterglow of successful investigating lasted until we were half-way through our entrees, when Alan walked into the restaurant in the company of an older couple. He saw us and nodded hello as they were shown to their table on the other side of the room.

We remembered that our self-congratulatory mood rested on the murder of his wife, and that he might have been behind that in some way, and that pretty much sucked the fun out of the evening.

"I wish we could sit Alan down for a chat," Suzette said.

"Me, too." Alan would know all kinds of helpful stuff, like what medications Rose had been on and how much of her money he would inherit. And whether or not there was a mistress in the wings. And whether he'd had anything to do with killing his wife, alibi or not. If he was innocent, I wanted to tell him what we were up to, and get his help. Until we knew that for sure, he was on the Do Not Trust list. A time might come to show our cards and see if they spooked him, but we weren't anywhere close to that yet.

*   *   *

When I got home, Val and Granimi—to whom I'd relinquished control of my Netflix queue—were on the couch with their feet up on the coffee table among a litter of red envelopes. Shadow nestled between them, paws tucked under his chin.

"We're having a Medium marathon," Val explained when I asked what they were watching. "We just started the third episode of Season One."

"Learning anything?" I asked.

"That poor woman never gets a good night's sleep," Granimi said. "I don't know how she keeps going."

"Probably she takes a lot of naps," I suggested, feeling yawny myself. I imagine they leave that part out when they dramatize it. I passed on joining the fun, reminding Val that she had swim camp in the morning and maybe shouldn't stay up too late.

Mom-ish duties done, I retreated to the kitchen and awakened my laptop from sleep mode. The excitement and sense of progress engendered by definitive brownie reports notwithstanding, I wanted to spend more time with my list of 421 Worth St. tenants before calling it a day. Many of the businesses at that address had their own websites. Unfortunately, none offered search functions capable of identifying "blonde woman seen with Alan Braska in downtown Laurelton this afternoon."

I was halfway through my list, checking out tenant websites for photographs of business owners and staff that might include and with any luck identify a slim, nicely dressed ash blonde in her early thirties, when I heard Val and Granimi winding down for the night. My pillow called, too, so I decided to defer any more cyber-sleuthing until morning, when a good dose of caffeine might reawaken my enthusiasm.

Val was just climbing into bed when I stuck my head into Olivia's room to say goodnight. "Did you call your Mom?"

She nodded.

"Did you tell her about your Medium marathon?"

Val blanched, and I immediately regretted teasing her.

"Just kidding, honey." Although it might be a good idea to check out what else had been added to my Netflix queue. "Hey, what did you find out about Tulip's job situation?"

"She works part-time at a health food store. I forget which one."

Val seemed surly, either annoyed by the bit about her mom, pissed that I expected her to dish about Tulip, or maybe just tired and cranky. Leaving her alone seemed the best course of action, so I did. Maybe she'd chatted with Granimi.

No such luck.

Granimi was also headed for bed. Or so she said. Sitting on the floor with an ankle behind one's head didn't much look like bedtime activity to me, but she claimed, as she released the foot and leaned forward to wrap both hands around her ankles and touch her nose to her knees, that she needed to work out the kinks from too many hours on the couch.

"That medium is something else," G. said. "Can you imagine, getting messages from dead people in your dreams?" She proceeded to stand on one foot, bend into a squat, and wrap the other leg around her knee and calf while crossing her elbows and wrists in a way that looked both tricky and uncomfortable, especially with that cast on. I'd fall over if I tried to do that.

"When are you going to take up yoga, dear?" She unraveled her arms and legs and wound them back up to the other side. "It's not too late to get started, you know. When you get to be my age you'll be glad you did."

When I get to be her age I hope I'll have earned the right not to twist myself into a pretzel before bed. I had to admit, though, that I felt the effects of a long day in a tight neck and tense shoulders. A good massage would take care of that, but with no in-house masseuse on call maybe some tips from an aging but agile yogini would help.

"Tell you what," I offered. "Show me something to loosen up a stiff neck and if I like it I'll let you teach me more tomorrow."

"Excellent." She grabbed a throw pillow from the armchair in the corner and set it down on the carpet. "You're probably very tight through the hips. The cushion will help you sit cross-legged."

Five minutes of shoulder shrugs and head rolls and arm stretches later I felt two inches taller and much looser around the neck. Granimi was right about my hips, if that's what made even a few minutes in a simple cross-legged position less than comfortable.

Granimi asked if that felt better and refrained from gloating when I admitted that her simple moves had made a difference. Maybe I should have let her talk me into this years ago. I was debating the wisdom of sharing that insight when I heard the faint familiar rumble of my neighbor's garage door in motion.

"Quick, turn out the light." I gestured at the wall switch by the door and creaked stiffly to my feet (and couldn't help comparing my lack of ease in that simple movement to how smoothly my grandmother got up and down). Granimi hit the switch and I moved to the side of the window and peeked through the mini-blind slats. Was he coming or going?

Going. Which meant he'd returned home from dinner and was headed out again. As he backed around at the end of the driveway there was a moment when the light from a streetlamp lit up the interior of his car and I saw he was alone.

"Where is he going this time of night?" Granimi wondered, peeking through her own gap in the blinds a couple of slats down.

"Hell if I know. He's not giving anyone a ride home, that's all I could tell."

"Perhaps he went to get cigarettes," she suggested. "Or ice cream. Or he needs something from a 24-hour pharmacy."

"Or he's got a date."

"Too bad we didn't know he was going to go out. We could have followed him again."

"Yeah." Too bad. Honestly, though, I was ready for my pillow and just as glad we'd missed that chance.

"Tell you what," I said. "Don't wait up or anything, but if you hear his garage door again tonight, take a peek at the clock so we'll know what time he came home."

"Okay, dear," she said. "I'm a light sleeper, anyway. I'll tell my subconscious to keep an ear out so I'll be sure to wake up."

Granimi is the kind of light sleeper who could snore through the apocalypse, so I wasn't confident she'd notice Alan's return. Not that I planned to drag an armchair over to the window to keep watch myself. I figured I'd only signed up for part-time detecting, and deserved a good night's sleep.

29

One of the calls I'd made while at the vet's office was to Alan's long-time secretary, now retired. I'd met Edith Stokely several times and remembered she was a Garden Club member. A chat with Edith was an opportunity to poke at the inner workings of the Garden Club and maybe ferret out some hints about whether or not Alan played around. The big question was whether Edith would talk to me once she realized what I had in mind.

Edith hadn't exactly jumped for joy when I'd called, but agreed I could come by her home at 3:30 on Friday. So, after the usual morning of driving Val around town, plus stops at Safeway and Whole Foods to refill the fridge, I pulled up in front of 83 Alcott Street mid-afternoon.

Edith's lawn was immaculate, her flower beds in glorious bloom, not a weed or dead blossom in sight. She'd made the most of the small lot, and two pots of lush geraniums flanked the steps to a tiny portico. A sign beside the front door indicated that a Notary Public resided within and could be called upon to perform official duties 9 AM to 3 PM, Wed & Fri. It was now after hours, so just as well I didn't need her to authenticate a signature.

Edith welcomed me politely and ushered me to an uncomfortable settee in her tidy living room. She was dressed in a conservative skirt and sweater set, flesh-tone stockings, and sensible shoes. No yoga pants and hoodie for Edith. Unless she'd dressed up for me, which made me wish I'd made more of an effort. I'd remembered to iron my chino skirt, but once settled on Edith's sofa I was showing a lot of bare leg.

Edith disappeared for a few minutes, returning with a tray laden with tea service for two. I'd have spent that time peeking at book titles and studying family photographs but the formal parlor she'd stashed me in was relentlessly characterless. The house was quiet, all the windows closed and the A/C on although it was not a hot day. I'd expected a lap dog but the room didn't appear to be sullied by so much as a single pet hair. I hoped I hadn't brought any with me, and made a mental note to get one of those lint-roller things now that I shared my couch with a cat. Edith settled herself on the other settee and asked how I like my tea. Not very much, but I pretended to enjoy it with milk.

"Rose was well-liked, of course," she said, passing me a delicate cup and saucer of very poor coffee substitute. "She was so refreshingly un-self-important for someone of her social position." Edith paused to pour herself a cup and add three cubes of sugar which she took from a bowl with a silver tongs and dropped, one at a time, into her tea before stirring thoughtfully. "Not like some of our members," she added, with a slight twist of her lower lip. "Although I don't like to name names."

"She'd been president of the Garden Club for a long time, is that right?" I took a sip of tea and wished I'd asked for sugar. Seemed impolite to add it now; Edith might think I found her brew on the bitter side.

"Oh yes. Rose led the group for a long time. That was before she got sick, of course. She hadn't been club president for several years." Edith took a sip of tea and paused with the cup in her hands. "When Rose stepped down Maisie Lomack moved in on that position like a rhino headed for a waterhole." She sipped again and put the cup down. "Fortunately, Maisie's very competent, although she can be a bit cavalier when delegating."

"So Rose's, ah, demise, didn't make a lot of waves."

"Oh no, dear. Nothing's changed at all. In terms of the Club, that is. Although we do miss her, of course. And we'll miss being her guinea pigs when she tested a new recipe. Oh, my goodness, I forgot to offer you these." She moved a pastry from the serving platter on her tray to a small plate and passed it to me along with a delicate linen napkin. "This is Rose's lemon bar recipe. I thought you might enjoy them."

Even though I knew it was the brownie that had killed Rose, not the lemon bar she'd also sampled that afternoon, it felt macabre to be offered one. Edith couldn't possibly have known. I lay the napkin in my lap and took a ladylike nibble, then spoiled my attempt at good manners by speaking with my mouth full.

"This is really good," I said, truthfully. Poor Rose. Too bad the last one she'd taken a bite of had been inedible. If she'd fed her sweet tooth one of these lemon bars perhaps she could have said no to that brownie.

"The only thing I've changed," Edith said, "is I add a quarter cup of ground almonds to the shortbread."

"They do add a nice flavor," I said, thinking it was nice but subtle. Add some chocolate, and it would be even less detectable. The bitter tea wasn't so bad, either, if you had something sweet to go with it. Would Edith be flattered if I asked for another one, or think me greedy and lacking in good manners?

"Do have another," she said, holding out the platter.

I smiled my thanks and took a second lemon bar.

Edith took another, too. Garden Club power plays, as expected, looked like a dead end. I wasn't sure how to proceed. I figured I had to stay at least another ten minutes before I could leave without seeming horribly impolite. Not that it mattered what Edith thought of me, but something about her made me feel held to a higher standard, a standard that it would do me good to live up to, even if doing so seemed tedious and unnecessary. Rose had had that effect on me, too.

Edith set down her empty tea cup and dabbed a few tiny crumbs from her lips with her napkin (something I didn't dare do for fear of getting lipstick on the embroidered cloth), and turned to look at me.

"Surely you didn't come over here just to ask about Rose's history with the Laurelton Garden Club," she said. "So why don't you tell me what's really on your mind."

"Oh. Okay." I put my tea cup down, still unsure how to spin things. "Well then, here's the thing. You know Rose died because she ate a brownie with some nuts in it." I waited for her to nod, then continued. "Everyone—I mean the police and the coroner and Rose's family—are choosing to call it an accident, even though there's some thought that she might have done it on purpose."

Edith seemed a teeny bit surprised by that theory, but remained silent.

"Apparently her condition had worsened again. So maybe she didn't want to go through a long decline. That's the theory anyway. I guess eating a brownie is as good a way to go as any."

"And you bring this up with me because...?" Edith waited for me to explain myself.

"Something doesn't feel right," I said. Geeze, that sounded lame. A chat with Edith had seemed like a good idea, but now I had to decide how much to tell her. It would be great if Edith knew something that would shed light on the Rose situation. But she'd worked for Alan a long time, so where did her loyalties lie? It seemed wise to assume that anything said here could make its way back to Alan.

I decided on the favor for a friend excuse. "The thing is, I know all the questions have been wrapped up and put away, but Rose's housekeeper, Hanna—do you know her?"

Edith gave a half-shrug that maybe meant she might recognize the woman if she saw her on the street.

"Hanna feels something's been overlooked," I said. "To tell you the truth, I'm not sure what she's concerned about, but I told her I would ask some people who knew Rose, like you, for their opinion. I think Hanna just wants someone to put her mind at rest."

Edith looked thoughtful. I felt she was on the verge of saying something, but she remained silent. She picked up her empty teacup and reached for the pot to pour a refill, then sighed and put the cup down.

"I'm going to switch to something stronger," she said, getting to her feet. "It's early for cocktail hour, but how does a gin and tonic sound to you?"

Not a whole lot better than tea, frankly. "That sounds like a fine idea," I said. If gin would loosen Edith up and get her talking, I was all for it.

Edith waved off my offer of help, which had totally been about getting a look at her kitchen, and carried the tea tray away. I was sorry to see the lemon bars go, but it was just as well. I didn't need to disgrace myself by reaching for a third.

I heard cabinet and fridge doors open and close and decided I'd had enough of the formal parlor. I followed the sound of ice cubes clinking into a glass and joined Edith in her kitchen.

"What a lovely room," I said, which it was: lots of sunny yellows and a windowsill bursting with African Violets. "Oh, don't bother with that," I suggested as she reached for a cocktail tray to put the highball glasses on. "We can talk just as well in here." I pulled out a chair from the table in her breakfast nook and sat down. "And I won't have to worry about spilling anything on your lovely upholstery in the parlor."

"Well, all right." Edith looked only slightly put out that I'd made myself at home in her kitchen. She set two coasters on the table, then finished making the drinks and passed one to me.

Sheesh, that was strong. Who was trying to loosen up whom here?

"So, what do you think happened, Edith?" I faked another sip. I'd have to drink slowly if I were going to drive myself home.

Edith sipped and considered. "I did hear the suicide theory," she said after a long moment. "Alan told me about it."

"Is that what he thinks?"

She sighed. "He seems to want to believe it. But the poor man is devastated that she didn't tell him how sick she was."

"You don't sound convinced. Do you think it's more likely Rose ate the brownie by accident?"

Edith took a good long sip and turned the glass in her hands. "I just don't see how that would happen," she said. "Anyone can see a nut brownie has nuts in it. So far as I know there was nothing wrong with Rose's eyesight. But suicide? That just doesn't seem like something Rose would do." She shrugged. "Who am I to say. I haven't had to face terminal illness. I might, if I were in Rose's position, do something out of character myself."

"In what way was it out of character?" Who wants to spend months enduring pointless treatments, or lingering in a hospice? Well, I guess some people do. Fingers crossed I don't have to make that choice for a while.

Edith thought about it, spinning the ice cubes in her glass. The alcohol did seem to loosen her up, and I risked taking another sip of mine. The gin-tonic-lime thing was growing on me. Maybe G&Ts have to be strong to be any good.

"Why was it out of character?" Edith said. "I'm finding it difficult to say. Maybe the fact that it happened in a public place. Well, as public places go, that one's pretty private. But leaving it to chance who would find her doesn't seem like Rose. She was very good at thinking through the details of things."

She drank again, and set the glass down with perhaps more of a thunk than she'd intended. "On the other hand, it makes sense that she would do it there, where so many of her family are. That place was very special to her, you know. I think to Rose it was like a private chapel. A place where she could go to be alone and think about things."

"That does make it sound more like something she might do," I said, "when you put it that way. If that is what happened, do you think she purchased the brownie at a bakery somewhere, and then went to the mausoleum to ... you know?"

"It's hard to imagine her not doing her own baking, but I know sometimes her arthritis made that difficult." Edith smiled. "I rather like the idea of her sitting there in her favorite spot, finally getting a chance to find out why so many people enjoy walnuts in their brownies. She often said that was the one thing she felt cheated by in life, that she was so well-known for her baking, and that a whole category of ingredients was off-limits to her."

Edith decided to freshen up her drink. I waved off the offer, showing her my glass was still half full.

"Finish that up before the ice melts," she advised. "A watery G&T's no good." Edith tossed her old ice in the sink and mixed herself a fresh drink. She seemed a bit unsteady coming back to the table with her refill. I was glad we'd met at her house, so I didn't have to worry about her driving anywhere.

"That Garden Club just isn't the same without Rose," she said, plunking down in her seat.

"I thought you said Rose's departure didn't change anything. What with Maisie being so competent and all."

"Oh, pssh." Edith dismissed Maisie with a wave of her hand that almost knocked her drink over. "Rose's departure won't change who chairs the meetings," she said. "But the tone of the club isn't the same." She made a look of disapproval again. "Some of our new members don't have an appropriate dedication to the mission of the Garden Club. They show up at meetings when they feel like it, sign up for a committee, and then just when you start to rely on them—poof!—they turn back into pumpkins."

Inconsiderate behavior, certainly, but nothing I cared about.

Edith looked off into the distance and tried to snap her fingers. "What was that woman's name? Well, you wouldn't know," she said, remembering I was there, too. "I do hope this sort of behavior doesn't become typical. So many of our members are older, you see. I'd hate for the Garden Club to fade away because a younger generation isn't truly committed."

"What did this younger person do?" I was barely mildly curious, but someone had given Rose that brownie, and it was someone who knew where Rose would be on a Monday afternoon, and maybe that someone had that knowledge because she was a fellow member of the Garden Club.

"Oh, she isn't all that young, I suppose," Edith said. "Probably about your age. She joined the club a few months ago, and seemed eager to be involved. She even volunteered to do Rose's shift at the cemetery a few times when Rose didn't feel up to it. Then she stopped showing up, just like that. She missed the last two meetings, and when June Esperson called her she was very abrupt and said she had more important things to do. Practically hung up on her, June said."

Edith frowned and gently rapped her temple with a fingertip as if to dislodge something. "Drat, I wish I could remember her name. It's right on the tip of my tongue. Funny how the mind works when you get to be my age. I remember that she wore a beautifully tailored suit to one of our meetings. She had her hair in one of those elegant French twists. Not a hair out of place. You don't see that so much these days. People walk around looking like they just rolled out of bed." Edith glanced my way, and I tried to remember whether I'd brushed my hair before leaving the house.

"She looked so polished and pulled together," Edith went on. "I remember thinking she looked like a successful professional woman. A lawyer, perhaps, or an executive of some kind, someone who took pleasure in dressing well for her job."

Edith's description perked me up because it sounded like the woman Granimi and I had seen with Alan in town yesterday. Her hair had been pulled back with a simple barrette, not up in a French twist, but she'd been well-dressed and tidily put together and, for the brief moment I'd seen her, appeared to carry herself with the kind of confidence that Edith might interpret as professional success. I wondered if the mystery woman Edith was thinking of had been a petite blonde.

Edith slapped the table. "Gillian, I think that was it. Such an old-fashioned name, don't you think? Has a nice, genteel ring to it. Gillian Tabor, maybe, or something like that. Well, that's of no interest to you."

She picked up her glass and swirled the remains of ice around. I tried to think of a subtle way to ask if she had ever known or suspected that Alan might be having an affair, while calculating how much longer I could stay before I had to pick up Val.

Edith sat up straight and took a deep breath. "I'm going to have another," she said, as though surprised by her own boldness. "I don't, usually, but it seems like that kind of a day. Would you care to join me or do you need to be on your way?"

"I can stay a while longer," I said. "Make mine weak, please. I have to drive home."

Edith excused herself to visit the little girls' room, and I perused the family photos on her fridge. A man of about Edith's age shared space with her in several of them.

"Is this your husband?" I asked, when she returned.

She nodded. "That's James. Nice days like today he goes fishing." She pulled a snapshot from the fridge and passed it to me to admire. "We'll have been married forty years next April. Forty good years."

She started to make the refills, but I waved her to a seat and insisted she let me take over. She'd think they were too weak, but she'd pass out if she had another the way she made them. I didn't want that to happen because she'd given me the opening I'd been looking for.

"Forty years." I passed her a wimpy refill. "I envy you."

And I did. Even if I found husband number four waiting for me in the car when I went to drive home, I'd be close to Granimi's age before we got to that kind of anniversary.

"Rose was lucky, too," I segued. "So many men Alan's age want to trade their wives in for a newer model. Especially considering how much older she was than him. But he was so devoted to her."

I watched Edith closely for her reaction, and saw something like a shadow flicker across her face.

"You don't agree?" I prompted, when it became clear she was not going to reply.

"I guess that depends on your definition of 'devoted,'" she said after a long pause.

"What do you mean by that, Edith?" I asked, feigning surprise. "Alan has always appeared to be a model husband."

She looked away. "It's really not my place to say," she said at last, toying with her coaster. "So I'll just say this: Alan and Rose had a, I guess you'd call it an understanding, for a number of years now. Ever since she got sick, you see."

"An understanding that… ?" it was clear what she meant, but I didn't want to make assumptions.

"That he would be discrete, of course," she said sharply. "Some men do feel entitled to have their… needs… looked after."

"So Alan looked elsewhere, and Rose looked the other way, and everyone was happy."

"I'm quite sure he remained devoted to her in all other ways."

I wasn't surprised that Edith came to Alan's defense, but that she'd done so with just a hint of reluctance was interesting. "Was there anyone, uh, special to him, do you know?"

Edith pulled herself up and set her glass down. "I don't know that I'd have any reason to tell you, if he did," she said. "I'm sorry if I come across as an old prude, but I don't feel comfortable discussing this any further."

I apologized and thanked her for her hospitality. The mood had shifted, and it seemed time to leave. I left Edith with my phone number and a request to let me know what the Garden Club decided to do in Rose's memory, so I could make a contribution.

There was no sign of husband number four hanging around when I went out to my car, so I drove off to pick up Val and think about what we would have for dinner.

What I was really thinking about was that the way to get Rose to eat the fatal brownie would be for it to be offered to her by someone she knew from familiar circumstances. Like the Garden Club. And that helping Rose with her regular Monday afternoon visits to the cemetery would be a good way to gain her trust and check out for yourself just how a good a location it was for committing an evil deed. And that if you were confident enough that you'd gotten away with it, you might not bother to keep up appearances with the Garden Club after the deed was done.

Gillian Tabor or something like that wasn't much to go on, but it was a start.

30

Between picking up Val, making a quick dinner, and corralling our group into the car to get to Raven's talk on time, I didn't have a chance to do anything about the possible Gillian clue until late in the evening. Ansel had shown up as soon as I returned with Val, wanting to continue whatever secret research the two of them had been doing.

"Aunt Lena, can Ansel and I use this?" Val stood in the kitchen doorway holding up the Ouija board.

"Sure, honey." Better them than me. The thing still creeped me out. If it stayed in this house I might be tempted to try to communicate with Brad, which was both distractingly appealing and the most terrifying idea I'd ever had.

"Hey Mrs. Wells," Ansel appeared in the doorway beside her. "Did Val tell you she scored really, really high on her sigh tests?"

I looked at the two of them, and wondered again what they'd been up to for the hours they'd been spending together lately. "What kind of test?"

"Sigh tests," he said. "We found a site online that has a bunch of them. Val's scores are way outside the statistical probability curve."

"Sigh tests?" I'd never heard of anything so absurd. Val did shrug and sigh a lot, but no more than any other adolescent. I hadn't realized it was a valid field of study. Who comes up with this stuff?

"You know, PSI," he spelled it out and I finally got it. "Like ESP and stuff."

Oh, that. Mental head slap. "Sounds interesting," I said.

"I'm really good at it!" Val said.

Not a big surprise from someone who could talk with ghosts. "Tell you what, I'd love to hear more about it, but Val we need to eat dinner now if we're going to get to that lecture on time. Can you fill me in while we eat? Ansel, you're welcome to join us, but more psi testing has to wait until later. Val, go find Granimi and tell her we're eating."

Ansel muttered something about mom expecting him home, while turning his nose in the direction of my kitchen. Then Granimi showed up and told him about our plans, which led to a quick call home and permission to hang with us for the evening.

Psi testing, huh, I thought, dishing out chicken and broccoli and buttered noodles all around. So long as the kids weren't making out and smoking pot while measuring Val's psychic abilities, I didn't see any harm in it.

*   *   *

Raven's talk drew a small crowd of about twenty-five people. Audience age was a mixed bag, with Val and Granimi bookending the outer fringes. Gender was solidly skewed toward the feminine, with three obvious repeaters there for a Raven fix, and two possibles. I didn't blame them. Raven had the kind of looks that would never grace a Calvin Klein ad, but he made graying hair look so good that for a few wild moments I considered evicting Miss Clairol from my bathroom cabinet. I decided that what made it work on Raven was his complete comfort in his own skin, a quality most people—including me, alas—do not possess. Maybe that's what made him attractive. He enjoyed what we all crave: freedom from self-doubt and insecurity.

The shamanic journey thing did sound more intriguing than I'd expected, even discounting the Raven factor. But, let's face it, kind of far out there on the anyone-can-be-spiritually-attuned woowoo scale for me. I hope I'm not a conventionally boring person—on a good day I've got the artist thing going for me—but this whole journeying for the masses concept seemed too much designed to make dull people feel special. Surely there was good reason only a select few did this sort of thing in indigenous cultures. Besides, was this kind of strictly codified method really necessary to anyone with a modicum of imagination?

On the other hand, let's see where my imagination has gotten me lately: in the painting department, goose-egg; in the detecting arena, remarkably slow progress and still a decent chance we were making mountains out of molehills; in terms of getting my life back on track, I'd been sidetracked, if not outright hijacked, by houseguests and suppositions. Maybe help from a power animal was what I needed.

I'd missed a good bit of what Raven had been saying, but that was okay. Some kind of shift had happened internally while my conscious mind wandered. By the time Raven drew the evening to a close and reminded us of the opportunity to attend his workshop the next day, I was eager to try this journey thing for myself.

As we headed for the car Val and Ansel and Granimi chatted about how much fun the workshop was going to be. I'd moved on to a deep contemplation of how a man can be hot without being handsome. And the even more burning question of how long I was going to tell myself I wasn't interested.

"I think my power animal is an owl," Val said. "Because they see everything. What do you think your power animal is, Aunt Lena?"

"Was I the only one who paid attention in there?" I countered. I'd listened to the part where Raven told us that, while power animals are sometimes an animal to which we feel a strong attraction, just as frequently they are not. A love of cats, he'd said, does not mean your power animal is a cat: keep your eyes and your minds open. "Did Raven not specifically say that we don't get to choose our power animals, they choose us?"

"Yeah," said Val. "But an owl would be cool. Or maybe a cat, like Shadow."

"I guess it's interesting what people think their power animal should be. A kind of one-question personality test."

"Mine's going to be a panther," said Granimi. "Strong and wild and slinky. Rrrowrr!" She swiped a paw at Val.

Wild and slinky? Sure G., whatever.

"Mine's a Tyranosaurus Rex," Ansel said. "Or maybe an eagle. I can't decide."

"Dinosaurs aren't power animals!" Val said.

"Why not?" Ansel asked. "It's a different reality."

"You can ask Raven tomorrow," I suggested, as Val opened her mouth to protest again. "I think a dinosaur would make a great power animal." If you didn't mind the pea-sized brain and destined-for-extinction aspects.

"What about you, dear," Granimi asked me. "If you could pick a power animal, what would be it be?"

I hadn't thought about it. So much for being a person of imagination. "Um, I don't know." I tried to think of something I wouldn't later regret mentioning. "A dolphin, maybe. They're great swimmers and they have a lot of fun."

"More likely yours is a parrot," Granimi teased. "They're colorful and talk a lot."

Val shook her head. "I don't think so. It's going to be something else for her."

Whatever. Dolphin, donut, I'd find out tomorrow.

Ansel went home to ask Tulip if he could attend the Saturday seminar with us, and Granimi and Val settled in the living room to continue their Medium marathon. I booted up my laptop to see if I could find a Gillian Tabor in town. After a few fruitless minutes of that I gave in to temptation and clicked over to Raven's website.

31

I imagine myself in the front hall of my childhood home. The house is quiet, empty. I go to my secret hiding place, the closet under the stairs, open the door and step inside. Although the space is small, I enter easily. Already proportion, dimension, and scale are fluid. This interests me and I file the observation away to be examined later when I am in front of the easel.

I look toward the back of the space, where the stairs rise up, and see another door. Opening it, I step through and follow a few rough steps down into the earth. The fecund smell of damp soil embraces me. I trail a hand along the tunnel wall and rub the dirt between my fingers. I want to paint this smell, this feeling of going down into the womb of the world.

Ahead, the tunnel ends, and I step into the Lower World.

Raven has instructed us to go slowly, to immerse ourselves in this virtual environment and take note of details. I've emerged beside a boulder the size of a minivan, at the edge of a grassy meadow. The air smells like sun-warmed grass, although I am also still aware—if I choose to be—of lying on a yoga mat on the floor of this community college classroom with its faint aroma of industrial cleanser and floor wax.

I remind myself to focus on the inner experience.

The meadow is dotted with small blue wildflowers. The sky is cloudless, a darker blue, the air remarkably clear. My eyesight is incredible. I can see details in the far distance, but remember Raven's advice to focus on what's near. I notice a path through the grass and follow it across the meadow toward a woods about a half-mile ahead.

A bumblebee buzzes up and hovers in front of me, curious.

"Are you my power animal?" I ask. Power insect?

It buzzes away. I guess not.

I have asked my power animal to meet me, as Raven instructed, and try also to follow his instruction to trust that it will happen. I hope I will not be one of those who fail at the first attempt and have to try again.

I will myself to go slowly, trailing my hand across the top of the tall grass bordering the path, as I did along the wall of the tunnel, feeling the scratchy tips of the grasses and the soft petals of wild flowers brush the undersides of my fingers. I wonder again if I will meet my power animal, and am curious to know what form it will take.

"Watch where you're going!" a voice scolds from somewhere around my feet.

I look down to see a small turtle in the path. I've almost stepped on it.

"Sorry," I say. I am about to move on, when I remember to ask, "Are you my power animal?"

"I have been." It looks up at me with an expression that I interpret as extreme patience.

I hear the turtle's voice in my mind clearly. This must be how Val spoke with Rose the other day. It seems easy and natural.

I crouch down to look more closely at the creature. I see it as luminously beautiful. "May I pick you up?" I ask.

It moves its head in a nod.

I place it in the palm of my left hand. It is small, the shell no more than six inches long, and weighs almost nothing. Tiny claws tickle my palm. I laugh, and feel happy, as though meeting a dear friend I haven't seen in years.

Turtle and I spend some time regarding each other. Because it is so small, it seems young, but its eyes are ancient, as though they witnessed the beginning of time.

I feel a love for this animal that is astonishing in its purity. The only other time I've felt anything like this was when I first held Olivia in my arms. And the time before that, with my first-born. The feeling I have now is staggering in its lack of complication. I am surprised to feel so profound an emotion, and realize this is why the work is so powerful. All of the crap that attaches to human relationships is stripped away, and we connect with something pure and essential within ourselves.

"What did you mean when you said that you 'have been,' my power animal?" I ask. "Does that mean you aren't my power animal any more?"

"I am still," it says. "But soon you will no longer need me."

I feel bereft at the thought of Turtle leaving me. "I don't want you to go. I've only just found you."

"I am not going away," it says. "A time will come when you no longer need me."

I ponder this. Raven has said that time as we experience it does not exist in the other worlds. 'A time will come' could mean tomorrow or in a future lifetime.

"What will I do then?" I ask.

"Others will assist you," it says.

In the distance, at the edge of the woods, movement catches my eye. With the clarity of my new vision I see a fox pause and turn to look at me as it crosses the path. Its appearance at this moment feels deliberate. It's odd to see such detail on something so far away, and I am aware that it looks tough and experienced, a creature of the wild, not some well-fed zoo animal. Its reddish fur is matted in places, and one of the ears looks ragged. Its eyes are a startling clear green. I know this animal, too, although it is a stranger to me. Then I remember how Shadow looked the night he appeared in my garage, and a shiver passes through me, as though this fox and the cat are the same being, existing simultaneously in separate incarnations in two different worlds.

Fox jumps from the path back into the woods. I am tempted to follow, but it is not the time for that. I wonder how I know this. This Lower World is complex beyond any possibility of comprehension, yet my experience here is notably clear and simple.

I remember to ask Turtle what special powers and abilities it offers me. Turtle responds by retreating into its shell. At first I think this means our session is over, then understand it is Turtle's answer. Turtle is showing me the shell of secrets and lies I pulled around me when I gave my child away, and from which I have never fully emerged. Then I remember the other question I've been coached to ask.

"What do I most need to do now, for myself?" I ask.

Turtle's head remains hidden, but its voice is clear: "Find the one who is lost to you."

I begin to cry then, my tears carrying the weight of decades of grief and regret. They fall into my cupped hands and glisten in the sunlight like splashes of quicksilver. My tears darken Turtle's shell and fill the pool of my palms and form a river that spills to the ground and runs in rivulets across the dust of the meadow path. Turtle is swept from my hands by the torrent and falls to the ground. I hold out my hands like a medieval saint displaying her stigmata and feel the river of emotion pour through me. Turtle has fallen upside down and flails tiny paws in indignation.

As suddenly as the deluge started it is over and I feel calm and cleansed. I crouch down once more and gently right Turtle and set him (her?) on its feet. Turtle lumbers off the path and into the grass without a backward look.

The drum beat changes, and I recognize the call to return. I retrace my steps to the boulder and creep up the tunnel to my closet beneath the stairs—

—and am back in my body.

Raven stopped drumming and advised us to lie quietly for a few minutes, to replay the details of our journey in our minds and fasten the snaps of memory while they are still fresh. After a short while I wiggled my toes and fingers and rubbed my face. I expected the damp aftermath of tears, but my skin was dry. I sat up and made some notes in the notebook I had brought for this purpose.

When we had all stretched and twisted our way back to this reality, Raven suggested a short break. There was a rush for the ladies' room, but I hung back. I felt thirsty, my cells parched. I drank most of a bottle of water and waited for the first rush to return to the seminar room, then made use of the facilities and splashed some water on my face. The water felt so good against my skin I rinsed my face several more times before blotting away the excess with a paper towel. Then I had to spend a few minutes repairing the makeup I'd so carefully applied that morning. It's not easy to achieve a "no makeup" natural look, but done right it's worth the effort.

Val and Granimi were chatting quietly when I returned, the gleam of successful journeys in their eyes. They asked if I had met my power animal and I said yes, and that I wasn't ready to talk about it.

Raven led the group in debriefing the experience, answering questions and reassuring the two participants who were unsuccessful that it is absolutely normal for meeting a power animal not to happen until a second or even third journey, a statement that was undermined by the majority of us who had no difficulty with the process.

A few eager beavers were bursting to tell us all about their success, but Raven intervened. "Some of you are eager to talk about this," he pointed out. "But don't be in a hurry to give away your power. This experience is yours alone. You do not have to keep it entirely secret, but journeys are like dreams. They are not as interesting or meaningful to others as they are to you."

Discussion continued for several minutes, then Raven talked about ways we could use the journey process for self-healing (using 'healing' in the broadest possible sense), and mentioned that in the afternoon session we would explore the role of the shaman as healer for individuals and the community, and then we broke for lunch.

The groupies massed around Raven as the rest of us gathered up our things and discussed the lunch question. I wasn't immune to the desire to be teacher's pet, but was way above jockeying for position. If the opportunity arose, I might try flirting after class.

Or not. It was a bit nice and a whole lot scary to admit I was drawn to him. Then there was the self-flagellation at my disloyalty to Brad. It had only been half a year. So why was guilt, not grief, holding me back? Was my possible interest in a new man an indictment of what I'd thought had been a good marriage, or was I just feeling the urge to couple? These questions were unsettling, and had my journey experience not been so intriguing and beautiful I might have bailed on the rest of the seminar.

One question that kept me around was curiosity about the degree to which my reluctant attraction to Raven might be reciprocated. He'd seemed to like me, too, but maybe he was a nice person who took an interest in everyone. Or maybe he'd pegged me as potential seminar fodder. If so, I had not disappointed. Not only had I shown up as promised, I'd brought Granimi, Val, Ansel, and Tulip—who'd decided it sounded like fun—with me. Maybe I should ask for a commission.

I told myself to stop overthinking and let the day unfold.

Our group divided into male-female for a pit stop, and when I emerged from the restroom Raven was talking with Ansel in the foyer. I'd noticed Ansel seemed glum after the journey session. He'd nodded yes when we'd asked him if he'd met his power animal, but hadn't looked happy. Now Raven had a hand on his shoulder and a reassuring smile, and Ansel had perked up.

The community college parking lot abutted a strip mall with a Panera outpost. As we straggled across the grassy median at the edge of the campus, my mind wandered back to the meadow I'd crossed in the Lower World and the rumpled horizon line of trees in the middle distance and the arc of clear blue sky above. In my memory, I saw a small dark bird dart across the sky. Was that something I'd seen but not noticed in my journey, or an element added just now by my imagination? My fingers itched to capture it on a sketchpad, but all I'd brought to the seminar was a small notebook of lined paper.

"Hey, Granimi," I said as we approached the counter at Panera to place our orders, "I'm going to get something to go, instead of eating here. I'll see you all back at class after lunch."

While my Santa Fe Chicken sandwich was being prepared I walked down to the OfficeMax that anchored the mini-mall and bought a sketch book and some pens and colored pencils. Not my preferred medium, but it would do. I picked up my sandwich and strolled back to the OCCC campus, where I found a shady spot under a tree on a slight rise behind the building where the workshop was being held.

I'd eaten half my sandwich and filled three pages in the sketch book and was working on a fourth when I became aware of someone strolling between the trees toward me.

"Are you a fellow picnic enthusiast," Raven asked, halting a few feet away and hoisting a paper lunch bag of his own, "or just seeking a few minutes of solitude?" He noticed the sketchpad. "Communing with your muse?"

"Yeah." But it's not something I can do with an audience.

He hesitated. "Shall I leave you alone?" He waved his bag at further stretches of campus greenery. "There are other trees I can sit under."

"No, that's okay," I said. "Have a seat." Now that I'd been interrupted I'd feel too self-conscious to keep sketching if he might be just a few trees over.

"I thought you'd be lunching with your groupies," I said as he settled in the cool shade and pulled a paper-wrapped sandwich, an apple, and a bottle of water from his lunch bag.

"Lunch is my chance to get away from the groupies," he said with a smile, unwrapping his sandwich. "One reason I bring my own."

We ate in silence for a few minutes. I tried to relax and enjoy the simple pleasure of a shady tree on a summer afternoon, but really I was waiting for him to ask me what I'd been drawing in the sketchbook or how my first journey session had gone. When he didn't I wondered if that showed courtesy on his part, or a lack of interest. Would I sound like a groupie if I told him I'd enjoyed the morning session?

"It was nice of you to talk to Ansel after the session," I said. "I could tell something was bothering him, but he seems to have bounced back."

"Happens all the time," Raven said. "The power animal he met wasn't as impressive as he'd expected. Tends to bother guys more. It helps if they know they have more than one power animal. He'll meet up with one he likes better, if he keeps up the practice."

"He was hoping for a dinosaur. Or something equally ferocious."

"You can't always get what you want," he said.

"But we get what we need?"

"The lucky ones get both."

How the kiss happened I'm not sure, and by the time I realized I was reciprocating, he was drawing back.

"I didn't mean to do that," Raven apologized. "My groupies would be horrified."

"I didn't exactly push you away." I'd definitely kissed him back. I hadn't even worried about my garlic-chipotle breath.

"Entirely my fault. Forgot to keep my professional distance."

"Don't tell me you're going to start treating me like a groupie."

"No chance of that."

That time I did see it coming. I might even take some credit for initiating. Too bad we weren't in that private meadow in my Lower World where we could roll around in the grass all afternoon.

Voices wafting over from the parking lot restored us to a semblance of decorum.

"That's my peeps," I said. My distance vision in the real world is not as acute as it was during my journey, but Granimi is hard to miss. "I'll see you inside."

I grabbed my things and high-tailed it out of there, waiting until I was no longer obviously leaving Raven's company before hailing and joining up with the others. If Granimi knew I'd been making out with Raven she'd start treating him like my boyfriend, and I was so not ready to go there.

I apologized for skipping the group lunch and explained that I'd wanted to capture the morning's journey in some sketches. It felt good to reclaim my artist's prerogative to defy social norms. As rebellions go, bailing on lunch was bush-league, but still, it felt good.

32

R aven did his part to keep a neutral distance as the afternoon session got underway, and I so studiously avoided any possibility of eye contact that I missed half of what he said. Raven explained that we would now go on a journey on another person's behalf, and asked us to pair up with someone we did not know well. We all shrugged and gave wry smiles to our seminar buddies and looked around for an unknown. I found myself agreeing to partner with the first relative stranger with whom I made eye contact: Tulie.

"This is good," she said with a smile. "We can get to know each other better."

I gave her a forced smile back and pretended it was going to be fun. The idea of Tulip skipping around in her Lower World on my behalf made me uneasy. Sort of the way I'd rather she didn't let herself into my house and poke around in my fridge: it was sure to be full of things she didn't approve of. Like the fact that I'd put her on the "blonde women who could be having an affair with Alan and might have killed Rose" list. And that, though it seemed unlikely, I hadn't crossed her off that list yet.

Maybe that friendly smile hid a fear that I'd discover her deep dark secrets, too. Maybe I would find out something interesting about her. So long as the mutual journey experience didn't make her think we were going to be friends.

Raven explained how it would work as we shuffled around and tried to think of a pertinent but not too revealing issue for our partners to journey on.

"Okay," I said, after some mental fidgeting, "I've got a question." My first thought had been to ask how to get my painting groove back, but my sketchbook already held the answer to that. My second thought had been to ask if I should sell my house. My third idea was the best one.

"I'm ready, too," Tulie said. "What's your question?"

"This is going to sound weird, so just trust that it means something to me."

She agreed, and I told her my question. She didn't get it, and we had to get past that, but the other pairs had settled down on their mats and Raven was scouting the room to see how close the class was to being ready to go.

"We're out of time," I said. "What's your question?"

She bit her lip and paused another long moment before taking the plunge. "Mine's rather sensitive, so promise not to say anything about it to anyone." She tilted her head toward where Granimi and Ansel were paired off and Val was with a plump young woman in a peacock blue sweatshirt. "I don't want this getting back to Ansel."

I made the zipped-lip motion. "Believe it or not, I'm very good at keeping secrets." Sometimes. Depends on the secret.

"Oh, good. Thank you. You know, I was really not sure I should ask this, but I feel I can trust you."

And if you get around to telling me what it is, we could get this show on the road.

"I want to know if my husband is having an affair," Tulip said quickly in a quiet voice. She'd noticed Raven circulating, and hurried to lie down and look composed. "Or maybe just feeling tempted."

Oh, thanks a lot, Tulip! You might want to keep in mind I'm a beginner at this. What if I'm no good at journeying for someone else? What does that do to your marriage?

"Everything okay over here?" Raven asked, crouching down.

"We're all set." I mentally rolled my eyes, embarrassed and annoyed at being the laggard of the class, but I wasn't the one who'd taken forever to spit her question out.

"Excellent," Raven said. I felt his palm rest for a moment on my shoulder. Was that a private signal or did he recognize that I was nervous about the journey-for-someone-else assignment?

"Okay," he addressed the entire class as he moved away, "let's get started. Remember, your first objective is to reconnect with your power animal. As you make your way to the Lower World, mentally ask your power animal to meet you. It's possible that some of you will meet a new power animal, or not connect with one this time. That's okay. If you do meet a new animal, remember to confirm that it is willing to help you before sharing any information. If you don't get an affirmative answer, keep moving until you meet a helper or gain information in another way."

Then the drumming began and I imagined myself in the room beneath the stairs again.

*   *   *

By the time the seminar ended I was so enraptured with vistas of the shamanic world that I was tempted to hand off my car keys to Granimi so I could huddle in the passenger seat with my sketch pad while she drove. I settled for getting us home safely, then left Granimi and Val in charge of making or ordering in the dinner of their choice while I retreated to Brad's study to call Suzette.

Who, as I remembered when I got bumped to voice mail, had plans with Bob. Darn, and I had news.

"Cross Tulip off the list," I said after the tone. "Call me if you wanna know why."

Brad's study was peaceful and quiet, his enormous leather chair inviting. I retrieved my sketchpad from the kitchen table where we'd all dumped our stuff, grabbed some art supplies from the garage, and told Granimi and Val that I would fend for myself when I got hungry. I then sequestered myself in Brad's den and gave expression to the virtual landscapes I'd traveled that day.

It had been nice to meet a power animal, but it was the place itself more than what I had experienced there that entranced me. When I'd captured sufficient fragments to fuel a dozen paintings it was after nine o'clock and I was overdue for a meal. Pausing at the foot of the stairs, I could hear the faint strumming of Val on her guitar upstairs. A peek into the living room revealed Granimi slumped on the couch, head back, snoring gently. She looked peaceful, and, with her lively spirit in temporary retreat, about a thousand and ten years old. I lifted off the reading glasses that were slipping from their perch atop her head and draped an afghan over her.

I believed Granimi was capable of taking care of herself, in spite of her wrist and my mother's concern, but she looked so ancient and fragile I felt acutely aware that she didn't have limitless years left. I hoped she would stay with me awhile so I could enjoy her loopy company while I had the chance.

I made a quick dinner wrap out of leftover chicken and salad, poured a glass of wine, and went back to my studio. Wait a minute, I thought, as I was about to step into the den, my studio's in the garage, right?

But what use did Brad have for a den these days?

I set my dinner on Brad's desk and looked at his huge TV and gigundo club chair. How long did I plan to keep this guy stuff in my house? If I sold the house it would all have to go and if I stayed, what was the plan, to keep this room as a shrine to my dear departed? Hadn't I decided to try getting on with life post-Brad, even if I had to do it in baby steps?

A bottle of Brad's favorite single malt graced a shelf below the goofballs, the burnished liquid a lovely amber in the room's soft lighting. Brad loved the stuff, but I'd just as soon sip kerosene from a dirty tennis shoe.

Maybe Alan would like it. I could take it over to him sometime when I needed a reason to follow up on a clue. If we ever got a clue.

Maybe Brad would enjoy a last drop before I gave the rest of the bottle away.

I poured him half an inch in a heavy crystal tumbler from a set we'd purchased on a trip to Scotland a few years ago. We'd enjoyed the time away from home and work and Olivia, who'd been a prickly 13-year-old with a mood repertoire ranging from sullen to surly. Thank God she'd come out the other side of that phase. I checked my watch. It was either too late or too early to call Italy.

"Here's to you, honey." I placed the tumbler on the shelf next to Brad's ashes. "Drink up, 'cause I'm taking over this space."

Custom cabinetry lined both side walls of the room, and the long wall housed Brad's enormous plasma TV. The room seemed smaller than it was because of all the oversized furniture. A mahogany partner's desk filled one end of the space, the huge leather club chair and matching ottoman—and side table convenient for placing the remote and a glass of scotch—the other. A large, deep-piled rug in shades of crimson and gold completed the men's club atmosphere.

If I've learned one thing from all the hours I've wasted watching HGTV it's that décor makes the room, and décor can be changed. I looked at the built-ins as useful storage space, and saw how during daylight hours the room would be bright with light from the oriel window high on the wall. Without the ginormous entertainment center I'd gain a lot of wall and floor area. Somewhere behind those dark plantation shutters—which hadn't been opened since Brad first settled into the deep satisfaction of his club chair and realized there was glare on the TV screen—was a lovely triple window.

How had I not noticed before what a wonderful painting studio this room would make? I felt a giddy smile creep up from somewhere deep inside and spread across my face.

33

Sunday morning I made a brief appearance in the kitchen to hand off the newspaper to Granimi, confer with Val about her schedule for the coming week, and refuel my coffee mug. Then I headed for the garage in search of a stepstool and the tool box. Shadow padded along behind me, whether curious what was up or hoping I would drop a mouse I couldn't say.

"You may remember that this garage hasn't been working for me as a studio," I told the cat, "so I'm taking over Brad's study." Shadow mrowped something that might have been approval or a request for more breakfast, and followed me back into the house.

Twenty minutes later the dark plantation shutters were down and the triple window of what would be my studio was revealed in all its glory. The shrubs along the front of the house had grown up, and the windows themselves were grubbier than I'd anticipated, but even so the room was now bright enough that I could turn off the overheads and move around without bumping into the furniture. Shadow sniffed at a shutter then jumped to the windowsill to see what birds might lurk in the bushes on the other side of the glass.

"What are you up to in here?" Granimi peered around the doorframe.

"I'm turning Brad's study into a painting studio."

"That's a wonderful idea, dear. Oh, look at those nice windows. It was so gloomy in here before."

"A few gallons of white paint will take care of that."

"Oh, Lena, it must have cost a fortune to put in all this cabinetry. Are you sure you want to paint over it?"

She was right, and I didn't care. "It's going to be my studio," I said. "And it's going to be white."

Granimi made an it's your party gesture and settled into the club chair for a test drive, easing her slippered feet onto the ottoman. "I feel like a child in this enormous chair. Was Brad really such a big man? I don't remember."

"Larger than life," I confirmed. "But not in need of this furniture any more."

If I couldn't sell the stuff I'd donate it to Goodwill, but hoped someone would fork over cash for it. I made a mental note to invite Bob over for a look-see. If he didn't want the guy stuff, he might know someone who would.

"If you cut those bushes back," Granimi said, "you'd have a lot more light in here."

"On the list," I assured her. "First I need to stash these shutters in the garage. No, you are not allowed to carry anything heavy. I'll take care of that." I looked around for a task that might keep her out of trouble. "Why don't you go through these books," I suggested, "and see if any are worth keeping. If it's about business or politics, or the words 'golf' or 'Tom Clancy' appear anywhere on the cover, put it in the 'to go' pile."

"That sounds like something I can do," she said.

"Great. I've got some boxes in the storage room you can put the books in."

The house phone rang as I returned from hauling shutters to the garage. I hoped it would be Olivia, who'd promised to call "over the weekend" but hadn't yet.

"Hey, what's this about crossing Tulip off our list?" Suzette wanted to know. "I thought you were going to prove that a conniving, adulterous bitch lurks beneath that sunny exterior."

"Yeah, I was. All that healthy eating and good cheer made me think the worst of her," I admitted. "But new information has come to light."

"Do tell! But make it snappy. Bob's out of the shower and eager for a man appropriate brunch somewhere."

"Couldn't get him to settle for a bowl of Special K, huh?"

"He refuses to eat, and I quote, 'chick flakes,' when Ken's House of Bacon is such a short drive away."

Can't say I blame him. I'd rather eat grease at Ken's Waffle House than Special K myself. "Guys need their bacon," I stated. Fact of life. Like girls need chocolate. Damn, now I wanted a big breakfast, too, with bacon, or maybe sausage links, and scrambled eggs, and something high-carb floating in a pool of maple syrup. Or maybe a Dove bar.

"Lena, snap-snap: the Tulip poop."

"She loves her husband and is afraid he's going to leave her and/or is having an affair."

"Maybe all he wants is someone who will let him eat bacon."

"My feelings exactly." Suzette was more accurate than she knew. "Anyway, no way is Tulip Alan's mystery mistress."

"I thought we thought it was that blonde you saw him with on the street."

"We do, but that could have been a business lunch or something. Which left Tulip in the game. Now we know she was also genuinely fond of Rose. If she weren't so busy smiling about how good it feels to be vegan she'd think something was up with that, too, just like us."

"I want to hear how you know that, but it'll have to wait. Just so I'm clear: now we like her, as in like her, not like, like her as a suspect?"

"If that's your idea of clear, Suze, we're in trouble, but yes, in my professional opinion Tulip is no longer list-worthy."

"Too bad. How many other women in this town are named after flowers?"

"Yeah. I'm bummed it's not her, if only for the name thing."

Suzette snickered. "It's eating you up, admit it."

"I so totally wanted to hate her," I whined. "What's life without a goody-two-shoes around to make fun of? Turns out, though, she really is nice. I feel like a toad for being snarky about her all week."

"There's plenty of snark bait out there, hon, I'm sure we can find you some. But I gotta go." Suze said she'd swing by later to check out the ultimate brownie bake-a-thon and report in on focus group progress, which she'd taken charge of. I went back to helping Granimi box up Brad's books for the next library sale.

"Find anything interesting?" I unloaded an armload of flattened shipping boxes and wondered what I'd done with the packing tape.

"As a matter of fact, I did." Granimi climbed down from the shelf she'd been clinging to like a monkey. I refrained from pointing out that, nimble though she was, confining her activity to somewhere in the general vicinity of the stepstool might be a good idea.

She handed me a large, musty, leather-bound volume and watched me open it. It was an old photo album.

"Look at that," I said of a 19th century couple, grim-faced and formal, posed in front of a photographer's backdrop of a European-looking vista complete with fake ruins. "I think that's a real tintype." I turned a few pages then flipped to the back where photos of more recent vintage—early 70s, judging by the clothes—resided. "Oh my god, that must be Brad's junior high graduation." Look at that hair!

I looked at another page or two then set the book aside, thinking it ought to go to Amanda or William. Maybe they'd know who some of the people in it were. Grandparents of the great-great-great kind, probably.

"And take a look at this." Granimi passed me a newer hardcover without a jacket. Song of Mississippi, according to the spine.

"This doesn't look like Brad's kind of ... oh." It was a fake book with a hollow compartment inside.

Granimi nodded. "A secret compartment book! I've always wanted one."

"It's your lucky day, then." I dumped the contents of the book into my palm and passed her the fake volume. "Put something fun in it."

The phone rang again. Hoping again that it was Olivia, I pocketed the dark blue velvet pouch I'd just palmed, trying to feel what was in it—a ring, maybe, and something bumpy—and picked up the hall extension.

"You're making things very difficult for me, you know," a man's voice said.

"I know lots of things," I replied cautiously, after a startled pause. "But who you are isn't one of them."

"Oh. It's Raven. Santiago."

"Ah, that Raven." Like I know lots of them. Shit, I was smiling. Not a good sign.

"If you had a picture phone you'd see I look chagrinned," he said apologetically.

"Who needs a picture phone when they've got an imagination?"

He laughed. "You're in fine form this morning."

"I am, actually. Thanks for noticing." It was a good morning, now that I'd noticed, too. I felt empowered by taking over Brad's study, plus a boy had called me on the phone. I felt better than I had since... you know.

The long pause almost felt awkward. I was happy that Raven had called, plus the thrill of being in a good mood for the first time in months.

"So how exactly am I making things difficult for you?" I asked. "Without even trying, I might add."

"Well, there's the fact that yesterday you expressed some interest in booking a Soul Retrieval."

"Since when are private clients not a good thing?" I could hardly believe I'd decided to go for the Soul Retrieval, but odd as it sounded it had felt like a good idea after the afternoon session. Even odder, I was looking forward to it.

"Since my interest in this particular private client is not entirely professional," he said.

"Oh." The kiss. Yeah, that had been a good one.

"Right. So, on the one hand I am calling to schedule your appointment for a Soul Retrieval, should you still feel that's something you want to do."

"It is. I think. Yes. Yes, I'm sure. I want to do it." Enough waffling already. Even though the flirtation was as terrifying as it was fun, I felt safe with Raven, confident he would be gentle with my secrets.

"Good. You mentioned afternoons are better for you, so how's this Wednesday at 1:45."

"That sounds fine." I'd have to drop Val at Nature Group early, but that wouldn't be a problem.

"Okay then. The session will take about an hour. My fee is two hundred dollars, which covers Dorothy's time as well. She's going to drum for us. I accept cash, check, or PayPal."

"Can I pay you Wednesday?" I didn't know how much I had in my PayPal account. The daughter sounded good. She could ward off inappropriate distractions.

"Of course."

More silence. "You handled that very professionally," I said.

"Good."

"So, was there an unprofessional part to this call?" I caught a look at myself in the mirror over the hall console table. That happy smirk made me look like an idiot. And my hair needed a trim. I turned my back to the mirror and fingered the velvet pouch in my pocket. Best guess: a key and a ring, and a lumpy oval something.

Raven ahemmed.

"Geeze," I said. "I haven't made a guy sound that awkward in years. I'm flattered."

"As you should be. I haven't felt this awkward in years."

"So, you could just ask me out and get it over with," I suggested. And I was afraid I'd forgotten how to flirt.

"Excellent idea. How's dinner on Thursday?"

I couldn't believe I was going to do this, but hell yes. "Sounds great."

Oh my God, I thought, as I hung up after scribbling down his address and directions for Wednesday's session.

I'd agreed to go on a date.

With a man named Raven.

What would Brad think of this? I imagined his spirit giving me a wry shrug and a thumbs-up. He wouldn't love the idea of another man in my life, but he'd want me to be happy. Eventually. Whether or not he'd agree that six months was a sufficient period of mourning I wasn't so sure. But what could he do about it? Haunt me?

Okay, regretting that thought.

The thing is, even though I felt that I still had all of one foot and half of the other in my marriage to a dead guy, hooking up with someone else was going to be part of my future happiness. I wasn't even 40 yet, after all, and being single for long doesn't seem to be in my genetic code.

Shit, what was I going to wear? Not only had I agreed to go on a date, but I had to look good for the Soul Retrieval, too. Without, of course, betraying any hint that I'd primped. I'd better get Suze over for a wardrobe and hair consult.

34

"Don't you look like the cat that ate the canary," Granimi said. I was still leaning against the console table in the hall in something close to a state of shock. She'd clearly been eavesdropping, not that I blamed her.

"Oh my God, G." I felt equally pleased and appalled by what I'd gotten myself into. "Not only am I having something called a Soul Retrieval, but I also just agreed to a date."

"Good for you, dear." She patted my arm. "You and Raven make a wonderful couple."

"Foot off the gas, granny! The Soul Retrieval thing is strictly professional, and the date is just a date. I'm recently widowed, in case that's slipped your mind. I'm not in any hurry to get paired up again."

"That doesn't mean it won't happen," she pointed out. "Besides, six months is long enough to mope around the house. Doesn't mean you're done grieving for Brad, but you need to get some sunshine back into your life, and the sooner the better if you ask me."

"Speaking of sunshine," I said, eager to change the subject, "how are you on washing windows?" I couldn't do much about the outside glass until the shrubbery was pruned into submission, but the inside panes were ready for Windex.

A roll of paper towels later the windows were sparkling, at least on one side. Granimi admitted to feeling over the cleaning thing and in a mood to update her blog, and I was wondering what to do with all the non-book stuff left on the shelves. Brad's collection of bronze animal figurines was probably worth decent money. He'd understand if I sold them.

The amateur golf trophies on the other hand—local small-time stuff, displayed with pride nonetheless—posed a challenge. I couldn't sell them, 'cause who would buy them? And it seemed disloyal to throw them away. I decided to pack them up in boxes for storage in the bonus space over the garage. By the time I next looked at them enough time might have passed that I'd be ready to consign them to the dump. Sorry honey, just keeping it real.

First task, move it all off the shelves so I can prep for paint. Not that I had paint yet, but with Val's activity list requiring so many trips around town it would be easy to swing by Home Depot. I'd rather hire someone to do it but they'd probably want to be paid.

The doorbell chimed: Ansel, wondering if Val were home.

"I think she's upstairs." I had an idea though, if he was bored and looking for something else to do besides rate Val's ESP ability. "Hey, can I interest you in being my research assistant for a couple of hours?"

"Uh, sure. I guess." He showed more interest when I said I would compensate him for his time. "Researching what?"

I showed him Brad's collection of bronzes, and explained that I wanted some idea what they were worth, and how I might go about selling them.

"See who's selling stuff like this on eBay," I suggested, "and what kind of prices they're getting. Also look for art galleries that specialize in this sort of thing."

I showed him that each bronze had a label on the base, with the artist's name. "So you can start making a list of those."

"Okay," Ansel said. "When do you need this? And can I do it at my house?"

"Wherever and whenever you like," I said, wiping down a shelf. What had I been thinking when I told Hanna not to bother cleaning in here? "It's not a rush job, so whenever you get to it will be fine."

I authorized three hours of Ansel's time at a reasonable-for-a-minor rate, and he took some photos of the bronzes and their labels with his phone, pointed out to me that the base of one was loose, then disappeared in the direction of Val's enthusiastic if not particularly tuneful guitar strumming.

I began to move the golf trophies off the shelves and onto Brad's desk so I could finish cleaning. When I picked up Brad's award from the 2007 Laurelton Invitational I discovered that base was loose, too. As I tipped it upside down for a diagnostic look, I managed to smack the tiny golfer's head against the edge of a shelf and it snapped off and fell to the floor. Oops. With a little careful handling, the question of what to do with these trophies would take care of itself.

Olivia finally called, and then Mom checked in to let me know that Olivia should spend more time with her boring grandparents instead of running off to Paris with her friends. Dad said he was staying out of it and otherwise having a wonderful time, too bad I hadn't come along. I returned to study conversion forty minutes later to find Shadow batting the plastic golfer's head around the floor of my future studio.

The head rolled to a stop against my foot. Shadow looked up at me and waited, tail twitching, until I kicked the head away so he could chase it some more. When I picked up what remained of the trophy to put it in the trash, the column on which the decapitated golfer posed came out of the base. What a flimsy piece of crap.

Turns out, the column was loose because someone, I presumed Brad, had inserted a small piece of rolled-up paper into it, and had mangled the reassembly step.

Getting the paper out of there required some patience and the use of my eyebrow tweezers. Eventually I was able to unroll and read it: "3-18-2" and the words "best day ever" in Brad's distinctive hand on what looked like ordinary scrap paper.

The 'best day ever' clue reminded me why those numbers were significant. One fabled day in the first or maybe second year of our marriage, Brad had risen before dawn to set out on the course at first light and had swung, chipped, splunked, splashed, plopped, plotzed, or whatever they called it when you chase a little white ball through three complete eighteen-hole games of a charity golf marathon. At the end of which he'd sauntered up to the clubhouse bar, fatigued and triumphant with an average of two under par. "Under par" is one of the few golf phrases I'm almost comfortable throwing around. It means you've done well, which is just one reason golf doesn't make sense. I don't pay much attention to sports, but I do know that usually the highest score wins.

Why did Brad preserve these numbers on a hidden scrap of paper? Did he fear dementia would someday erase that fabled day from his memory? Did he not realize that even his devoted but golf-immune wife—having heard the story many, many more times than she'd cared to—would be able to provide details on demand, even in her sleep, no matter how ancient and decrepit she might become? Besides, if his mind could no longer remember those numbers how did he expect to remember where to find the paper on which he'd written them down?

I was surprised Brad hadn't commemorated the glorious day with something permanent, like a tattoo. Then again, if he'd been a tattoo kind of a guy I'd never have married him (been there, done that: husband #2). Brad had his idiot moments but on the whole was an astute and intelligent man. Something was up.

The obvious conclusion: it's a combination to something. Something locked, to keep other somethings inside it from prying eyes. Something like a safe.

Which reminded me of the thing that felt like a key in the velvet pouch I'd stashed in my pocket. I pulled out the pouch, saw it was worn and threadbare now that I took a closer look, opened it, and placed the contents on Brad's desk.

"What do you make of this?" I asked Shadow, who had jumped up on the desk. I pulled him into my lap and held him there in case he thought these might be fresh toys: a brass key (antique); a delicate gold ring (small, engraved with a viney pattern and set with a dark red stone that was probably garnet); and the lumpy oval object that turned out to be a cameo carved with a rose motif.

Shadow wasn't interested in any of it, but the ring fit my pinky, barely. Pretty, but not my style. Neither was the cameo. I wondered if the rose was significant, and couldn't imagine how, even given the current Rose situation. As for the key, it probably unlocked something. Although I also had a code that looked like a combination, so what did I need both for?

"Brad, you doofus," I said aloud. "You couldn't just leave a sealed envelope with your lawyer, 'to be opened in the event of my death'? Or a note to your wife: 'Darling, if anything happens to me, here's the combination to the safe'?"

Sheesh. This is what happens when guys don't outgrow their fascination with secret decoder rings.

Okay, I'm looking for a safe or other combination lock (unless the numbers are a code for something else) and for something that opens with a key. Maybe the thing that opens with a key was in the safe.

If there was a safe.

Of course there was a safe. Brad was the kind of guy who would have wanted a secret safe even if he had nothing to put in it. Why hadn't I thought of that before? Or maybe Brad had left me a clearly worded "in the event of my demise" note in his desk and I hadn't thought to look for it until now.

The drawers in both Brad's desk and his file cabinets had locks, but the key from the pouch didn't fit them and they were all unlocked anyway. Nothing in any of them opened with a key. Nothing manufactured in the last hundred years, probably, opened with that key.

What I did find in the top right-hand desk drawer was a fat manila folder full of mail. Mail that had arrived after Brad's death. I'd tossed obvious junk and opened anything that looked like a bill. Everything else I'd set aside to go through when I got around to it, figuring if I overlooked anything truly urgent someone would eventually let me know. I had a vague memory of moving the mail pile off the kitchen table and into this drawer and, as the inflow slowed to a trickle, adding to it less and less often.

I really ought to have gone through this stuff. So much for the virtues of cleaning up: if I'd let it pile up in the kitchen I would have done something about it by now.

No time like the present, Mom would say. I was tempted to take the express route and toss the whole lot in the trash, but felt I should at least glance at contents before moving things to the circular file. Most if it was bank and credit card statements that I don't look at anyway because I keep my eye on things online. Those could be filed until aged enough to shred. Everything else was, as suspected, of no interest or importance.

Except one envelope, near the bottom of the pile, that contained a check. Not a big check—$218.72—but a check nonetheless, dated a week after Brad's death. More interesting was the account holder name: Zaff Investigations, with a PO box in Orchard City. Curiouser and curiouser. I set the check aside to take to the bank, and turned to the several sheets of paper in which it had been wrapped.

One was a statement that showed initial payment of $5,000 on Job 2467, and itemized a week or so of services rendered, various small expenses of the parking and postal variety, and "balance of deposit returned: $218.72." A hand-written note on a sheet of letterhead added, "Please accept our condolences on the passing of Mr. Wells."

What was Job 2467? Two possibilities came to mind: 1) it's work-related; 2) it's not. Not meant personal, which implied... me?

Why would my darling husband investigate me? Even if I wanted to cultivate an air of seductive mystery and hint at a secretive past, I doubt I could pull it off. I get a few points for secrets, but they're of the youthful indiscretions and embarrassing mishaps kind, well short of murder, mayhem, and assorted felonies.

Let's assume work-related, then. Brad was, I'd thought, pretty good about sharing a general picture of those things that amused, irked, or stressed him about his day. If questioned about why he looked so tense (or peeved, or twinkly, as the case might be) he'd oblige with something more detailed than, "I don't want to talk about it."

I'll be the first to admit that I didn't always pay the closest attention to what Brad shared about his work life, but I'd thought I was up to speed on most developments that transcended business as usual. It did not escape my attention now that although Zaff Investigations was on the check and letterhead, it was not on the envelope, which had been sent to our home, not to Brad's business address. Brad had played something close to the vest.

One easy way to find out what this was about. "What do you think, should I give this guy a call?" I turned to look for Shadow's response, but he'd wandered off. If you want devoted attention, get a dog.

I squinted at the phone number on the letterhead and had started to dial Brad's desk phone when I noticed the line was dead. Right, I'd had it disconnected months ago as part of my cut-the-fat approach to budget management. I grabbed the cordless from the hall and retreated back to Brad's desk, closing the door behind me for privacy.

I was mentally composing a message to leave on voice mail, when the call went through.

"Zaff Investigations. Kevin Zaff speaking."

"Oh, uh, hi. I didn't expect anyone to be there on Sunday."

This is where you pause to let the other guy say something like, "Thought I'd come in to catch up on paperwork while it's quiet," or "We're open 24/7 ma'am," or whatever, but he wasn't going for it.

"This is Lena Wells, Bradford Wells's wife, uh, widow. I guess you know that Brad died a few months ago."

"I was sorry to hear he'd passed," Kevin Zaff said with a neutral tone. "What can I do for you, Mrs. Wells?"

"You can tell me about this check you sent over some time ago for," I reached for the check, "two hundred eighteen dollars and seventy-two cents."

"That sounds about right."

"Says here on the statement that it's a balance of deposit on job number 2467?"

"That sounds about right."

That sounded a bit tight-lipped, but I guess that's a good quality in an investigator.

"I'm curious what job 2467 was," I said. "There are no details on the statement."

"We provided Mr. Wells with a written report at our meeting on," pause for keyboard sounds, "December 9 of last year."

Written report, huh. Was that somewhere here, too? A quick flip through the rest of the miscellaneous-addressed-to-Brad file turned up nothing. Maybe it was in the file cabinet. Or in the safe, if there was a safe. Mustn't forget to look for that.

"The report hasn't turned up yet," I said, as if I'd been searching for it for days. "Perhaps you could shed some light on the matter."

"No offense, Mrs. Wells. but you are not my client, and we take our confidentiality agreements very seriously."

"As I hope you would," I said agreeably. I'd noticed that the check was accompanied by a photocopy of Brad's original deposit: a check drawn on our Fidelity account. "Thing is, Brad hired you with a check drawn on a joint account of which I am now the sole account holder. I haven't cashed your refund check yet, which could mean, should you look at it this way, that you're still on the job, and that I am now your client."

The pause was longer this time. I pictured a balding guy in a wrinkled shirt with the sleeves rolled up, ample gut framed by worn suspenders, twisting his swivel chair from side to side and wishing he still smoked as he considered the possibilities, both pro and con, of being just a tad more forthcoming.

He sighed deeply.

I waited.

"Okay. This isn't how I'd ordinarily handle things, but that was shaping up to be an interesting case. If you want me to take it a step further I'll see what I can do. Two hundred bucks will buy you a couple hours of my time."

Dude, seriously. "I'm not prepared to tell you to 'take it a step further,'" I tried to hide my growing exasperation, "until you tell me what 'it' is."

This call had been a mistake. I should have cornered him in his office on Monday; maybe he was the kind of guy I could bat my eyelashes at. Or I could pull Distraught Widow out of mothballs and give her another shot at the limelight. It was harder to pull off over the phone. Plus, that role was feeling old.

"How 'bout," I suggested, "we start with what, or who, Brad hired you to look into. Was this a background check on a potential employee, or something else? Because it seems to me that if it was ordinary work-related, he would have paid you by company check and had your mail sent to his office. So I'm guessing it was something he didn't want his partner or assistant to know about."

Pause.

"How'm I doing so far?"

"Not bad."

Doing pretty well reining in my frustration, too, but that grip was slipping.

"Look, Kevin." I infused as much warmth as I could summon into my voice. "Let's try something really easy. Yes or no: were you looking at me?"

"Uh, no ma'am. You were not the subject of our inquiries."

Good. Didn't think so, but nice to get that out of the way.

"Always good to start with the obvious," he conceded.

Wow. Progress. If Mr. Zaff didn't watch it he might slip right over into informative.

"Okay, next most obvious. Yes or no, were you looking at Martin—" shit, what was his last name? I always thought of him as Mahvelous Mahtin, "—ah, what's-his-name. Brad's assistant."

Come to think of it, when had he quit? Probably after Brad had hired this guy. Had Mahvelous Mahtin been helping himself to the petty cash?

"Nope."

Good. I liked Martin. Let's see, who's next. Oooh, got it: "His ex wife was causing trouble again."

"Nope."

He actually sounded amused by that guess. Clearly he'd never met Alicia. I haven't either, but her antics are legendary. Okay, business. Brad ran a small ship, partnering with others as necessitated by the specifics of each project. The big one, at the time he'd died, was the one he'd fallen from.

"Alan Braska, then."

"Bingo."

"Oh. Cool." Funny how I felt like a winner when it had taken four tries to get it right.

"Why cool?"

"Uh, because I finally got something from you."

"Ah."

"Are you saying that something uncool was going on?" I'd learned not to rush the master of the ponderous pause.

"Define 'uncool.'"

Oh, you've got to be kidding me. "Gee, Kevin, it would be so much easier if you would just talk to me." At this point he had to be stalling for the fun of it. "Okay, let's see, I'd define 'uncool,' in this context, as anything from, say, sneaky-bastard behavior to the illegal, immoral, unethical, and/or litigious."

"That would about cover it."

"Come on, Kev. We're getting along so well. Tell me what 'it' is already."

He considered that. "'It,' in this context, is more on the sneaky-bastard end of the scale, with some immoral and unethical thrown in, and—the main reason for your husband's concern—possible illegalities."

"I heard that chuckle, Kevin. I know you're toying with me."

"I take my fun where I can find it, Mrs. Wells."

"So glad I could brighten your day."

"It's much appreciated. Spending a summer Sunday in the office because the paperwork has piled up isn't my idea of a good time."

Okay, that was weird. Somehow we'd gone from unforthcoming to what could maybe, almost, be called a flirtatious tone. I figured Raven had filled my flirtatious phone call quota for the day, and besides, the mental image I'd formed of this guy wasn't appealing.

"It might interest you to know," I said, "that Mr. Braska's wife died recently, under what some might think are suspicious circumstances."

I'd say that shut him up but probably I shouldn't take credit, given his penchant for lengthy pauses.

"How about that," he said at last.

"Yeah, how about that."

"Somewhat suspicious circumstances, you say."

"I do."

"You know." He sighed as though it was gonna kill him to say it. "I don't want to get into this over the phone—"

What, he thought Alan was tapping my line?

"—so what say we meet up and I'll share what I know."

Really? I wasn't entirely confident, based on our conversation thus far, that Kevin Zaff defined "share" the same way I do. Probably he was stalling because he wanted to check me out first. I couldn't fault the guy for being careful.

"Okay. We could do that. When and where?"

"Let's say Tuesday, mid-day. You're still in Laurelton?"

I told him I was. "Prospect Heights neighborhood, but I can meet you in town somewhere, or even come to Orchard City."

"In town is good. You know that bakery on Elm, added a café a few years back?"

"SweetiePies." Oh yes. Third-best brownies in town, and I can say that definitively.

"That's the one."

"Perfect. Is one o'clock okay?"

"Make it twelve-thirty," he said, "and you've got a deal."

"Great. I'll see you then. Oh, wait. Let's exchange cell numbers, just in case."

We did, and look at that. I had a meeting with a genuine, real-life PI on Tuesday. This could be fun. Suzette would want to come along, but I didn't think Kev would go for that. I'd have to meet him alone.

35

I was eager to look for Kevin Zaff's report but while I was on the phone Hanna had arrived for our brownie baking extravaganza. The report, and the safe—if there was one—would have to wait. For the first time in my life I felt reluctant to participate in an activity involving baked goods.

Hanna brought extra mixing bowls, baking pans, and cooling racks borrowed from Rose's kitchen. We got organized—refusing kitchen entry to Shadow, who appeared intent on getting cat hair in the brownies—and started in. As we measured and stirred, I filled Hanna in on our plans to conduct a geriatric taste test. She agreed it was an excellent idea and suggested recording the sessions, which was even better. Ansel could be in charge of that.

"Here's something odd," I said, as we settled into a mix-and-bake rhythm. "The other night, at about 10:30, I heard Alan's garage door open and saw him drive away. I wondered where he would be going at that time of night."

Hanna paused in her fruitless attempt to keep the kitchen tidy as we went along, and gave me a blank look. "I never think what they do in the evening," she said. "I know they don't go out so much since Mrs. Rose get sick. That's late to leave the house, yeah?"

My sentiments exactly. "So you don't have any idea where he might have been going?"

She shook her head no. "I only know what happen when I'm at the house. Latest I ever stay, maybe eight o'clock. Usually I leave a lot before then." She bent down to crack open the oven door and peer in. "These ones ready to come out."

Either she didn't have any more of a clue than I did, or she didn't want to say.

By two o'clock cooling brownies covered every surface in my kitchen and chocoholics in the next county were sniffing the air and wondering what was up. Hanna advised that, tempted as we might be to hold a private taste test immediately, the brownie flavors would develop as they cooled and sat overnight.

Suzette showed up just in time to miss the massive cleanup effort, after which we moved to the pool deck with a late lunch of bacon and avocado sandwiches and a pitcher of iced tea. Suze filled us in on focus group plans—on for Tuesday at 3:00 at Woodside Meadows—and asked about the journey seminar. I stuck to generalities and omitted certain lunchtime events. Suze could hear about Raven developments later, when it was just the two of us. I did hoot a bit about artistic inspiration gained from the journey experience, and gave in to Granimi's entreaties to see my sketchbook.

"You didn't tell us your power animal is a turtle," Granimi said as she admired my drawings.

I hadn't intended it, but Turtle made an appearance in many of my sketches. I tried to downplay it in an attempt to forestall the inevitable; if I became known for a fondness for turtles the deluge of turtle-themed gifts would begin. I noticed as Granimi and Suzette admired my sketches that Hanna looked unhappy. When I asked if she were okay, she said the journey business, "does not sound like what a good Christian would do," which shut me up.

Hanna broke the awkward silence by getting to her feet and saying she had some things to do at home, so I accompanied her inside and helped pack up the borrowed baking equipment. I felt I should apologize for making her uncomfortable, but wasn't going to. I could have paid more attention when she'd mentioned coming over "after church," but still. Was it really God's plan for people to be so closed-minded? Seems to me that anyone with the vision and ability to create an entire cosmos in a week—and have a full day left over for napping—would appreciate curiosity and a sense of adventure.

Never mind. Hanna had been a great help with the brownies, and said she'd assist with the focus group on Tuesday afternoon and would be back on Wednesday to clean, so we left it at that.

The house was suspiciously quiet as I shut the front door behind Hanna. A call-out for Val got no response. Last I'd noticed Ansel was headed upstairs to interrupt her guitar practice, hours ago. Had they had lunch? And if the sequential aromas of baking brownies and sizzling bacon hadn't lured them into the kitchen, where the hell were they? Ansel's house, most likely.

"Where'd the kids disappear to?" I asked Granimi when I returned to the lunch table.

"They were talking about a bike ride," she said. "Ansel offered an extra bicycle for Val to use, and I thought it would be good for them to get away from the computer and get some fresh air and exercise."

Yeah, until they get into trouble. How long had they been gone, and did the extra bike for Val come with an extra helmet? I called Val's cell, and was relieved when she answered.

"We're at that park by the river," she said. "Ansel's teaching Fiona a new trick."

"Does Ansel's mom know where you are?"

"She's the one who said to take the dog with us."

"But does she know where you are?" Honestly. Kids.

"We told her we were headed over here. I bought us ice cream, is that okay?"

"Yes, honey, ice cream is fine. It's not fine that Granimi and I didn't know where you were. Next time call me before you go anywhere, even if Ansel's mom is in on the plans, okay?"

"Okay!"

"Good. Now, are you going to ride back here, or do you want me to pick you up?" I'd be tired if I rode to the park and back, but Val was probably in better shape than I am. And it's residential all the way, safe streets and not a lot of traffic on a Sunday afternoon.

"We're fine," Val said, as though being offered a ride home was the ultimate in dorkdom. "Really."

"Okay, but don't stay out much longer."

I could feel her eyes rolling through the phone. Fine. I'd trust the kids to take care of themselves. At least she hadn't ventured off on her own.

I knew I wouldn't really relax about Val until she got home, and tried to put mom concerns out of my mind by telling Granimi and Suzette about my journey experience with Tulie.

Yeah, I'd promised to keep it confidential, but Granimi and Suzette don't count.

* * *

I'd imagined my way through the earthen tunnel to the Lower World, hoping I'd return with relevant information. At first I'd been hesitant that a beginner could journey on someone else's behalf, but as I emerged into the meadow I realized my task was simple: just wander around and allow something to unfold. When the journey was over Tulie could tell me what it meant.

As I walked the meadow path a bright spot of red caught my eye. I moved closer to it, and saw that it was a tulip. Cool. Okay, what next? I looked around some more. For no good reason other than the impulse to do so, I left the path and after a few minutes of aimless wandering came to a large oak tree.

As I neared the tree I saw a pair of squirrels moving around on the bare ground near the trunk. I stopped to watch them. The female (how I knew that I don't know) appeared to be sorting a pile of nuts. The male squirrel moved purposefully in a wider circle. He frequently paused to look at the female, and from time to time he would look away, into the distance, and step a bit in that direction, then he would turn and move closer to her. He licked her face but although she paused to allow his attention soon she was moving and sorting and judging her stash of nuts, and he turned away.

"What do you think it means?" Tulip had asked when I described the journey to her.

"Me?" I'd said. "I thought you would tell me what it meant."

"Yes, I know that's the idea, but you seem to have a knack for this, so I'm curious what you think."

"Oh. Okay. If the squirrels are you and…" I'd forgotten her husband's name.

"Michael."

"Right. If the squirrels are you and Michael, then I think he worries about living up to your high standards. I think the looking away was him wondering if maybe he'd be happier elsewhere. I didn't get the impression, though, that he wanted to leave. He seemed to want to make you happy, but you don't slow down enough to let him do that."

"Oh God," she said. "That's so true. He takes pride in working hard to support us, and lately he hasn't seemed happy. I just don't know how to please him."

"I don't think he wants you to please him," I said. Where did that come from? Was I talking about the squirrel or her husband? I'd hadn't even met the guy. "I think he just wants to be able to relax, and you make that hard for him."

"Relax? That's all he wants? Just to relax?"

"Honey, we all need a day off sometimes. Let him know he doesn't have to spend every minute of the time he's home making it up to you for being away so much. Run him a bath. Tell him to go play golf instead of mowing the lawn. Feed him a pork chop."

Tulip gave me a horrified look.

Had I said that out loud? Well then, "You know what, Tulip? That's what my intuition had to say: maybe he just needs some guy food. Next time he's home, ask him what he really, truly, wants for dinner. If it's something radically non-vegan that you can't deal with cooking, go to a restaurant. Let him know you love him no matter what he eats."

"You think he doesn't want to be vegan anymore?" She looked more upset by that than anything else I'd said.

I made a valiant effort not to roll my eyes. "Tulip, for all I know he dreams about tofu and raw kale. All I'm saying is ask him what he wants. Then make sure he gets it, with lots of smiles from you."

By the time I'd finished my tale Suzette and Granimi were laughing so hard they had tears in their eyes.

"I can't believe you went on this grand esoteric journey and your advice was to feed the man a pork chop!" Suzette guffawed. "But what does that have to do with why she's off the maybe-she-did-it list?"

"Because, one, we've decided the most likely reason Rose died was to get her out of someone's way, and Tulip wants her own husband, not Rose's."

Suzette grimaced. "Can't say I blame her. Alan's on the dull side. Not to mention on the old side."

"Some women like older men," I pointed out. I hadn't meant me, but come to think of it, Brad had been older by almost 10 years, and Raven was probably—no, not going there. "Maybe Alan's had the money wife and now he wants a trophy wife. That can't be Tulip: trophy wives don't wear socks with their Birkenstocks."

"What was your other point, dear?" Granimi asked.

"My other point," I said with some satisfaction, "is that while I journeyed for her, Tulip was journeying for me. And my question to her was, 'Who gave Rose the brownie?'"

That shut them up. For about a nanosecond.

"You came right out and *asked* her?" Suzette was appalled. "Why would you do that?"

"Because if it was her, she would have been startled or scared," I said, "and I would have seen it. I realized yesterday that Tulip is so smiley and friendly because she's genuinely a happy, friendly person most of the time. She's not good at hiding her emotions."

"What was her reaction to your question, dear?"

"She didn't know about the brownie. She truly didn't get why I would ask her to," I made air quotes, "'waste the journey experience on something so trivial.' And then she was upset that I 'didn't trust her enough to ask a serious question.'"

"So what happened?" Suzette prodded. "Did she get an answer for you?"

"I'm not sure," I admitted. "The thing about this journey stuff is that it's metaphoric. You just saw that. I mean, Tulip asked me to find out if her husband was unhappy in their marriage and I saw squirrels scurrying around."

"What did Tulip see when she journeyed for you?" Granimi asked.

"She saw a house with rose bushes and a FOR SALE sign in the front yard. What does that tell you?"

"That Rose was planning to sell her house?" Suzette wondered.

"Maybe Rose's money is in real estate," G. suggested. Which at least some of it was, as she was the primary owner of the River Bend Terrace property.

"Maybe Tulip picked up on the question I didn't ask, about whether I should put this house on the market," I said.

"Oh." Granimi looked disappointed.

I shrugged. "That was what I was going to ask, before I got the idea to poke Tulie with a stick, so to speak, by asking about the brownie."

"So you think Tulie got an answer to what was on your mind," Suzette said, "even though that's not what you asked about?"

I shrugged again. "Maybe. I'm hardly an expert on the process."

"I bet that's what happened," Granimi said. "If you were thinking about the house, that question would be in the quantum field and Tulip could pick up on it. But why would you want to sell this lovely house, Lena?"

"We can discuss that later." If I told Granimi I had financial concerns she'd want to help out. Inheriting money from a dead husband, or even a dead grandmother, is one thing, but accepting bailouts from living family members makes me itch.

"The thing is," I went on, "Tulip didn't think she was any good at journeying. She apologized for not being helpful."

Then I grinned at them. "And then we got talking about real estate, and to reassure her the journey info wasn't a dud I explained that I'd almost asked her about selling my house. And she gave me her real estate agent's card. Said she'd been really happy and impressed with her, and I should give her a call."

"Why is that such good news?" Suzette asked.

"Because," I pulled the card out of my pocket, "remember what Edith Stokely said? About some woman named Gillian Tabor 'or something like that,' whose interest in the Garden Club was suspiciously self-serving."

I passed the card to Suzette.

"'Lillian Haber'? That's your big clue?"

"There is no Gillian Tabor in town," I said. "At least not that I could find in the phone book or online. Gillian Tabor, Lillian Haber… you don't think they could be the same person?"

"I suppose," she admitted. "It seems a bit flimsy."

"Suze, everything we've got so far is flimsy. We're going to let that stop us now?"

"I bet she's that blonde we saw with Alan the other day," Granimi said. "There was a real estate office in that building they went into. I remember that. Oh, this is exciting!"

"Bingo, Granimi!" I showed her the 421 Worth Street address on the card.

"Don't you see?" I said to Suzette. Maybe all that quality time with Bob had scrambled her brains. "We think Alan has a mistress. We saw him with a blonde. We got a real estate clue from the journey, and— here's something else—one of the mug shots on the Century 21 website looks like the blonde Alan was with, who also seems a good candidate for the Garden Club poseur Edith mentioned. So, of all the theories we've come up with, don't you think we should move 'Alan's mistress wanted his wife out of the way' to the top of the list?"

"Okay, I'm with you." Suzette said. "We should check her out. Any ideas how?"

"I'm going to show the headshot from the website to Edith," I said.

"See if this Lillian Haber is that Garden Club dropout she was talking about. Also, I could call the woman, tell her I'm thinking of selling and ask her to come look at my house. But other than good news or bad news on the home valuation front, what would we get from that, other than meeting her in person?"

"We could arrange for Alan to come by at the same time," Granimi suggested. "Invite him over for a home-cooked meal, and see how they act with each other."

"That's a great idea," Suzette said. "Can I come, too?"

"Of course," I said. "Hey, we could pretend we're trying to set you up with Allan, see how she reacts. No, that won't work. It's too soon for that."

"I'll keep an eye on things from my window," Granimi said. "We should be ready to follow him if he goes out at night again. Maybe he'll go to her house."

"It would help if we knew where she lives." I wondered if Ms. Haber was in the phone book. Could it be that easy?

"If we follow him and he goes to her house, we'll find out," Granimi said.

"We could follow her home from work," Suze suggested.

What are the chances we could successfully follow anyone anywhere? Slim to none, probably, though I was willing to try.

"I vote for seeing if she's in the phone book, first." I called information on my cell, and learned Lillian Haber had an unlisted number.

"Plan B: we follow her home from work. Once we know where she lives, it will be easier to follow Alan at night to see if that's where he goes."

"He might notice," Suzette pointed out, "if you pull out of your driveway right after he does late at night."

She had a point. "How about this," I suggested. "I'll call the real estate office tomorrow toward the end of the day, find out if blondie is in. If she is, we'll follow her home. Then, next time Alan leaves his house at an odd hour, Suze can drive over to Ms. Haber's place and see if Alan shows up there."

It felt good to have a plan, even if I wasn't sure we could pull it off.

36

After dinner Val, Shadow, and Granimi returned to the couch to commune with Netflix and I returned to searching Brad's study. The idea of a safe was enticing, but I most wanted to find that Zaff Investigations report. I started with Brad's desk and moved on to the filing cabinet. Thirty minutes later I hadn't found anything resembling a report from Zaff Investigations. So maybe it was in the safe. Assuming there was a safe.

I did a slow spin in the center of the room. If I were a safe where would I be? I'd recently seen a crime show on TV that featured a safe in the floor, but Brad's huge rug made that unlikely. It would take two brawny men to move that TV, so I was confident nothing was hidden behind it. Most of the rest of the wall space was covered with built-in cabinets and shelving.

I was disappointed not to find a section of shelves that swung open on hidden hinges, like you see in the movies. But that didn't seem to be it. Surely a secret shelf hinge wouldn't be disguised so well you couldn't find it if you were looking for it. Which left one of the two paintings in the room. Yeah, I should have started there, but the idea of a secret compartment behind the shelves had been too good to resist.

One painting was a work of mine, and 3-18-2 seemed to refer to golf, so I turned to the other. That picture captured early morning light on a golf course somewhere. I was sure Brad had commented (more than once) on which famous course it was, but that's not the sort of information that adheres to my memory cells. I lifted the painting down and, sure enough, recessed into the wall behind it was a small safe. It looked exactly like a safe is supposed to look, with a large numbered dial and a lever handle that grants access when the dial is properly spun.

Brad, you sneaky bastard.

Not that I'd been 100% forthcoming. I'd thought I would tell him, someday, about my other child. The one I'd given away when I was seventeen and unprepared to be a mommy. But that's not the kind of topic that comes up a lot, and by the time you're on husband number three you've stopped believing that wedding vows mean you tell each other everything. I wondered whether Brad still existed out there somewhere as some form of disembodied consciousness. And if that were so, whether that state of being conferred omniscience, and if that were so, what he thought about the secret I'd kept from him. Pointless to wonder, 'cause I'd never know.

3-18-2 did not open the safe. Not right-left-right or left-right-left, or 2-18-3, or any other combination I could make from it.

Dammit, Brad. Why'd you leave clues if you didn't want me to get in there?

Okay, let's assume it's a three-digit-number. I gave up on the code and tried my birthday, Brad's birthday, our anniversary. Nada.

The best day ever... what date was that?

I examined the golf trophies I hadn't gotten around to packing up yet. Surely the best day ever had involved some kind of trophy. Golf competitions always involve trophies.

Aha: Laurelton Chamber of Commerce Charity Golfathon, July 17, 2004. Looked just like all the others, but for the event and date on the plaque.

Let's give it a go: 7-17-4.

7-17-24

Maybe it was a four-number combination: 7-17-20-04

Crap.

71-72-4?

Nope.

I left the room for a glass of water and when I returned the golf course painting, propped on Brad's desk chair, caught my eye.

Scotland. That frickin' painting was of a golf course in Scotland. Maybe European date format would work.

Let's see, that would be 17-7-4, right?

I tried the lever again.

Holy crap, I was in!

"There better be something good in here," I said to Brad. "Or I'm flushing your goofballs down the toilet."

The chamber inside was smaller than I'd imagined, but that didn't matter because underneath a couple of file folders and a manila envelope I saw money. Cash money. Bound stacks of $100 bill cash money.

I ignored the files and pulled out a sheaf of US legal tender and riffled the edges. The paper band holding the wad together said I had $10,000 in my hand.

Holy Toledo.

"Thanks, Brad," I said. "This will come in handy."

There were what looked to be two dozen stacks in the safe. If this single bundle was ten grand, all of that together must be … a shitload and a half.

Yippee.

Maybe not my best day ever, but wow. Best day in a long time, that's for sure.

I pulled two, make that three, bills from the pile in my hand without noticeably reducing its heft (and a nice feeling that was) and put them in my pocket. Using these at Whole Foods instead of whipping out my debit card would do a lot for my cash flow.

Man, what a thrill it was to have a secret safe full of money! Part of me wanted to get Suzette and Granimi in there and show it off, but the rest of me didn't want to show it to anyone. Ever.

I almost understood why Brad had kept it secret. It occurred to me then to wonder where the money had come from and what he'd had in mind to do with it. Was it simply a grandiose emergency stash or—

For several long and horrid moments I worried that the money might not belong to Brad and that scary dudes with more muscles than morals would want it back. But it had been six months already, and no one had come looking for it (that I was aware of, but mostly I'd moped at home which limited opportunities for anyone else to poke around the place looking for it). Probably that was a good sign.

Crap, what if it was unreported income? Shit. No way did I want to bring a tax hell down upon my head.

"Brad, honey, what the hell were you up to?" I asked aloud. I thought about Eugene LeJeune and wondered if my beloved husband had been involved with some unsavory underside to the construction business. I didn't want to think it, but was it really impossible?

Not liking that scenario, so what else could explain all this cash?

Uh oh, what if it was counterfeit?

I'd better Google how to identify counterfeit US currency, pronto.

I spent some long minutes fondling the bundle of bills in my hand, asking myself how much I wanted to know what all this money was about and where it had come from and what it was doing in Brad's safe.

The conclusion I came to was that ignorance is bliss and if the money was legit it was mine anyway (pending IRS issues, but I'd think about that some other time), and if it wasn't legit probably silence was the best policy. If someone came asking, all bets were off, but I'd deal with that when it happened. Assuming the stuff was real, I'd rein in the spending, be discrete, only use it for part of my grocery money.

I had to count it. Having moved all those damned golf trophies off the shelves and onto the desk, I had to move them again to clear space for looking over the contents of the safe.

The money made a nice pile. A $239,700-sized pile. Plus the 300 bucks in my pocket made 240 grand. Almost a quarter of a million dollars. Sweet. It made me nervous, but still: sweet. I indulged in a few more minutes of appreciation, then turned my attention to the documents Brad had stashed with it.

The files appeared to be papers relating to the River Bend Terrace mill-to-condos project. Worth a look, if only because I'd found them in the safe, not in a file cabinet, but not as sexy as the money or the contents of the manila envelope, which, as I'd hoped, contained the Zaff Investigations report.

I was halfway through reading the report when a knock on the study door startled me. Shit. All that lovely money was in a heap in front of me, in plain sight.

"Aunt Lena?" Val called from the other side of the closed door.

"With you in a minute, honey!" I called back. I grabbed the wastepaper basket and swept the cash in there, then shoved the canister out of site under the desk.

I lurched for the door and opened it as casually as I could. "What is it, sweetie? You're up late."

"I'm going to bed," she said. "Granimi fell asleep on the couch. Can we go to the mall tomorrow, after my guitar lesson?"

"Sure honey, we can do that."

I ushered her off to bed and went to check on Granimi.

"Hey, G.," I said softly, touching her shoulder. "Wake up. Guess what I found in Brad's, uh, desk."

Granimi wobbled awake and fumbled for her glasses. "What's that, dear?"

"Proof that Lillian Haber and Alan Braska were having an affair. And look at this." I showed her the info I'd copied onto a scrap of paper. "Her home address."

Granimi congratulated me on my discovery, and asked for a few minutes to freshen up. While she did that, I called Suzette.

"I have her address." I said, when she picked up, not trying to hide the self-congratulatory tone in my voice.

"Whose, that Lilliput person?"

"Exactly. I have her address. We don't have to follow her around town to find out where she lives."

"That's good news, I guess." She sounded disappointed.

"I thought you'd be excited. This is so much easier."

"Duh. Of course it's easier. I was looking forward to tailing someone. I had it all figured out: we would take two cars, and keep a cell line open, like a walkie talkie, and switch off who was the lead car and who followed."

Clearly I was not the only person on this call who watched too much TV. "Tell you what," I said. "Someday when this is over and we're both bored we'll pick a car at random from the mall parking lot and follow it."

"That could be fun," she said.

I thought probably it was among the worst ideas I've ever had, but I'd deal with that later. "In the meantime, I have an idea for tomorrow."

"Do tell."

"Granimi should make an appointment with this Lillian person to look at houses tomorrow afternoon. She can say she's moving here to be closer to family. That way, we'll know the woman is occupied, and you and I will go check out her house."

"Good idea. Can we look through her garbage? I've always wanted to have a reason to look through someone's garbage."

"Be my guest. I'll stand upwind while you do."

"Mimi should look at condos, though."

"Condos?"

"Yeah. Instead of houses. People your grandmother's age want to downsize, go low maintenance, avoid stairs."

"Good point. I'll give you a call tomorrow when it's set up."

Granimi wandered back in as we were wrapping up. "Got what set up, dear?"

"Plans have evolved." I reminded her that we now had Lillian Haber's home address. "So we don't have to follow her home from work tomorrow."

"Why would Brad have that woman's home address?"

"Uh, one of his real estate things." I felt reluctant to share details. Perhaps it was the seductive lure of secrets. Or maybe, although I think of Granimi as spry and sharp for her age, it was because she seemed spacier these days, and occasionally a little more foggy-brained than I'd remembered. I guess that happens to us all eventually. Some days I feel 82 myself, and I'm not even half that old yet.

"Oh, that makes sense, dear. So what's this new plan you mentioned?"

"The plan is that you'll make an appointment with Ms. Haber tomorrow, pretend you're in the market for a condo here in town. Tell her you want to downsize, be closer to your granddaughter. Then, while you keep her busy, Suzette and I will take a look at her house."

"Why do you need to look at her house, dear?"

Um, "Because on TV the detectives always check out where the suspect lives." Wasn't that reason enough? "We'll peek in the windows and maybe go through her trash."

"That sounds smelly. I'll be happy to leave that one to you two girls."

"Maybe we'll find something interesting."

"Maybe you'll find chicken bones and coffee grinds. No thank you."

"Good. Then you won't mind spending a few hours in the company of a possible murderess?"

Perhaps I should not have put it quite that way.

Granimi frowned. "Isn't that funny," she said. "I hadn't thought of it like that." Then she smiled and her eyes twinkled. "Good thing I'm old and kooky. She'll never guess I'm on to her."

Uh oh. I gave her a stern look. "Granimi, your job is to keep her busy and away from her house for an hour. Not to get in her face in any way. Please, please, please promise me that you will not grill, interrogate, insinuate or in any other way investigate her or tip her off. Just be the sweet, zany old lady we all love."

"Of course I'm not going to tip her off!" she protested. "What kind of fool do you take me for?"

Great, I'd insulted my grandmother. "I don't think you're any kind of fool, G.," I promised her. "I'm feeling very aware that until now we've been having fun with this among ourselves. Now we've got a possible suspect. If we're right, she's already killed one person and thinks she got away with it. The time may come to shake her piñata, but for now it's sneaky snooping at a distance. Okay?"

Granimi nodded and patted my hand. "I think that's a very wise position, dear. We'll leave the dangerous stuff to the detectives on TV."

Good. Granimi was clearly tired so I trundled her off to bed. In fact, bed was an excellent idea. I was in my jammies and brushing my teeth when I remembered I'd left $239,700.00 in the trash basket under Brad's desk.

Oops.

I rinsed and spat and scurried downstairs to return the money to the safe, where it belonged. Temporarily. Until it made its way into my wallet a few bills at a time. I figured if I used it to defray, say, eight grand a year in household expenses, that would free up an equivalent amount from my declared income to go into my retirement fund. There may be more exciting things to do with a fat wad of found money, but in my experience excitement is overrated.

Since I was back at Brad's desk again, maybe I'd take a quick peek at the rest of these papers before heading to bed.

Why were these particular files in the safe? I don't know a lot about converting a 19th-century mill building into Laurelton's idea of luxury apartments, but I'm confident it generates a staggering amount of paperwork. So what made these documents special? Brad had often done some work from home, but a quick flip through revealed that none of these papers had been current immediately prior to his death; most were at least a month old at that time.

Alan was the obvious person to ask, but until the Rose thing unraveled he would stay on the Do Not Trust list. He'd made the list because the first rule of homicide investigation is "maybe the spouse did it." But maybe Alan deserved a top spot on the DNT list for other reasons, too. Was something hinky hidden in the fine print of these pages? Brad had hired a PI for a reason. A reason that Kevin Zaff implied involved more than the potential bad publicity of an extra-marital liaison.

What had Zaff said? Something about unethical and possibly illegal behavior on Alan's part. Maybe that's why some of these papers were building inspection reports signed by… yup, Eugene LeJeune. Building inspections were the sort of thing Brad usually handled. Alan was mostly a figurehead partner, but sometimes he'd stuck his fingers in the strudel saying he wanted to learn Brad's side (i.e., doing the real work) of the business. Brad wouldn't have hired a PI if he'd been up to something underhanded himself. So maybe Alan had wanted in on the daily details for a reason.

I pondered what that reason might be and came up with nothing more specific than a vague idea that Alan might have cut himself in on the kickback action with Eugene somehow. I did remember that not long before Brad died there had been some tension in his relationship with Alan. I'd let it go, figuring it would blow over, that Brad would either figure out how to repair the rift, or the friendship would drift apart. It happens. It wasn't any of my business.

I was making it my business now. I knew Brad kept a copy in his home files of any document that bore his signature. So somewhere in this file cabinet I ought to find all the River Bend Terrace contracts, agreements, documents, and whatevers that he'd signed.

They made a substantial pile, once I'd pulled them from the file cabinet, but it struck me that something was missing. I did a rough sort into contracts and everything else, looking for the deal that Russell, Brad's money guy, had told me about: the one that swapped Brad's interest in River Bend Terrace LLC for a 30-acre parcel of undeveloped land outside of town. By the time I'd decided I couldn't find it, it was past my bedtime and way past my attention span for corporate documents. I put all the papers in the safe and locked up for the night.

I remembered that Ansel's dad did something in finance. Maybe he'd know someone who could review all this stuff and tell me what was amiss.

37

Granimi called Lillian Haber first thing Monday and made an appointment for three o'clock that afternoon.

"She sounded very nice," G. said, pocketing her iPhone.

"That's how the sneaky ones get you," I warned. "They sound nice, so you trust them, and then they take advantage. If she offers you something to eat, don't accept it."

Val had made enough friends at swim camp that I'd been able to arrange for her to carpool. I'd be on duty later in the week, but today it freed up my morning to work on turning a home office into a studio.

I took another quick look through the papers in the safe, but they didn't reveal any more in the light of day than they had at midnight. I put them away to await a more expert set of eyes, and turned my attention back to making Brad's space my own.

By the time I'd boxed up almost everything from the shelves and file cabinets and had lugged the boxes to the storage room I was hot and sweaty and envied Val her hours of fun in a cool swimming pool. How convenient that I have a pool of my own to jump into. I wrestled into a tank suit that had somehow become a size too small, then dove in and swam a few laps.

I was puffing and gasping my way toward the end of lap twelve when something pinged my shoulder. I stopped to look around and, ploop, another something hit the water a foot away. What the... ? I ducked my head under and saw several pieces of gravel on the bottom of the pool and another tumbling past my face. I hauled myself out of the water and reached for the towel I'd left on a deck chair.

Here came another gravel mini-bomb, crashing through the leaves of the sycamore, accompanied by a muffled "whoop" from the other side of my fence.

"Ansel?" I called out, more curious than annoyed. "What are you up to over there?"

"Oh, hi, Mrs. Wells." Ansel's grinning face with more freckles than sense popped up over the top of the fence.

"Check this out!" He fired another piece of gravel across my yard with a formidable looking slingshot. "Awesome! That one went over the Braska's garage!"

I winced at the tink of gravel hitting window glass. "That's pretty cool, Ansel," I said, trying not to rain too heavily on his parade. "Until you break a window. And you're getting gravel in my pool."

"Sorry. I was aiming for a squirrel."

"Ansel! Don't shoot at animals." Or people, for that matter, although I didn't think he'd go that far. "You could hurt something with that thing."

"Mom says squirrels are rats with furry tails," he protested. "She said it's okay if I chase them away."

"I guess that's alright, then." I wondered if I should read something into Tulip's squirrel antagonism. "But pay attention to what's in the range of fire, like my pool, and anyone in my yard."

Ansel looked at his new toy as if maybe it weren't so wonderful after all. Which is why he's a good kid: low thug potential.

"How 'bout target practice?" I suggested, feeling I should make up for being a killjoy. "You could set up soda cans and try to hit them from the other end of your yard."

"We don't have soda cans."

Of course not, what was I thinking. I'd offered Ansel a toaster pastry a couple of days ago and he'd looked as if I were trying to poison him. Although he ate brownies without complaint.

I invited Ansel to meet me in my garage so we could see what kind of target appropriate beverage containers lurked in my recycling bin.

"That's an impressive slingshot," I said when he got up close. It had a wrist brace, and looked serious and not like something Tulip would condone. "How long have you had that?"

"Just since this morning. I was washing Mr. Braska's car, and this was in a box of stuff in the trunk. He said I could have it."

"That was nice of him." What on earth was Alan doing with a slingshot?

"He didn't even know he had it!" Ansel took practice shots at the house across the street.

Imagine having something that cool in the trunk of your car and not knowing about it. "Where did it come from, then?" I wondered.

Ansel shrugged and aimed at a passing car. "He said he stopped by a friend's house on the way to Goodwill, and she gave him some stuff to drop off, too. Then he forgot about it."

"Lucky for you."

"Yeah. He didn't even look in the bag. This was right on top!"

"Wow. His loss, I guess." My snoop meter pinged off the dial. A 'she' friend gave Alan stuff to take to Goodwill? I bet it was Lillian Haber. I wondered why she'd had a slingshot, and what else was in that bag.

"Did Alan say what he was going to do with the rest of it?" I asked.

Ansel gave me that mystified look kids get.

"I could take it to Goodwill for him," I said. "I've got some things of my own to get rid of." I heard a neighbor's car start up and my heart jumped. Oh please don't be Alan taking his junk to Goodwill.

I hustled Ansel out of the garage with a trash bag full of Fresca and Diet Pepsi cans and took three steps toward Alan's front door when I remembered I was dressed in a damp swimsuit and a faded pool towel. Maybe I should put some clothes on first.

* * *

Alan looked like death on toast. His color was so bad it was freaky. I wanted to despise him for the mistress thing, and for whatever he might have been up to in his business dealings with Brad, but it was hard not to grant sympathy points to someone so pathetic looking. He'd lost weight, too. I remembered that. I'd lost nine pounds on the Amazing Heartache Diet in the two weeks after Brad's death. It had been the one silver lining in my cloud until the syndrome morphed into a severe chocolate dependency that put the pounds back on, plus some.

"Alan, hi. I stopped by to see how you're doing."

"As well as can be expected," he said. He tried for a smile, but it didn't take.

"Pretty miserable, huh." Gee, for a guy who had a hot mistress in the wings, he didn't look happy.

"That's life," he said. "We can't avoid the bad stuff forever."

"That's for sure." Granimi was right. I should be a good neighbor and feed the man. "Alan, would you like to come over for dinner later in the week? Maybe Friday? My grandmother and niece are visiting, but it will be totally casual. Just a family meal at my house. Unless you'd rather not socialize, of course." I hoped he'd say no, but by Friday anything could happen.

"That's very kind of you, Lena. Dinner sounds lovely."

"Great. Six o'clock sound good?"

"I'll be there."

"Wonderful. Oh, hey, Ansel showed me that slingshot you gave him."

His eyes brightened. "He did look pleased with it."

"He's having a great time. Anyway, he said you have some other things for Goodwill? I'm taking some stuff down there myself. So I could drop yours off as well, save you the trip."

"That's very kind of you Lena, but really not nece...." He paused mid-refusal. "Actually, that would be helpful," he said. "I teach a Monday night class at the Community College Summer Extension. My students might appreciate it if I took some time today to refresh my memory of what I'd planned to teach them. I've had to cancel class the past two weeks."

"I didn't know you taught a class, Alan. Good for you."

"'Real Estate Law for Beginning Investors.' Rose badgered me into it," he confessed. "I think she wanted to get me out of her hair one night a week. She said I had too much knowledge up here," he tapped his noggin, "not to share it with a younger generation."

"Sounds like an excellent idea," I said. Because, yay, it meant Alan would be out of the house for a couple of hours that night and a terrible, horrible, wonderful idea had taken shape in my brain. "Where's this box of treasures?"

"In the garage. Come in and we'll go through the kitchen."

I followed him through the house. "Wow. What a clean garage." Where did the Braskas keep all their miscellaneous crap?

"The garage is a house for the car, not a personal landfill," Alan said. "That was my father's policy, and I try to live up to it."

"You're doing a fine job with that." I'm of the personal landfill school, myself, one reason my garage is less than ideal as a painting studio.

"Here it is." He walked over to his Lincoln and opened the trunk. Which was also very clean, and empty except for a mid-sized cardboard box with the flaps folded in and a rumpled Macy's bag on top. "Rose asked me to take care of this months ago. I was driving her car while mine was in the shop, so I put it in her trunk and forgot about it."

"That's one advantage of an SUV," I said. "You can see what's in the cargo space."

Alan grunted as he lifted the box, and I hurried to take it from him. It wasn't heavy, so the fact that he struggled with it was not a good sign.

"Are you okay, Alan? I don't mean to pry, but your color isn't good."

"I'm sure I'll be fine, Lena. Thank you for your concern. And thank you for taking care of this for me."

He opened the garage door so I could carry the box home without detouring through his house. I turned to wave goodbye from the driveway, but had my hands full. "We'll see you Friday, then. Take care, Alan."

I made as sedate a mad dash for my place as I could manage and put the box on the dining room table. I'd pulled the Macy's bag out by the string handles when all that TV-watching experience kicked in.

Chain of evidence. Fingerprints.

"Granimi, are you available?" I called out. I set the Macy's bag down beside the box. The edges were crumpled in, so I'd have to open it to see what was inside.

Granimi appeared in the dining room archway. "Of course dear, what I can I do for you."

I grinned at her. "Look what I scored!"

She walked over and peered at the box of Rose's old clothes. "Have you been thrift shopping, dear?" She reached into the box and pulled out a grandmotherly floral cardigan. "This doesn't look like your style at all."

"That's something of Rose's," I said. I recapped my encounter with Ansel and my suppositions about the provenance of the Macy's bag. "If I'm right, these are Lillian Haber's castoffs."

"Oh!" Granimi perked up and reached to look inside the bag

"Not so fast, G.," I cautioned. "We don't want to mess up any prints she might have left on it, in case we ever have to prove the bag is hers."

"I see your point." Granimi held her arms by her side and leaned over to try to peek into the bag. "Should we take pictures of it, too?"

"Oh, good idea." I found my digital camera in my second-guess location, then grabbed cooking tongs and a wooden spoon from the utensil jar beside the stove and a pair of rubber gloves from under the sink.

I cheated and put the shopping bag back on top of the box so I could take a photo of it in situ, then snapped one of it out of the box.

I put the rubber gloves on and uncrumpled the top of the bag. Then I passed the tongs and wooden spoon to Granimi so she could hold the sides of the bag open while I took a photo of what was inside. Then I pulled out the contents and lay them on the table for study.

Item #1: a black cashmere cardigan from Nordstrom, size S, with a row of tiny pearls around the neck.

"This is gorgeous!" I held it up after I'd photographed it. "And expensive. Who in their right mind would get rid of something like this?"

"That is lovely," Granimi said.

I could tell she wanted to take it from me, and fingerprints on cashmere didn't seem likely to be an issue, so I handed it over.

She inspected it expertly, examining the seams and hemline and holding it up to check the shape.

"The elbows are a bit stretched out," she said. "And a couple of these pearls are loose. And there's a tiny hole developing at the corner of the tag, here. Those can all be fixed." She shook her head. "Young people today have no idea how to maintain a wardrobe. With proper care a garment like this should last decades. I'm tempted to keep it myself."

She held it up again, considering. "It's a bit somber," she decided. "At my age black is too funereal."

Maybe, but it smelled good.

"What's that fragrance, G.? Do you recognize it?"

She raised the sweater to her nose and inhaled. "I don't smell anything."

"You don't smell perfume?" I asked. "Flowery, kind of like…," roses?

"It's not coming from the sweater." Granimi lay the cashmere on the table and sniffed the air. "A heavy rose note," she said. "Well, some people like that. It's a bit old fashioned for me."

"Uh, yeah." I wondered if that was a heavy Rose note in the air and wished Val were around to get a visual. I tried to scan the room with my peripheral vision, willing my genes to wake up and jump-start whatever freaky ability might run in the family, but all I saw was my dining room. And the loot on the table, which included:

Item #2: Very nice ivory gabardine slacks, size 2P, with a brownish-red stain on one knee. Tres chic if worn with that black cardigan. I wondered if the stain would come out. Not that I'd ever fit into them.

Item #3: Denim jeans, dark wash, gently worn, tiny. I didn't recognize the label but guessed they were the $300 kind. I wear $30 jeans from Wal-Mart. These were nicer, but not ten times nicer. At a certain point jeans are jeans. This pair was also a petite size 2, which I'm nowhere close to.

"These might fit you, G.," I said. "Do you wear jeans?"

"Not very often," she said. "I'm partial to yoga pants for casual wear."

"Off to Goodwill with them, then."

Item #4: A pair of black pumps, also from Nordstrom's, also in excellent condition; two-and-a-half inch heels with a pointed toe and a vamp low enough to show toe cleavage. Size 5-1/2 narrow. That was a shame. If they were an 8-1/2 I'd be trying them on already.

"Oh, those are nice." Granimi leaned in for a closer look. "I don't wear heels like that anymore, though. What size shoe does Suzette wear?"

"Nine-and-a-half double A." Girlfriends who shop together know these things.

I turned them over to look at the soles. Only lightly scuffed. If they'd been worn more than twice it had been on carpeting. Something about the shoes niggled at me, but my hands were sweaty in the rubber gloves, and there were more things in the bag, so I set the shoes aside to reconsider later.

The remaining items were a twill skirt with a missing button, good quality but nothing to yearn for, and a couple of paperbacks: The Red Tent and The Secret Life of Bees. Too reading-groupish for me.

That slingshot didn't go with the rest of this stuff at all.

"Have we learned anything?" Granimi asked.

"I don't think so. Except that she's a petite size 2 and has good taste in clothes."

"That's not very exciting," she said. "What's in the box?"

"The box is Rose's stuff." Grandmotherly garments in size 14. I felt like Goldilocks: those are too small and these are too big. Also in the box: a few hardcovers that looked like Alan's weekend reading; a pair of men's casual shoes; a saucepan but no lid; four rather pretty teacups with three saucers. Plus two silk scarves so prim and matronly they'd strangle me with boredom. I lamented the loss of my lovely orange scarf, and thought maybe I was done with scarves forever.

The last item was a brooch in the shape of a seahorse, missing a few rhinestones. We heard the front door open and Val wandered in, back from swim camp and looking for lunch. She took a fancy to the seahorse pin, so we let her have it.

"You should keep those shoes." She pointed at the black stilettos. "And the black sweater, and those slacks."

"Honey, I'm flattered you think they'd fit me, but really, not a chance."

"Not keep them to wear. Just keep them."

"Why?"

She shrugged and pinned the seahorse to her T-shirt. "I don't know. You just should. Can we have lunch now? I'm starving!"

38

The plan was to take Granimi to the real estate office for her appointment, deposit Val at her guitar lesson, and then Suzette and I would check out Lillian Haber's house. If the woman's cast-offs were any indication, she had a great closet. Not that we planned to break in. Just a peak around from the outside, for no other reason than that it seemed like something we should do.

Things went according to plan until we'd dropped Granimi off, at which point Val leaned over from her seat behind me and asked, "What are you and Suzette doing while I'm at my guitar lesson?"

"We've got errands to do," I said. Val has her talents, but she's twelve, and I felt we should keep her out of it as much as we could.

"Shoe shopping is never just an 'errand'!" Suzette exclaimed with pretend outrage. "Especially when Macy's is having a sale."

Macy's is always having a sale, but I played along. "Expect to see shopping bags in the car when we get back," I said. "Can we bring you anything from the mall?"

Suzette glared at me and I realized I'd gone too far. If Val said 'yes,' we'd have to squeeze in a side trip before picking her up in an hour.

I glanced in the rearview and caught Val frowning at me with her arms crossed.

"You're lying," she said. "You're not going to the mall."

"Of course we're going to the mall," Suzette said. "Macy's is the only place to get decent shoes around here."

"You said we could go to the mall after my lesson."

Oh, right. Oops.

"You're up to something," Val insisted. "I can tell."

I tried to deny it, but she wasn't convinced. "What do you think?" I asked Suzette. "Should we tell her?"

Suze turned around in her seat to face Val. "While Mimi's meeting with that real estate agent, Lena and I are going to scope out where she lives."

"Why? Do you think she killed Rose?"

So much for subtlety and discretion. "Some of the information we have seems to point in her direction," I said. "At this point we're guessing."

"I should come along," Val said.

"You're not coming along."

"I can help. I know it."

"Val, you have a guitar lesson."

"You're going to need me."

I couldn't imagine how. On the other hand, she did have abilities neither Suzette nor I possessed. We were two blocks from the guitar guy's house. I pulled over and got my cell out of my purse. I didn't have his number. I couldn't even remember his name. Gary something. Or was it Jerry?

Val was already thumbing her phone. "Here," she said, handing it up to me when she'd dialed. "It's Gary."

"Hi, Gary?... Yeah, this is Lena Wells, Valerie's aunt. Listen, I'm sorry to cancel at the last minute, but we've got a, ah, family situation, and need to reschedule... No, Val's fine. Not bad news, just a bad day. ... I understand. ... Friday at 2:30 will be fine."

I gave Val her phone back. "You're rescheduled for Friday," I said, in case she'd missed that. "And we owe Granimi for a missed lesson."

*   *   *

I peered in Lillian Haber's window at the cleanest kitchen I'd ever seen. Where were the grimy oven mitts, the rumpled dishtowels, the disorganized spice rack, the pile of unopened mail? The woman didn't even leave a dirty coffee mug in the sink. She and Alan were a good match in the neatnik department.

We'd parked at the curb a couple of doors down in front of a house with a FOR SALE sign in the yard. As a formality we'd rung Ms. Haber's doorbell, waited briefly, then strolled around to the back as though we had every right to do so.

"She sure is neat." Val balanced on one foot on a hose spigot as she peeked in a bedroom window.

"And she doesn't cook." Pod people. They're everywhere.

The house was a split-level ranch, not what I'd expected for a woman who wore silk and cashmere from Nordstrom's, but typical for the neighborhood and well maintained. The landscaping was mature and meticulous, the generous deck on which I stood a nice upgrade to the back yard. The bay-windowed breakfast nook looked like a recent addition, too.

We peeked around some more, but the trip so far seemed pointless. Kinsey Milhone would pick the lock—not something I know how to do or wanted to try—and invite herself in. I was nervous enough just peeking in the kitchen windows while Suzette whimpered in frustration at being locked out of the garage and therefore denied access to Ms. Haber's trash bins. It's not like we'd find a Duncan Hines Brownie Mix box in there. That would have gone out with the trash sometime last week.

"What are you doing?"

I practically fell over, but it was just a kid on a bike watching us from the driveway next door.

"Ms. Haber didn't answer the door," I said. "So we thought maybe she was in the kitchen and didn't hear us knock."

"She's not home." The kid looked about seven years old, so depending on his upbringing and TV habits either easy to fool or a half-second away from yelling for his mom. Judging by expression, he was a yeller.

"Oh well," I said with a casual shrug. "I'll give her a call later."

Suzette and I waved goodbye and ambled off in the direction of my car. It wasn't as if we were learning anything useful. Loitering any longer seemed pointless unless we were going to evade the vigilant kid and break in, which no way was I up for.

I assumed Val tagged along until I heard her say from some distance behind us, "I like your bike. Do you live here?"

Chat up the neighbors, always a good idea. Except when you don't want your quarry to know you've been asking around. But two kids? Who would notice?

Suzette and I struck casual poses beside my car, pretending to be friends who'd run into each and were having a sidewalk chat.

"Unlock the car already," Val said a minute later, jogging across the street and tugging at the passenger door. "We should go."

"That was a colossal waste of a missed guitar lesson." I pulled away from the curb and pointed the car toward the mall.

"Nuh uh," Val said.

"What? The kid knew something?"

Val said the kid had said Ms. Haber would be mad we were looking in her windows, but he wouldn't tell because she was a meanie. His mom didn't like her either. "And guess what? She made brownies recently."

"Really?" How on earth had that come up in a 90-second conversation with a seven-year-old?

"Yeah. Something about a block party. The mean lady gave them brownies. She said she didn't want them because she's on a diet. He thinks that was a lie, because she's already skinny."

Sounded like a lie to me. No one on a diet bakes brownies.

"How did you get all that from him so quickly?" Suzette asked.

Val shrugged. "He said she was a meanie, so I asked if she'd ever done something nice."

"How did you know to ask that?" I wondered.

Another shrug. "I just did."

Fair enough. Val was right; it was good we'd brought her along.

"Did he say if the brownies tasted funny," Suzette wanted to know.

"I asked him that, too," Val said, looking pleased with herself. "He thought they did and his mom said there was coffee in them."

"What about nuts? Did he mention nuts?"

"His said his sister's stupid, because she insisted they had nuts in them, but he could see they didn't. Then his mom came to the door, and I thought maybe I didn't want to talk to her, so I ran over here."

"Val, you are amazing!" I said. "I take it back. That was totally worth missing a guitar lesson for." The timing of the brownie event wasn't definitive, but we weren't after definitive. We were after enough to get the cops interested again. I was confident a date could be nailed down by someone with a reasonable right to inquire about such things.

As our scoping out of Ms. Neatnik's house had taken all of twelve minutes, we ended up at the mall with an hour to kill before meeting Granimi. I called her cell to say we were done but happy to amuse ourselves for as long as necessary. G. said there was one more place she wanted to look at and she'd call when she was done.

"I think my grandmother is maybe taking this condo thing too seriously," I said to Suzette as she pulled me toward the Macy's shoe department. "She sounds like she might really buy a place." Not a bad idea, though. Granimi's San Francisco house is a monstrosity, and way too big for her. And worth a fortune. She could buy a dozen condos for what she'd get for that place, even in today's market.

39

Tulip called a few minutes after we got home to ask if Ansel could hang out at my place while she and Michael went to dinner. At a steak house.

"Oh, good for you Tulie," I said. "I hope they'll have something you can eat, too."

"I'll be happy with a salad," she said. "Even a steak house will have some kind of greens on the menu."

I couldn't imagine munching on greens while my dinner companion cut into a juicy tenderloin, but whatever. I said that would be fine if she didn't mind Granimi being in charge of the kids for a short while—probably less than an hour—while I went out.

I'd called the Community College office, pretending to be one of Alan's students, to confirm that his class would meet at its regular time (6-8 PM) that night. Which meant Alan would be out of his house from around 5:30 to 8:30 or later.

Suze and I quizzed G. on the ride home what Lillian was like, but all Granimi'd said was that Ms. Haber had been "perfectly nice," "very professional," and, "certainly a polite young lady, although not with what you'd call a warm demeanor," followed by, "None of which means she isn't a killer."

Val and Granimi went upstairs and I pulled Suzette, who hadn't yet headed home, into the study and shut the door.

"What are your plans for the evening?" I was so nervous about what I had in mind that I'd probably pass out two minutes after stepping across the threshold and would need someone to carry me home.

"Laundry and TV," she said. "Unless you've got something better going on."

Suzette already knew, of course, that I'd found Lillian Haber's home address, but I hadn't told her the whole story.

"Holy Tuscaloosa!" she said, when I filled her in on the Kevin Zaff angle and his hints that Alan had been up to some kind of no good. The safe, and cash, I was keeping to myself. "Brad hired a private investigator to spy on Alan? And that's how you got this bimbo's address?"

I nodded.

I explained how something appeared to be missing from Brad's home edition of the paper trail on the River Bend Terrace project.

"When Russell, our accountant, went over the money stuff with me after Brad died, he said River Bend Terrace LLC was up to its eyeballs in debt and likely to lose its financing and that Brad was lucky to get out when he did. He said Brad traded his stake in the project for a piece of land outside of town."

"I remember that," Suze said. "We drove out to look at it. Not impressive."

"That's what makes the story work. It proves the company was in deep financial doodoo, because otherwise the deal's a total rip-off and no sane person would go for it. The thing is, Brad bailing on a project 'cause he thought it was going to tank? That's not like him. He'd never admit that he couldn't find a way to make it work. That was his thing: he never let a problem get the best of him."

Suzette nodded me along.

"So that bothers me. That, and he didn't tell me about it. It's not like he told me everything, but backing out of that big project? Because of money problems? Nothing Brad said implied things weren't okay on the money end over there. Yeah, he would have downplayed it if things had been bad. But it would have come up. I was just so flipped out when Brad died I didn't question anything Russell said. I was all, 'Just tell me where I stand now.' I was too busy grieving to care about details."

"I'm not sure I follow. You're saying Russell lied about the whole thing?"

"I don't know yet. Maybe. Maybe not, in which case it is what it is and my imagination has gone totally bonkers. But if Alan pulled a fast one, which I'm starting to think maybe he did, Russell had to be in on it. And Russell and Alan go way back.

"So anyway, I've been going through Brad's files. I found the original partnership agreement, no problem. But nothing that changes it. Plus, remember all that stuff in the paper about Eugene LeJeune?"

"How could I forget: kickbacks, payoffs, extortion, and a skanky, homicidal mud-wrestler? It'll be decades before anything that exciting happens around here again."

"I think Alan was mixed up in that somehow."

"No way."

I nodded. "Brad was pissed at Alan for mishandling something that he should have let Brad take care of. And Eugene's signature is on some of the documents I found. I don't know more than that, but if Alan was involved in something as sleazy as the Eugene mess, maybe he's capable of a major rip-off." We already suspected the guy of maybe offing his wife, why not throw financial malfeasance at him, too, and see if it stuck?

Suzette looked thoughtful. "If they lied about the River Bend corporation, or whatever it is, having money trouble, and it's not, how much would Brad's stake be worth?"

I shrugged. "I don't know. The original building belonged to Rose. He didn't own any of that. His deal was to handle the renovations in exchange for a share of the profits. Once the condos were sold he stood to make big bucks. Maybe not so big as they thought, given the state of the economy, and maybe not enough to solve my money problems forever, but it would take care of me for a while, that's for sure."

"And all you've got to show for it is a crappy piece of land no one wants."

"Maybe. I don't know yet. The fact that I didn't find a buyout agreement in Brad's files doesn't mean it doesn't exist, or that the project isn't about to go belly-up, or that anybody ripped Brad—and me—off. But it makes me think maybe they did."

"Well, shit, girlfriend, let's find out!"

I grinned at her. "That's what I plan to do tonight, while Alan's out of the house. I figure he'll have copies of important stuff like partnership agreements in his home office now, since he retired in January. And if he and Russell did pull a fast one when Brad died, you can bet they'll have a fake paper trail handy to cover their tracks. I don't want to start any kind of official fuss until I'm sure I'm not barking up an imaginary tree."

"So what's the plan? Will Hanna let you in, or did you scare her off with the shamanic journey thing?"

I shook my head. "We don't need Hanna. As a trusted neighbor called upon to bring in the mail and water plants when the Braskas are on vacation, I have a key."

"Magdalena Wells!" Suze had her hands on her hips in mock outrage. "Are you planning to abuse the Good Neighbor Covenant?"

I grinned again. "How would you like to blow off your laundry plans in favor of unlawful entry?" I explained what I had in mind and Suze said, "Count me in!" with a little more enthusiasm than might be appropriate for someone who's dating a cop.

Then I showed her the stuff I'd retrieved from Alan's garage. I figured it might make up for not being able to get at Lillian Haber's trash that afternoon.

Suzette was thrilled with my find, and thought it a good omen. She listened with suitable admiration to how quick-witted and clever I'd been to track the stuff down and obtain it for myself, and then we left Granimi in charge of the kids and headed next door.

Before we left, I used the hall phone to call Alan's house, holding my breath until the machine picked up. Good, he'd left already.

"Alan, it's Lena," I said after the beep. "I thought I heard some noise over there a few minutes ago, and wanted to make sure you're alright. Sorry if I'm being alarmist about nothing." I waited a moment, as if I hesitated to hang up, then disconnected.

"Okay," I said to Suzette, who applauded softly. "That's our official reason for going over and letting ourselves in. Let's hope we don't need it."

Suzette grinned at me as we stepped out the door, practically hopping with excitement.

"Settle down!" I hissed at her, feeling close to ill with dread. "You look like a six-year-old on her way to the circus. We don't want to attract attention." Good thing we hadn't invited Granimi along. She was worse than Suzette at feigning subtlety.

40

I used my good neighbor key to let us in the Braska's front door. Once inside, I closed the door and paused, listening, trying to coax my pulse into something that felt less like a panic attack. Suzette looked excited; I was so anxious I prayed I wouldn't pass out. If Alan came home while we were in his house they'd have to carry me out in a body bag.

The Braska's home was of similar, although not identical, layout and style to mine. Their office/den is also at the front of the house, but entered from the living room rather than the hall. Alan, like Brad, had gone for an über-male dark wood and leather scheme, accented with a staid navy plaid.

"Remind me again what we're looking for?" Suzette said as we stepped into the study. The room smelled strongly of cigars and whiskey, traceable to the cigar stub and almost empty lowball glass on Alan's desk. I resisted the urge to raise his wooden Venetian blinds and open a window.

"First and foremost, the file cabinet." The light in the room was dim, a floor lamp beside the desk on its lowest setting. I flipped on the overheads so we wouldn't bark our shins on the coffee table. "I'm looking for papers about River Bend Terrace. Specifically, anything with Brad's signature on it, and even more specifically something dating from last fall or early winter that could be a buy-out agreement."

"This looks like household stuff." Suzette had opened the top drawer of a file cabinet in the corner. "Car insurance, homeowner's policies, copies of tax stuff. Wow, being a fuddy-duddy pays well. Wanna guess how much Alan made last year?"

I waved that I didn't care. What I hoped was that, if my suspicions were correct and Alan had done something uncool, he'd covered his ass by manufacturing proof of innocence and keeping it where he could get at it. So far his desk hadn't yielded anything interesting. If he'd done a Brad and stuck the important documents in a safe behind that rather awful portrait of Rose we were out of luck.

"Oh my god, look at this!" Suzette pulled a file out of the second drawer.

"Don't take anything out unless you can put it back in the right place!" I admonished. Sheesh, had she paid any attention when I'd told her we wanted to be in and out without leaving a trace? "What is it?"

She splayed the manila folder open and I recognized the telltale curves of underwiring. Suzette held up the lingerie up by a shoulder strap and I could see it was a very expensive-looking black lace balconette.

"Tres sexy, non?" Suze put the manila folder on top of the open drawer of files, and held the bra closer to the light to read the tag. "Oooh, La Perla!" She raised her eyebrows at me. "What does a LaPerla like this go for, three hundred bucks? I wish someone would buy me a bra like this. It's a 32B, though."

It couldn't be Rose's. Rose was at least a 38D.

Suzette held the balconette up against her chest. "I'm a 34, but for LaPerla I'd squeeze into it."

"Suze!"

She shrugged and dropped the bra back into the folder, returning it to the drawer. "I wonder if there are more where that came from."

"We don't care how much Alan spent on mistress lingerie," I said. "We're looking for stuff that involves Brad, not scrawny blondes. We need to keep an eye on the time, too. Alan's class is supposed to go 'til eight, but the sooner we're out of here the better."

I turned on the copier, in case we found something worth copying. I'd brought my digital camera, too, but the test paperwork shots I'd taken at home were illegibly out of focus. I took over at the file cabinet, and found some River Bend Terrace documents in the third drawer down. Behind them, in a separate folder of their own, were the papers I was looking for. It took a while to realize that's what they were, as I tried to skim through the legalese as quickly as possible while also going slowly enough to pick out some sense of what each document was about. When I understood what I had, I flipped through the pages again for dates and signatures.

When I found them, I did a little hop of anticipation. Could I have been right, after all?

Brad died soon after we'd taken an impromptu long weekend in Palm Springs. He'd golfed. I'd shopped and swum in the pool and spent more than I'd budgeted at the hotel's day spa. And over dinner on Saturday Brad had opened up about his growing dissatisfaction with Alan, how the partnership wasn't working out as well as he'd hoped, and how he wouldn't work with him again once the River Bend project was done. What he hadn't mentioned was any kind of looming financial disaster, or any thoughts of asking Alan to buy him out.

I looked at the date on the documents again. I'd have to check last year's calendar, but I'd rebooked our flight home so we could stay an extra day, and I felt sure that extra day was the date next to Brad's signatures on these pages. Which meant either Brad had been less than truthful with me, or he hadn't known about this deal.

Suze came over to see what so engrossed me. "Is that what you were looking for?"

"I think so." I showed her the documents and explained what they were. "This is a buyout agreement. One that cuts Brad out of profit participation in River Bend Terrace LLC and saddles me with that parcel of unlovely land out on Route 20. This looks like Brad's signature," I said. "But the date's wrong. We were in Palm Springs that day."

Suzette didn't seem to find that as alarming as I did. "Probably he signed them while you were there, and had them notarized when you got back," she said. "Or maybe he went to the office after you got home."

I shook my head. "Our flight was delayed. We didn't get home until dinnertime. He didn't go out that evening, and no, Alan didn't stop by the house. I think Alan faked Brad's signature."

"But why would he go to all that trouble then pick a date Brad was out of town?"

Karma. By picking that date Alan had set himself up for a bite in the ass from his own bad behavior. I tried not to smile, but man, it made me happy.

"I don't think he knew," I explained. "We were supposed to fly back Sunday but decided to stay an extra day. Brad made a few calls Monday morning to check in with his crew, but Alan wasn't around the jobsite much. There's no reason he would know we hadn't come back as planned."

Then I had another thought and my knees went all wobbly and the room spun, and I sank down onto the leather sofa and put my head on my knees.

Why had it not occurred to me until now? We suspected Rose's "accidental" death had really been murder. Had Brad's accident been engineered, too?

"Lena?" Suzette was beside me, her hand on my shoulder. "Lena?" she gave me a gentle shake. "Are you okay?"

I lifted my head. "What if Brad was murdered, too?" I squeaked.

"What? What are you talking about?" Suzette looked confused and concerned.

"I've been assuming, if Alan really did come up with some clever rip-off scheme, that it was a crime of opportunity. That when Brad died so suddenly he had the idea to fake these papers so he could keep Brad's share of the business for himself. But what if someone made that chance happen?"

"Oh my God. Do you think—?"

"I don't know. The cops thought I might have pushed him. Maybe someone else did." It was too horrible, too overwhelming. "I can't think about it now. It's too much. Let's make copies of these and get the hell out of here."

I had placed the photocopies of the documents into the tote bag I'd remembered to bring along when I heard a siren in the distance. I froze, my dread increasing as it approached. "Shit!"

"Oh my god!"

We looked at each other in horror. My heart, which seemed to have stopped entirely for a moment, started up again at a rapid pace. I fumbled to turn off the copier and dropped the originals back into their folder and shoved it into what I hoped was the right place with shaking hands. I was wrestling with the copier dust cover when Suzette held up her hand.

"That's not the police," she said. "That's an ambulance."

"Are you sure?" Police, fire, and ambulance sirens are each distinctive in our town, but I couldn't seem to access whatever corner of my brain knew which sound was which.

Suzette nodded. "Positive."

I sidled over to the window and lifted a slat of the blind to peer out. The siren hiccuped to a stop somewhere close by but not in front of the Braska's house.

"Not us." I collapsed against the window frame. I had my cell with me and Granimi would have called if Val had slid down the banister and cracked her head open.

"Oh my God, Suze, I am so not cut out for this."

Suzette laughed. "I'm having a great time," she said. "Other than the bad news about Brad's partners ripping you off. Where's your sense of adventure?"

"I don't have one." I regained the use of my limbs and checked my watch, appalled at how quickly time had passed. "Shit. We should get a move on." I was a wreck; if Alan came home early no way could I talk us out of this.

"Don't you want to look in his computer while we're here?"

I considered the keyboard and monitor on Alan's desk. "I'm reluctant to mess with it." If we turned it on and poked around in there, would we be able to exit without leaving signs that we'd snooped? Better to leave it alone.

"Real detectives would make a copy of his hard drive," Suze suggested, looking under the desk for the CPU tower.

"Real detectives would know how to do that," I countered. Surely you'd have to copy it onto something. Could be that's what thumb drives and USB ports are for, but I only have a hazy idea what those are.

"Hey, look what I found on the floor." Suzette showed me a small black plastic remote. "What do you suppose it's for?"

Unlike Brad, Alan did not have a monster TV in his study. Suze waved the remote around the room, clicking the power button on and off.

"Do that again." I'd heard something that could have been a faint electronic whirr from somewhere behind me.

Suze waved and clicked again, and I turned around and opened a louvered closet door to reveal a camcorder on a tripod.

"Sneaky bastard," Suzette said, with what sounded like admiration. "I wonder if he had Miss black lace balconette on the desk and wanted to capture the moment."

"Ewww," I said. "That is so tacky."

"Nothing is too tacky for a guy with a hard-on," Suzette pointed out.

"It's not recording now, is it?"

Suze leaned over my shoulder. "I don't think so. Here, let's have a look."

I stepped aside and let Suzette at it.

"It's off," she said. "And it was kind of leaning over. It looks like someone shoved that box in here," she nudged a cardboard carton with her foot, "and knocked the tripod off-center. Okay," she'd detached the camera from the base, and backed out of the closet. "Let's see if we can get it to play back. Here we go."

We stood shoulder to shoulder, staring at the camcorder's tiny screen, waiting for an image to appear.

"Oh wait. I didn't rewind."

We discovered that the camera, unable to right itself, had recorded mostly the louvers of the closet door and, through the spaces between them, part of the study wall on the other side of the room. The image sporadically included the top of a blonde chignon and, when the woman turned, the upper part of her forehead. Alan, being taller, came and went with most of his face visible. Their argument sounded like something more than a lover's spat.

"Don't think you can brush me off, Alan," the woman, I assumed Lillian H., said. "All of this was as much your idea as mine, and if you mess things up for me I will make very sure people know that."

"I don't want to mess anything up for you, Lily," he said. "And I will take full responsibility for my actions if a time comes when that's necessary. But I will ask you to bear in mind that my wife of many years has recently died. I'd like some time to mourn her properly without being pestered by you to rush to the next step."

"Uh oh," Suze said.

"Are you calling me a pest?" Lily's voice achieved the frequency of a dog whistle.

"No, Lily, I am not calling you a pest—"

"Yes you are," Suze admonished with a shake of her head. "Men."

"—but I have a class to teach in half an hour and it would be best to continue this conversation another time."

"What a pompous jerk."

"Shhh!" I said. "I want to listen." If this was from earlier that day, Lillian (Lily: flower!) must have come to see Alan after her appointment with Granimi. It was weird to think she'd been in this room while I was next door fondling her cashmere sweater.

There wasn't much more to hear, though. Alan must have left the room because we heard Lillian saying, "Do not walk away from me, Alan," in a diminishing voice, then faint sounds of a continuing argument, and then nothing.

"Don't you hate when men walk away while you're still talking?" Suze said. "Why do they do that?"

"Because they don't know how to shut us up."

We waited, but Alan and Lily didn't come back, and after ten seconds or so of a static image of the back of the closet door, Suze turned the camcorder off.

"I wonder what that was about," I said. "What does she think he'll mess up for her?"

Then a terrible thought occurred to me.

"Suze."

"Yeah?"

"Push PLAY again. We may have turned it off too soon."

"You think there's something else on here?"

"I'm really hoping there isn't."

There was. After another short stretch of nothing, a blip of transition, then two figures moved past the closet door and a familiar voice said, "Remind me again what we're looking for?"

"Oh, shit!"

"Yup."

"It got us, too!"

"Yup."

"Oh my God."

"Suze."

"Yeah?"

"We have to erase that."

She examined the camcorder. "It's digital tape," she said. "We could record over it."

"How? If it turned itself off after they left, and then we're on it, that means there's a motion or voice sensor somewhere. If we just set it and leave, won't it turn off again after whatever the delay is?"

"Maybe." She turned it over in her hands. "How much do you know about how these things work?"

"Hardly anything." For a moment I allowed myself to consider calling Ansel for advice, but we were way past the kind of stuff we could involve a kid in.

"No biggie." Suzette popped the cassette out and slipped it into the pocket of her hoodie. "Problem solved."

I must have looked appalled.

"What?" she said. "It was your idea to let yourself in, go through the man's files, and make copies of whatever caught your eye. It's gonna bother you if we walk out of here with a camcorder cassette?"

When Alan's phone rang I was gratified to note that, for all her professed cool, Suzette jumped just as high as I did.

Alan, like me, had a phone extension and answering machine on his hall table. The volume was set high, and with the study door open we heard it clearly:

"Alan, this is Beth Wrigley. I just got a call that you didn't teach your class tonight. I understand your situation at home, but we need to keep the needs of the students in mind, too. Please call me when you get in."

"Holy shit." I placed a hand on Suze's arm. "If he didn't teach his class, he could be home any minute! We've got to get out of here."

Suzette put the camcorder back on the tripod and shoved the closet doors closed while I grabbed my tote bag and glanced around to make sure we hadn't left any glaringly obvious signs of our presence. There'd be a cassette missing from the camcorder, but I wasn't going to worry about that. I flicked off the overheads, and we left the room.

Suze headed for the front door, but I stopped her. "Let's go out the back."

"Right. Don't wanna be stepping out the front just as he turns in the driveway."

As we passed through the kitchen I noticed the key pegs beside the back door, and paused to find Alan's set of keys to my house and take them back. I hoped he'd never abused the good neighbor covenant the way I just had, but even if he hadn't I was revoking his privileges. I'd rather transfer the honors to Tulip. I wouldn't even mind if she let herself in and looked through my fridge.

Suzette and I went out the back door and crept along the side of the garage. I heard a car approach and ducked back, bumping into Suze behind me. I motioned her to stay still, and pressed my back against the garage wall.

I heard the car drive past, and had moved toward the street again when Suze hissed at me to wait up. I turned and saw her looking in the small window in the side wall of the garage.

"How many cars do Alan and Rose have?"

"Two. His and hers sedans." I'd seen them myself that morning.

"If he's gone out—" Suzette stepped back and gestured me to take a look, "—why are there two cars in the garage?"

I stepped closer to peer in the window. The streetlight in front of the house cast a yellow light through the narrow windows at the top of the garage doors, reflecting off the two cars at rest inside. I looked at Suze.

"He took a cab? Someone gave him a ride?" I didn't want to believe what this meant.

I remembered how gray and ill Alan had looked that morning.

"We have to go back in," I said.

41

We found him on the floor of the master bedroom, a splotch of blood beneath his head. Suzette and I cowered in the doorway until a feeble round of rock-paper-scissors determined I would be the one to feel for a pulse. I tiptoed over to him and crouched down. It was clear up close that he was dead, but I placed my forefinger against the side of his neck, just in case. He wasn't cold yet, but no living person's skin is as cool as that. Or as colorless.

I looked back at Suze and shook my head.

"Oh. My. God." Suzette said.

"Uh huh." I retreated to the doorway. All that anxiety about when he would come home and he'd been there the whole time, dead.

Alan was dead. Right in front of me. Dead.

"Please tell me he's been dead for a while," Suzette said, and I realized that dead might not be the worst of it.

"Oh my God." I almost threw up at the thought: what if he'd been lying there, still alive, as we'd let ourselves in, and we'd spent the past hour rummaging through his office instead of calling an ambulance and saving his life?

Suzette looked at me, face white, eyes wide, all the excitement of doing something naughty gone from her face. "What do we do now?"

What else: "Call Bob again," I said.

* * *

"Are you kidding me?" Bob said when we opened Alan's front door to let him in an eternity and a half later. "You found another body?"

Suzette burst into tears and he stopped being a cop long enough to wrap her in his bear hug until she calmed down. "Sorry honey. Didn't mean to be insensitive. I do hope you're not going to make a habit of this."

"What happened this time?" he asked me over Suze's head.

We'd had the presence of mind, while awaiting his arrival, to get our story straight. Knowing my voice message was on Alan's answering machine, and that there really had been an argument in the house, I stuck with that, saying I'd heard something next door that had sounded like a loud argument, and had called Alan, who had looked very unwell earlier in the day, to ask if he was okay. Getting no answer, I'd debated with Suze and we'd decided to check on him. I explained why I had a key to the house, and that we'd let ourselves in and looked around and found Alan.

Within minutes the house went from creepily empty to bustling. Bob guided us to a couch in the living room and told us to stay put. An ambulance arrived (no rush, no siren), and the EMTs carried a stretcher upstairs. Bob reappeared long enough to say it looked like Alan had fallen and hit the back of his head on the corner of the glass-topped dresser. No signs of foul play, most likely a heart attack or there'd have been a lot more blood.

Suze and I exchanged sorrowful looks. We wanted to feel reassured, but they'd thought Rose was 'no signs of foul play,' too. I felt numb and dazed with adrenaline fatigue, and wanted to go home and crawl into a hot bath and stay in there until my skin sloughed off.

Then the ambulance crew made their way back down the stairs with their burden and I heard one of them say, "Two calls in an hour to the same block, how often does that happen?" And a muffled question from probably one of the cops, and the reply, "old lady next door had a stroke."

I was off the couch and into the hallway before I realized I was in motion. "Old lady?" I asked, my heart racing again. "Next door which side? Spiky hair, pink cast?"

They reached the bottom of the stairs and released the stretcher undercarriage. "Yeah," one of them said. "You know her?"

"Oh my god." I turned back to the couch to grab my things. "That's my grandmother, I have to get to the hospital. Oh god, where are the kids? Suzette, run over to my house, here, take my keys—" my hands shook so hard I dropped the keys. I headed for the door, forgetting that my car was at my place. That I'd just handed my keys to Suzette. That my purse was on the table in my kitchen.

"Whoa, whoa. You're not going anywhere like that." Bob put a firm hand on my shoulder. "You don't look in any shape to drive. I'll take you wherever you need to go, so just hang on for a sec, okay?"

"Where are the kids?"

"We gave them a ride to hospital," one of the EMTs said. "Not supposed to let minors in the back, but the girl insisted. We took your grandmother to Orchard City Memorial. They've got a Stroke Unit there, so she's in good hands."

Bob arranged for one of the other officers to take over. I calmed down enough to get out my cell phone, and of course discovered I had turned it off and that Val's frantic calls to me had gone to voicemail. I tried calling Val, but either she hadn't taken her phone with her or they'd made her turn it off at the hospital.

Oh god, this was all my fault. If I'd stayed home and looked after the kids like a good stand-in mommy none of this would have happened. I called the hospital, and was waiting for someone in Admissions to pick up when Bob said he was ready to go. Suze wanted to tag along, but Bob told her to hang tight until he came back.

Bob drove while I tried to elicit an update from the hospital. I finally learned Granimi had been moved to a room on the third floor. The Stroke Unit nurse would only say that Granimi was stable, and that Val and Ansel were in the waiting room.

* * *

Granimi, I was told when I got to the hospital and found her room, was sleeping, and would be okay. Probably. Mostly. The stroke, much as it seemed a really big deal to me and the kids, was considered by those in the know to be not that serious. Because the kids had acted quickly to call the ambulance and get her to the hospital, damage had been minimized. As much as these things go. She'd fallen again—onto the thick carpet in the living room, fortunately—and had some discomfort in her hip. Could just be a bruise, or it might be a hairline fracture. Their hip guy would take a look tomorrow.

Motor control on the left side had been slightly affected, but might come back. We'd know in a few days. Worst case scenario: Granimi would need physical therapy, and maybe some speech therapy as well. Verbal comprehension appeared unaffected, but the left-side motor control issue made it difficult for her to speak. They wanted to keep her for a couple of days, for tests and observation. She'd probably be able to come home with me by the end of the week. Doctor Warren was concerned, though, that at G.'s age, where there was one stroke, others might follow. Doctor Stephenson, their stroke man, would do rounds in the morning. I could talk with him after that.

Val said it had been scary, but I knew from a brief conversation with the nurse that she and Ansel had received lots of praise from the EMTs and ER staff for keeping cool heads and doing the right thing, and by the time I'd found her for an emotional clinch she was calmer than I was.

"Val, sweetie, I'm so sorry I wasn't there. I feel terrible that you had to go through this." I hadn't mentioned anything about what had happened next door. So far as Val and Ansel were concerned, I'd gone over to Suzette's for an hour.

"Why didn't you have your phone on?"

I apologized profusely for my carelessness and inattention. I was mentally black and blue from kicking myself for not calling home as soon as we'd heard an ambulance in the neighborhood.

Now that I was around to blame for everything, Val's mood descended rapidly.

"It's not fair. You make me carry my phone everywhere so you can check up on me, then you wander off whenever you want and no one can reach you!"

"It won't happen again. I promise," I said for the eighty thousandth time. If I weren't feeling so guilty I'd be getting crankier by the minute, too. None of us had had dinner and clearly we needed food. And it was time for the kids to go home. I wanted to stay, but no way I was sending Val back to my place alone. Fortunately, a call to Suzette revealed that she was already en route. She'd had the presence of mind to stop by my house to grab my purse and lock up. She'd drop my stuff off, then take the kids to Olive Garden for dinner, "Dope 'em up with carbs," as she put it, admitting she could use a hefty serving of comfort food herself. After dinner she'd take Ansel home, and Val could either spend the night at her house, or Suzette would sleep over chez moi.

"Do whatever you need to do there," she said. "And don't worry about Val. She's a tough kid. She's probably a lot less rattled than you are right now."

By eight o'clock I was alone in the third floor lounge, wondering how so much could have happened in just two hours. The nurse assured me that Granimi was still sleeping, and let me peek into her room again to see for myself. I wanted to go sit beside her and hold her hand, but didn't want to disturb her. I needed to call my parents in Italy, but in the wee hours anything I told them about Granimi's condition would sound many times worse. Better to wait and call them at an hour when they'd be up. Which would be when, here? I stared at the time readout on my cell and couldn't figure out the time zone thing. I've been calculating the time difference to and from Italy every summer for twenty years. At eight PM here, it was… some other time over there. Forget it. I'd deal with it later, when I'd had something to eat and my brain was back on duty.

I pestered the nurse one more time to be sure to let Granimi know, should she wake up before I got back, that I'd been there and would return as soon as I'd found some food. And chocolate. Lots of chocolate.

I sat at a table in a corner of the hospital cafeteria with a cup of chicken noodle soup and felt like a terrible, terrible, horrible person.

That's it for me, I thought. I'm out. Suzette could turn our brownie theory and findings over to Bob and waggle her tits at him until he agreed there was something to it. I'd turn the Brad-Alan-Russell thing over to… somebody. I wasn't feeling particularly kindly toward lawyers (Alan) or accountants (Russell) at that moment, but I'd dig up a couple of trustworthy ones and they could unravel that mess for me. Count me out. I would sit at Granimi's bedside for as long as she needed, and then I'd go home and hug Val and finish turning Brad's study into my painting studio and leave the heavy shit for more qualified personnel. No more snooping for me.

42

I woke up in a chair beside Granimi's bed when a nurse came in for a six AM vital-signs check. Dear god I was stiff. I wished I could remember those yoga moves she'd shown me a few days ago. I'd fallen asleep without calling Mom and Dad, but the nurse said Dr. Stephenson would be by in a bit and I decided to wait until I'd heard an expert opinion. I hung around long enough to say reassuring things to Granimi, then another nurse came in and wanted a few minutes with the patient, which was my clue to go in search of a very large coffee.

Dr. Stephenson was alarmingly young but seemed to know his stuff. He flirted with Granimi and while he didn't tell us anything I hadn't already heard, he told it more authoritatively. Came down to the same thing: Granimi had clearly not had enough of an ordeal last night and must spend the day being wheeled around the hospital for one test after another. I hoped she had good insurance; the lab bill alone was going to be a whopper.

I warned Dr. Stephenson that my mother would want to talk to him, but he shrugged it off and said that dealing with pushy family members was part of his job. "They teach a course on that in medical school," he said, which I figured was maybe his idea of a joke. He did recommend that if Mom wanted to get through to him she should call between three and four-thirty that afternoon. I wondered if he was maybe maneuvering for the time zone advantage or planning to be out of the office by then. Points to him, either way.

"Bottom line, Doc, first thing Mom's going to ask is should she hop on a plane back here. What do I tell her?"

He shrugged and looked at Granimi to see what she thought.

G. shook her head and grimaced. "Shay therr," she said. "Peesh." She rolled her eyes and Dr. Stephenson and I both laughed.

"Tell her your grandmother will be fine, but that she needs to rest and the fewer visitors the better for now."

"Ankewe," G. got out. "Uver, bu shoo mush."

"You love her, but she's too much?" the doctor asked.

Granimi nodded. "Taygh pissher, sheessee fye."

"Take a picture, she'll see you're fine?"

Geeze, I hoped the speech therapy worked, or we'd have to hire Dr. S. as a full-time interpreter.

I told Granimi I'd snap a picture later—after I brought a hairbrush and some makeup from home—and followed the doc into the hall.

"Anything I should know that you didn't want to say in front of her?" I asked, before he could get away.

"I don't see any immediate cause for concern," he said. "But she's 82, and she's had a stroke. Perhaps not the first one, just the first that anyone's noticed."

In fact, he said, some of the occasional spacing out I'd mentioned, perhaps the loss of balance that had led to her broken wrist, might be indicators that she'd had a series of very small strokes leading up to this one. If that was the case, she should not be living on her own. "We'll know more after the tests. If all's well, she can go home with you in a few days."

"What about recovery? Mobility, speech, all that good stuff?"

"Too soon to say. I can tell she's a live wire compared to most folks her age, so there's a good chance she'll recover better than most, too. To what degree—," he shrugged. "We'll know when we know."

Great.

By the time I'd thanked the doc for his time an orderly had arrived to wheel Granimi off to her first round of tests. I trundled along to Radiology, wished her luck, and figured this was a good time to spread the news. Especially since using a cell phone gave me reason to step outside and breathe something that wasn't hospital air for a few minutes.

I spoke to Dad first, which was good. The man enjoys supernatural unflappability, something I could use more of. Talking to him made me feel more grounded, a good set-up for talking to Mom. It wasn't easy convincing her that Granimi did not require a bedside vigil. Of course she wanted to talk to G.'s doctor herself.

"Dr. Stephenson seems very capable," I assured her. Just as well she couldn't see how young he was, or she'd insist he fax her a copy of his med school diploma. "He says a good time to call is between three and four-thirty this afternoon. That's local time here. He assured me it's completely unnecessary for you to cut such a wonderful vacation short."

Mom finally mellowed as she grasped that Granimi's condition, though unfortunate, was not dire, and that she didn't need to hop on a plane this minute. I told myself I should check voice mail before calling Olivia. I hate voice mail—it seems to just add more things to my to do list—but it has its good points. Such as I could listen to a barely coherent, borderline hysterical message from Hanna, listen again to make sure I got the gist of it, and not have to deal with or even talk to her in person.

Hanna had shown up at the Braskas as usual that morning, flipped out over the bloodstained carpet and disarray in the master bedroom, and totally freaked when our neighbor across the street told her that Alan had died. "This too much for me," she said in her message. "Can't be part of this kind of thing. I go away for a while."

Maybe she thought we were engaged in the Devil's work and she'd better vacate the range of influence. Maybe she was in or a fugitive from the Witness Protection Program, which might explain the weird accent and unconvincing backstory. I felt bad that Hanna was frightened and fleeing, but also figured it was her problem. I couldn't muster up the energy to worry about her. Selfish of me, but between family stuff and self-recrimination I felt stretched thin. Usually I like feeling thin, but not this way.

Olivia and pals had migrated to Barcelona, where I reached her on her cell and indulged in ten uninterrupted minutes of listening to my cutie ramble on about what a great time she was having. She reminded me to check out her flickr page for new pics, "I got some great ones yesterday," and apologized for not sending me daily email updates.

Olivia yelped when I told her the Granimi news, and was furious I hadn't alerted her straight away. I didn't care that she was pissed I'd let her talk before spilling the bad news; listening to my daughter's happy chat about her travels had been worth it.

"There's no reason for you to come home," I said. "Granimi will be furious if you give up roaming around Europe on her behalf. She'd love it, though, if you'd send a video message to her email and tell her what a great time you're having. Get Tina and Rory in there, too. You know how she likes us all to be surrounded by friends."

Many 'luv you's' were exchanged, and then I realized it had become Tuesday, and I'd agreed to do something on Tuesday and oh, shit, I was supposed to meet Kevin Zaff at SweetiePies in… fifty-three minutes. I know, I said I wasn't going to snoop any more and could have and maybe should have cancelled. I rationalized that finding out more about KZ's snooping was not the same as doing more snooping myself. Besides, how often do I get to have lunch with a private eye?

I sprinted back to Radiology, explained my dilemma to Granimi who, mercifully, was not at that moment entubed in an MRI machine or whatever they next had planned for her, then panicked because I couldn't remember where I'd parked, and finally remembered my car was at home. Thank god for taxis, and for Orchard City cabbies who don't mind driving a fare all the way to the far side of Laurelton (for a small fortune, of course, but I had $300 in my wallet), and who don't try to make conversation all the way. I grabbed one that had just discharged its passengers and hightailed it home for the quickest shower on record and a change of clothes.

*   *   *

SweetiePies was a cheery haven of sunny windows, red vinyl booths, and the heavenly mingled aromas of warm pie, hot grease, and coffee. By some miracle I was only three minutes late. I had no idea what Kevin Zaff really looked like and didn't see any solitary guy who resembled my idea of a PI, so I took a booth by the front windows. A waitress sensed my desperation and took my order of coffee and a grilled turkey and swiss on rye with mustard, coleslaw on the side. There was pie in my future, too, but I was following a grease-before-sugar plan. Besides, they have a lot of pies and I didn't want to make a rushed decision about the most important part of the meal.

I'd barely begun to refill the caffeine reservoirs when a preppy-looking guy in his early 30s swung around on his counter stool, looked me in the eye, and smiled as if he knew me. He picked up a 9x12 manila envelope and a black leather zippered folder and walked over to my booth.

No way. The Kevin Zaff in my mind was 52. At least. On the short side. Beefy turning to fat. He wore cheap shirts that had been laundered so many times the collars were frayed. The Kevin Zaff in my mind had a bushy mustache and a receded hairline and was overdue for a haircut.

He had a history with cheap cigars and didn't believe in teeth whitener.

"Mrs. Wells." The Kevin Zaff in SweetiePies slid into the other side of my booth.

"Mr. Zaff." I took a nonchalant sip of my coffee.

He wasn't what you'd call holy-cow hot, but trim and nicely put together. Neatly groomed, short hair, clean shaven. Dressed in pressed chinos and a light blue polo shirt. He looked like he'd stepped out of a J.Crew catalog. And was so much younger than I'd expected.

"Couldn't pick me out of the crowd, huh?" he said.

I gave a casual shrug. "You're the investigator. I figured you'd find me."

The waitress brought my sandwich over and looked at him and he said he'd have a chef salad and could he get two hard boiled eggs with that, house vinaigrette on the side.

"Something's wrong with this picture." I peeled open one of my sandwich halves and stuffed it with coleslaw. "Isn't the girl supposed to order the salad?"

"I watch what I eat," he said. "Don't want to turn into that overweight guy you were expecting."

I took a large bite of my sandwich, without admitting I'd had him all wrong in my head. Oh, man, that was good. I might have whimpered. Ordinarily I'd feel self-conscious about stuffing my face with grilled cheese and coleslaw while a guy watched me eat, but I was hungry and not in a flirtatious mood.

"That looks like rough-day food," he observed.

I didn't reply because I had a mouthful. I chewed and swallowed, unwilling to be rushed. I washed it down with the rest of my coffee.

"You don't know the half of it," I said when I could speak.

"I like mine with pickles," he said, as I forked in some more coleslaw.

"Whatever floats your boat." Inferior choice, but he was entitled.

His salad arrived and he dug in and we ate in silence for a few minutes. By the time I reached for the extra napkins I'd had the waitress bring over I couldn't stand the suspense any longer.

"So, what's in the envelope? I hope it's for me."

"Tell me why you're eating rough-day food, and you can have it."

Geeze, this guy never gave anything away.

Okay. He'd asked, I'd spill. "Let's see, first, my BFF Suzette and I snuck into Alan Braska's house last night. I have a good neighbor key, but it's not like he invited us in. And, what else… oh, I found some business papers in Alan's study which look like they have Brad's signature on them, but I'm pretty sure that's forged. Which I think means Alan ripped Brad and me off for a ton of money. There was something else… oh, yeah. Turns out Alan wasn't teaching his Monday night class at the Community College, like we thought. The whole time we were in there, riffling through his papers? He was upstairs, dead. They're saying cardiac arrest, but gee, given who he's been hanging around with, I don't know."

Not only did Kevin Zaff look impressed, he also appeared to have been rendered speechless. Involuntarily. That was a nice change.

"There's more." I made him wait while I signaled the waitress for a coffee refill. "While we were in there illegally," I added, "my grandmother, who was babysitting my niece and the neighbors' kid at my house, had a stroke. She's doing okay, but they're twelve, which is a little young to deal, you know?"

"Gee." He finally found his voice. "Is one sandwich going to be enough? Maybe you should order something else."

"I'm getting pie in a minute," I assured him. "Probably á la mode. The worst thing is, when the ambulance went by, we heard the siren and I didn't even realize it had stopped at my house, which is right next door. I thought it was the cops coming to arrest us. Closest I've come to peeing my pants since I was nine and Jimmy Clement dropped a frog down my back."

"You seem remarkably cool about it."

I shook my head no. "That's the sedative effect of grease. Inside, I'm still shaking. I am not cut out for this skullduggery stuff. The entire time we were in there I thought I was going to pass out or throw up or both. Put so many stress hormones in my system it probably took years off my life."

He laughed, but something in his look said it wasn't about my stress hormone concerns.

"What's so funny?"

He smiled. "Your husband said you could be a hoot."

I gave him my best I-don't-think-so look. "I'll have you know," I corrected, "that Brad consistently rated me 'a hoot and a half.'" And then all the missing him came back and the fun was gone.

"I only met Brad a couple of times," he said, "but he struck me as an okay guy. I can see you'd be good together. I bet you miss him."

I nodded, tearing up. Dammit. I was glad for the remaining extra napkins. I didn't have to worry about smearing my mascara, because I hadn't had time to apply any.

He gave me as much time as I needed.

"Sorry," I said, when I had things under control. "The more time passes, the more I think I'm getting a handle on it, and the more it catches me off-guard, you know?" I deposited a wad of damp napkin on my plate. "So, that's why the rough-day food. You owe me whatever's in that envelope."

He passed it over and I took a look while he worked on his salad. Most of it was a duplicate of what I'd found in Brad's safe, with some added details.

"Your husband hired me," Kevin explained between bites, "because he suspected this guy Alan was fooling around. He didn't care so much about the affair, but he was concerned it was affecting the business. He thought the woman Alan was seeing, this Lillian Haber chick, was up to no good. So the first thing I did for him was get evidence of the affair. Then he asked me to look into Ms. Haber more, dig around in her work history, reputation around town, that kind of thing. So that's the report you have there. Other than a fondness for well-heeled older men, and a curious lack of marital history, not much to go on."

I flipped through the folder, trying not to feel majorly miffed that Brad had had this dirt on Alan and not told me.

"She's not well-liked," Kevin went on. "Considered 'cold' and 'standoffish.' Usually that just means the person isn't interested in making friends. But sometimes people don't want to make friends because they have things to hide."

I nodded him along, reminded of Hanna. Probably I'd never know what that story was.

"So, at around this point, I left a couple messages on your husband's cell, asking if he wanted me to keep digging, but I didn't hear back from him. When a week had gone by without an answer I called your house to see what was up. A very efficient lady answered, told me Brad had died."

"Probably my mother." I complain about her a lot, but if you need someone to take care of shit like answering the phone, because no way can you hold it together, she's your gal.

"I gotta tell you, I wondered at first what had happened, thinking maybe I hadn't been as discrete in my inquiries as I thought, and maybe that had led to an unfortunate reaction."

"The cops had their doubts, too," I assured him. "Although their suspicions were aimed at me." I wondered now if they'd been right to be suspicious, but had faced the wrong direction.

"I heard about that," he said, "through a friend on the force. Glad they didn't pursue that angle."

"Yeah. Me, too."

"So, no client, no case," he summed up. "I tallied up the bill, wrote out a check, and put it in the mail. But I was curious. So now and then, when I've had some time, I've poked around. Started all the way back." He unzipped the leather folder and passed me another sheet, which turned out to be a concise bio.

Holy cow, look at that: Lillian (Lily) Haber. Place of birth: Peru, Indiana.

"Peruvian Lily," I said to myself. The Ouija clue had been right. I shivered. It creeped me out more now than it had that night.

"Something wrong?"

I looked up from the report. No way I was getting into the Ouija board scene with this guy. "Uh, no. Peru, Indiana, huh? Sounds like a small town."

"It is. She grew up there through high school. Here's something interesting: she was an archery champion her senior year. Won some kind of national title for her age group. Good with a slingshot, too. I just found that out last week."

"Slingshot?" That explained Ansel's new toy, though not why she'd tossed it in a donation bag with a cashmere sweater.

"Yeah. Hard to picture isn't it? She's petite, around five-two. Athletic, looks like she could be a gymnast, maybe, but archery? That's not a typical girl sport."

"I didn't even know it was a sport." I put the bio sheet on top of the report pages. "I want to run something by you," I said. "See what you make of it."

"Okay. Shoot."

"I happen to have in my possession some personal items that a female friend reportedly gave to Alan on the understanding that he was going to drop them off at Goodwill along with some stuff of his own."

"With you so far."

"The fun part's in how I got 'em."

"Do tell."

"A while back Alan was driving Rose's car because his was in the shop. He was supposed to do the Goodwill thing, but forgot. So the stuff sat in the trunk of Rose's car, but she didn't drive much and no one looked there. Yesterday morning my neighbor's kid, a budding internet gazillionaire whose mom makes him put his online earnings in his college fund..."

"I'm with mom on that one," he said, when I paused for breath. "He'll thank her when he's older."

"...and who wanted to earn some pocket money, offered to wash and clean Alan's cars."

"An offer no good neighbor can refuse."

"Exactly. Even if the cars don't need it. So Ansel, that's the kid, finds the stuff that was supposed to go to Goodwill."

I paused again for breath and coffee, and to flag down our waitress and order a slice of blueberry pie with vanilla ice cream.

Kevin declined dessert. Too bad. He was showing potential as a banter buddy. But the no dessert thing; even if he were irresistibly cute it could never work between us.

"Okay," he said when the waitress had departed, "that explains how the kid found the stuff. How did you get it?"

"A couple hours later," I said, "I'm swimming in my pool and something dings me on the shoulder. I look around, and plop, there's another one hitting the water. It's gravel. Ansel's on the other side of the backyard fence with his new toy, a competition grade slingshot, taking pot-shots at a squirrel in my sycamore tree."

"So you ask him where he got it?"

"So I ask him to please cut it out, because he's getting gravel in my pool. Then I let him show it off to me while I pretend to be interested. And he tells me where he got it."

"From the stuff that was supposed to go to Goodwill that was in the trunk of Rose's car."

"Exactly. So I go over to Alan's and say, 'I'm going to Goodwill, I can take your stuff, too, save you the trip.'"

"And he said, 'Why thank you, Mrs. Wells, that's very thoughtful of you.'"

"Close enough, yeah."

"So now it's in the trunk of your car."

I shook my head. "Nope. Now it's spread out on my dining room table. And one of the things in the bag—" I flipped through the papers he'd given me until I found the photo I was looking for, and tapped it with a finger, "—is this sweater."

"How about that."

"Yeah, how about that."

I pictured Lillian Haber's garments as I'd left them on my dining table. It occurred to me that I'd better clean up in there before Friday night rolled around, because I'd invited Alan over for dinner. Then I remembered that Alan wouldn't be eating dinner at anyone's house, ever again.

43

I told Kevin Zaff what else had been in the bag, and he looked
thoughtful. Then he pulled out his cell and asked whoever took his
call if they could push it back a couple of hours.

"You got any problem with me coming over to your house?" he
asked.

I shook my head. "Happy to have you take a look." I had to go
home anyway, check in with Val and get some things to bring to Granimi
in the hospital.

Suzette was in my kitchen when we got to my place, packing up
brownies for the focus group with help from Val. I gave Val a quick
hug and asked about her night with Suzette (fine) and assured her that
Granimi was doing well and would be home in a few days. I suggested
that, if they could spare a few brownies, Granimi might like to sample the
options, too. Val could bring them to her for a private taste test during
evening visiting hours.

"That's a lot of brownies," Kevin said.

"Oh my god," I realized. "I haven't told you about Rose and the
brownies yet!"

"What about Rose and the brownies?" he asked, while Suze made
faces at me that most likely meant who's this cutie you're bringing home,
and what's going on that I don't know about?

"Come in here and we'll tell you about it." I led Kevin through to
the dining room, whispering to Suzette to come along and leave Val in
the kitchen. If Val found out there was a PI in the house she'd be all over
him. When we were adults-only I introduced Kevin, and got a thumbs-
up from Suze when she learned he was the PI Brad had hired.

"We think Lillian Haber killed Rose," I explained to Kevin. "By
feeding her a brownie with disguised nuts in it." I gave him a quick recap

of the least-woowoo aspects of our investigation to date, including the upcoming focus group. We'd considered canceling, given the testimony of Lillian's neighbor and my family emergency, but it was something for the kids to do, get their minds off the events of last night. And if our disguised-nut brownies fooled enough elderly palates we'd go back to Bob with our solidified theory. Or Suze would. I reminded myself I was staying out of it.

"Now that you've confirmed the affair," I said to Kevin, "I'm guessing Lily wanted Rose out of the way so she could be with Alan."

"Be with Alan's bank account is more like it," Kevin said. "I doubt there was a whole lot of love going on there."

"Doesn't matter now. He and his money are both out of reach."

"Doesn't make sense she'd have killed him," Kevin pointed out. "If she wanted his money."

Suzette shook her head. "Bob called a few minutes ago," she said. "It was a heart attack. Alan hit his head on the corner of the nightstand on his way to the ground."

"Definitely?"

"Bob says totally, absolutely, not a chance they're wrong, cardiac arrest. Heart first, head second. I didn't press for details, but it's the kind of thing they're always figuring out on CSI."

"He did look ghastly when I saw him yesterday morning." I didn't know whether to feel relieved that Alan hadn't been murdered after all—although the argument captured on tape might have done him in—or frustrated that another path to pinning blame on Lily was closed, or even worse than I already did because I hadn't forcibly driven Alan to his doctor yesterday morning when any fool could see the man wasn't well.

I tried to focus on the present by gesturing at the table. "In the box is Rose and Alan's stuff. It's ignorable. The rest is what was in Lillian Haber's bag."

"I have my eye on that sweater," Suzette said. "If it's ever up for grabs."

"It's a size small," I reminded her.

"Cashmere is stretchy. Some people would say there's no such thing as a cashmere sweater that's too small."

Kevin gave Suze the once-over. "I think that sweater would fit you just fine," he said with a grin.

"Knock if off, you two." I glared at Suzette and turned to Kevin. "So, what do you make of this stuff. Plus the slingshot, of course."

"First thought? Looks like she maybe was dumping an outfit—those shoes and slacks and the sweater—tossed the other stuff in to fill up the bag so it would be less obvious."

"That's what we thought. But how do we know she wasn't just cleaning out a closet?"

"You ever clean out a closet?" he asked.

"Sure."

Suzette snorted. "Not recently."

"You're one to talk." My closets are a study in zen minimalism compared to Suzette's. She admits the mess is a feng shui no-no, and claims she's going to do something about it. Some day.

"Everyone has clutter," Kevin said diplomatically. "And sooner or later they make a pile of stuff to take to Goodwill."

"I even use Macy's bags for it," I said. Probably the largest accumulation of Macy's bags outside of Macy's is Goodwill stores.

"And if someone looked in those bags," Kevin asked, "what would they find?"

All kinds of shit. "Books, shoes, clothes, accessories. DVDs. Stuff my kid's outgrown. Kitchen things I never use. Half the gifts my grandmother gives me."

"And what struck you about this selection?"

"That she's a skinny bitch and I hate her?"

"Other than she's a few sizes smaller than you."

Suzette gasped and I glared.

"I'm not saying anything negative about your shape or size. Personally, I think it would be a shame if you lost those curves. I'm just sayin'."

I let it go. "What struck me is there's not enough here to make up a convincing donation bag." Then I remembered our pathetic attempt at reconnaissance the day before. "But, you know, Lily is one of those freaks of nature who doesn't have clutter. I've looked in her windows and neatnik does not begin to describe her. So maybe this is convincing, by her standards. Which maybe supports the dumping-the-evidence theory?"

"But what's it evidence of?" Suzette asked.

"Dunno yet," Kev said. He picked up one of the shoes and examined the sole.

"Someone explain to me why she didn't just toss it in a dumpster," Suzette said. We'd tossed that question around yesterday and hadn't come up with an answer.

"Personally? A dumpster would be my first choice." Kevin moved on to peer at the stain on the trousers. "But there was a case last year in Orchard City. Some homeless guy goes dumpster diving, fishes out something the cops have been looking for and walks around town for a week with it sitting on top of his cart. A sharp rookie recognizes what it is, asks where he got it, and they catch the bad guy. Story made the front page of the paper and was all over the evening news."

"So if she'd noticed that story," I surmised, "she might think twice about a dumpster."

"And you don't put evidence in your own trash," Suzette added. "Everybody knows that."

"But wouldn't Goodwill be risky?"

"Depends if anyone's looking for these items," Kev said. "If not, it's clever, especially if Alan's doing the drop off. Worst case, he's caught with the stuff and she can say it was all his idea."

"All what was his idea?"

"Whatever. Don't get hung up on it."

"Once this stuff hits the rack at Goodwill it would go fast," Suzette said, "even with that spot." She held up the slacks. "I'd take these to a tailor, have them made into city shorts."

"And there goes the evidence," Kevin said. "Now someone else is wearing this stuff—"

"—saying, 'Look what I found at Goodwill for five bucks!'"

"By the time they question Goodwill, if they ever do, it was just another drop-off," Kevin said.

Suzette put the pants back on the table. "I wonder what else is in that shop. Lena, when was the last time we went thrifting?"

"I don't thrift," I reminded her. Strangers' old clothes: ick. And another feng shui no-no, by the way, which doesn't seem to slow Suze down any. "Okay, I get that it wasn't such a bad idea to dump these at Goodwill. But I'd never sleep again if it were me doing it. I'd lie awake every night worrying."

"That's because you're a wuss," Suzette said. "Some people would lie awake every night thinking about how clever they are."

"A scheme like that takes confidence," Kevin agreed. "And confident people make good criminals. Until they get caught."

If they get caught. We'd made progress with the brownie theory, but Lillian Haber was still out there, showing condos to rich old ladies who wanted to move closer to their grandkids. It was nice to feel that the clothes were important, and that I'd been both clever and incredibly lucky to intercept them, but what did they mean? If we couldn't sell the cops on our brownie theory, how would Lillian Haber's cast-offs help us get her into handcuffs?

"I want to know what she was doing when she wore these," I said, "that she doesn't want anyone to know about."

"She wouldn't have been wearing that sweater when Rose died," Suzette pointed out. "In June? She'd get heat stroke."

"Plus, we know the stuff was in Alan's car for a while." I wondered how much of a while. Brad had died in cashmere-appropriate weather. Had I been wrong to blame my heartache on him, to be so furious at his idiocy and carelessness? Had some size 2 bitch been responsible all along?

I felt dizzy again, and pulled a chair out from the table to sit down before my knees gave out.

"Do you think it's possible to kill someone with a slingshot?" I asked.

"Sure," Kevin said. "Ever hear of David and Goliath?"

The doorbell rang and Val thumped down the hall to answer it. It was Ansel, with a plate of the vegan brownies Tulip had insisted on contributing to the taste test. Explaining why we didn't need them hadn't seemed worth the effort.

Suzette looked at her watch. "If we're going to do this focus group," she said, "we ought to go. Where's Hanna? She said she'd be here at one forty-five and it's after two."

"I forgot to tell you. Hanna left me a voicemail this morning. She backed out."

"Gee, Lena, thanks for the heads up."

"It gets worse."

She glared at me. "You're backing out, too?"

"Can you handle it on your own? I should get back to the hospital. I feel like I've abandoned Granimi. We could still cancel, you know."

Val and Ansel had wandered in by then, wondering why we weren't on our way yet.

"We want to do it," Val protested. "Right, Ansel?"

Ansel, who'd been fiddling with his camcorder, looked up. "We're all set to go, Mrs. Wells."

"Fine, we'll do it," I said. "But you'll have to do it without me. Suzette will be in charge, okay?"

I tried not to take it personally that they appeared to think trading me for Suzette was an improvement to their day.

* * *

"You got a minute?" I asked Kevin after the others left. He did, so I showed him the original River Bend Terrace partnership agreement from Brad's files and my photocopy of the swap-out documents I'd found at Alan's. I explained Russell's version of the story and why I thought maybe that wasn't what really happened.

I could tell by his expression when I'd finished that he was intrigued but not convinced. I couldn't blame him; that's how I felt about it, too.

"For every Donald Trump," Kevin said, "you gotta figure a hundred guys lose their shirts in the development game. Way the credit market's been lately, it's entirely possible something went kerflooey on the money end. Brad may have been very smart to get out of it."

I reminded him of the "let's stay another day in Palm Springs" wrinkle.

"I agree the date is suggestive," he said, "but I doubt you'll be able to make anything of it. You prove Brad was out of town that Monday and they'll just say, 'Oh, but it was Tuesday; nobody noticed the date was off.'"

"So how do I find out if there's anything to this?" I hoped he could suggest a next step. Preferably one that minimized active involvement in my part.

"Easiest way? Sue your accountant for fraud. The money stuff will all come out in discovery."

"I'd really hate to do that if I'm wrong," I said. "I just don't see using a law suit as a fishing expedition. Isn't that kind of behavior part of what's wrong with this country?"

"Some people would say your right to abuse the legal system to your advantage is what makes this country great, but I take your point."

"What do you think about this notary business?" I pointed out that the original LLC documents were date-stamped by the state's business registration office, but did not require notarized signatures, whereas the buyout deal that Brad had allegedly managed to sign on a day he was out of town had been notarized.

Kevin shrugged. "A corporate attorney would know whether or not it's required. Certainly it validates the signatures."

"Which would kind of be the point, don't you think, if one of these signatures is a fake? Especially if the documents don't otherwise require it."

He saw it the other way. "The point is that from a legal standpoint it proves the signatures are genuine."

"You're relying on the honesty of the notary," I said. "Maybe that's a mistake."

He didn't think that was plausible until I pointed out that notary Edith Stokely had been Alan's devoted secretary for many years. And that I suspected she might be susceptible to manipulation by her long-time employer.

Which is how we ended up ringing her doorbell twenty minutes later.

44

I could tell when Edith opened her door that she'd heard about Alan. Her face was blotchy, her eyes red, clothing somber. If you didn't know her you'd think her hair looked fine, but I could see entire strands out of place. She waved us in without saying hello and showed no curiosity about who Kevin was or why he was with me.

"I'm so sorry about Alan," I said when we were seated in her parlor and I'd introduced Kevin by name only. Mr. Stokely appeared briefly in a doorway, but Edith waved him away.

"It's kind of you to stop by," she said. "I was Mr. Braska's secretary for more years than most people stay married these days. To lose both him and Rose in such a short time&hellip." She sniffed and dabbed at her nose with a rumpled handkerchief.

"Edith, please forgive us intruding at a sad time," I said, "but some documents have come to our attention that we hope you can help us with." I'd worried she would ask us to leave, but the opportunity to be of service and to think about something other than the death of her friend and employer seemed to perk her up.

I showed her the papers with Brad's signature and the questionable date, pointed out that she had notarized them, and asked if she remembered them.

"My goodness," she said, giving them a cursory glance, "we handled so many real estate transactions in that office. I don't know that I could remember a specific document."

"This is from the week before Brad died," I said. "It was a Monday?"

That seemed to mean something to her, but she had to consider it for what felt like an hour before deciding she recalled something specific.

"I hope you don't mind my saying this," she began, "but in my experience Mr. Wells did tend to over-schedule. He was forever running late and doing things in a rush."

That was true. I'd given up attempting to help Brad better manage his time when I figured out he liked to be in a hurry. Not one of the qualities that most endeared him to me, but I'd learned to live with it.

"I remember this now," Edith said, "because my hairdresser appointment caused so much trouble."

I've had troublesome hair appointments myself from time to time, but didn't see what a bad cut had to do with anything.

"I have a standing appointment for the second Monday of every month, you see," Edith explained. "I always took a long lunch break on that day. Of course I made up the time by coming in early the rest of the week."

Kevin made a face at me. I was thinking the same thing: most people would call it a dentist appointment and expect to get away with it.

"I didn't know anything was amiss until Friday of the next week. That's when Mr. Braska found these documents in his office. They should have been notarized and filed with the county before then, and he was quite angry they'd been overlooked. When it became clear I didn't know what he was talking about, he reminded me that Mr. Wells had come in the Monday before—the day of my hairdresser appointment, you see— to sign them. They'd waited as long as they could for me to witness the signatures, but Mr. Wells had another appointment and had to leave before I returned from my lunch break. Mr. Braska was quite put out that I didn't remember, but I'm certain he hadn't said a word to me about it. We finally figured out that Mr. Braska had made the appointment himself at the last minute, which is why it wasn't in my copy of his book."

Kev opened his mouth to speak and I shook my head at him. Edith had been directing her comments to me, and I didn't want interruptions from a stranger to disrupt her narrative.

"But you notarized these," I said, pretending to be confused, "with the Monday date."

"That's right, dear. Because on that Monday, when Mr. Wells left before I got back from the hairdresser, Mr. Braska put the papers aside, thinking he'd ask me to notarize them when I returned. It's not how things are supposed to be done," she admitted. "But with long-time clients sometimes the rules get bent a little for everyone's convenience." She looked at me then as if it had just occurred to her that perhaps our visit meant there was cause for concern.

I kept my face neutral and spoke as reassuringly as I could. "That's totally understandable," I said, "with clients you've known for such a long time." I'd expected her to relax once I'd indicated it was no biggie, but she looked displeased with her memories.

"So on the Friday," she explained, "Mr. Braska asked me to notarize the documents retroactively. I wasn't comfortable with that, because some time had passed and of course Mr. Wells had died by then. But Mr. Braska was so upset, and it was clearly important, so I made an exception. I would never have done it except that I knew Mr. Wells's signature. I didn't like being made to feel responsible for the situation, though. That's why I remember it so clearly now."

"What do you mean?" I asked. "Clearly it wasn't your fault the documents were misplaced."

"I've had the same second-Monday hair appointment for over a decade," she said with a trace of exasperation. "But even though I reminded Mr. Braska I'd be taking a long lunch hour that day, and had put it in his calendar as I always did, he scheduled that meeting with Mr. Wells expecting I'd be back at my regular time."

Edith struck me as the sort of person who took her lunch break at precisely the same time every day. Probably went to the same lunch room, too, and ate the same thing. My guess: half a chicken sandwich on white and a cup of tomato soup.

"Mr. Braska said that if I'd come back at my regular hour that Monday, the crisis would have been avoided. He did apologize later for getting so worked up about it. He explained that if the papers didn't get filed that afternoon, on the Friday that is, he'd miss… I don't remember what exactly, a financing deadline or something like that. And," she paused and sighed, "perhaps this doesn't reflect well on me, but I didn't want to be in a position where Mr. Braska might blame me if the signature was invalidated or an important deadline was missed. He could be like that, you know. Sometimes you just had to do things his way."

"It's good that you were flexible, then," I said. "And the papers got filed on time?"

"I presume so," she said. "That was the last I heard of it, until now. Usually I was the one who took things to the County Clerk's office, but if I remember correctly Mr. Braska mentioned he'd be near there that afternoon and would do it himself." She paused and then nodded again. "Yes, I'm quite sure that's it. I remember thinking the rest of the day would be busy, and was glad I wouldn't have to make a trip to the county office."

Well, there you go.

"It's a good thing Alan isn't around any more," I steamed, after we'd thanked Edith for her help and the front door had closed behind us. "I'd like to put on a pair of pointy-toed cowboy boots and give that man a vigorous kick in the tush." What a lying, scheming, manipulative piece of shit. "Taking advantage of a prissy old fart like Edith Stokely. That's just not right."

Kevin couldn't repress a snicker.

I glared at him. "What?"

"That's the first time I've heard 'prissy old fart' used as an endearment."

"I don't have to like her to feel sorry for her," I pointed out. "She's grieving for that son of a bitch. Now we know why Alan picked that date to use on those documents. Forgot she was taking a long lunch that day—I don't think so."

"You're pretty steamed about this."

"Do you have any idea how much of a shit I've been feeling all day? For sneaking into the man's house and going through his files when he was lying on the floor upstairs, dead? All frickin' day I've been telling myself, 'Alan wouldn't do anything that sneaky and underhanded. Alan wouldn't have ripped Brad off like that. You're blowing this waaaay out of proportion.' Now I find out he does not deserve my sympathy."

We were standing at the curb by then and I kid you not, I was so ticked off I kicked a tree.

"Ow! Remind me not to do that in sandals." I hopped on one foot until I was sure I hadn't broken a toe. I patted the tree. "Sorry. That wasn't meant for you."

"You win," Kevin said, when he'd stopped laughing. "'A hoot and a half' it is." Then his cell rang and he turned away and I heard him say, "I'm on my way."

"I gotta run," he said. "I'll make you a copy of this—" he pulled a digital voice recorder out of his pocket and I gaped my admiration for his sneakiness, "—and get some names for you. I can recommend a documents guy who'll take a look at that signature, and I'll ask around who'd be a good lawyer to advise you how to proceed."

I thanked him and he said it had been fun and wished me luck, and then he drove off. I called the Stroke Unit at Orchard City Memorial and learned Granimi was through with tests for the day and back in her room, but sleeping, so I got in my car and headed for Woodside Meadows to see how the brownie focus group was coming along.

*   *   *

"At least half of them said the vegan ones were really good!" Val collapsed in her chair, giggling. I ought to maybe censor my opinions around her more stringently, give the kid a chance to develop prejudices of her own.

"Wishhun issat?" Granimi poked at the bite-sized morsels on the plate we'd placed in her lap. "I ligu dryid." Her pronunciation was a little better, which I took as a good sign. We both had a dusting of brownie crumbs down our fronts.

Val had had a great time at the taste test, and I was glad we hadn't cancelled it. Ansel had practically teleported home, he was so eager to write up a report, and I'd taken Val out for an early dinner before evening visiting hours. The nurse said it was okay for Granimi to eat sweets "in moderation." I figured the brownie bites were small so they ought to qualify.

Val picked out the vegan one for G., who offered to share it with me. What the hell, why not?

We nibbled, and Granimi made a lopsided face of moderate approval. I had to admit it wasn't bad. I missed the depth of flavor you only get from real butter, but the texture was good and the chocolate very intense. I've had bakery ones that were worse.

Suzette came by at the end of visiting hours. She'd had dinner with Bob, and was purring with satisfaction that he'd said our updated brownie theory was much more convincing than the first rendition. He'd even asked for a copy of Ansel's report. Suze had given Bob a selection of duplicitous brownies to try out on his Lieutenant in the morning, maybe take some over to the DA's office in Orchard City. It looked like we'd done right by Rose, though Bob warned it might be a day or two before they had enough ducks in a row to bring Lily in, and that if she was as slippery a bitch as we suspected getting charges to stick might be tough.

I wasn't going to worry about it. I'd retired from duck-wrangling and was happy to let the professionals take it from there.

Which doesn't explain why I made an appointment with Lily to see a condo the following afternoon, but sometimes a temptation is irresistible.

Per Granimi's request, one of the items I'd brought from home was her iPhone. Which she couldn't use in her room, so she showed me how it worked and I took it outside and checked voicemail for her. Lillian Haber had left a message. She had another condo Granimi might be interested in: 2 bedrooms plus den in a newly renovated 19th century mill building just north of the commercial district. The only doorman building in town; great location; walking distance to shops, restaurants, parks; large rooms; high ceilings; great light; river views. Elevator. Indoor parking. One of the two penthouse units had just fallen out of escrow.

Only one place that could be. I had to see it. I returned Lily's call, introduced myself as Mimi daGiovanni's granddaughter, and explained that my grandmother would be unavailable the rest of the week but I had a very good idea what kind of place she was looking for. That penthouse she'd mentioned sounded perfect. Would it be possible for me to take a look at it?

We're on for 2:15 tomorrow.

An hour later I remembered I'd booked a Soul Retrieval with Raven for 1:45 Wednesday. Shit. He might take it the wrong way, but I'd have to reschedule. And somehow I'd let Kevin Zaff drive off without getting any feedback from him on the "What if Brad wasn't an accident?" question.

Visiting hours were over but I'd bribed the nurses with brownies to turn a blind eye to my presence for another hour. Suzette had driven Val home, and I'd promised to follow in a bit. I should sleep in my own bed and be around when Val got up in the morning, but Granimi, who'd slept half the day, was showing no signs of drowsiness. Having bailed on accompanying her to most of the day's test procedures I felt it would be cruel to leave her wide awake and with no one to talk to. She was supposed to be taking it easy and I suspected that if I left she'd get up and wander the halls until she found a fellow insomniac to befriend.

The TV in her room was on with the sound turned to just barely audible. Granimi nudged me and pointed to the screen. "Why-ee," she said, smiling.

I looked up in time to see a travel commercial featuring flower-draped hula dancers waving their hips, handsome surfers riding waves, and a couple dining al fresco while an orange sunset glowed beyond the fronds of palm trees.

Hawaii. I've never been there, although Brad and I had talked of going. For no good reason we'd taken our trips elsewhere. "We'll do Hawaii next year," we'd say, then end up in Barbados instead.

"Wahgo bag," Granimi said. She looked sad now, and very old.

"You want to go back? To Hawaii?"

She nodded, and I saw tears in her eyes. "Lass shance," she said. "Beh way du long."

"You've been away too long?"

She nodded again.

"Can I come with you?"

That got a big smile, and she looked like Granimi again. "Thabee wunnefuh," she said.

Granimi told me, with many pauses for me to confirm I'd understood correctly, that in her journey to the Lower World she'd found herself in the Hawaii of her childhood. Walking over the fallen orange blossoms of tulip trees, she'd followed a stream until she came to a dirt road through a sugarcane field, where she'd met Myna, a fierce-looking but gregarious bird like those that had chattered and quarreled in the yard of the house where she'd grown up.

"Come home," it had said to her.

"When was the last time you were there?" I asked.

1967, for her parents' funerals. She wasn't counting a 48-hour stopover in Honolulu in 1983, on their way home from Australia.

We had a good laugh at her attempts to pronounce Honolulu, and I asked why she'd stayed away so long. She said she'd had no family there to go back to, and so many other places to visit with Grandpop. And eventually she hadn't wanted to go back because she knew it would have changed so much, and she didn't want to see that.

"Ray doo see dow."

"Ready to see it now?"

She nodded.

"You should practice all the Hawaiian names you can remember," I suggested, "as speech therapy."

Granimi thought that was a great idea, and tried one, but after half a dozen guesses on my part she gave up and wrote it out for me: Queen Lili'uokalani.

"I think we should both get a break on that one," I said.

She asked about my Lower World journey and I told her about almost stepping on Turtle, and my river of tears.

"Wha you gry fo?"

I hesitated, tempted to withdraw into my shell, to say it was nothing. "I was crying for my baby."

I told Granimi how much he'd been on my mind lately, how over the past months I've had difficulty sometimes distinguishing who my tears have been for. Many of the times I'd cried for Brad, I'd been crying for my lost son, too.

"I'd like to find him," I said.

Granimi smiled and let me know she was cool with that. But it's problematic. It was a private adoption. When I found out I was pregnant just after my high school graduation, I'd run away to San Francisco, to Granimi and Grandpop. Friends of theirs had a son and daughter-in-law unable to conceive again after the difficult birth of a daughter, and craving a second child. So they became my son's parents. Granimi had kept in discrete touch with them for years, but gradually they'd withdrawn and she'd respected their desire to keep their family to themselves. A year or so ago she heard the couple had died. She didn't know where my son, now 20, was. Maybe Kevin Zaff could track him down. That thought cheered me up.

Granimi said her face was tired from the effort of talking semi-clearly, and switched to paper and pen for communication. Too bad her handwriting's so awful. I told her it was time for me to go, and gave her a hug. She motioned me to wait and wrote something else—neatly, in large letters—on a piece of paper that she tore from her pad and handed to me.

"Don't think about how much you miss him, or how sad that makes you feel," I read. "Be happy that soon you will see him, and know that he will be happy, too, to meet you."

"Thanks, G.," I said. "I'll do that."

* * *

I called Raven Wednesday morning and told him about Granimi—no, it wasn't serious, but had been scary for everyone and they were keeping her for a few days of tests and observation. He understood that I'd have to reschedule the Soul Retrieval and maybe take a rain check on Thursday's dinner. We'd see how things went.

"Would Mimi like a visitor?" Raven asked. "My afternoon just opened up, and I could come by."

I was about to say Granimi would love that when I realized that, duh, he'd expect to see me there, too.

"I think she'd like that," I said, "in a day or two. She's a little out of it still, and we're supposed to limit visitors." I felt bad about it, because I knew G. would enjoy a visit from Raven. I wouldn't have minded hanging out with him myself.

Val and I had brownies for breakfast. We'd over-baked, it turned out, for the taste test. Even though some extras had been given to the participants a remarkable number of brownies had found their way back to the Santa tin.

When Val left for swim camp I turned to cleaning out Brad's study. My first impulse had been to get rid of the golf course painting and put up one of my own, but when I went to take it down I changed my mind. It would be nice to have something in the room that reminded me of Brad.

I was taking a break from cleaning, sitting at Brad's now-empty desk to make a list for Home Depot, when I heard a muffled thud from across the hall. I went to investigate and found Shadow had knocked one of Lillian Haber's shoes off the dining room table and was pushing it around the floor.

"Mrowp," the cat announced, looking at me and twitching his tail.

"Something going on here I should know about?" I asked, picking up the shoe and putting it back on the table.

Shadow jumped up on the table and sniffed at the other shoe.

"I think it's time you went out." Shadow allowed me to pick him up, and I opened the front door and deposited him on the front step. "Go catch a mouse or something."

I went back inside but instead of returning to the study I found myself in the dining room looking at Lillian Haber's shoes. We'd accepted clues from a Ouija board, why not hints from a cat?

"Glad they didn't pursue that angle," Kevin Zaff had said over lunch at SweetiePies. The angle that maybe I'd given Brad a push. There'd been suggestive woman's footsteps in the construction dust near where he'd been standing, but it turned out the cops had underestimated my shoe size. The footprints that matched my Cole Haan loafers led to the far end of the building where I'd seen lights downstream and had a horrible feeling.

The other footprints turned out to be a dead end because Alan had shown a real estate agent around that afternoon who'd walked all over the place, mentally calculating her commissions and admiring the views. A female real estate agent. With small feet.

I thought about it, then looked up something online and made a couple of calls. It took a few tries to reach the person I needed, but it turned out one of Brad's dry-wall guys had a thing for petite blondes and well-dressed, out-of-his-league women. He'd noticed the cute real estate agent—had asked her if she'd like to have a drink with him sometime and got shot down—and he remembered what she'd been wearing: "White slacks that showed off her butt, and a black sweater that made me want to nibble the buttons off it."

What a sleazeball. I thanked him for his time and sprayed my phone with Lysol.

"I think she came back," I said, when I reached Kevin Zaff on his cell. "I think the little bitch came back and knocked Brad into the river."

It took a few minutes and some backtracking on my part for Kev to catch up, but he agreed to the possibility.

"It's suggestive that she was wearing those clothes that day," he said. "But didn't the police decide the footprints were inconclusive? That they didn't get close enough to where Brad had been standing for someone to have pushed him?"

"That's where the slingshot comes in," I said. "She wouldn't have had to leave the stairwell."

He thought about that. "Brad was a big guy," he pointed out. "Armed with a golf club."

"Yeah, so was Goliath."

"Goliath had a golf club?"

"You know what I mean."

"I'm trying to picture it," he said. "That little blonde taking on an armed, six-foot-plus, 200-pound guy, with a slingshot."

"You forget he was facing the river," I said. "If she snuck up the stairwell and waited until he'd finished his swing and was watching how far he'd kicked that ball's ass, she would have had a good target and he would never have seen her."

"Jesus," Kevin said. "She'd be taking a huge risk, though. There's no guarantee he'd fall into the river. She couldn't be sure she'd even knock him out."

"I looked it up online," I said. "How 'bout I take a shot at you with a competition class, Model Z-52 WristRocket and a 12mm steel ball at a range of, say, 10 yards, and we'll see if it smarts."

"Ouch. Remind me to stay on your good side."

"I bet a close-range head shot would at least hurt like hell and knock someone off-balance," I said. "If it didn't knock them out. Or worse."

He was silent for a while. "Okay, devil's advocate: What if he doesn't fall out of the building, how's she going to move an inert mass twice her body weight to tip him over the edge? What if that steel ball ricochets off into the building and she doesn't see it, and investigators find it? What if she doesn't do more than piss him off, and he comes after her? What if it all works out as planned, and the coroner says, 'Huh, where'd this ding in his head come from?' She's a smart, calculating woman. How do those odds add up in her favor?"

"Confidence."

"What do you mean?"

"If she's smart, calculating, and cocky, the numbers will add up to whatever she wants them to be."

"You could have a point there," he admitted. "Okay, here's the clincher: Why? What's her motive? What does she gain from killing him?"

"Maybe she knew you were investigating her."

"Give me some credit," he said. "I know how to investigate without getting caught."

"I'm not saying she was on to you," I explained. "I've been looking at this report you wrote up for Brad. There's enough here for an astute reader to conclude she's a gold-digger and not to be trusted." I told Kevin about the conversations I'd had with Brad during our weekend in Palm Springs. "Brad wasn't happy with how Alan was handling business decisions. He was specifically pissed that Alan had given exclusive sales rights to River Bend Terrace to a real estate agent Brad thought was not a great choice. And you told me over lunch that Brad's concern wasn't the infidelity so much as that Lily was a bad influence on how Alan was conducting business."

"That's correct."

"I can see Brad going to Alan and saying, 'Hey, pal, I don't like your girlfriend.' Maybe he said or implied that the partnership—and the project—would be in trouble if Alan didn't break things off."

"Could happen that way."

"And maybe Alan, who has turned out to be not such a nice guy after all, over-thought it and came to the conclusion that Brad was trying to edge him out."

"You think Alan was behind it?"

Kevin couldn't see me shaking my head, but that was the part I had doubts about. It's a big step from playing fast and loose with the paperwork to offing a guy you've been golf buddies with for twenty years.

"I think it's more likely Alan said something to Lily that made her think they'd be better off with Brad out of the way, and she took matters into her own hands."

"I'll buy that," he said. "I think Lily's capable of anything. Still, it's a lot of 'what ifs.'"

"What ifs are my specialty."

"You given any thought to what you'd like to do about this?"

"As a matter of fact," I said, "I have. Lily is showing me a River Bend Terrace penthouse at 2:15 this afternoon. Wanna come?"

I'd had plenty of time to realize that meeting Lily on my own might not be such a great idea. Suzette would be in a snit for a while when she found out I hadn't invited her, but she'd get over it. And let's face it, Kevin is a guy and probably a lot more capable of handling things than either me or Suze would be, should the situation devolve in an unpleasant way.

Kev thought it was a terrible idea. He reminded me I have known temper issues, and was of the opinion that being face to face with Lily might be more than I could handle.

I told him I could rein it in when I had to, but as it turned out, Kevin was right.

46

"Honey, come look at this view."

Kevin, introduced to Lily as my husband, joined me at the master bedroom window.

"Nice. I can almost see my office from here."

Not hardly, but he was good to play along.

"He was standing right where you are when he fell," I whispered, looking to make sure that Lily was giving us space to talk ourselves into wanting the condo.

"Stop checking on her," Kev whispered back. "Shit, that's a long way down."

It was hard to stop checking on Lily because she was wearing a beautifully tailored suit (pencil skirt, peplum jacket) of ivory silk twill with an ice-blue handkerchief linen shell and matching stiletto sandals and I really wanted to pull one of those sandals off her size 5-1/2N foot and whack her over the head with it. I wondered how hard I'd have to hit to draw blood. Probably if I tried to find out she'd fight back, which could make getting a definitive answer difficult. Maybe Kev could hold her down for me.

"I mean it," Kevin hissed. "Ignore her. She's just a real estate agent. All she should see when she looks at us is a fat commission check."

We admired the view some more, then had to compare it to the other exposure, in the second bedroom.

"How many baths are there again?" I asked when Lily poked her head in to see how we were doing.

"Two and half. There's an en suite for each bedroom, and the half is this powder room, over here.

I followed the click-tap of her sandals around the corner to a half bath cleverly fitted in behind the kitchen, equally accessible from the living room, dining alcove, and den.

"And laundry facilities are here."

Lily opened the door to what I'd thought was a closet. Full size washer and dryer, nice. Those stacked units most apartments have may fit in small spaces but they take an hour to dry one towel. Too bad any condo I might be in the market for wouldn't be nearly as nice as this. Then again, Kevin had given me the name of a lawyer who, he said, "eats sharks for lunch," so maybe I could get this place in a settlement.

"Would you excuse me?" Lily asked, checking the caller ID on her cell. Her ring tone was subdued, classy. "I really should take this."

She walked to the far side of the living room for privacy while Kevin and I admired the den. More walls of built-ins. Probably Brad's idea. His furniture would look good in here.

"You need any oversized guy furniture?" I asked Kevin.

"I'm not planning to move in," he said. "I'm just here to keep you out of trouble."

Good luck with that. "I'm selling a large desk, ginormous leather club chair with matching ottoman, and a big-ass TV," I said. "And a very nice rug. Stuff of Brad's I'd like to unload. Good price to the right buyer."

Kevin made a face like he might be interested. "I'll come take a look."

My tummy rumbled, reminding me I'd been too wound up about this appointment to eat any lunch. "Let's check out the kitchen."

The kitchen was nice, too. Viking stove, SubZero fridge, lots of well-thought-out counter space and cabinets. Everything about the condo was beautifully laid out. If I didn't like my house so much I'd want to move in. I knew Brad deserved the credit for that, and felt sad that he couldn't see how well it had turned out. The kitchen was a little too stainless-steel modern for me, though. I'm more of a French Country type when it comes to kitchens.

"Honey, I'm starving," I said, loudly enough for Lily to hear, should she be eavesdropping. "When we're through here let's get something to eat."

"Honestly, Lena," Kev said, keeping in character, "I don't see why you can't manage your blood sugar. Don't you have a snack in your purse?"

Just the opening I needed. I reached into the oversized satchel I carried and pulled out the Santa tin.

"You carry a cookie tin in your purse?" Kevin whispered. "What's wrong with a protein bar or an apple?"

"It's not cookies." I grinned at him and pried off the lid.

Kev wanted so much to go ballistic I thought his ears were going to fly off. "Put those away," he hissed. "Now!"

"How are we doing in here?" Lily's timing was so perfect I almost wanted to kiss her.

"Would you like a brownie?" I took one for myself and held out the tin to her. "I'm taking these to my grandmother later, but she won't mind if we have some."

Lily waved them off with a brittle smile. Could be that's why she's a size 2 and I'm not, or maybe she associates brownies with bad behavior.

"Do have one," I pressed. "They're my secret recipe. Kevin loves them."

Kevin stood behind her shaking his head at me in disgust. Or maybe he was telling me not to push it.

Lily hesitated. I knew what she was thinking: The market's in the toilet, don't blow the biggest condo sale of the year by turning down this woman's brownies.

"Oh," I said, pulling the tin back just as Lily reached for one. "I should have asked if you're allergic. They have nuts in them."

They didn't look it. They were the taste test winners by a wide margin. According to the report Ansel had brought over around eleven that morning, 72% of tasters had identified them as nut-free.

"I call them Espresso Macadamia Surprise."

Kevin was so furious he had to leave the room.

Lily blanched, and almost wavered on those stiletto heels, and I could tell she forgot to breathe for a moment but she didn't collapse in a heap, weeping and confessing all and begging for mercy. Probably that had been too much to hope for.

"Have you seen the master bath yet?" Lily squeaked. "It's one of the unit's best features."

* * *

I rubbed the duct tape around my wrists against the edge of a built-in dresser. At this rate there was a chance we'd get loose before Season 85 of Biggest Loser started. If we hadn't starved to death by then.

Kevin groaned and came to and swore for a while when he remembered what had happened and figured out we were locked in the larger of the unit's two walk-in closets.

"Are you okay?" I asked. At least we weren't in the coat closet. That would have been cramped.

"No, I am not okay. I've been knocked out and tied up and now I'm locked in a closet with an idiot."

"You're calling me an idiot? I don't recall seeing anything in your report about her expertise at tai kwon do or whatever the hell that was. I thought you investigated her."

"Go ahead, blame this on me," he said. "You're the one who offered the woman a brownie. What the hell were you thinking?"

"I was thinking if we rattled her she'd do something stupid and between the two of us we could take her, 'cause she's a shrimp, and then the cops could charge her with something more serious than baking with intent."

"Jesus. Next time you come up with a scheme like that let me know first. Better yet, leave me out of it."

"Fine. Wouldn't want you to get beat up by a girl again."

Silence.

"Sorry."

More silence.

"Seriously, you didn't know about the martial arts thing?"

He sighed. "I thought she was going to yoga class. That's the only thing I can think of it could be."

I considered that. "Which studio?"

"Lotus something. Lower Mill Street, second floor, across from a playground."

I nodded. "Suze tried to get me to take a self defense class there."

"Wish you'd gone. I could have used some backup."

Lily thought she'd left us in the dark, but we'd been in the closet long enough for me to find the light switch and turn it on with my elbow. Kevin had a nasty lump at the hairline and somewhere on his sternum was the imprint of a size 5-1/2A stiletto heel, delivered with an impressive combination of a roundhouse something and a donkey kick. I don't know how she pulled it off in a pencil skirt, but whatever that move was and however she'd done it the kick had sent Kevin flying and knocked the air out of him. After that he'd barely had a chance.

Lily had taken me out of action the old-fashioned way, by pulling a gun. She carried a large satchel of her own, and it was way better than mine because not only was it a Vuitton, it had the aforementioned personal firearm and a roll of duct tape in it. I'd tell you what kind of gun it was but I have no idea. It was small, and very, very scary.

And I'd felt so clever pulling a tin of brownies out of my Dooney&Burke.

"You missed the part where she pulled a gun," I told Kevin. "She'd knocked you out by then."

"Oh."

I'd tried to take her out myself, with the Santa tin, but it hadn't gone well. There were brownie fragments all over the place out there and I hadn't even managed to smudge Lily's white suit.

"She took my cell phone. Yours, too."

"She's not stupid."

"Do you think I'd be any good at martial arts?" I couldn't see it, myself.

"Yeah," he said. "I do. I saw how you went after that tree."

"Huh." Usually my idea of self-defense is to eat a carrot stick instead of a cookie.

Kevin didn't speak because he had wriggled his hands under his butt and up around his feet so his hands were in front, and was gnawing his way through the duct tape that bound them together.

Oooh, good idea. Why hadn't I thought of that? I tried the same maneuver and couldn't get my wrists under my butt. I told myself that was because my arms are shorter than Kevin's, not because my butt is so much bigger than his. Plus, I'm not very flexible. If we ever got of that closet I was going to take up yoga.

"What kind of woman carries duct tape and a gun in her purse?" I complained "She couldn't just lock us in the closet? She had to tape us up, too?"

"As soon as I get this tape off me I'm putting it over your mouth," Kevin said. He didn't mean it, though, because when he broke through the tape on his wrists he just tossed it aside and started on his ankles.

"Building's not occupied yet," I said. "I don't think they've finished more than a couple of units." I didn't bore him with what I knew about how thick the floors were, or how soundproof they'd planned the units to be. "Nobody's gonna hear us if we yell for help."

"Shhh. You hear that?"

I listened. Nothing. I skooched over to the door and lay my ear to the crack. Faint clippety-tap sounds. Someone was pacing back and forth on the certified sustainably harvested, formaldehyde-free bamboo flooring in the condo's living room.

"She's still out there! I thought the point of locking us up was so she'd have a head start on getting away."

Oh, shit. If Lily was still out there, maybe she was waiting for someone. Someone big and tough and with a ruthless approach to problem solving. I wished I hadn't thought of that.

"Can you hear if there's anyone with her?"

"I think it's just her." The clippety-tap got louder and then stopped. "Shit, she's headed this way." I skooched over to the other side of the door and tried peering through that crack. Kevin unwrapped his ankles and moved over to work on me.

Lily paced back and forth in the master bedroom, cell to her ear. Her footsteps had stopped because the room's carpeted. Lily muttered to herself loudly enough that I could hear. "Come on, come on. Damn it, Russell, pick up."

"Russell!" I whispered at Kevin.

"He's out there, too?"

"No, she's trying to call him. He's not picking up."

"Russell's the accountant, right?"

"Yeah." He had to have been in on the Brad deal with Alan, but I hadn't thought to put him together with Lily. I'd been so busy thinking about what Alan had been up to, and so indignant on my own and Edith Stokely's behalf, that I'd forgotten about Russell.

"We should have paid more attention to Russell," Kevin whispered.

No shit.

"Hey, go back to what you said about Lily's purse," he said.

"Uh, that she had a gun and duct tape in it?" I said. Big satchel bags are handy, but there are limits to what sane people carry around in them.

"That makes me think she knew who we, or at least you, are before we got here. And that she knew we're on to her."

I peered through the crack. Lily was still in the bedroom, but father away now. "How is that possible?"

"Google, probably, and maybe Edith Stokely."

Kevin's theory was that Lily Googled people who made appointments to view high-end properties. "That's what I'd do, if I were showing a million-dollar condo to someone I didn't know," he said, finishing with my wrists and starting on the tape around my ankles. I could have taken over at that point, but it was nice to be looked after.

"I'm confused. To her I'm Mimi daGiovanni's granddaughter. I didn't even say a last name. And my brownie stunt may have been stupid, but it did suck the color out of her."

"She didn't know we were on to the brownie thing," Kevin said. "She knew we were on to the land switcheroo."

I thought about that. "She was in on that, too?"

"Makes sense she at least knew about it, if she's calling Russell."

"But where does Edith come in? I thought she was Alan's dupe."

"Me, too. But if our visit made her think she might be in trouble for misuse of her notary seal, she could have called someone for advice."

"Russell?"

He shrugged. "I'm just guessing, but if he and Alan were tight and go way back she might have called him to say, 'Lena Wells is asking questions about some River Bend Terrace documents Alan made me finagle, what should I do?'"

"And Russell called Lily, because she's in it, too."

"And Lily said, 'That's interesting 'cause I've got a Lena no-last-name wanting to see a River Bend Terrace apartment this afternoon.' She might have tugged a little harder at the Mimi daGiovanni connection."

"Granimi's got a blog," I said. "And she posts tons of photos to flickr. Family holidays, vacations, it's all up there."

"So Lily could have found your picture online."

I nodded. "And she'd recognize it. There's a photo in Alan's office of the four of us—me and Brad and Alan and Rose—at some charity dinner. It's a good likeness." I don't look much different all dolled up than I do in daily life, because there are limits to what I'm capable of doing with my hair. "If she was hanging around Alan, she's sure to have seen it."

It freaked me out to think the gun and duct tape had been special just for me. I liked it better when I'd thought Lily was such a badass she always carried stuff that like around.

Lily's classy ring-tone chimed again. We pressed our ears to the door.

"Russell, thank God … What the hell do you mean, you can't make it? I can't handle two … Okay, okay, I'll calm down … Okay … Are you sure, because … "

It went on like that for a while as she paced around, and then she hung up and paced some more, and then she left the room.

"Any idea what that was about?"

"She went to get the gun," Kevin said.

We moved away from the door.

*   *   *

Lily kept the gun on us from a safe distance as she explained how things were going to go. It was the kind of plan that doesn't sound like it will work, but when someone like Lily points a gun at you it's a good idea to do what she says.

"Lena, I am begging you," Kevin muttered as Lily gestured us out of the closet and toward the condo door, "do not try anything stupid. She's an amateur, we'll get our chance."

How he could think Lily was more of an amateur than I am, I had no idea. And even though I'd declined the self-defense classes I know you never, ever, let the perp get you into her car. When you're talking abductions, cars equal death.

So I did the only thing I could think of that might work.

I offered her the money.

47

Lily took the bait.

I told her Russell was out for himself and had no intention of coming to her rescue. That fate had cheated her when it dealt Alan a heart attack, and she deserved to walk away with something. Something like the $240,000 in Brad's safe. Yeah, it was a few bills short, but I didn't figure she'd wait around to count it.

"I know it's not much," I said, thinking it was a hell of a lot and I'd really like to keep it. "But it's yours if you let us go. It won't make all your problems disappear—" I'd told her a warrant had been issued for her arrest, which maybe had been jumping the gun a little, "—but it's enough to help you disappear, and isn't that almost as good?"

I also mentioned that Alan's garage housed two potential getaway cars that no one would be looking for, that keys to said cars were on a hook inside the kitchen door, and that getting into the house wouldn't be a problem.

Lily seemed to like the car idea, but first we had to get to the other side of town. She took us down in the service elevator and tried to make us crawl into the trunk of her Mercedes coupe but one look and it was clear we wouldn't fit. Two munchkins, maybe, but not full-sized adults.

I was feeling extremely disappointed in Bob by that point in the adventure. I'd told him that, should he be overcome by the urge to run out and arrest someone, I knew where Lillian Haber would be at 2:15 that afternoon.

I hadn't shared the details of my idiotic plan to him but Bob knows me well enough by now—or ought to—to suspect I might need some help. So where the hell was he?

"Lily, we can take my car," I said. "You sit in back and hold the gun on Kevin, and I'll drive. I swear I won't try anything stupid."

Lily seemed to think I didn't mean it about not trying anything stupid. She made Kevin drive while she held the gun on me. Kev and I locked eyes in the rearview every chance we got during the drive from River Bend Terrace to my house. I'm not sure if he was trying to send me messages or just keeping an eye on me. I hoped he wasn't still so pissed off at me that he'd try something stupid himself.

Traffic was a bear, which didn't help anyone's nerves any. By the time we turned the corner to my block I was close to panic because it was bad enough I was in a mess, but if Val were home she'd get caught up in it, too. When I'd left the house to hook up with Kevin for our condo tour Val and Ansel were heading out on their bikes. But they might be back by now, and which house they'd end up at was a toss-up: Ansel has Wii tennis but I have better snacks. Val had promised she'd check in, but my cell had disappeared into Lily's bottomless satchel. So much for never turning my phone off again.

We pulled into my garage and the door rumbled down behind us. Lily got out first and gestured Kevin to climb into the back cargo area. She called me over and handed me the roll of tape and supervised as I trussed Kevin up again, more securely this time. Lily childproofed the door and window controls and borrowed my clicker to lock him in.

She waved me ahead and I unlocked the kitchen door with shaking hands. If Val was home I wanted to alert her that something was wrong so she could run or hide or call for help, but if Lily didn't know anyone else was in the house a surprise might work to my advantage. I was dithering what to do when Lily prodded me in the back with something that felt like the gun and told me to get a move on.

We stepped into my kitchen. The knives were on the other side of the room and I couldn't think of any good way to maneuver myself within reach of one. Besides, prior experience implied that trying anything stupid would be a mistake.

As we passed through the room my terrified senses were so heightened it really did seem that time slowed down. A glint of sunlight reflected off the surface of my swimming pool, and through the kitchen slider the framed view of my backyard looked so tranquil and perfect I almost wept. The floribunda roses by the back fence were in riotous bloom, the most exuberant flowering they'd delivered in years, and even through the closed sliding doors it seemed their idyllic scent caressed the air.

Rose, I thought, if you're still hanging around, I could really use some help here.

"Keep walking," Lily hissed.

"The cash is in here," I said, and led the way to the study. It occurred to me, too late, that I could have told her the money was in a safe at Alan's house and we could have played this out over there. What an idiot. I almost deserved to be shot.

Lily stood inside the study door, far enough away that I wouldn't get away with a crazy stunt like winging the golf course painting at her.

Getting the safe open wasn't working out so well, either.

"Hurry up!" Lily hissed at me. "What the hell is your problem?"

"My problem is you're scaring the shit out of me." My hands shook and I couldn't remember the combination.

"You have thirty seconds before we go back to Plan A," she said. "When you've unlocked it, open it and step away."

"Okay, okay," shit. July something, '04, day first. It took three tries, but I finally got it. For a horrible moment I was convinced the safe would be empty, but when I swung the door open it was all still there. Part of me wished Brad was the kind of guy who kept a gun in his safe, but I wouldn't have known how to use it or even if it were loaded and it seemed a good bet Lily not only knew how to use hers but it probably had bullets in it and she might not hesitate to pull the trigger.

Lily motioned me further to the side then walked over to the safe to look in it, but she's short and the safe was at high eye-level for me and recessed into the wall. She looked around and saw the stepstool Granimi and I had been using to clear off Brad's shelves. She told me to bring it over and back away again. She looked like a kid, climbing on a stool to peek in the safe. A very cold and mean and dangerous kid. You might think that would have been a good moment to try something stupid but the tiny hand holding the gun on me didn't waver as Lily took a quick look and hopped down again.

I'd hoped she would tell me to put the money in her satchel and maybe I could palm my phone, but she was on to me.

"Take the money out and put it on the desk," she said.

When I was done she gestured me away and checked I hadn't left anything interesting in the safe.

"Now put the stool over there and sit on it."

I did as I was told. Lily put her huge purse on the desk and took out the duct tape. She tossed it to me and supervised as I perched on the stepstool and taped my legs to the sides. Then she bound my wrists behind my back and taped my mouth shut. Kev would be happy. I was sorry he wasn't there to see it, and wondered if he was having any luck getting loose in my car.

Once I was out of action Lily returned to the desk and put the money in her purse. I was closer to the hall, and my heart sank when I heard a faint sound that might have been the kitchen slider opening. No, no, no, please god don't let Val come home. I listened as hard as I could, but didn't hear anyone moving around out there. Could be I'd been mistaken.

"Where's your powder room?" Lily asked.

Hah, even criminals have to pee sometime. Next door to the right, I directed with my head. I had to pee, too, but it didn't seem like a good time to think about that.

"Don't try anything while I'm in there, or I'll go after your grandmother," she said.

I didn't try much. Wriggling my hands and feet was ineffectual, and I almost went over when I tried skooching the stepstool across the carpet. That wasn't going to work.

Then movement in the living room across the hall threw me into a panic. I shook my head vigorously and tried to yell through the duct tape to tell Val and Ansel to get the hell out of there. They were crouched down behind the couch, Ansel with Fiona in his arms, a hand on the dog's nose to keep it quiet. Val put her finger to her lip to tell me to keep quiet and ran barefoot across the hall into the study. When I saw the paring knife she'd grabbed from the kitchen counter I freaked because I thought she planned to try to use it on Lily, but she crouched behind me and cut at the tape around my wrists. Ansel pointed a finger at the powder room door and I nodded and he made a gesture that I think was supposed to mean I should stay put. As if I had a choice in the matter.

I struggled to sit still while Val worked on my bonds. The paring knife was dull, and it was slow going. Shit, shit, shit, shit, shit, I wished they would leave me and get the hell out of there. I prayed the kids had thought to call the cops.

Just as Val got my hands free we heard Lily flush. I shrieked at Val to run but with my mouth still taped shut it didn't sound like much, and she stayed behind me, sawing at the tape around my left ankle as I scrabbled at my right one with what felt like paralyzed fingers. Mobility seemed more important than voice at that moment and I didn't want to waste even half a second ripping the tape off my face.

I didn't think two kids and one clumsy adult had much of a chance against Lily, but I hadn't counted on their secret weapon.

I heard the powder room door open and saw Ansel move the dog from his lap to the carpet. I stood up and took a step to the side and discovered the stool was still attached to one leg. It hampered me a little but didn't stop me from grabbing the bronze figurine of a charging bull that hadn't been boxed up yet. Lily appeared in the study door and saw me loose and Val beside me and fury swept across her face. She raised the gun and had taken a step into the room when a bright fluff of orange fur darted across the hall, glommed onto her right leg, and started humping.

Lily shrieked and tried to turn and kick Fiona off at the same time and the heel of her sandal caught in the thick nap of Brad's carpet and she windmilled her arms and went down. As she fell she swung the gun toward Val and I hurled the bronze figurine at her.

48

What is rose, what leaf, what stem, what thorn? This bounce, that glide, a swoop, a tickle.

Deep in the floribunda all is delight, is rapture, is oneness, is flower.

Then the glimmer of whatever had held her dissolves and she is summer, she is sunlight, she is petal, she is perfect.

She is light, is air, is song, is gone.

My aim with the bronze bull wasn't very good, and it didn't help that it was the one with the loose base, but probably that was for the best because it was hefty and might have killed Lily if I'd hit my target. I did manage to knock her out with it, and open up a nasty gash on her temple. I'm sure a self-defense plea wouldn't have been a problem given the circumstances, but as the aftermath unfolded it was convenient that Lily ended up injured and talking rather than among the silent ranks of the dead.

After we'd trussed Lily up with her own duct tape—in case she came to before the cops arrived—I told the kids to take my car keys and a sharper knife and go free the guy they'd find taped up in the back of the CR-V, then wait for me in the kitchen. I had just enough time to retrieve the money from Lily's satchel and lock it back up in the safe before the police arrived. I wasn't confident I could claim the money had been honestly come by, but that didn't mean I wanted it to disappear into an evidence locker. I told the cops the money had been a bluff.

Val and Ansel, it turned out, had been next door when Val announced they were urgently needed at my house and should bring the dog. How they knew to sneak in and stay quiet they couldn't say other than it seemed like the right thing to do. Ansel admitted Fiona was trained to hump on command, but I forgave him. I even went online and ordered Fiona a gift basket of the very best organic doggie treats.

I suspected Kevin's pride was bruised that we'd been rescued by two twelve-year-olds, but he'd done pretty well, managing to squirm his way out of the cargo area and halfway into the front seat by the time the kids showed up in the garage. Another few seconds and he'd have been S-O-S-ing the horn. Given that all the excitement was over by the time he made it into the house I was surprised when he urgently requested a phone. Turns out the worst part of Kev's day was he missed meeting his fiancé at Macy's to look at china patterns. I guess it wasn't the first time that sort of thing had happened, because last I heard she hasn't returned the ring yet but is refusing to set a date until they've "reached an agreement" about the conflict between his profession and her feelings. I've met her, and she's okay, but I think he can do better so I've kind of got my fingers crossed it doesn't work out.

We had a few minutes of downtime as the cops and EMTs dealt with Lily, which I used to strike a deal with Kev that if he did some investigating for me on a personal matter I'd never, ever, tell anyone he got beat up by a girl. We had to fudge some details in our version of how things had gone down at the condo, but the fact that Lily had a gun meant no one much cared where the lump on Kevin's head came from or how we'd ended up in the closet. Kevin's been good about his side of the bargain, and thinks he's close to finding my son but the kid travels a lot and is proving hard to pin down. Kev will get a lead on him soon, I'm sure of it.

Lily recovered, and once Russell had been brought in and they'd both lawyered up it was a race to see which of them could blame the other faster. Turns out Russell and Lily were the masterminds behind the land swap thing, and the real couple, or had been. They won't be seeing much of each other in prison. Edith lost her notary license, but she was so clearly a prissy old fart who'd been taken advantage of they left her out of the conspiracy to defraud charges.

We'd been right that Lily wanted not just Alan's money, but Rose's, too, and had run out of patience when my kindly neighbor's health had appeared to improve when she started taking the herbal formulas. Lily stonewalled for a while, but eventually admitted to feeding Rose the lethal brownie. Once Rose was dead the plan was for Lily to marry Alan. Nobody specifically said, but if Alan hadn't croaked when he did I suspect an unfortunate accident would have followed soon after the honeymoon. How Russell believed that walking into the sunset with Lily would have ended with anything other than an unfortunate accident for him someday I didn't understand but it could be he really loved her. The funny part is Russell hadn't bailed on Lily intentionally when he'd called to say he couldn't make it to the condo to help her out; he'd been caught in the same horrific snarl-up as Bob and his crew, who'd been diverted to deal with a seemingly more urgent convenience store robbery gone bad that resulted in the largest traffic meltdown Laurelton has seen in years.

Kevin's suppositions about how Lily had been on to us turned out to be accurate. What we were way off on was the how-Brad-fell-into-the-river theory. Lily insisted, and it was verified, that she'd been at a cocktail reception on the other side of town at the time. The stain on her trousers turned out to be Merlot, and she had some choice things to say about the idiot who spilled red wine on her best white slacks. She insisted the cashmere sweater was a little shabby and said the shoes, while she liked them, pinched her toes. The slingshot wrist brace wasn't comfortable so she'd replaced it with a model that was a better fit. Not that she'll get a chance to use it, where she's headed.

So it turns out Brad was careless and stupid after all. I'm not quite over being mad at him for that.

Suzette was miffed she'd missed the fun, so I offered her the cashmere sweater, but once she heard the details of Lily's past and recent behavior she decided it would be bad feng shui to wear it. Which is why I don't thrift. You never know where that stuff has been or who's been doing what in it.

The lawyers and accountants are still wrangling over spreadsheets and depositions but it looks like I could own a sizeable chunk of River Bend Terrace, along with Rose's kids. The idea of being in business with that Anna daughter and Stewart the lush gives me hives, so my shark-eating lawyer is negotiating for them to buy me out. For real this time. It's gonna cost them a bundle, but they have major bucks from their mother and can afford it. It looks like my money problems are going to be solved for at least the next decade, which means I won't have to sell my house. I still own that parcel outside of town, but it doesn't even offer a good picnic spot so I'll probably offload it to the first person who makes a halfway decent offer.

Granimi's made a good recovery. Not 100%, but closer than expected. We went back to River Bend Terrace the week after all the shenanigans and had another look at the condo. Granimi wasn't interested in buying it after what had happened there, but she wanted to see where the action went down. She talked me into shutting her in the closet for a few minutes but I drew the line at timing how long it would take her to get out of duct tape. The agent who showed us the place carried a reassuringly tiny purse, and, as best I could tell, had never even heard of tai kwon do. I don't know who cleaned up the brownie mess, or what happened to the Santa tin. I have a reindeer one I can use for this year's Christmas cookies, but it won't be the same.

Granimi's been back and forth to San Francisco a few times because getting her house there ready to go on the market is a huge undertaking. The place is enormous, and full of stuff. She hasn't entirely given up on the condo in Laurelton idea, but for now she's enjoying my guest room and I have a feeling she'll be here for a while. She'd say hi, but she's online right now booking us a trip to Hawaii for February.

Val ended up staying through the second week in August. She has a standing invite to show up on my doorstep any time. Everyone should have a place to go where they'll welcome you with a hug and feed you brownies. The good news is her mom's engaged now and that's mellowed her out considerably. She didn't even make a fuss when she showed up to take Val home and discovered her daughter came with a cat. I'd secretly hoped that Shadow would have to stay with me. I'm still picking cat hair off the sofa cushions, but it feels like something's missing from the house now.

I never did have that Soul Retrieval, but I did go out with Raven. Several times. What we did and what time I got home isn't any of your business. There's chemistry there, which is fun, and I'm tempted, but I've decided to try not dating for a while. I tend to lose sight of priorities when I'm deep into a guy, so it seems like a good idea to … excuse me a sec.

Sorry, that was Raven on the phone. We're getting together later.

So? I'm not very good at resisting temptation. If you haven't learned that about me by now, you haven't been paying attention.

Where was I?

Brad's den is white now, and makes an excellent studio. Carlos came by recently to see what I've been working on, and wants six of my journey paintings for a group show. He swears my work will be in the main gallery, by the way, not in that back room.

William, Brad's son, is back from Shanghai and came for a visit last weekend with his new girlfriend, Cassie, an Aussie girl with a great laugh and an uncanny resemblance to the Duchess of York. Will loved the old photo album, and had a few guesses who some of the ancients were. There's a lovely picture in there of Brad's maternal grandmother, probably taken when she was about my age. If you look closely, you can see she's wearing the rose cameo and the garnet ring Granimi found in that hollow book. The key's still an unknown, but chances are it's just a memento.

Saturday was one of those spectacular fall afternoons that makes you want to go play outdoors, so we took Brad out for his final golf game. Cassie and I tooled around in a golf cart and got ~~smashed on~~ acquainted over a thermos of Suzette's famous Cosmopolitan Lemonade, which is both tasty and lethal. Will and Suzette did the golfing. Will's pretty good—he got the golf bug from his dad—and Suzette was some kind of junior champion when she was Val's age. Then she grew five inches and developed curves and that threw off her center of gravity and ruined her game. She says even at that age she was more interested in boys than golf and didn't mind giving it up. She's still got a nice swing, though, and can hit that ball pretty far for a girl.

Both Will and Suzette insisted that ash-filled goofballs would be utterly unplayable, but they had a lot of fun trying to prove each other wrong. They didn't get to play all 18 holes, though, because at some point we ~~got so rowdy~~ were having so much fun that we ~~were evicted from the Country Club~~ decided to move the party to my house. Olivia, who's started her junior year at Laurelton High and was at band practice at the time, heard all about it and still hasn't forgiven me for embarrassing ~~her~~ myself in front of her friends' parents.

I don't care, because it was the best game ever.

Heartfelt thanks go out to my early readers, especially Abby, Rebecca, and Gay, for their encouragement and helpful suggestions. Thanks are also due to National Novel Writing Month (www.NaNoWriMo.org), without which a first draft might never have made it onto the page, and most of all to my beloved husband, whose dedication and support made it possible for me to neglect so many other responsibilities while nurturing this story into its present form.

Stephanie Serrano is the author (as Stephanie Roberts) of the *Fast Feng Shui* book series, *The Pocket Idiot's Guide to Feng Shui*, and *Clutter Clearing from the Inside Out*. *Lethal Blossom* is her first novel. Stephanie lives on the Big Island of Hawaii with her husband and two cats.

Visit her at www.StephanieSerrano.com.